Lindsey Kelk is a *Sunday Times* bestselling author, podcaster and internet oversharer. Born and brought up in Doncaster, South Yorkshire, she worked in London as a children's editor before writing her first book, *I Heart New York*, and moving to Brooklyn. Lindsey's novels include the I Heart series, *The Christmas Wish* and *Love Me Do,* as well as her YA fantasy debut, *The Bell Witches*. She lives in Los Angeles with her husband.

You can follow Lindsey on Facebook, X or Instagram @LindseyKelk, and sign up for her newsletter at www.LindseyKelk.com.

Love Story

LINDSEY KELK

HarperCollins*Publishers*

HarperCollins*Publishers* Ltd
1 London Bridge Street,
London SE1 9GF

www.harpercollins.co.uk

HarperCollins*Publishers*
Macken House, 39/40 Mayor Street Upper, Dublin 1,
D01 C9W8, Ireland

Published by HarperCollins*Publishers* 2024

24 25 26 27 28 LBC 5 4 3 2 1

A catalogue record for this book is available from the British Library

ISBN: 978-0-00-868769-4 (PB B-format)
ISBN: 978-0-00-869548-4 (PB, US, CAN only)

This novel is entirely a work of fiction.
The names, characters and incidents portrayed in it are
the work of the author's imagination. Any resemblance to
actual persons, living or dead, events or localities is
entirely coincidental.

Typeset in Melior by Palimpsest Book Production Ltd, Falkirk, Stirlingshire

Printed and bound in the UK using 100% Renewable Electricity by CPI Group (UK) Ltd

MIX
Paper | Supporting
responsible forestry
FSC
www.fsc.org
FSC™ C007454

This book contains FSC™ certified paper and other controlled sources
to ensure responsible forest management.

For more information visit: www.harpercollins.co.uk/green

This book is for you.
I'm so happy to be here, reading and
writing HEAs with you.

CHAPTER ONE

'Romance novels are *so* hot right now.'

I looked up at Malcolm, both my cheeks hamster-full of lamb biriyani and nodded.

'Gen Z can't get enough,' he said, digging through his lunch with vigour. 'They're out there this very second, inhaling them, tearing through books like locusts! They can't get enough. They're insatiable.'

It wasn't a particularly appealing visual, thousands of young women swarming around their local Waterstones, devouring everything on the 'as seen on TikTok' table. I poked sadly at my lunch having suddenly lost my appetite.

'And your bloody book.' Mal pointed at me with a chunk of tandoori chicken, the tines of his fork shining through the neon red meat. 'Soph, I've never seen anything like it.'

'Well—'

'It's unprecedented!' My publisher interrupted before I could even get started. 'We can't keep the book in stock, the audio and the ebook are outselling everything else in the industry and for the love of god, don't tell anyone this, but we've had to "borrow" some of the paper assigned to a very famous author's print run, just to keep the supermarkets stocked. And believe you me, he wouldn't be happy if he heard about it.'

'I bet,' I replied.

'I can't tell you who it is.'

'Then don't.'

'I wish I could.'

'I don't want to know.'

He looked around the quiet Indian restaurant I'd chosen for lunch and mouthed the name of an unbelievably successful, notoriously humourless, male literary author before slapping both of his hands against his cheeks, *Home Alone*-style.

No pressure there then.

'Oh,' I replied weakly. 'That's nuts.'

'Too bloody right it's nuts,' Mal said, reaching for his second icy cold Kingfisher. 'Which is why I need to know when I'm getting the sequel.'

'Right.' I reached for my glass of water, took a gulp then forced a smile. 'The thing is—'

'And I don't want any excuses. "It needs one more read-through, I'm not happy with the ending, I've been busy at work", I've heard them all before, Soph.'

'In fairness, you haven't given me a chance to say anything, have you?' I pointed out, dropping the smile. 'I don't think I've finished a sentence since we sat down.'

He looked at his empty plate.

'Then how come I've almost finished my lunch and you've barely touched yours?'

'Because you talk with your mouth full and it's

2

disgusting. Besides, they're not excuses. I know it's not what you want to hear but it *does* need one more read-through, I'm *not* happy with the ending and I *have* been busy at work.'

The look on Malcolm's face was not a happy one.

'*Butterflies* has only been out six weeks and it is already one of the top ten fastest-selling debuts MullinsParker has ever seen,' he replied. 'You're a *Sunday Times* and *New York Times* bestseller, a Reese's Book Club pick, a Book of the Month, you've already got translation deals for twenty-nine languages—'

'Thirty-two,' I corrected quietly.

'Thirty-bloody-two languages?' he repeated. 'Christ almighty, Sophie. I don't know the exact numbers but surely the movie deal alone must be worth twenty times your annual salary? Are you really going to sit there and tell me you can't get the sequel in on time because you've got to teach a bunch of little kids their ABCs? Don't take this the wrong way but what the bloody hell is wrong with you?'

It was a fair question, even if it wasn't presented in a particularly pleasant manner. Malcolm Jennings wasn't just my publisher at MullinsParker; he was also one of my parents' oldest and best friends, and my godfather. Mal was the one who bought me the full set of Beatrix Potter books the day I was born and, every time he came to visit, I demanded he read my bedtime story because he always did all the voices. When I was a teenager, it was Mal who slipped me all the cool, edgy books my parents said I couldn't read until I was older, and when I graduated from Durham with a first in English, it was Mal who offered to help me find an internship in publishing. It wasn't until I sent him the

3

first draft of *Butterflies* that he'd even come close to forgiving me for turning him down to go into teaching instead.

'Mal.' I pushed my plateful of food away, inspiring a bowtie-wearing waiter to immediately spring to life and clear it off the table. 'You know I appreciate everything you've done for me.'

He harrumphed into his beer but, underneath his annoyance, I could still see the avuncular affection I'd known and loved my whole life.

'Aren't you the one who always says no author should jack in work on their first book, no matter how successful they are?'

'Yes, but that's because I had no idea you were going to outsell the Bible,' he squawked, loud enough to attract glances from all around the restaurant. 'When The Beatles said they were bigger than Jesus, everyone went bananas but you, Sophie Taylor, could say it and right now, according to sales figures, it would be true!'

'That doesn't mean I want to rush the sequel and let the readers down,' I countered, hunching over the table and lowering my voice. Malcolm loved drama and attention, I did not. 'Or that I even want to give up my job, I've been offered head of year next term. Maybe I like being a teacher.'

He coughed, choking on his beer. 'There are people who actually like teaching?'

'Wild, I know, but yes, there are and I'm not ready to explain to the headteacher how I spend my evenings and weekends writing very spicy romance, let alone the parents.' I tapped the limited edition, pink-sprayed edge, foiled-board, hardback Spice Rack subscription box exclusive edition of *Butterflies* that sat in the middle of the table and shuddered. 'Would you be happy with the author of *this* educating your six-year-old?'

'I'd be happy with Charles Manson educating my six-year-old if thought he'd come out of it in one piece,' he replied. 'Manson, that is.'

'Xavier is a handful,' I admitted, keeping the thought that marrying a woman thirty years younger than you and having a baby at the age of fifty-nine was asking for trouble very much to myself. I liked Rosa a lot. I liked staying on Mal's good side even more. 'But I don't think the majority of parents would share your opinion.'

He wiped a hand over his face and let out a resigned sigh before he could even say what we both knew he was going to say next.

'I suppose that answers the next question I wanted to ask you.'

'Mal, I know what you're going to say,' I replied. 'The answer is still no.'

'I've got everyone from *Good Morning America* to Oprah bleedin' Winfrey wanting to talk to "Este Cox" about her book!' He slapped the table so hard, he made the papadums jump. 'Why are you so determined to stay anonymous?'

'I would rather set myself on fire than let people know I wrote it,' I answered immediately, pushing away my book with the tip of one finger, afraid even to be seen with it in public. 'You told me it would be OK.'

'Again, something I agreed to before I knew we were working with one of the biggest-selling books I've seen in my career,' he said with a groan. 'You know I only want the best for you but honestly, it breaks my heart to think you aren't out there enjoying all your success. Why are we hiding away in a Brick Lane curry house so we won't bump into anyone from the industry when we should be showing off and showering you with champagne at The Ivy? And I do mean the proper one in Covent Garden, not one of those shitty chain offshoots.'

'As lovely as that sounds,' I said, even though it did not sound that nice, 'I'm very happy with the way things are. I don't want anyone to know I'm Este Cox.'

He sat back, arms folded, and lowered his chin, inspecting me over the rim of his glasses.

'This is about your parents again, isn't it?'

'No,' I replied too quickly. It wasn't *only* about my parents.

'I understand why you wanted to keep things quiet in the beginning but if you ask me, I think they would be chuffed to bits for you if you told them now.'

I gave Mal a grateful look but we both knew he was wrong. My dad, Hugh Taylor, was a world-renowned book editor and publisher at the MullinsParker imprint, Anaphora, famous for his exquisite taste in literary fiction. In his long and storied career, he'd acquired and edited countless prize winners; Bookers, Nibbies, Neustadts, Costas, Pulitzers, two of his authors had even been awarded the Nobel Prize for literature, all of which was to say, my father was not well known for his love of the romance genre. In fact, it was entirely possible that the only two people on the planet who held it in lesser regard were my mother, well-respected and greatly feared literary critic, Pandora Taylor, and publishing's current favourite moody boy author, CJ Simmons.

Also known as my ex.

Three perfectly good reasons to keep the authorship

of *Butterflies* a secret from now until forever as far as I was concerned.

'I'm not ready yet,' I said, leaving out the part where I never would be. 'You know I never wanted to be famous, I just wanted to write a book.'

'And what a bloody book.' Malcolm picked up the special edition and flicked through the pages in awe. 'I still don't think you understand how good it is. You're not an overnight global sensation for nothing.'

Good was one word for it. Spicy was another. Filthy. Smut-filled. An affront to all that is holy. Just some of the descriptions I'd spotted when I took a peek at the Goodreads reviews. First and last time I ever did that.

'Clearly you haven't read the reviews,' I muttered into my water glass.

He admonished me with a cluck. 'There are ten times as many good reviews as bad ones. Sod everyone else, *you* should be incredibly proud of it. Of yourself.'

Easy for him to say, trickier for me to believe. Most parents were disappointed in their kids for smoking or drinking underage. Mine would've been thrilled to see me puffing on a Marlboro Red as long as I was reading *Crime and Punishment* at the same time. Neither of them batted an eyelid when they found my fake ID when I was sixteen but the horrified look on Mum's face when she came across my secret stash of Jackie Collins novels was something I'd never forget.

'Ultimately, it's all up to you.' He pushed the book back towards me and I felt the furrows between my eyebrows deepen. 'But even if I can't plaster Este Cox all over the media, I still need the sequel. I've held the dogs at bay as long as I can.'

'And you'll get it,' I promised, trying not to let my

7

eyes slide to the tote bag slung over the back of my chair. The last thing I needed was for Mal to know the manuscript was within grabbing distance. When I woke up, I had every intention of handing it over but, somewhere between Kings Langley and Watford Junction, a niggling feeling in my gut made me take out the stack of pages and give it another once-over. It wasn't ready. I couldn't quite say what exactly but I was certain there was something missing.

'Give me one more week,' I said, slinging an arm over my chair with forced casualness. 'You'll have it by next Friday.'

It wasn't as though he could argue with me really. What was he going to do, steal my laptop, cut off my hand to get the fingerprint and wade through the dozens of weirdly named drafts until he found something he could publish? I gulped and tightened my grip on the bag. Judging by the scowl on his face that was a possibility.

'You're sure that's enough time with the big party this weekend?' he asked, picking up his beer and wiping the sweaty bottle across his generous forehead.

'More than,' I confirmed. 'As long as you're sure you aren't going to feel strangely compelled to tell Mum and Dad about my secret identity.'

Malcolm leaned across the table and lowered his voice.

'Sophie Taylor, I have kept more publishing secrets than you've had hot dinners and I will take them all to the grave. Did I ever tell you about the time Kazuo Ishiguro and I ended up on a ferry to the Isle of Man after the British Book Awards?'

'No,' I whispered, eyes wide open.

'And I never will,' he replied sternly. 'Your secret is

safe with me. If I can keep quiet about the author who has to have a baby bottle full of warm milk brought to his room every night on tour for more than twenty years, I think I can get through your dad's birthday party without spilling the beans.'

'One day I am going to get you so drunk and you're going to tell me everything,' I threatened as he finished his beer then laughed.

'Please, you forget who you're talking to. I remember when publishing was still a three-martini lunch game. I could put away enough whisky to down an elephant and I still wouldn't utter a word,' he said with a wink. 'But if you go on *Good Morning America*, I'll tell you everything.'

You couldn't blame a man for trying.

'Thank you so much but I couldn't eat another thing,' I said, ignoring my groaning stomach and immediately reaching for my spoon when the waiter put two bowls of kulfi down on the table. 'And I don't think we ordered them?'

'They were sent by the gentleman over in the corner.'

He discreetly inclined his head towards the far left side of the room and, as I leaned all the way out of my chair, I saw the shadowy shape of a man raising a beer bottle in my direction.

'But I don't know the gentleman over in the corner,' I said, puzzled.

'I do,' Malcolm said in a voice that was not promising. 'Bloody hell.'

The silhouette stood and the first thing I saw was an electric smile light up the darkness.

'Joe bloody Walsh, our new senior creative director.'

Mal plucked his napkin from his lap and threw it over my book. 'He does your covers. Bloody genius when it comes to books but, in the words of my dearly departed grandmother, he's both a cad and a bounder, so keep your wits about you. Half the girls in the office are under his spell and I'd say a fair number of the men as well.'

It was very easy to see how Joe Walsh qualified as a cad, a bounder and the official MullinsParker office heartbreaker. When he stepped into the sunlight, I almost gasped out loud. The man looked like something off the cover of a romance novel and not one of the modern ones with the cute illustrations that were, according to some very angry people in my DMs, seriously misleading about the content inside. Oh no. This man belonged on a proper, old-school romance novel, something overtly sexy with 'rogue' in the title. Or duke. Or pirate. He'd make an excellent pirate. Dark, dishevelled hair, square jaw, broad shoulders, the sleeves of his white button-down shirt rolled up to the elbow, revealing strong, muscular forearms, and all of it set off by piercing blue eyes that seemed to see through my dress and directly into my soul. If he was one of the characters in my book, I'd have described him as rugged but sensual, unbelievably handsome with an edge of mischief in his eyes and every movement bursting with barely restrained sexuality.

Joe Walsh was the man of every romance reader's dreams.

'Don't you worry about me,' I told Mal as the cover model approached, my sex most assuredly not on fire and nary a single millimetre of my skin aflame. I was impervious to good-looking book boys with bad attitudes, one was enough to last a lifetime. 'I'm cad-proof and bounder-resistant.'

'That's what they all say, Sophie,' he muttered back. 'That's what they all say.'

CHAPTER TWO

'So this is where you're hiding.'

Without asking permission from one of the waiters, Joe Walsh dragged a chair away from another table and pulled it up to ours, seat facing outwards. He straddled it confidently, arms crossed and resting on the high back like the cool substitute teacher in a bad nineties movie about a tough inner-city high school. He had the costume down, tie already loosened, shirt rumpled and un-buttoned at the throat, and on anyone else his brown corduroys would have screamed 'double geography' but the way they strained against his thick thighs suggested he spent less time studying boulders and more time casually picking them up and throwing them around.

'What are you doing here?' Mal asked sharply.

My head flicked back towards my godfather. I couldn't think of another time I'd known him to be so agitated, not even when he babysat my little sister and she filled his shoes with used cat litter because he refused to sit through *Twilight* for a third time in seven hours.

'Best chicken dhansak in London,' Joe replied, his

unabashed eyes still on me. I glared back but he didn't look away, unbothered by our silent exchange.

'We missed you at cover art,' he said to Mal, picking up a teaspoon and helping himself to my kulfi. He closed his eyes and moaned in soft ecstasy, pulling the spoon slowly out from between his full lips. 'Clearly you were busy.'

'Joe Walsh, this is my goddaughter, Sophie Taylor,' Mal said by way of explanation. 'Sophie, this is someone I work with who wishes he could join us for a cup of tea but sadly can't because he's far too busy.'

Joe laughed, a deep, mellifluous sound that went straight to the ovaries.

'Good news. I can absolutely join you for a cup of tea. The department heads meeting was cancelled because, according to your assistant, you're out all afternoon on a very important secret meeting with a very important secret author. Should we be ordering champagne?'

'I don't drink in the daytime,' I lied before Mal could spontaneously combust. 'So no thanks.'

Joe shrugged and reached across the table and nudged Mal's napkin aside, revealing the special edition copy of *Butterflies*. Slowly, intentionally, he turned it over in his hands like a detective with a smoking gun and my stomach dropped all the way through the soles of my comfortable shoes.

'Big fan of Este Cox, are you?' he asked.

'No,' I said.

'Yes,' said Mal.

Both at the exact same time.

One corner of Joe's mouth flickered upwards.

'I'm not a big fan, I'm a huge fan,' I corrected, hitting my godfather with the world's finest side eye. 'Malcolm mentioned there was a special edition coming out and I begged him for a copy.'

'Huh.' Joe flicked through the pages with a look of easy disdain. 'Three hundred pages of wish fulfilment fantasy for women who need to get out the house more often. Or stay in more often, if you catch my drift.'

It wasn't a difficult drift to get a hold of.

Mal said nothing, I said nothing. Instead I clenched my jaw tightly and felt my teeth grinding against each other.

'Two fresh mint teas?'

The toxic silence around the table was broken by our waiter.

'Mint tea sounds good, I'll have one too,' Joe said as the waiter put down our cups, eyeballing the awkward situation he'd walked in on.

'No problem, you can have both of ours.' Mal rose to his feet, pulled out his wallet and pressed his credit card into the waiter's empty hands. 'I've got to be getting back to the office, busy afternoon.'

'Except the department heads meeting is cancelled,' Joe said.

'I've got a call scheduled with an author.'

'Your assistant said your diary was empty.'

'Pamela is a PA, not a mind reader.'

I watched the action volley back and forth between them as though I was watching a particularly heated game of tennis and not two grown men bickering until the waiter returned holding a card machine, waiting for a break in the posturing to present it to Mal.

'If I could get your PIN, sir.'

There had never been a more apologetic man than that waiter.

'So, Sophie Taylor.' Joe said my name slowly, trying it on for size to see if it fit. 'You're Malcolm's goddaughter, are you?'

'That's right,' I replied, sucking in my cheeks and tamping down the desire to kick him in the shins.

'And this is a nice, friendly catch-up lunch?'

Tightening my jaw, I did my very best not even to glance at my book as he dropped it heavily onto the table.

'What else would it be?'

'Can't imagine,' he answered with mock confusion. 'Just seems a bit odd that Malcolm would be paying for lunch with his goddaughter with his company credit card, that's all.'

Me, Mal and the waiter froze as the little white receipt reeled silently out of the card machine.

'This really is delicious,' Joe said as he dipped back into the kulfi. 'What is it, pistachio?'

The waiter nodded.

'Yes, sir. We make it ourselves, my grandmother's recipe.'

'Incredible. Malcolm, you really should try it before you rush off to your busy afternoon.'

'Thanks but I'll pass,' Mal replied, shoving his credit card and the receipt back in his wallet with no small degree of irritation. 'Sophie, shall I call you a car to the station?'

I waved off his kind offer as I stood and slung my tote bag over my shoulder, shooting daggers at his co-worker. 'Don't worry about it. My train isn't until six, I've got ages.'

'Plenty of time to sit down and eat dessert with me then,' Joe piped up.

There are roughly one million things a person can do in London on an average Thursday afternoon. Even when I factored in my little wheelie suitcase, heavy tote bag and the sultry late August heat there were still endless ways for me to entertain myself until it was time to catch the train. Museums, cinemas, art galleries, an infinite number of coffee shops where I could hole up with my latest draft and try to work out what was missing from my book. I could go to the zoo. I could take an open-top bus ride around the city. London was mine for the taking.

But when Joe Walsh stood up, pulled out my chair and patted the seat, something inside me clicked. Not in a good way, like a puzzle piece slotting into place. More like someone taking the safety catch off a gun.

'You know how the trains are,' Mal said, speaking far more loudly than necessary. 'Maybe you ought to get to St Pancras nice and early.'

'St Pancras?' Joe echoed. 'I live right by there. Don't worry yourself, I'll make sure she gets to the station in plenty of time.'

'I'm a big girl, no one needs to get me to the station,' I said when Mal opened his mouth to argue. 'Thank you for lunch, Malcolm. I'm going to stay and finish my tea.'

It was very obvious he wasn't happy but he could read my expression just as well as I could read his. I wasn't going anywhere. As far as I was concerned, the only thing more irritating than the kind of man who went out of his way to get a rise out of you, was letting said man know he'd got under your skin. Joe Walsh clearly thought he was the cleverest person at the table.

Joe Walsh was about to find out otherwise.

Mal fought his way into his suit jacket, aggressively tightening his tie as Joe hopped back into his empty seat. 'Text me when you get home,' he instructed gruffly. 'And don't forget what we agreed about the other thing.'

'Other thing?' Joe leaned forward with his chin in his hands. 'That sounds interesting.'

'It is,' I replied, meeting his intrigue with steely resolve. 'But it's also nothing to do with you so maybe you should mind your own business.'

'Oh, Christ.' Mal sighed, shaking his head as he gave my shoulder a warning squeeze. 'I'll see you at the weekend. Behave yourself.'

'I always do?!' I replied, genuinely offended by the implication.

'Bye, Malcolm! See you Monday!' Joe called cheerily as Mal stalked off towards the door, still chuntering under his breath.

When the door was closed and we'd both watched Mal storm away down the street, Joe looked at me and smiled. In no rush at all, I reached for my cup of still-steaming tea and stirred, searching for the chink in his arsehole armour.

'Why Monday?' I asked as he claimed Mal's tea as his own. 'Don't you work on Fridays?'

'Most Fridays I do,' he answered. 'I'm off tomorrow.'

'Doing anything fun?'

'Could be.' He picked up his cup and blew. 'But it's nothing to do with you so maybe you should mind your own business.'

So it was going to be like that, was it? Let the games begin.

'Mal says you're the creative director,' I replied

17

politely. With a man like Joe, you couldn't play your cards too early otherwise they flounced off in a huff and where was the fun in that? 'That sounds so interesting. What does it entail exactly?'

His Adam's apple bobbed up and down as he swallowed his tea before responding. 'Anything and everything. I don't edit but I'm involved in every other aspect of a book's publishing journey. This one, for example.' He picked up the copy of *Butterflies* again, the book practically purring when he brushed the pad of his thumb against every single soft page. 'Malcolm brought it in, Sera on his team did the edit, but after that, it's all me.'

I nodded slowly with a thoughtful expression, taking my time as I considered his statement.

'So you're a cover designer with a fancy title?'

Joe flinched. My first blow had clocked him right in the ego.

'There's a lot more to it than that,' he replied, his tone pricklier than before. 'It's the cover, the typeface, the paper stock, special finishes, the marketing, the social media – anything and everything that has to do with the brand comes through me. I am the person who communicates the book's message.'

'Funny,' I said. 'I'd have thought the author communicated the book's message.'

'Funny,' he replied. 'I'd have thought you would know the author doesn't want anything to do with the publishing process. What with you being such a big fan.'

One point to Walsh.

'The author writes the book,' Joe said while I focused every atom of my being on not giving the game away by blushing. I would not give him the satisfaction.

'But a hundred thousand words floating around the world on their own aren't going to get read. You need the right cover, the right marketing, the right brand strategy. That's where I come in. My job is to explain what the book is about, who it's for and why they should buy it.'

'When you put it like that, it's almost as though you don't need the words at all,' I replied, snatching my book from his hand, automatically scanning the back cover copy even though I must have read it at least a thousand times before.

Jenna Johnson has only one goal for the summer; to get as far away from London and her ex as possible. A trip to Texas with her best friend sounds like just what she needs, a whole month of fun, sun and American accents, but when her friend drops out at the last minute, Jenna finds herself all alone in Austin . . . until she meets stoic cowboy, Eric Hall, another lonely heart looking for distraction. Irresistibly drawn to each other, the two make a pact – spend the month together without falling in love, something Jenna's ex claims she's incapable of. When their powerful physical connection unexpectedly turns into something more, Jenna begins to wonder – was her ex right about her icy heart or is she finally feeling butterflies?

'The words might make it harder to sell something like that,' Joe said with a chuckle. 'As I said, wish fulfilment for sexually frustrated women. It's like shooting fish in a barrel.'

'If that's true, there must be an awful lot of sexually frustrated women out there,' I replied, my fingers curling protectively around the spine as he held up his hands in mock surrender.

'Don't blame me. I can't be everywhere at once, I am only one man.'

'And very possibly the actual worst one,' I retorted. He was enjoying this far too much. 'So what if that's part of it? How come when a woman writes about sexual frustration she's the butt of a joke, but when a man writes about his sexual frustration, he gets an Oscar?'

'Look, I didn't like *The Joker* either,' he replied, unexpectedly defensive. 'All I'm saying is, this kind of book, as popular as it may be, it's not that complex, is it? Not exactly Dickens. More like dick-ins, if you know what I mean.'

'Oh, I think I do.' I stood so abruptly my chair toppled to the floor behind me. Enough was enough. 'Now I think about it, St Pancras is pretty far from Brick Lane,' I said. 'I'd hate to miss my train.'

'The one that leaves in four hours?'

'That's the one,' I confirmed. 'I'd love to say it's been a pleasure but it really hasn't.'

'OK, I'm sorry, I'm sorry.' Joe spoke quickly but got to his feet slowly, confidently, like he knew I would wait. He wasn't about to be rushed, not even in his apology. 'I went too far. I didn't mean to offend you, it was a joke, I was teasing. There's nothing wrong with a book about a woman who needs a shag.'

'Could you have tried any harder to miss the point?' I asked, so frustrated. 'That's not what the book is about at all.'

'That's what chapter five is about,' he replied. 'And chapter eight and chapter ten and chapter thirteen and—'

'It's fine, clearly you don't understand it,' I told him before he could list every sex scene in my book. 'Not that I'm surprised, it wasn't written for you. The sex is what happens in the book, not what it's about.'

'You really are a passionate fan,' he said, refocusing on me. 'Remind me, what is it that you do?'

'I'm a teacher,' I mumbled. 'I read a lot.'

'English teacher?'

'Primary school.'

'Really?' He looked surprised, responding with one raised eyebrow. 'Single?'

My spine stiffened. 'What does that have to do with anything?'

Joe Walsh brushed one hand through his hair, dipped his chin and trained his ocean blue eyes on mine.

'Everything.'

There was no doubt in my mind that move would work on ninety-nine out of one hundred women but it wasn't going to work on me. All he was doing was proving my point.

'What I'm trying to say is, you don't understand the message of the book,' I shot back. 'It's not about a woman who just needs a good seeing-to. It's about all the frustrations women have to put up with every day, all the things we're expected to get on and do without complaint to make everyone else's lives easier, all while our needs go unfulfilled which, yes, very often includes our sexual needs. We've been trained to be grateful for what we're given rather than ask for what we want, not *only* in bed – but maybe you're right. If there were a few more men who tried a bit harder, perhaps there would be a few less books like this.'

When I slapped my hand on the table to punctuate my sentence, I was out of breath, my chest heaving, and two red spots had appeared in Joe's cheeks. We both stared at the powder-puff pink book in the middle of the table, the recessed lights in the restaurant ceiling making the silver foil title shimmer.

Butterflies.

'Excuse me.'

A panic-stricken waiter stood before us, two full-to-the-brim liqueur glasses in his hands.

'These are from the manager,' he said as he placed one in front of me and one in front of Joe, never spilling a drop. 'It's an Irish cream liqueur.'

'Thanks,' Joe replied with a flash of his winning smile. 'You can give me both, she doesn't drink in the day.'

Without a word, I swiped both glasses, downing one and then the other.

'I'll have another,' I said, wiping the back of my hand across my mouth as Joe watched on in silent shock. 'And so will he.'

CHAPTER THREE

'They don't have "Since U Been Gone" but they do have "Before He Cheats",' Joe yelled over the tinny karaoke backing track of 'Tainted Love'. 'Or we could do Britney, they've got all of Britney.'

'It's "Love Is a Battleground" next,' I shouted back, squinting at the blurred screen suspended from the ceiling and jabbing at a sticky remote control. 'Then it says "My Humps" by The Black Eyed Peas?'

'My speciality,' he replied with a shallow bow. 'Trust me.'

As the first few bars of the Pat Benatar classic filled the tiny, red-walled room, I tried to remember the exact chain of events that led to me being locked in a karaoke booth somewhere in King's Cross with a man I wouldn't have spat on if he was on fire two hours earlier. First there was Baileys, a lot of Baileys, which I wouldn't have thought of as a good summer drink but, it turned out, if you put enough ice in it, Baileys is good any time of year. Joe apologised for being an arsehole and

23

insisted he didn't mean what he'd said, which I didn't really buy, but by the time the third Baileys hit, it didn't seem to matter as much. Then the restaurant told us they were closing to prep for dinner and Joe suggested we move to a pub near St Pancras but an unexpected singalong to Beyoncé on the way there saw him divert our black cab to his favourite karaoke bar, and now I was standing barefoot on a built-in zebra-print banquette holding a microphone they'd have to prise out of my cold dead hand, there was an almost empty bottle of overpriced prosecco on the table and another one on its way. I was hot, sweaty and ecstatic, and I couldn't stop staring at Joe Walsh.

'What's wrong?' he asked as I clambered down from the sofa and tipped the remains of my drink down my throat. 'You missed your cue.'

'Hot,' I muttered, rolling the glass over my face. 'It's hot in here.'

'It is but you are also dressed like you're on your way to mass,' Joe said, refilling my glass. 'It's summer, woman. I know that doesn't always mean much in London but have you not noticed the heat wave?'

I pulled at the high collar of my dress, rivulets of sweat snaking down my chest and seeking refuge inside my bra.

'You try dressing for a meeting in London, a three-hour train ride and a visit with your parents when you will literally set on fire if the sun touches your skin and see what kind of outfit you come up with.'

'What meeting?'

The soft edges of my mind moved more slowly than usual, flickering gently instead of clicking away with rapid-fire responses.

'Lunch,' I amended. 'I meant lunch.'

'Right,' he replied, pushing his own damp hair away from his face. 'Lunch. With Malcolm.'

'That's right. Busy day. And I still have to get the train to Chesterfield then a taxi to my parents' house because my sister could come and get me but it's too much effort so she won't and Mum and Dad will be busy organising the party and god knows what everyone else will be doing but well, yes, busy day.'

I was rambling, desperately trying to keep the conversation moving without really saying anything. Just because we'd sung a duet of 'I've Got You Babe' didn't mean I was about to spill my deepest, darkest secrets to this man. Joe might not be as terrible a human as I initially suspected but I trusted him about as far as I could throw him and, since he was at least a foot taller and many solid muscular pounds heavier than me, that was not very far at all.

'To be honest, I'm not really looking forward to it,' I added, in case it wasn't clear.

The door creaked open and before the server could even step inside, I leapt down from the bench, grabbed the open bottle of prosecco out of the little silver bucket and filled my glass. The door closed quickly. 'Family, you know. Can be tricky. Tricky tricky tricky.'

'I hear that.'

He held out his glass and I poured until sparkling wine spilled over the top and trickled down his hand. He brought his fingers to his lips, catching my eye as he licked it off.

'My parents are divorced,' Joe said. 'Mum's in Scotland, Dad's down here. Twice the stress, double the visiting, half the fun.'

'Scotland's nice though,' I replied in a high-pitched voice. Joe's face changed completely when he wasn't smiling. His bottom lip was the tiniest bit fuller than the top giving him a perma-pout, and the two little lines between his eyebrows, slightly closer to the left than the right, gave the impression he was always deep in thought. I only hoped he wasn't thinking the same things I was or else I could be in real trouble.

'Scotland is nice,' he agreed after taking a deep drink of prosecco and reducing the amount in his glass to a more manageable level. 'Except Mum decided it would be fun to move as far north as it's possible to go without getting wet. It's a trek. Can't blame her for wanting to stay clear of my dad though.'

'You don't get on?' It was possibly the most redundant question ever.

A small half-smile appeared on his face and that little crease between his eyebrows ironed itself out.

'My dad is a lot. Best enjoyed in small doses. Mum put twenty years into trying to change him before she gave up and legged it to America. She and I moved to Boston when I was sixteen.'

'Fancy,' I commented as the very loud music echoed around us. 'What brought you back?'

He looked away, vaguely shaking his head. 'Lots of things.'

'Did you go to school in America?'

'I did. A little place called Harvard.'

Something in the room changed and our easy back and forth shifted into something else, an interview rather than a conversation, less sharing and more stating. His genuine half-smile was swallowed up by the louche, smug grin that had put my back up at lunch. My defences sprang back into action and I was forced to remind myself just because a man knows all the words to 'Crazy in Love' doesn't mean he's a good person.

'Have you ever heard of Harford – Harford-on-the-Water?' I asked, backing across the room and searching for the glass of water I hadn't touched since the first bottle of prosecco arrived. I needed to hydrate. I needed to keep my distance. 'That's where my parents live. It's beautiful. Bit boring, very quiet, but beautiful. It's on the river, lots of limestone cottages, even more sheep.'

'Sophie Taylor.' Joe said my name slowly and, in spite of everything, this time I did not hate the way it sounded as it tripped off his tongue. 'Wait, your dad isn't Hugh Taylor, is he?'

I groaned inwardly and blanched outwardly; there was no need to confirm or deny, my expression said it all for me.

'I should have known,' he exclaimed, raking his hair away from his face. 'Malcolm's your godfather. You're Hugh and Pandora Taylor's kid.'

'One of. I have a younger sister and an older brother,' I replied in between glugs of water but Joe wasn't listening. His face tensed with concentration as he worked through something in his head.

'Isn't it his big birthday party this weekend?' he asked as I started on his glass of water after finishing my own. 'That's why you're going up north?'

The backing track played on and Pat's lyrics scrolled merrily across the screen, completely unaware they were being ignored. No promises, no demands.

'That's why I'm going up north,' I said, his self-congratulatory Sherlock Holmes smile melting away as

27

I spoke. 'I know everyone in publishing worships them, I'm sure you've got some amazing story you can't wait to tell me about how one of them once imparted some words of wisdom and changed your life forever. Go on, get it out your system.'

'Call me crazy.' Joe leaned against the closest wall, just a couple of feet away. All the walls were close, the room was tiny and getting smaller by the second. 'But I get the feeling you have a conflicted relationship with them.'

'Everyone has a conflicted relationship with their parents,' I replied before quickly correcting myself. 'No, I don't, they're great parents. Amazing, best parents who ever lived. Is it me or does it feel like they've turned the heating on in here?'

'Then why did you say you weren't looking forward to going home?'

'I hate travelling,' I lied. 'Trains are a nightmare, taxis cost a fortune. It really is getting very warm.'

Joe watched my futile attempt to fan myself with a damp napkin, finished his drink then reached for the prosecco to top off his glass.

'You're not going to believe this but,' he said, laughing as though he couldn't believe he was really about to say what he was about to say, 'when I first saw you with Malcolm at lunch, I thought you were Este Cox.'

My water glass slipped out of my hand, fell to the floor and shattered into a thousand pieces. Well, three pieces. It was a cheap glass.

'Come on, it wasn't that far-fetched an idea,' Joe said, draping himself over the zebra-print seats. 'You and Malcolm, book on the table, clandestine meetings in back alleys.'

'We were having lunch in a curry house in the middle of the day.'

'A secret lunch,' he amended, 'and you were both extremely shifty when I came over.'

'Because you were acting completely normal?' I replied. 'Watching us like a weirdo then emerging from the shadows like some sort of shit spy.'

'Obviously Hugh and Pandora Taylor's daughter would never write anything like *Butterflies*,' Joe chuckled, shaking his head at the very thought. 'God, imagine the look on your mother's face if she had to explain *that* to her friends.'

I felt like I was going to be sick. It was one thing to think that kind of thing myself but it was another to hear someone else say it out loud. My eyes welled up with tears and I wiped them away with surprise, slowly sinking to the worryingly sticky floor. I couldn't remember the last time I'd cried and here I was, seconds away from bursting into hysterics in front of an absolute tosspot who had no idea what he was saying.

'Sophie?' Joe squatted down in front of me, a very real-seeming look of concern on his stupidly handsome face. 'Are you all right?'

'No,' I replied as I dragged myself upright to find my feet again. Was the room spinning when we came in? I wasn't sure. 'I'm not all right and neither are you.'

'Come again?'

'When will I learn to trust my instincts?' I asked myself out loud, shame steadily finding itself eclipsed by disappointment. Disappointment in him for proving me right and disappointment in myself for thinking I might have been wrong in the first place. 'You're an arrogant, ignorant, insensitive arsehole, so wrapped up in your own privilege, you can't see past the end of your own nose. Not everything is about you, not everything is for you.'

'Me?' he exclaimed, clearly stunned as he looked up at me from the floor. 'You think *I'm* privileged?'

'Unless you were part of a Harvard diversity programme where they mix up the rich Americans with some posh British boys for a bit of balance?'

'What about you?' Joe launched back, rising unsteadily to his feet, his face flushed. 'Where did you go to university?'

I wrapped my arms around my body and squeezed. 'Durham.'

'Interesting. Isn't that where your dad went? In fact, isn't that where he still guest lectures *every year*?'

'You know a disturbing amount about my father,' I replied, chin raised. 'Is there something you want to tell me?'

'Only that you're just as privileged as me, sweetheart.'

All traces of jokes or sarcastic asides were gone. He was angry. Joe tossed back the rest of his prosecco and slammed the glass back down on the low table, a dull crack piercing the synth-heavy backing track. Two hours of karaoke, two bottles of prosecco and two broken glasses. This was going to cost a fortune.

'Life must be so hard for you with your university education and your amazing parents,' he ranted, 'teaching at some fancy private school—'

'Ah-ha!' I cut in. 'It's not a private school.'

He paused, an expectant expression on his face.

'But it is quite hard to get into,' I confessed into my chest.

'You don't know me as well as you think you do but

I've got your number,' Joe went on, moving closer as he continued with his tirade. 'Let me guess, school was easy, you probably got accepted into Durham before you even took your exams, could've walked into a cushy publishing job but that sounded too much like hard work so you decided to rough it for a bit, teach some rich shits' kids their ABCs until you land a rich shit of your own. But Mr Rich Shit still hasn't appeared so you spend all your nights alone, reading books like *Butterflies*, wondering why no one has fallen for your silky hair and rose petal lips and your terrible, terrible singing voice, and—'

'I spend all day, every day dealing with children but you, Joe Walsh, are the biggest child I've ever met,' I yelled, poking a finger into his solid chest, so mad I barely even heard what he was saying. 'Ooh, look at me, I'm so clever and well read. Ooh, look at me, I went to Harvard so I know better than everyone else about everything. Ooh, look at me, I'm handsome and tall and probably played lacrosse and . . . and . . .'

Through the red mist of rage, I couldn't quite find a way to finish the sentence. We were so close, I could see the flare of his nostrils and the quiver at the corners of his mouth, but when I reached his eyes, instead of the anger I was anticipating they were full of something else entirely.

Lust.

Joe Walsh was looking at me like he wanted to eat me up and, I realised, as the white hot fury burned out from my chest and slid down into the pit of my stomach, settling somewhere unexpected, below my belly button, there was nothing in the world I wanted more.

'Sophie—' he began, reaching one hand towards me.

'Excuse me.' I jerked backwards before he could make contact and grabbed hold of my suitcase. 'I have a train to catch.'

I was out the door and on the street before the song had even finished.

CHAPTER FOUR

The train from London to Chesterfield was not good.
Not that there were any good train journeys any more,
only OK ones and godawful ones, but this had to be
one of the worst.

Every carriage was packed with human soup since
the two trains scheduled before mine had been cancelled
and I made it through the turnstiles with one minute
to spare. As we pulled out of St Pancras, I shuffled
down the overcrowded carriage, banging my shins on
stuck-out suitcases, only to find three different people
fighting over my seat and one already sitting in it since
the conductor thought it would be fun to void all reser-
vations. Too exhausted to join the fray, I carried on to
the end of the carriage and crammed myself in with
two muddy mountain bikes and a towering stack of
overflow luggage.

The train was hot, the train was slow, I was fighting
a fast-moving hangover, my phone battery was at twelve
percent. I didn't have *any* snacks, let alone an M&S
cocktail in a can, and to top it all off, the toilets weren't

working. It was the worst train journey anyone had ever endured but there was something that bothered me even more than the horribly embarrassed man in a very nice suit who kept apologising as he peed into an empty Lucozade bottle three feet away from me.

I couldn't stop thinking about Joe Walsh.

The scent of his spicy aftershave still lingered on my dress from where he'd hoisted me into the air during our *Dirty Dancing* duet and I could still feel the firm grip of his hands around my waist, hear the raspy laugh that accompanied his singing. It was a long time since I'd spent that much intimate time with a good-looking man in a sweaty darkened room. A man who looked like he could crush walnuts with his thighs and tear phone books in two with his bare hands. Did they still make phone books? The one that lived on the little table in my parents' hallway could well be an antique. Maybe he could have a go on the ten-thousand-word instruction manual that came with my air fryer instead.

Not that it was my fault, this was his plan all along. I considered myself a fairly intelligent, reasonably savvy woman and I'd still been easy prey. If I had to choose who would win a fight between Joe Walsh and a bear, I would back Joe Walsh. Not because he could reasonably defeat a bear in a show of strength but because he'd find a way to flatter it into submission then deliver a knockout blow when it wasn't paying attention. The thought of him and his smug face working anywhere near my books made me so angry, I almost wanted to ask the man in the suit if I could keep the Lucozade bottle and courier it to Joe as a lovely way to start his weekend. Thankfully, as long as Este Cox stayed anonymous, I would never have to go into the MullinsParker office which meant, thankfully, I would never have to see him again.

But that didn't change the fact that every single time I closed my eyes, I heard him say my name and saw his mouth inching closer to mine. And every single time, my whole body burned.

When we finally rolled into Chesterfield station, I stumbled off the train, gasping for air like I'd escaped Shawshank prison.

'No offence, Soph, but you look like warmed-up dogshit.'

Blinking into the low evening sun, I looked around to see who had so damningly and accurately described me.

'And she's lost the power of speech. That should make the drive easier.'

'William!'

Never in my life had I been so happy to take my brother's abuse. I flung myself at him, suitcase slow-motion toppling off the pavement and into the road, earning us both a disgruntled honk from a man in a Mazda.

'Wanker,' William said with a smile, shaking his hand in the matching gesture once the car was safely down the road. He stooped to retrieve my fallen suitcase with me still clinging to his lanky frame like a baby koala.

'How did you know I was here?' I asked, giving him the biggest, strongest hug I could given the fact my arms were about as strong as used toilet paper.

'I'm psychic?' He patted me on the back to signal the acceptable amount of sibling PDA time had passed. 'Also your arrival time, along with your departure time, arrival station, departure station, phone number, email,

Instagram, Facebook *and* TikTok handles were all on the official Hugh Taylor Big Birthday Weekend Bash shared spreadsheet.'

'Dad's on TikTok?' I said with a shudder. It was a terrifying thought.

'Dad's big on TikTok,' he said with a grim nod. 'He mostly sticks to CleaningTok but he's sent me more than one Catluminati video. He stays away from BookTok, obviously. Right now he's mostly into capybaras.'

'Who isn't?' I replied. 'Makes sense that he steers clear of BookTok . . .'

'Imagine what would happen if someone said a word against Faulkner,' William chuckled. 'He'd hunt them down and beat them to death with his first edition of *The Sound and the Fury.*'

'Wait a minute, what spreadsheet?' I said, rewinding his sentence.

'The spreadsheet detailing every second of every minute of every hour from the day the party was announced until the final second when the last guest fucks off back home. You didn't get it?'

'I did not get it,' I confirmed, what little air left in my lungs seeping out until I was fully deflated. 'Dad didn't include me on the party spreadsheet.'

'So weird,' he said, scratching his beardy chin. 'I assumed you were ignoring it because—'

He stopped himself altogether too suddenly but I caught the shifty look on his face before he could wipe it clean.

'Because what?'

'Doesn't matter, don't worry about it, let's get in the car.'

'William.'

My voice carried the unmistakable threat of getting kicked in the balls by your little sister in a town centre car park. It wasn't an empty threat either, I'd done it before and I'd do it again.

'OK, I'll tell you but don't shoot the messenger or knee him in the nut sack or whatever else you're thinking about,' he said, reading my mind. 'The reason you're not on it is probably because CJ is.'

'And why would my ex-boyfriend be on my dad's official Big Birthday Weekend Bash shared spreadsheet?' I enquired.

'Would you like me to lie to you?'

'Yes, please,' I replied, the last shot of Baileys bubbling in my stomach and threatening a dramatic comeback.

'Because Dad definitely hasn't invited him and he definitely isn't coming.'

Perfect. This was just perfect. I'd spent the whole afternoon drinking with one publishing wanker I never wanted to see again and now I had to spend the entire weekend with another.

'How mad would you be if I threw up right now?' I asked, rubbing my stomach unhelpfully.

William pointed at a black car in the corner. 'Soph, it's after eight in Chessie train station. As long as you puke on that Tesla, it's fine by me. *But*,' he paused for added emphasis, 'allow me to share a theory as to why you shouldn't be stressed about it in the least.'

'Go on?'

My stomach gurgled and I took one side step towards the Tesla.

'You broke up what, two years ago?'

'Yes.'

'And CJ is so insecure, he's still clinging to his ex-girlfriend's dad to protect him from the big bad publishing bullies? That's just sad.'

'Say more things like that,' I suggested.

'He's obviously still single.'

'So am I.'

'Yes but CJ is utterly insufferable and, yes, he might have written one poncey, literary flash-in-the-pan book but he definitely doesn't have the bestselling debut novel of the year that's already been sold in twenty-nine languages.'

'Thirty-two,' I said quietly and he swiped a palm down his face.

'Really? I should know that, shouldn't I?'

'Might be helpful,' I agreed. 'Since you're supposed to be my agent.'

William pressed the key fob in his hand, the taillights of his vintage BMW flashing obediently.

'Este Cox's agent,' he corrected with a toss of his shiny chestnut hair, the exact same colour as mine. 'If I'm correct in assuming you're still not ready to tell Mum and Dad.'

I shook my head as my stomach settled itself. 'This is hardly the right weekend, is it?'

'What are you saving it for? Christmas? Wedding anniversary? Deathbed confessional?'

'Mine or theirs?' I said as he led me towards the car with one arm wrapped around my shoulders as though I were a frail old lady incapable of making it there herself. 'I swear I'll tell them. Just not this weekend.'

There was a reason my big brother was the only person besides Mal I'd trusted with my secret and it wasn't only because he was one of the best literary agents in the business. William was honest, loyal and kind. He never sugar-coated anything and he had an uncanny knack of always putting everything into perspective. Also, I was the only one who knew it was him who'd got drunk and smashed the conservatory window by driving through it on a dirt bike when Mum and Dad were on holiday twenty years ago, and not Richard Filby from Year Thirteen who conveniently moved away right before they got back. Yes, two decades had passed. No, I was not about to give up that kind of leverage.

'Seriously, Soph, are you ill? You do look awful.' He pulled his arm away and shoved me halfway across the car park. 'You're not contagious, are you?'

'No, you arse,' I replied, bouncing off the boot of a Fiat 500. 'I'm fine. I had a couple of drinks at lunch, that's all.'

'Of what, cyanide?'

'If I had to choose between cyanide or CJ, I'm not entirely sure I know which one I'd go for,' I admitted. 'Is it too late for me to go home?'

'Yes,' he replied. 'Get your shit together. This weekend is going to be a circus.'

He opened the back passenger side door to put my suitcase in the backseat of his precious car as I let myself into the passenger seat. Once upon a time it belonged to our dad and it still smelled like the school run and summer holiday drives to the seaside.

'If I'm being completely honest, I have felt better,' I said as I closed my eyes and relaxed into the nostalgia. 'So if you felt compelled to stop at the drive-through McDonald's, I wouldn't be mad about it.'

'I've never knowingly turned down a Big Mac when someone else is buying.'

'Did I say I was buying?'

He flashed me a vicious look as he closed the door on my suitcase.

'Why, thank you, William, for getting off your arse and driving all the way to Chesterfield to pick me up even though you could've been doing literally anything else with your evening like sitting in front of the TV with your hands down your pants, watching twenty-year-old episodes of *Frasier*.'

'You know, you aren't always the best advertisement for marriage,' I replied, earning myself another filthy look. 'All right, I'm buying. But you're not having a milkshake.'

'At this time of night?' He gasped as he dropped into the driver's seat. 'That much sugar and dairy before bed is asking for trouble and yes, before you say it, I know, I've changed. So has my metabolism. It's called getting older.'

'Didn't say a word.' Fastening my seatbelt with a decisive clunk-click, I sighed happily and visions of nuggies danced in my head. 'No one would believe you're a day over forty.'

'I'm thirty-eight, you cow.'

I bit my lip to hide my smile. There really was nothing like riling up your big brother to put a happy cap on a shitty day.

William looked over his shoulder into the backseat, my handbag nestled in my lap, my head resting against the seatbelt.

'You're travelling light for a change,' he said, gently coaxing the car into life. 'Only one suitcase? Must be a new record.'

And that was the exact moment when my heart stopped.

I twisted in my seat so quickly, every muscle in my body pulled in protest. There it was, my little wheelie suitcase, happily relaxing against the beige leather seats. My handbag was still in my lap and the footwell was completely clear of everything except for my feet.

My tote bag was nowhere to be seen.

The tote bag that contained the special edition copy of *Butterflies*, a printed-out copy of the unfinished sequel complete with scribbled edits all over it, my laptop, and just for good measure, a handful of post I'd picked up as I ran out that morning. Post with my real name and address all over it in big bold letters.

As William turned the vintage engine over, I watched the train I'd arrived on chug slowly out of the station, taking with it what felt like my last shred of composure, and, for want of any other kind of response, I burst into tears.

CHAPTER FIVE

'Oh, come on, Soph,' William grumbled, staring straight ahead as he steered us out of the car park only to be stalled by a trainee bus driver having trouble with the roundabout. 'It's not going to be that bad, it's only a party.'

'It's not the party,' I replied, gulping down lungfuls of air that did nothing to calm me down. 'I think I left my bag on the train.'

'Ohhh, I've done that before, it's so annoying,' he said with as much empathy as a man gagging for a McDonald's could muster. 'Still, hardly the end of the world. What was in it?'

'My laptop, a load of post with my real name and address on it, a copy of *Butterflies* and a printout of the unfinished sequel.'

'Ah.'

'Tell me it's not a big deal,' I pleaded. 'What are the odds of someone going through the bag, figuring out I'm Este Cox and telling anyone who cares? Tiny, right? Minuscule, non-existent.'

He glanced over at me with a terrible grimace hiding behind his beard.

'The *Mail* is still offering a ten grand reward if anyone can confirm your identity. But since when could you believe anything you read in the *Mail*?'

'I think I'm going to be sick,' I whispered into my hands, the static car suddenly whirling around me.

William patted me awkwardly on the arm and I could see the wheels of his mind turning while my dehydrated brain continued to shrivel and shrink, peeling itself away from the inside of my skull until it was the size of a peanut and ready to escape through my ear.

'There's not much we can do about it now,' he reasoned. 'The ticket office is closed and the train's gone. Let's get you home and I'll make some calls and please don't throw up in my car, you know you never really get the smell out.'

'Why is this happening to me?' I wailed. 'I'm a good person.'

'Well.'

'Not to you, you're my brother,' I said, sobbing freely. 'But in general, I am. I donate to charity, I picked Mum and Dad up from the airport that time they landed in the middle of the night, and I never once complained about how much Cara at work expected us all to pay towards her hen do even though it really was a lot of money and the spa was shit.'

Another reason I'd told my brother my secret and no one else. William was very good at making it seem like everything was going to be OK, even when it was deeply untrue.

'Did I ever tell you about the time I left my laptop

on a train to Edinburgh?' he asked with encouragement before pulling out onto the roundabout. 'Someone handed it in at Waverley and they called me before I even realised it was missing. There are good Samaritans still out there.'

'That or they took a peek at your search history and shit themselves.'

'Oh look, you're feeling better already.' He grinned, shifted gear and put his foot down. 'One phone call and it will all be sorted. You're right, the odds of someone finding your bag and putting two and two together are tiny. Most likely they'll just nick your laptop and leave the rest.'

I sniffed sadly, too far gone to admit it was an uplifting thought.

'Tell you what,' William said. 'I'll pay for the McDonald's.'

'OK but I'm having a milkshake,' I warned, brushing my lank hair away from my face. I couldn't show up at Mum and Dad's looking like this and expect them not to ask questions.

'Anything you want. With the obvious exclusion of an apple pie. I'm not taking you to A&E when you burn the inside of your mouth. Again.'

'It's a deal,' I said as I stared out the window at the darkening sky, doing my ultra very best not to panic.

High on chicken nuggets, sugar and existential dread, we arrived home forty-five minutes later, a shared smile of solidarity on both our faces as we pulled into the driveway.

Until Mum got pregnant with my little sister, Charlotte, nineteen years ago, (a thrilling, midlife surprise, according to Mum who was forty-two when she had her), we'd lived in a small three bed semi in the suburbs outside London, but with a new addition on the way, they decided to sell up down south and invest further north. Dad was more than happy with the long commute and Mum only went into the office once a week for meetings so it didn't make any sense to stay in the city when they could move to Harford and live out their *All Creatures Great and Small* fantasies with five bedrooms, a gorgeous kitchen and a beautiful sunroom on the back of the house that opened onto a garden so huge, my dad had bought one of those ride-on lawn mowers to take care of it. The garden was so big, I sometimes felt as though I needed a staff, half a dozen sheep and a packed lunch if I wanted to go all the way down to the bottom.

After university, I moved back down south, sharing a flat with William and his husband, Sanjit, until I got my job at Abbey Hill School in Tring, and William and Sanjit stayed in London until the year of banana-bread-and-support-bubbles that we'd all agreed never to discuss again. Despite spending every second of his teens desperate to get out from under their roof, William now lived five minutes around the corner from our parents and altogether too far from me for my liking.

'Go on,' William instructed, parked up in the driveway and already dialling National Rail. 'I'm going to find your bag, you save your energy for Mum and Dad.'

'And if Mum sees you eating McDonald's, she'll tell Sanjit and he'll divorce you.'

'It's not my fault he's got high cholesterol,' my brother

mumbled through a handful of fries. 'But feel free not to mention this to him ever.'

I kissed him on the cheek, ignoring his theatrical show of revulsion, then climbed out of the car, grabbed my suitcase and rolled it awkwardly down the gravel driveway. It would be all right. Everything would be good. William would talk to the right people, find my bag and get it back. There was nothing to worry about.

'Hello?' I called loudly, letting myself in the front door. 'Anyone home?'

'Sophie, is that you?'

Mum's head popped around the kitchen door and right away I felt a million times better than I had in the car, but that could've had less to do with Mum's soothing presence and more to do with the way William had sped down the country lanes at seventy miles an hour, driving one-handed while housing a Big Mac.

'I think so,' I replied, flashing back to one particularly hairy head-on challenge from a double-decker bus. 'Can't quite say for sure.'

'Come here and give me a hug, I've got my hands full.' She beckoned me into the kitchen with a head toss. 'I'm icing the cake for your dad's party.'

Well, maybe there was still one thing to worry about.

Pandora Taylor was not known for her abilities in the kitchen. She was known for being one of the fiercest and most well-respected literary critics in the business, cutting the greats down to the bone if she saw fit, ending careers and creating stars overnight. When she wasn't busy intimidating the literary crowd, she took time out to terrify everyone in her children's lives. My teachers never looked at me the same way after she took my primary school to task for 'failing to challenge young minds' when I came home and performed what I thought was a very impressive rendition of 'I'm a Little Teapot'.

'The cake is fine, it's red velvet,' she said, piping bag in hand. 'I'm having some trouble with the buttercream.'

'Some trouble' was an understatement. The entire farmhouse kitchen, sage green cabinets, grey slate floor and white quartz countertops, was covered – *covered* – in brown buttercream icing.

'I don't want to alarm you,' I said from the safety of the doorway. 'But it does look a little bit like someone's had an accident in here and not with buttercream icing.'

Mum groaned and pushed her glasses back up her nose with the crook of her elbow, the only part of her not smeared with sugar, butter and brown food colouring. 'I don't know what happened. I followed all the instructions. It's supposed to be the Sorting Hat.'

I stared at the brown mound in front of her and drew my lips together tightly.

'It doesn't look like a hat, Mum.'

'I know what it looks like,' she said with a dissatisfied grunt. Her signature silk scarf slipped off her head, releasing her silvery grey hair and floating down to her icing-sugar-speckled shoes. 'Charlotte is going to be so disappointed.'

'Charlotte?' I replied. 'Isn't it Dad's birthday?'

'Yes but your sister saw it on one of those "is it cake?" shows and she loved it so much I said I'd have a go.'

Not that my little sister was spoiled in any way. Not that I didn't love the bones of her, she was clever and funny and very resourceful, but she was also impatient, stubborn, had an answer for everything and that answer was usually 'you're wrong'. I still hadn't recovered from the withering look she gave me at Christmas when I asked how she felt about the latest Marvel movie. People had died from less severe injuries.

'Obviously I wasn't about to put more money into Rowling's pockets by paying an arm and a leg for an official one.' Mum wiped off her hands and picked up a length of black fabric. 'Do you think, once I put the ribbon on . . . ?'

'Mum, let it go, the patient cannot be saved,' I said, tipping my head from side to side to consider every angle but each one was more horrifying than the last. 'If Charlotte loved it so much, why isn't she making it?'

Throwing up her hands in defeat, my mother shoved the cake across the counter where it wobbled precariously before slumping sadly to one side. It needed to be sorted into the bin.

'She's out. I've hardly seen her all summer, she's so busy.'

'New love interest?'

'No.'

'Did she start another dog-walking business and lose all the dogs again?'

'That only happened twice,' she replied with an unconcerned tut that reminded me why we'd never been allowed pets as kids. 'She's working. You know she's very big on TikTok.'

'I did not know she's very big on TikTok.'

My father *and* my sister on the clock app. This was a concerning development. I pulled out my phone and searched for her name but nothing came up.

'Don't bother looking for her, she's got the whole family blocked,' Mum said as though this was perfectly acceptable even though I wasn't allowed to buy a diary with a lock on it until I was fifteen. 'One of the girls in the office follows her and sends me any videos she thinks I ought to see.'

'I dread to ask but what exactly is my eighteen-year-old sister doing on TikTok?' I asked, immediately and reasonably anticipating the worst. Dancing? Make-up tutorials? ASMR? Please, I prayed, please let it be ASMR.

'She reviews books.' An echo of undeniable pride swelled through the kitchen. 'I can't say I completely understand all the videos but she's got thousands of followers. One of them had a virus.'

'You mean it went viral,' I replied and she shrugged in response. Her refusal to get on board with social media was infamous. How she was coping with Dad's sudden conversion I did not know but at least that made more sense now.

'She's not shy with her opinions,' she said, positively glowing. 'One of the editors at Hawkshead called her *scathing*.'

Perfect. Another sibling merrily following the rest of the family down the approved path of literary greatness while I taught primary school by day and wrote secret smut by night.

'She's quite astounding, your sister,' Mum added over the sound of running water as she rinsed her hands clean of what I had to keep reminding myself was buttercream. 'At the beginning of the summer she came to us with a proposal and honestly, Sophie, she put together a very accomplished and ambitious business plan. Your father and I were both incredibly impressed.'

'A business plan for what?' I asked, almost certain I didn't want to know the answer.

She turned to look at me, her cheeks flushed and her eyes alive. She couldn't have looked more thrilled if she'd just found out Hanya Yanagihara had written a prequel to *A Little Life*.

'A bookshop.'

'This is Charlotte, the eighteen-year-old who *just* finished school?' I spoke very clearly to make sure I hadn't misheard or inadvertently slipped into an alternate dimension. 'Mum, please tell me you haven't bought her a bookshop.'

'Don't be silly,' she replied with a laugh. 'We haven't bought a bookshop.'

I shook my head at myself. Of course they hadn't, what was I thinking?

'We've rented one.'

I suddenly longed to be back in William's car, having a breakdown over my lost laptop and facing certain double decker bus death.

'Do you remember Gwendoline?' Mum asked, chatting away as though she hadn't just said the most insane thing I'd ever heard. 'She ran the greengrocer's across from the post office? She wanted to retire so we've taken a one-year lease on her place. Lottie has done all the research, there's a young girl out in California who opened her own shop and she's doing tremendous business. I talked to some people at the paper and your father had a word with publicity at MullinsParker, they're all keen as mustard to work with her once she gets going. She's even designed all her own merch. That's tote bags, T-shirts, that sort of thing.'

'Yes, I know what merch is,' I replied, steadying myself on the one remaining inch of counterspace that wasn't smothered in shit-coloured frosting. 'But how is Charlotte going to run a shop? Has she ever even had a real job?'

Mum looked far less concerned about this than I felt and, for a brief second, I wondered if she was joking. Or drunk. I hoped she was drunk.

'The business plan was very comprehensive,' she answered as she dried her hands. 'One of the girls who worked for Gwendoline is going to stay on to work the till but your sister is selecting the books, running the social media, the marketing, the online store, all of that. She's been taking business classes online.'

'And she's going to run the shop remotely from Durham, is she?'

For a split second, my mother's shoulders seized up then she opened the fridge and pulled out an open bottle of white wine, refilling a glass hiding behind the KitchenAid mixer.

Ah-ha.

'She's taking a year out.'

I couldn't believe what I was hearing. There was just no way. My parents were obsessed with education. *Obsessed.* The pair of them had such a fearsome reputation, my GCSE English teacher actually hid on parent-teacher night and when William got an A in English language and not an A*, they insisted on reviewing the school's curriculum to 'ensure the same travesty didn't impede the future of any other children'. Now Charlotte was taking a year out to run a bookshop across from the post office. I couldn't make it make sense.

'All right, I'm on to you. First you're baking cakes and now you're letting Charlotte defer uni for a year?' I said. 'Who are you and what have you done with my mother?'

After adding more wine to the glass she set the bottle down with a shaky hand.

51

'It's only one year and I'm completely on board.'

I wasn't sure who she was trying to convince, me or herself.

'The only thing is . . .' She leaned against the sink, nursing her wine. 'I can't say I'm entirely supportive of the books she's decided to sell.'

'Which are?'

'She's focusing on YA.'

'That makes sense,' I replied. 'Since she is a YA.'

'YA and . . .' My mother took a large mouthful of wine to give her the strength to complete her sentence. 'Romance novels.'

A sob escaped the back of her throat as I considered grabbing the glass right out of her hand. My need was definitely greater than hers.

'All because she's obsessed with this one godawful book,' she went on, shaking her head. 'The bloody thing is never out of her hands.'

'What book?' I asked, really not wanting to know the answer.

Mum sharpened her eyes and summoned all her venom for the book that had corrupted her precious youngest daughter.

'*Butterflies.*'

CHAPTER SIX

One of my favourite things about the summer were the long, light nights and even though Harford was only a couple of hours further north, the nights were even longer and lighter here than they were at home. The evening shadows stretched lazily across the golden grass by the time I finally escaped Mum's unrequested TED Talk on how books like mine were destroying the youth of today, the sun finally surrendering to the night and slipping away over the horizon. My head was swimming with everything I'd been through in the last twelve hours: meeting with Mal, karaoke with a wanker, the train ride from hell, Charlotte's bookshop, Mum's disgust. Not to mention the Baileys, prosecco and a McDonald's milkshake. I felt worse than her cake looked and if William didn't come running out to declare my bag had been found and secured, I'd be joining it in the bin.

'As I live and breathe, if it isn't the world's greatest teacher, Sophie Taylor.'

The silhouette of a tall, stout man rose up against the

paling horizon, flat cap on his head, work boots on his feet. Not William but almost as good. My dad.

When he lived in London, Hugh Taylor was strictly a suit and tie man. Polished shoes and freshly pressed shirt from Monday to Friday, only dipping into something more casual on the weekend, maybe a polo or rugby shirt teamed with chinos and a respectable loafer, and while the rest of us had silently agreed jogging bottoms were acceptable apparel in almost all circumstances, Hugh Taylor clung to his belted trews like his life depended on it. But something had changed in the last six months. As his sixtieth birthday loomed, my dad was trying his hand at all sorts of new experiences: TikTok, oat milk, trousers with lots of pockets, and rumour had it, there was even a hoodie lurking in the back of his wardrobe. Mum wasn't sure he'd ever worn it but she definitely saw him slip it into the trolley at Tesco.

'World's greatest is a bit of a stretch,' I said, giving him an enormous hug. Even if he'd changed up his wardrobe, he still smelled the same, same deodorant, same fabric softener, same cheeky cigarette he'd had at some point in the afternoon and still thought none of us knew about. 'I'll accept Hertfordshire's greatest though. I've been offered head of year next term.'

'Soph, that's marvellous. Moulding young minds. Setting the next generation off on the right path.'

'Or at least trying to convince them there are other career aspirations beyond dancing on the internet or appearing on a reality dating show.'

'How old are the kids you teach again?'

Dad's forehead crumpled, trying to work out whether or not I was telling the truth.

'Six to eleven and I wish I was joking,' I replied. 'We had to send out new uniform guidelines for next term clarifying that the no-make-up rule includes false eyelashes and nail extensions. Ten-year-olds aren't what they used to be, Dad.'

'Neither are eighteen-year-olds,' he muttered, kicking away a clump of dirt at his feet.

'Mum was just telling me,' I replied. 'I hear my little sister has decided to become the next Jeff Bezos.'

'She'll be a billionaire by Christmas,' he said then tapped me on the arm and started down the garden. 'Come and see the cottage.'

Dad claimed that, once upon a time, the cottage had been a perfect little rustic dwelling, stone walls and a thatched roof, roses round the door, the whole Snow White shebang, but the previous owners had let it go to ruin and now it was more of a horror story than a fairy tale. When my parents moved in, the crumbling limestone building was crammed full of useless junk – boxes of broken tools; a lawnmower without an engine; three kids' bikes without wheels or saddles; a very concerning device that looked an awful lot like a torture rack (after Dad plucked up the courage to take it to the tip, we all agreed to pretend it never existed – a Taylor family speciality) – but somehow the cottage was even more terrifying once it was empty. I didn't know if it was the caved-in roof, glassless windows or the thrilling smell of rotten wood and mould but it gave me the creeps, and while I personally wouldn't have chosen it as a place to give birth and raise a family, the fox population of Harford apparently felt very differently, claiming squatters' rights the moment it had been cleared out. Mum, William and I had voted to knock the whole thing down and start again but we'd been overruled when Dad insisted he was going to restore it to its former glory. Just as soon as the foxes were gone. Which I assumed would be never.

'Can we have a look in the morning?' I replied, casting a reticent glance towards the shadowy building hiding underneath the trees.

'Are you sure?' he replied, sounding just a little bit disappointed. 'I've been working on it.'

Exactly what he told me at Christmas when he dragged me down there only to be surprised by a distinctly unfestive rat.

'Positive,' I said with a shiver. 'Let's go back in and get the kettle on. I want to hear all about the big birthday party plans.'

Only slightly dejected, Dad turned around and followed me back towards the house. 'We'll have to do a tour in the morning before the hordes arrive.'

'You're looking forward to it then?'

'Mostly,' he said, smiling. 'As long as everyone behaves, it should be fun. I've got some surprises planned for you all.'

'Yes,' I frowned, remembering the unwelcome addition to the guest list. 'I heard.'

When we got back to the house, William opened the door, still on the phone. Hope fluttered lightly in my chest.

'Any luck?' I mouthed, letting go of Dad who marched merrily in his muddy boots.

He shook his head and my momentary optimism crashed and landed with a thud at my feet.

'Not yet. The train is in the depot, they're cleaning it now. I'm sure they'll find it soon.'

'Thank you,' I said, leaning into his half-hug. 'I'm sure you're right.'

Or at the very least, I hoped he was.

The living room was one of my favourite parts of what William and I would always call the new house. It was so cosy, with its low ceilings and old, wooden bookcases, every piece of furniture selected for comfort rather than visual appeal, but somehow the higgledy-piggledy design worked. You had the choice of an old leather sofa or two oversized Liberty-print armchairs with mismatched mid-century modern footstools, all of them loaded with cushions, pillows, blankets and throws, begging you to settle in with a good book. And books were the one thing my family would never run out of. Everywhere you looked, not just the bookcases, but every available surface was covered in hardbacks, paperbacks, manuscripts and bound proofs, there were two Kindles on the coffee table and, in the corner, I spotted the Alexa my dad had adopted to read his audiobooks out loud to him. He'd resisted at first, convinced it was spying on him (it almost certainly was), but now more or less considered it a fourth child.

In the armchair closest to the window, still with a smudge of brown buttercream on her cheek, Mum was curled up, completely absorbed in an advance copy of a book I knew wasn't coming out for at least another year although, from the look on her face, the author might want to push the pub date back a few months more.

'Pandora, love, there's something on your face,' Dad said from a safe and horrified distance.

'It's icing,' I said quickly, allowing him to breathe out

with relief as I tapped my own face to guide my mother's hand to the right spot.

'Too much butter in the buttercream,' she grumbled as she licked her finger clean then set her reading to one side. 'And too many similes in this bloody book. It's every other bloody sentence. Bloated, sloppy.'

'What I'm hearing is, you don't love it.'

I reached for the proof but she slapped away my hand.

'They made me sign a bloody NDA for that tosh. Don't sully your eyeballs with it.'

She snatched it away and tossed it in her massive handbag, the brooding photo of the author mooning out at me from the back cover. Poor man, he had no idea my mother was sitting in her living room, preparing to end his illustrious career with chocolate icing all over her face.

'Sophie wants to know the plan for the weekend,' Dad announced, settling himself on the highest leather chair and pulling a super-slim laptop from between the frame and the seat cushion.

'Yes, because Sophie just found out Sophie wasn't included on the shared spreadsheet,' I replied as I flopped down on the sofa. 'So Sophie hasn't got a clue what's going on.'

He tapped away at the keyboard, lifting one hand to wave away my concerns.

'You're always so busy with school, the last things you want to concern yourself with are guest lists and catering and marquee rentals,' he replied. 'All you need to worry about is enjoying yourself.'

'That's exactly what I'm worried about,' I said. 'Also, marquee rentals?'

'Maybe not quite a marquee but a tent.' Dad's eyes glittered. 'A very big tent.'

'He's lost his bloody mind,' declared Mum. 'It started out as a nice afternoon barbecue with the family until him and Mal got together and suddenly it was an entire long weekend affair, then that dreadful bloody Gregory Brent got involved somehow and they might as well have hired PT Barnum as a party planner. He won't even tell me half of what he's got planned.'

So William hadn't been joking. This weekend *was* going to be a circus.

'Gregory Brent is coming?' I enquired lightly and my mother rolled her eyes. Depending on the day, Gregory was either my dad's best friend or worst enemy.

'He's coming,' Dad confirmed. 'I imagine to try to poach another of my authors.'

It was a story we knew all too well. 1998. Dad and Gregory were both senior editors at Anaphora. Dad's favourite author, Nelson Allen, was looking for a new publisher for his next book and while my dad was at lunch with Nelson, passionately expressing his love for his work, Gregory took his top-secret manuscript to Herringbone, their biggest rival, negotiated himself an enormous pay rise and a promotion, then offered Nelson's agent double the Anaphora advance. Nelson took it.

Not that my dad still held a grudge or anything.

'I doubt he'll poach so much as an egg at your birthday party, darling,' Mum pointed out. 'But I did tell you not to invite him. I don't want you skulking around after him all weekend. It's supposed to be fun.'

'It will be fun,' Dad replied, suddenly gleeful. 'Especially when he finds out we've signed Genevieve Salinger to a three-book deal.'

59

'Isn't that the Peruvian author who wrote the book about the man trapped in the body of a llama?' I asked with a wrinkled nose.

A reverent sigh of confirmation slipped from my mother's lips. '*Llama Glama*. A masterpiece. Made me see the world through completely new eyes.'

'Right,' I agreed. 'The eyes of a llama.'

'A thrilling treatise on the human condition, *The Metamorphosis* for the twenty-first century,' Dad added. 'Gen is the new Kafka. Mark my words, they're going to change the world with their writing.'

'As long as they don't turn me into a llama, we're all good,' I assured him.

It wasn't that I thought *Llama Glama* was a bad book, I actually thought it was a lot of fun, but even though it was lauded by the critics, including my mother, it hadn't found a home with readers. The writing was dense and weirdly accusatory, like it was somehow the reader's fault the main character had woken up inside the body of its pet llama, and strangely enough, most people popping into their local bookshop for a sweet summer read weren't super into that. When I thought what Dad must've paid to secure a three-book deal, my chicken nuggets threatened to come back up again.

'Gen is coming to the party on Saturday,' Dad said. 'I hope it won't be too upsetting for Gregory.'

The expression on his face did not match the words coming out of his mouth.

'So, if the big party is on Saturday night, what are we doing tomorrow and the rest of the weekend?' I asked, keen to move the conversation on.

Mum clucked dismissively. 'It's the school holidays, what else would you be doing?'

'Literally anything?' William suggested as he walked in, phone still in hand. 'Just because she isn't in school doesn't mean Soph isn't busy.'

'Right,' I agreed, raising my eyebrows hopefully at him, only for my whole face to crumple when he shook his head again. 'I'm very busy. Doing. Stuff.'

'How eloquent. So glad we spent all that money on your education,' Mum said with disapproval as she snatched Dad's laptop and scanned the party planning spreadsheet. 'Right, Friday. Your Aunt Carole and Uncle Bryan should be here in the morning and we're expecting Gregory around – what time did he say, Hugh?'

'He's taken the day off work, so he said around lunch,' Dad replied darkly. 'So anywhere between seven a.m. and midnight.'

'Perfect.' Mum carried on scrolling without looking up. 'Your father has now decided to throw a barbecue tomorrow evening for family and a few close friends, because hosting a hundred people on Saturday night isn't enough work. I'd appreciate your help getting all that ready if you don't mind?'

It was presented as a request but we both knew it wasn't really.

'Saturday, we thought it might be fun to take the visitors out and about, show them the sights,' she added. 'There's a summer fête in town, that should be fun for your aunt and uncle and the Londoners.'

'She must know different Londoners to me,' William muttered, sitting down on the arm of a sofa.

'You won't need me to go to that though?' I said, my statement turning into a question as my mother narrowed her eyes.

'Why not?'

'Because I don't want to go to a summer fête with Aunt Carole and Uncle Bryan?'

'Saturday night, all the hoopla kicks off,' she went on, not even dignifying me with a response. 'Sunday morning it'll be bacon butties for the hangers-on then fuckity bye to the lot of them. Your father has invited all of Harford and half the publishing industry so you can both consider yourselves on call all weekend.'

'As wonderful as that sounds, we've still got Sanjit's parents staying with us while they have their new kitchen fitted,' William said, snapping his fingers with disappointment. 'I might not be available *all* weekend.'

'Sanjit's parents sound like a Sanjit problem,' replied Mum, spearing her son with a pointed look. 'I will need you here.'

Whatever he mumbled under his breath, he had the sense to keep completely inaudible. Thirty-eight or not, our mother was still terrifying.

'Speaking of the invitees—' I began but, before I could finish my sentence, William shot up out of his seat, car keys in hand.

'Would you look at the time!' he exclaimed. 'Better get back, Sanjit'll be wondering where I've got to.'

'Are you sure he won't be wondering how much longer he can enjoy the peace and quiet without you stomping around the house?' I enquired sweetly.

'If I get a call from the station, I'll tell them to keep the bag, shall I?' he replied.

'Bag?' Dad asked, blinking at me from behind his glasses. 'What bag?'

'Never mind, doesn't matter,' I said as William planted a kiss on Mum's cheek then patted Dad's shoulder on the way out. 'Unlike the fact you've invited CJ to your party.'

'Only Saturday night,' Mum said with a kindness that bordered on condescension. 'Don't overreact, Sophie. I know things didn't work out between the two of you but we couldn't exactly invite all your dad's other authors and not CJ. You can survive for one Saturday night.'

Dad cleared his throat.

'Well,' he started, searching for the non-existent right words. 'As it happens, he called this morning to ask if it might be all right if he possibly popped up early. Since he's coming all the way from London.'

'How early?' I asked.

'Tomorrow. For the barbecue.'

'Tomorrow for the barbecue,' I repeated flatly.

'And, I didn't think it would be a problem since the two of you stayed such good friends—'

'According to who?!'

'But he asked if he could stay here,' Dad finished, as meek as the world's meekest mouse on International Meek Mouse Day. 'Apparently the pub is full. And I told him he could.'

Mum squinted at me from across the room as I recalibrated my definition of Worst Day Ever. 'Are you feeling all right?' she asked. 'You've gone very pale. Is it your blood sugar?'

'I think I might go to bed,' I replied, each word tight and controlled. If I didn't watch exactly what I said, there was every chance I would scream so loudly, every window in the house would shatter into a million pieces, and that would probably take the shine off Dad's big weekend.

'You're in the back bedroom,' Mum called as I sloped down the hallway to retrieve my suitcase. 'Carole and Bryan wanted the en suite and I thought it better to keep CJ downstairs, out your way.'

'Appreciate it. See you both in the morning,' I called back, concentrating all my energy on putting one foot in front of the other. There was no fight left in me. For now.

'Told you she wouldn't mind,' I heard Dad say as I trudged upstairs to my designated bedroom with my suitcase. 'CJ said it would be fine.'

'Hugh,' Mum replied. 'I love you but you're an idiot.'

I couldn't have said it better myself.

CHAPTER SEVEN

'It's not *my* fault you don't *understand*.'

I paused outside the kitchen, the sound of my sister's voice cutting through the morning air like a cheese grater. Whatever she and Mum were arguing about, it was too early for it and I did not want to be dragged in the middle. But my desperate need to caffeinate was stronger than my instinct for self-preservation, so I quietly opened the door, keeping my head down as I crept inside.

'Are you genuinely trying to tell me I don't understand a book?' my mother said, ignoring me as I skulked across the room. 'Charlotte, sweetheart, you do realise my entire career is based on my understanding of books?'

My sister, all five foot two of her, sat on a stool at the kitchen table, spine straight, eyes bright and hair an interesting shade of peach. The only way to describe Charlotte was adorable, with her button nose and impossibly long eyelashes, but she didn't look adorable right now. She looked thoroughly pissed off.

'Sophie, can you back me up?' Mum asked as I

dumped a third teaspoonful of sugar into my mug. 'Your sister seems to think I'm an imbecile with no taste.'

'Mum's not an imbecile,' I replied robotically. 'And Reese Witherspoon once told her she had excellent taste.'

'All right, no need to name-drop,' she said as though she didn't bring it up at every possible opportunity. 'But I do think thirty-five years of experience ought to count for something. I'm only trying to help you.'

I took my first sip of coffee and waited for it to work its magic.

'You're not trying to help,' my sister replied. 'You're trying to tell me which books I should be stocking in Charlotte's Bookshop.'

'Is that the name or have you started referring to yourself in the third person?' I asked, immediately regretting the decision to open my mouth.

She hit me with a glare that woke me up faster than any cup of coffee ever could.

'Yes, it's the name, and it's perfect. Clear, concise, easy for social media, it'll look great on merch and it centres everything around me.'

'Naturally.'

'Which works for the PR angle,' Charlotte finished, glowering at me from her stool.

'I don't have a problem with the name,' Mum said in her most cajoling tone. 'All I'm asking is that you reconsider your purchasing strategy. It's all well and good buying things that are trendy now but what happens six months from now when you're stuck with a stockroom full of flash-in-the-pan nonsense you can't shift?'

'I send it back to the publisher?' Charlotte's smooth

forehead wrinkled momentarily as she gave Mum a look of complete disgust. 'I know how returns work.'

Mum slid off her own stool and stalked across the kitchen, refilling her own coffee, and I stole her seat, observing their back and forth. Aside from the conservatory-window-dirt-bike incident, me and William had been the best-behaved children on the planet, at least as far as I could remember. I would never have spoken to my mum that way when I was eighteen, I wouldn't even speak to her that way now, and I was equal parts horrified and deeply impressed.

'It's not as easy as simply returning the books,' Mum explained, stirring one half-spoonful of raw sugar into her coffee. 'You've got to think about cashflow. Publishers don't refund you immediately, the money doesn't appear back in your bank account overnight, and your stock-room is tiny. You don't have space to hold that many returns.'

I peered into Charlotte's mug and saw her coffee was black and strong. God help us all, the last thing she needed was more energy.

'But there isn't going to *be* any extra stock because I'm going to sell *everything*,' she insisted.

'And how are you going to do that?' I asked.

She didn't miss a beat. 'By getting all my friends on BookTok and Bookstagram to promote me, and I'll be holding virtual and IRL events with loads of authors.'

'I'm not trying to be an arsehole but lots of other bookshops do that,' I said as gently as I could. There were an awful lot of weapons within arm's reach.

'But they don't have my secret weapon,' she replied, her tone victorious.

'Which is?'

'I'm going to reveal the identity of Este Cox.'

Spitting my own coffee across the kitchen table was probably a bit dramatic but I couldn't exactly take it back once I'd done it. Silently, my mother handed me a wad of paper towels to clean up my mess.

'Well said,' she commented as I dabbed at the mess on the old wooden tabletop. 'My thoughts exactly.'

'How can you reveal the identity of Este Cox?' I asked with only mild hysteria in my voice. 'No one knows who she is. She doesn't have social media, she hasn't done any interviews.'

'Please, I'm eighteen, me and my friends can find out anything on the internet if we really put our minds to it,' Charlotte scoffed. It was a terrifying and believable thought.

'But you don't actually know who she is right now?' I pressed, fingernails biting into the palms of my hands. A sullen look came over her pretty face and she scowled.

'Not yet. But I'm close. If I have to, I'll get Dad to find out.'

I breathed an internal sigh of relief, safe for now.

'Dad doesn't know, she's at a different imprint, and even if he did he wouldn't say. You know how seriously Dad takes his job.'

'Then I'll ask Uncle Mal. Or CJ. *Someone* must know.'

It was hard to say which part of this I hated the most. The sour look on my mother's face, my little sister unknowingly trying to crack my secret identity, or the mere mention of my ex-boyfriend. It was deeply unfair of them both to make me deal with all of this before I'd had at least seven coffees.

'You know there's one theory that it's Taylor Swift,'

Charlotte said. 'It would make sense, right? With all the Swiftie Easter eggs in *Butterflies*?'

'Or maybe the author was listening to her a lot while she was writing,' I replied, mentally locating my phone, still charging upstairs on the bedside table. My Spotify Wrapped would out me in a second.

'There's one girl I know who's convinced it's another author and that's why she doesn't use her own name. Like it's Maggie O'Farrell or Donna Tartt. My friend, Indhi, thinks it's Colson Whitehead.'

'Give me strength,' Mum whispered to the heavens. 'You think Colson Whitehead is writing secret romance novels?'

Charlotte nodded.

'He probably gets bored writing all that wordy, literary stuff.'

'Sophie, please leave the room and take your sister with you,' our mother croaked. 'I don't want my daughters to see me cry.'

'It doesn't matter who she is,' Charlotte said, burning with single-minded determination. 'As long as she is my first author event. She's the key to everything. If Este Cox does her first ever event at my bookshop, it's guaranteed to be a success.'

Across the room, Mum glared at the both of us.

'The only thing that her attendance will guarantee is a gaggle of overly hormonal young women who wouldn't know a good book if it fell on their head. I'm sick of hearing about that book and I'm sick of hearing about its author.'

'In case you couldn't tell, Mum's not a fan,' my sister drawled. 'Even though she hasn't even read it.'

Mum glared at her, disgusted. 'No, I haven't read it.

Why would I waste my time when I know exactly what it is? Predictable, badly written, misogynistic nonsense.'

'Ow,' I breathed. 'Don't hold back.'

It was exactly what I'd imagined she might say about my book but hearing the words come out of her mouth hurt in a way not even I could have predicted.

'It's offensive, all this "good girl" nonsense,' she went on. 'If a woman were to say "good boy" you would assume she was talking to a dog. Don't tell me you've read it?' She looked aghast at the very thought. 'Sophie, I thought better of you.'

'I skimmed it?' I offered, high-pitched with embarrassment she happily accepted for the wrong reasons. 'One of the other teachers had it in the staffroom, it's not as though I bought my own copy.'

Not technically a lie but not technically the truth. I hadn't bought my own copy and I had skimmed it in the staffroom, but not because one of the other teachers had it – *all* the other teachers had it. *Butterflies* was the Abbey Hill Primary staff book club pick for July.

'Mum doesn't know. She hasn't read a single page.' Charlotte held her coffee mug in one hand, her phone in the other, sipping, scrolling and arguing all at the same time. 'The irony of you accusing a book of misogyny when you haven't so much as scanned a word.'

'I don't need to read erotica to know it perpetuates harmful ideals against women. Let me guess, she's sad and single, meets a man, it's love at first sight, the sex is orgasmic from the beginning, then the couple break up for some absurd reason, most likely a tedious miscommunication that was entirely unnecessary and wraps up with them getting back together when the man makes a grand romantic gesture.' Mum was almost ranting. I hadn't seen her take against anything in publishing with such vehemence since Brooklyn Beckham's photography book. 'A denouement that traps the protagonist in a patriarchy-approved, heteronormative relationship, takes away her agency and denies the woman any room for growth.'

Not even Nadine Dorries's books had raised this much ire in her and in all honesty that did not seem entirely fair.

'You've got it all wrong, *Butterflies* doesn't have a miscommunication trope,' Charlotte challenged as I searched the kitchen for a hole to climb into and hide. Maybe the oven? It would be a tight fit but I'd be able to get all the essential bits in there.

'It's a strangers-to-lovers, forced-proximity, he-falls-first, small-town love story,' my sister sniped. 'And it's romance, not erotica.'

'Lottie, if it looks like a duck and it quacks like a duck, it's a duck,' Mum said with a sigh. 'Call me old-fashioned but I don't think there's anything romantic about extremely graphic sex scenes. I lived a good long while without knowing anything about pegging.'

'Please don't say that word ever again,' I begged, the oven looking more and more inviting by the second. Could you off yourself in an electric oven? Where was Sylvia Plath when you needed her.

She gave me The Look, a patented signature expression that all mothers kept in their back pocket and only pulled out when it was time for their child to shut up immediately.

'The very fact you could boil this book, any book,

down to a list of tropes tells me everything I need to know about it. It's frivolous at best, genuinely harmful at worst.'

'You are so out of touch,' my sister huffed. 'Do you know how successful *Butterflies* is? How many women will have a happier life because they read a book that showed a healthy relationship with boundaries and communication, and encouraged them to expect the same? That sounds like the opposite of misogyny to me, *Mother*.'

I should've known The Look didn't work on Charlotte. 'Is that really what you thought when you read it?' I asked, an unexpected smattering of surprise cutting through my overwhelming shame.

'That's what everyone I know thought when they read it,' she replied, still defensive as though I needed to be talked around like Mum. 'It's a book that teaches women to ask for what they want out of life instead of accepting what they're given.'

Mum clucked dismissively.

'Only if what they want is to know about pegging.'

'There's no pegging in *Butterflies*!' I yelled at the top of my voice.

Both of them stared at me, Charlotte with a Cheshire Cat grin and Mum with a recognisable look of disappointment.

'So you *have* read it,' Charlotte crowed. 'Super-swot Sophie, curled up at night with her smut. I love it.'

'And she's too embarrassed to admit it as she should be,' Mum said with a superior smile. Both of them were claiming this as a win but there were no winners, just one big loser. Me.

'Maybe you should read it again,' Charlotte suggested

when my shoulders sagged. 'You're so uptight, sissy, it could do you some good.'

'Thanks,' I said, scraping back my hair and knotting it around itself. I'd been awake for less than half an hour and I was ready to go back to bed. 'I'll consider it.'

'Let me know if you need more recommendations,' my sister called as she sailed out the room. 'Or if you want me to do something with your hair.'

'She's a monster,' I muttered into my mug. If there was room for me in the oven, Charlotte would certainly fit.

'But she's right about one thing,' Mum said on a long, frustrated exhale. 'You do need to do something with your hair, love.'

An untethered strand fell down in front of my face on cue and I tucked it behind my ear. When was the last time I'd had it cut? I couldn't remember. I really had been very busy for a very long time and personal care hadn't exactly been a priority. No point in wasting time getting haircuts when all you ever did was work.

'Mum, do you really hate *Butterflies* that much?' I asked, even though I knew she wasn't about to do a complete one-eighty on the most fervently held opinion I'd heard her express since she reviewed the TV adaptation of *Lessons in Chemistry*. Hopefully Brie Larson missed it and never had to endure the pain I just had.

'I don't hate it,' she replied easily. 'I don't respect it.'

'Oh,' I replied. 'That's much worse.'

'There's a reason the author doesn't want anyone to know who she is,' she continued, blissfully ignorant. 'Pseudonyms might be common but complete anonymity isn't. Whoever she is must be deeply, deeply ashamed.

73

Books like this and the women who read them set back feminism a hundred years.'

'Good to know, sorry I asked,' I said, sliding off my stool to refill my coffee. It wasn't like I'd ever be able to sleep again anyway, might as well give myself a caffeine headache while I was here.

'Not as sorry as Charlotte will be if she doesn't drop this nonsense,' Mum replied, nudging her glasses up her nose with the back of her wrist when the doorbell rang. 'Can you get that? It'll be your aunt and uncle, they said they were getting here early and I need to have another stab at this cake.'

'Stabbing it would be a mercy,' I assured her, Mum pulling the abomination out the fridge as I schlepped down the hallway. They weren't exactly my favourite people and our feelings about the world didn't always align, but at least Aunt Carole and Uncle Bryan wouldn't denounce me as a global disgrace and after what I'd just been through, I was prepared for anything they could dish out.

Or at least I thought I was until I opened the door to see a tall, rugged man on our doorstep, a huge smile on his handsome face.

'You've got to be joking,' I said as he took in my cat-print pyjamas, fluffy bunny slippers and the much-maligned state of my hair.

There was one other thing I wasn't prepared for and it was standing right in front of me.

Joe bloody Walsh.

CHAPTER EIGHT

'What are you doing here?' I squawked as Joe slid past me into the house, carrying an overnight bag in each hand. 'And where do you think you're going?'

'Hello, Sophie, nice to see you again, Sophie,' he replied cheerily. 'Nice PJs, very sexy. Think you missed a button.'

'They're not meant to be sexy, they're meant to be comfortable,' I said, heat rising in my semi-visible chest. 'Not that I care what you think. I happen to love these pyjamas.'

But I did care. As soon as I saw him, it all came flooding back: the red walls of the karaoke room, the hot, sweaty air that made it so hard to breathe, his face coming closer to mine until my lips prickled at their proximity.

'Something else that isn't for me,' he grinned as I fastened my missed button. 'Don't worry, I get it.'

'Where's the birthday boy?'

A voice boomed down the hallway and a tall, tanned man, who looked to be somewhere in his sixties despite his neon yellow Air Force 1s and ultra-distressed jeans, strolled in like he owned the place. Without thinking about it, I took a safety step backwards. His energy was off. I couldn't put a finger on it but there was something I didn't like about his extremely shiny white teeth and even shinier diamond earring, and it was only when he pulled off his enormous sunglasses to hit me with the full force of his piercing blue eyes I realised who it was. Gregory Brent. Dad's favourite frenemy and, I realised when the two of them stood side by side, Joe's dad.

'Little Sophie Taylor, is that you?' Gregory asked, failing to notice my extreme discomfort as he launched himself at me in a slightly too long hug. 'I haven't seen you since you were in knee-high socks.'

'Gregory, hi.' I pushed him away and took another, much bigger step backwards. How much aftershave could one man wear? He was more potent than a Lush store and didn't even come with the possibility of a bath bomb to ease my suffering.

'Lucky you for getting the lion's share of your mother's genes,' he said with a leer. 'Bet you could still pull off those knee socks.'

'You're Joe's dad,' I stated, ignoring the deeply unpleasant implication.

There was no denying a fact. Same blue eyes, same square shoulders, almost the same height. They even had the same dark, dark brown hair but where Joe's was glossy and full of life, Gregory's was flat and matte. A tell-tale sign of the overzealous application of Just For Men.

'For my sins,' Gregory guffawed before slapping his son on the back so hard that Joe stumbled forward and rattled the umbrella stand with one of the weekend bags. Both were made of leather, one shiny, black and covered in debossed designer logos, the other one almost as dark brown and weathered as his dad.

'Surely you don't remember Joseph? You were tiny the last time the two of you met. But that's a Brent man for you, we've always known how to make an impression on the ladies.'

'Quite,' I agreed. 'So it's Joseph Brent, not Joe Walsh.'

'No one calls me Joseph except for Dad,' Joe explained as his father began picking up everything within touching distance in the hallway. My dad was going to go spare when he saw his fingerprints all over his framed letter from JRR Tolkien. 'Walsh is my mum's name. I changed it when—'

'When she fucked off to America and took him with her.'

From the way Joe closed his eyes and shook his head, I had to assume that wasn't exactly how he would have put it. It made perfect sense for noted cad and bounder, Joe Walsh, to be the devil spawn of Gregory Brent but why hadn't he told me yesterday?

'Where is everyone?' Gregory asked, picking up then putting down a photograph of my parents in the 1980s and striding past me down the hall and into the kitchen. 'Isn't this supposed to be a party? Pandora, my angel, what have you got there? It looks like a giant pile of shit.'

Joe and I hung back by the bottom of the stairs and, for the first time since we'd met, he seemed to be struggling to meet my eyes.

'You're Gregory Brent's son,' I said accusingly, crossing my arms and adding a silent 'well, well, well' to my sentence. 'Isn't that interesting?'

His reply was tight and tense. 'No more interesting than you being Hugh and Pandora Taylor's daughter. Whoever my dad is or isn't has no bearing on who I am.'

'Probably has a bit of bearing on what you do though, doesn't it?' I suggested with just the tiniest touch of smugness. 'Or did you get your fancy creative director job by bravely soldiering on through the trenches of publishing, succeeding solely on your own merits and keeping your family connections quiet?'

'You're one to talk.'

When he looked up, I saw the beginnings of a smile playing on his lips and the sound of distant alarm bells rang in my ears.

'Joseph! Get your arse in here and say hello to Pandy!'

'Please excuse me,' Joe replied. 'I need to get my arse in there to say hello to Pandy. We'll pick this up later.'

'No, we won't,' I said, both hot and bothered. 'And Mum hates being called Pandy so if you don't want her to spit in your coffee, I'd think twice about saying it to her face if I were you.'

He backed off down the hallway, his grin growing bigger by the second until he turned to disappear into the kitchen, leaving me pressed up against the wall, breathing heavily. Joe Walsh was in my house. Joe Walsh who definitely hadn't appeared in one of my weird, restless night dreams, along with a desert island, a carton of Ben & Jerry's and, for some reason, my Great-Aunt Maeve's toby jug collection. I pressed a hand against my clammy forehead and stared up at the ceiling. It would take more than a tub of Ben & Jerry's to cool me down now.

'Sophie?'

Jumping right out of my skin, I turned to see my aunt and uncle standing on the doorstep. Bryan's bald pate glistened in the morning sun and Carole had her lips pressed together so tightly, they completely disappeared into her overly powdered face.

'Are you having a funny turn? Your dad said you were coming up from London,' Carole said, Bryan nodding enthusiastically beside her. 'You can catch all sorts down there, you don't know where anyone's been.'

'Or where they've come from,' Bryan added ominously.

I squeezed my eyes shut as I searched for the correct response but there wasn't one. Was it even a family party if there wasn't a touch of xenophobia?

'Now I think about it, there was that man rolling around on the floor screaming on the tube,' I said as I bundled them both into the house and planted very wet kisses on their cheeks. 'I didn't think much of it until he started frothing at the mouth but I probably should see a doctor, the rash on my backside can't be normal.'

They stared at me with dread, scrubbing the skin from their cheeks.

Maybe there was a correct response after all.

It wasn't even half-past ten on a Friday morning and it felt like the day was turning into my very own Agatha Christie novel. Everyone milled around the kitchen, shaking hands, but who would be found face down in the duck pond? Pandora Taylor, respected literary critic but failed baker? Hugh Taylor, celebrating his birthday and holding a lifelong professional grudge? Or Gregory Brent and his son, Joe Walsh, a pair of complete and utter dickheads who honestly could do with a good dunking?

'Oh my god, everyone's here already!'

Charlotte bounced into the kitchen like Tigger after one Red Bull too many, prancing around as she presented herself for hugs and kisses. At least until she got to Gregory who she avoided like one of Taylor Swift's ex-boyfriends. My sister could be annoying when she wanted to be but she wasn't an idiot.

'And who are you?' she purred, looking up at Joe from under her eyelashes.

Well, not a total idiot but she still had a lot to learn.

'He's a twat who's twice your age, that's who,' I answered on his behalf.

'We love a man with experience,' Charlotte replied. Subtle she was not. At least Joe had the decency to look mortified.

As she turned, a tiny black handbag swung from her shoulder.

'Where did you get that?' I grabbed for the bag but ended up with a handful of air as she skipped around the table to nestle into our mother's open arms.

'It was in your room.' Charlotte held the handbag aloft. A perfectly square, quilted black leather handbag, dangling on a long gold chain, tell-tale interlocking Cs on the clasp giving the game away without anyone saying a word. It was the one nice thing I'd bought myself since *Butterflies* blew up and I'd regretted it every day since. Finding the courage to walk into the Chanel boutique on Bond Street had been difficult enough and the snooty sales assistants hadn't made the experience any less stressful. It was easier getting a mortgage than it had been to buy that bag, but things like this happened when you watched *Selling Sunset* on your phone on the way into town and drank one too many pink wines at lunch, after which your friends all went home to their families and partners, leaving you alone and very suggestible.

Even though I knew it was ridiculous, I couldn't bring myself to leave it alone in the flat while I was away, so I'd brought it with me, like a pet. A very expensive, wildly impractical pet. I was terrified to take it out in public and couldn't even get my phone in the damn thing but the only thing I could think of that might be more humiliating than buying it was the thought of trying to take it back.

'What were you doing in my room?' I demanded as Charlotte and my mother pawed at the soft lambskin. 'That was in my suitcase, I haven't even unpacked.'

'I was looking for something,' she answered, waving a vague hand around. 'There's no way you can afford Chanel. Did you steal it? Do you have a sugar daddy? Are you on OnlyFans?'

'What's OnlyFans?' asked Uncle Bryan.

'That looks like an expensive bit of kit, Sophie,' Dad said, holding out his hands for the bag and pushing his glasses up on top of his head to examine it more closely. 'You're not getting yourself into debt to keep up with the Joneses, are you?'

'More like the Carter-Knowleses,' Charlotte answered before I could say anything. 'That's got to be worth what, three, four grand?'

Everyone gasped except for Joe.

'For a handbag?' Auntie Carole shrieked while basting herself in hand sanitiser.

'All right, Oscar Wilde,' Mum muttered. 'Sophie, can

you please tell your sister you didn't spend four thousand pounds on a handbag?'

'Yes, I can,' I replied, even though it was a lie. That was exactly how much it cost and I almost wept every time I thought about it. 'It's—'

'A fake,' Joe announced. He reached for the bag, turning it over in his hands and inspecting the tiny stitches, so small I assumed they had been made by magical mice who were under a spell. It was the only reason I could think for the bag to cost as much as it did. 'It's clearly a fake.'

'Are you sure?' I said, snatching it back. 'Are you sure I didn't borrow it from one of those designer rental agencies?'

'That would also be a good explanation,' he replied, tipping his head from side to side.

'Yes,' I agreed. 'It would.'

'But it's definitely a fake.'

That clinched it. Joe was going face down in the duck pond first.

'I don't know how I feel about you buying fake handbags,' Mum said, taking my bag baby back once again. I shuddered at the thought of all those unwashed hands touching my precious child. It just wasn't right. 'These counterfeit rings are into all sorts of nasty business, I read about it in the *Guardian*. Organised crime, drug trafficking, child labour—'

'And they're full of disease,' Uncle Bryan chimed in. 'That's how the black plague got here.'

'In a knock-off designer handbag?' I replied. 'Really?'

Charlotte snatched it out of Mum's hands and held it tightly to her chest, the shape of the bag protesting only slightly at the strength of her love.

'Can I have it?' she said, for some reason speaking to my mother instead of to me. 'I don't care if it's fake, it's the best replica I've ever seen. They've lined up all the diamonds and got the correct number of stitches in each one and there's even a microchip inside. Please let me have it?'

'How do you know so much about Chanel handbags?' I asked, my heart pounding altogether too fast for this time in the morning. I really should check what brand of coffee my mother was brewing.

'I've watched all the videos on TikTok. Please, Sophie, I've always wanted a Chanel bag. Mum, tell her?'

'Always? You're eighteen!' I exclaimed. 'The last time I checked, the only thing you'd always wanted was a pony.'

'Well, you don't have a pony but you do have a fake Chanel bag.'

I recognised her wheedling tone and knew I was fighting a losing battle. Charlotte had already convinced her parents to back her business, for fuck's sake, they weren't about to lay the law down now. 'Oh, Soph, don't be such a miser.' Dad draped his arm around his youngest daughter's shoulders and winked. 'Look how happy she is. Let Lottie have this one and I'll give you the money to buy a new one. How much could it cost anyway?'

'They were practically giving them away on Canal Street last time I was in New York,' Joe offered unhelpfully. 'What was it, Sophie, fifty? A hundred?'

'A hundred pounds for a fake bloody bag,' Mum grumbled as Charlotte bounced around the kitchen with glee, her bag slung across her chest, while I eyed the knife block, wondering which one would cause Joe the most agonising pain when I ran him through with it. 'I thought we'd raised you better than that, Sophie Taylor.'

'Apparently not,' I replied, Joe's bemused gaze burning into the back of my head as I stalked out the kitchen door and into the garden.

CHAPTER NINE

In the morning sunshine, my parents' garden was a completely different place to the night before. The long shadows had been replaced with a children's paintbox full of colour; green grass, blue sky and every colour of flower you could think of, red, pink, purple, orange, pansies, petunias, delphiniums, geraniums, hollyhocks. The scent of honeysuckle, rose and an ever expanding lavender bush at the bottom of the garden filled the air with the kind of perfume I spent a fortune on trying to replicate in candle form, and the tall, elegant silver birches towered above me, nodding in a breeze that was too high in the sky to bother me and my pyjamas. It was the kind of garden that transported you back to a time when people could be easily tricked into thinking fairies existed and the worst thing that could happen to you was having your sleeve nibbled on by a passing sheep from the neighbouring farm. But I could survive a bit of sleeve nibbling. What I couldn't see myself surviving was this weekend.

Leaving the house and its inhabitants behind, I

ventured down the garden and curled up on a bench hidden between a rhododendron bush and a sycamore tree, cursing myself for leaving my phone inside. William could be trying to call me to let me know about my bag. For all I knew he was at the train depot right now with my perfect little laptop in his hot sweaty hands. He might already have the manuscript, covered in slashes of scarlet pen with the words 'fix this – it's shit' scrawled in the margins of every other page.

Above me, I saw the tree twitch and a pair of bright green eyes peeked out from the branches of the syca-more. A tiny grey tabby cat with a white bib and paws shuffled into view and miaowed.

'Hello there,' I said. 'Cute whiskers.'

The cat did not return the compliment. Instead, it gave me a dismissive once-over before it began the very serious business of grooming. I couldn't help but feel a little bit judged.

'Just so you know, some of us haven't had a chance for self-care this morning,' I grumbled. 'Some of us have been very busy trying to make it to—' Pausing, I checked the time on my watch. 'Is it really only half-past ten?'

The cat blinked once then stuck its back leg straight up into the air.

'Show-off.'

I buried my chin in my chest and slumped back until my spine curled, shoulders hunched and my tailbone teetering dangerously close to the edge of the bench. The internationally recognised sulking position.

Three days.

I was stuck here for three long days.

All I had to do was not kill my sister, pray that William was able to locate my bag with the manuscript before someone published the sequel on Reddit, avoid my ex, survive the rest of the family, keep my secret identity a secret, come up with a better ending for my book and never, ever let myself be alone with Joe bloody Walsh. How hard could it be?

'Morning.'

It could be impossible.

There he was, same smug grin on his face, same thick thighs and bulging arms stressing the seams of his jeans and T-shirt. What was wrong with this man, could he not buy clothes that fit?

'Fuck off,' I said, primly straightening the collar of my pyjama top.

'Spoken like the daughter of two literary luminaries.'

Joe raked a hand through his dark hair like something out of a shampoo ad but made absolutely no move to fuck off.

'Did you want something?' I asked, eyes on the ground. It wasn't safe to look at him, like the Ark of the Covenant or the sun or the sell-by date on a bag of Mini Eggs you find in November when you're on your period. There were some things we were better off not knowing.

'Yes,' Joe said. 'A fresh start.'

I considered his request for a second.

'No. Fuck off.'

'As much as I'd love to, that's going to be tricky since I'm here for the whole weekend.'

'That doesn't mean I have to talk to you,' I replied as his hulking frame moved directly in front of me and blocked out the sun. 'I think we both made our feelings perfectly clear yesterday, I can't see any need to antagonise each other further.'

He dug his hands deep into his pockets and shrugged. 'I'm willing to let bygones be bygones.'

'And I'm willing to shove those bygones right up your—' I stopped myself before I could finish the sentence. I would not give him the satisfaction.

'Look, we clearly got off on the wrong foot,' Joe said, digging the toe of his brown suede desert boot into the ground. 'We both had a drink, we both got carried away, I can't see any reason why we can't forget yesterday happened and try to be friends.'

He was unbearable. I looked up to see his mouth curved up into an insufferable half-smile.

'If you wanted to be friends then maybe you shouldn't have gone for a full-on character assassination during Pat Benatar yesterday,' I suggested as his eyes flared with annoyance.

'Me? You're the one who flew off the handle about nothing!'

'And you're the one who didn't mention you were coming to my dad's birthday party, you total psycho!'

'I didn't know!' Joe protested, sliding one hand across his chest to the tense muscles in his neck. 'I really didn't, it was a last-minute thing.'

Risking a glance into his eyes, I searched for the truth. How could they be so blue?

'After you ran out, without paying your half I might add, I had dinner with my dad and he mentioned he was coming up for the party,' he added. 'He asked if I wanted to come, I said yes.'

'Why?'

'Because I can't say no to a sixtieth birthday party?'

'I bet old people love you,' I guessed. 'They're probably the last generation that find your nonsense charming.'

'I do quite well with the septuagenarian set,' he admitted.

'At least you're self-aware,' I said with a sniff. 'But I still don't believe you.'

Joe let out an exasperated sigh. 'What, you think I changed all my weekend plans then begged him to bring me along exclusively to torment you?'

'Yes.'

'Didn't have you pegged for arrogance,' he replied with a click of the tongue.

'No, you had me pegged as a sexually frustrated, spoiled baby, half-arsing a teaching job until I find a rich man to marry,' I reminded him. 'It's the twenty-first century, not the nineteen fifties, you chauvinistic arsehole.'

He dug his hands deep into his pockets and sucked in his cheeks as they shifted to a shade Farrow & Ball might have called 'Mildly Ashamed Pink'.

Before either of us could go in for another jab, the conservatory doors opened and Gregory Brent strolled out of the house with my father close behind, carrying both weekend bags Joe had brought in with him.

'Here, Mr Taylor, give me those.'

Joe rushed back up the garden to grab them, his father standing, hands on hips and a pout on his face as he surveyed the garden.

'Call me Hugh,' Dad said with a happy grin. 'Very good to see you, Joseph, it's been an age.'

'And you call me Joe,' he replied, smiling back. 'Feels like yesterday to me. Running around your back garden, chasing Sophie through the sprinklers. And who could forget your famous chicken?'

'Ahh, get on with you,' Dad gushed. 'Imagine remembering that.'

You could practically see the heart eyes emojis floating above his head. Complimenting my father on his barbecue skills was the quickest way to win his love. Or any man's love, really.

'We're thrilled to have you.' He patted Joe on the back like he'd just returned from the Hundred Years' War before linking arms with me and dragging me down the garden with them. 'The more the merrier, even if we are fully booked up. I hope you don't mind a sofa bed.'

'I'm sure I've slept on worse,' Joe assured him as the four of us made our way down the garden.

'Don't speak too soon,' I said as I realised where we were headed. The dreaded cottage. 'The only place I've ever seen that's more disgusting was my third-year uni house.'

'She lived with three lads,' Dad said with grim recollection. 'Very nice, very clever, completely oblivious to the concept of bleach. I still have nightmares about that bathroom.'

I smiled in spite of myself and shook my head, same memory, different lens.

'Strongest immune system I ever had,' I told him, shooting a threatening look in Joe's direction. 'And living with the boys taught me how to take care of myself.'

No need to mention all three of them were absolute wimps and I even had to set up the internet myself.

Dad flapped his hand in my direction then pulled out a set of shiny silver keys. 'Don't let Sophie scare you, her bark is worse than her bite.'

'Happy to put that to the test,' Joe replied quietly.

'And the cottage has had a bit of a makeover since

she was last here,' Dad continued blithely as I fought the urge to beat Joe to death with my fluffy bunny slippers. 'I've been working on it all year.'

'Dad, I love you but it needed a fairy godmother, not a makeover,' I said.

'Just wait and see,' he replied with a laugh. 'You might be surprised.'

Surprised was not the word.

Shocked, maybe. Stunned. Convinced I'd passed into a parallel dimension where up was down and the sky was green. The dark, dirty, cobweb-filled shed I'd avoided like my life depended on it had been transformed. From the outside, I could just about tell it was the same cottage but the centuries-old limestone walls had to be the only thing that remained. Yellow roses grew around the brown stable door and on either side there were two new windows, square panes with white trim sparkling in the sun.

'You did all this?' I asked my father in amazement.

'It's amazing what you can accomplish when you put your mind to it,' he replied, watching on as we each wiped our feet on the mat. 'Your mum thinks I might have missed my calling.'

'Mum might be on to something,' I breathed. 'Bloody hell, Dad.'

All the gardening equipment, broken bikes, stringless tennis racquets, deflated footballs and rusty pogo sticks had disappeared and in their place was the most charming country cottage I'd ever seen. A snug, cosy place with low ceilings and polished floors, the inside every bit as inviting as the flower boxes that hung outside the windows. Everything was perfect, from the kitchenette and squishy, cream-coloured sofa to the thick rugs on the floor and tiny, tiled fireplace already full of chopped wood. But most impressive of all was the bed. Brass frame, fluffy duvet and gigantic marshmallows for pillows, it looked like heaven. A heavy, knitted blanket rested over the frame, begging to be wrapped around my shoulders on a chilly winter night and it took everything in me not to run across the room and dive-bomb under the covers. I was already in my pyjamas, after all.

'Charlotte says it's *folklore*-coded which was apparently a compliment,' Dad said. 'What do you think, Soph?'

'I think you did a deal with the devil,' I replied, flexing my toes inside my slippers. 'There's no way this is the same cottage.'

'It's very nice,' Joe commented even though no one asked him. 'Have you ever thought about going into renovation professionally, Mr Taylor?'

'*Hugh*,' Dad said, blushing like a schoolgirl. 'You haven't seen the best bit yet. Come on, this way.'

The three of us followed him out of the large, airy room and through a second stable door, Joe rattling on about the finishes and fixtures, me mentally planning my summer cottage staycation and Gregory absently poking at things and muttering under his breath.

'Here it is, the highlight of the tour.'

Dad stood to one side and unveiled his masterpiece with a flourish.

'Sorry, Dad, I'm never leaving,' I announced. 'I'm moving back home.'

'You most certainly are not,' he replied, unable to keep the pride out of his voice. 'But I didn't do a bad job on the bathroom, did I?'

He had done an incredible job. There were all the usual things you find in a bathroom, toilet, sink, towel rack, but they weren't important. All that mattered was the massive, cast-iron claw-foot bathtub that sat next to the window, looking out over the rolling fields behind my parents' garden.

'Never really been one for a bath,' Gregory said, twisting the sink taps. 'Where's the shower?'

'Glad you asked. Behold the pièce de résistance!'

Dad crossed the room and opened a door to the garden on the other side of the bath. Outside, jutting out from the side of the cottage, was a rainfall shower the size of a dinnerplate with a smooth pebble floor beneath it and honeysuckle-covered rough stone walls enclosed the space. Two plush bathrobes hung on brass hooks, along with towels so thick the thought of how long they'd need in the drier whenever I washed them made me feel faint. Wafting us back inside, Dad turned on the taps and, immediately, the space filled with lavender-scented steam.

'Malcolm treated us to a weekend away at Soho Farmhouse for my birthday,' Dad explained, his glasses all fogged up. 'Your mother was like a pig in shit the whole time, couldn't get her out the bloody bathroom so I thought, why not recreate it at home?'

'It's very impressive, Hugh,' Joe said with what sounded like genuine enthusiasm. 'Much nicer than Soho Farmhouse, I'd say.'

Of course he'd been to Soho Farmhouse. Probably went all the time. Probably with an influencer called Haeyleigh who only wore Lululemon and made him take her photo seventeen thousand times until she was happy with her duck face pout and peace sign combo.

'This is all well and good,' said Gregory, backing away from the shower spray as though he might melt on contact with the water. 'But surely you don't expect me to stay down here?'

Dad's smile slipped and he looked over at his friend, crestfallen.

'You don't like it?'

'It's very . . . rustic,' Gregory replied, glancing down at his yellow trainers. 'I can't get in and out of that bath with my back and not to be rude but there's no way on god's green earth you're getting me in an outdoor shower. Are you trying to kill me? We're in England. It's chilly at night. What do you do about nosy neighbours? What if there's an unexpected storm while I'm soaping up and get struck by lightning? Best-case scenario, Peeping Toms. Worst-case scenario, flash-fried Gregory.'

'There are no storms forecast and it's perfectly warm out here.' Dad pointed at heating panels hidden in the overhanging roof of the cottage as he turned off the water. 'And it's completely private, there's no way anyone can see in.'

But Gregory held firm.

'No, I'm sorry. If this is all you've got to offer, I'm going to have to head home. I wish you'd told me you were planning to have me camp out in an ancient shed when you offered me a place to stay.'

Gregory was now and always had been a knob. He didn't mean it, he just wanted to take the wind out of my dad's sails, but I knew Dad wouldn't thank me for pointing it out. I didn't realise how tightly I was keeping my mouth closed until I noticed the muscles in Joe's jaw ticking exactly the same as mine. Both of us were biting our tongues.

'You can't leave before the party tomorrow,' Dad insisted, looking to me in a panic. 'Perhaps you could swap with Sophie?'

'Swap?' I repeated. 'You mean, Gregory gets my room and I get to stay here? All weekend?'

'If you don't mind moving your things.'

I could've passed out from joy. Ditch the overcrowded house and hide out down here, soaking in the tub, reading by the fire and handfeeding squirrels and deer and any other number of Snow White-themed-activities?

'Works for me,' I said, already planning my bath schedule. 'Gregory, you're welcome to my room. I'll clear out my stuff right now.'

'Then it's settled,' Dad announced before his so-called friend could comment. 'Gregory, you're up in the house, and Sophie and Joe will stay in the cottage.'

CHAPTER TEN

'Absolutely, positively, one hundred percent not.'

I glared at the three men in front of me and they stared back. Dad seemed perplexed, Gregory looked annoyed, but Joe? He was delighted.

'I'm not sharing a bed with him,' I said, pointing at the world's most smug man.

'Noone's asking you to share the bed,' Dad replied, leading us back through the cottage and pointing at the two pieces of furniture, on opposite sides of the small living room. 'The sofa pulls out. Joe can sleep on that.'

'You can't seriously expect me to share a bedroom with a man I don't know,' I returned, furious with how flustered I sounded.

'But you do know him,' Dad said. 'It's Joseph.'

'Just because I know who he is doesn't mean I want to share a room with him!'

It was a perfectly rational argument, no one should have to share a sleeping space with someone if they didn't want to, and yet, my usual logic and composure had abandoned me completely. It was very obvious from the looks on my dad and Gregory's faces my tone had hit the level of shrill where men stop listening altogether, no matter how valid any woman's argument.

'Soph, there's nowhere else for him to sleep.' Dad lowered his voice, speaking slowly as though I was the one who didn't understand. 'What do you want him to do, kip on the floor?'

'Yes?' I threw up my hands in despair, why was he not getting this?

'I could always sleep in the car,' Joe offered, mirroring my body language as though he was truly searching for a viable compromise. 'Unless there's a hotel nearby?'

'Nonsense.' Dad clasped his hands to his chest, the thought of sending Joe off to the Travelodge an arrow through his heart. 'They're all full last we checked and there are two perfectly good beds in this room.'

'Sofa bed is more than good enough for me.' Joe dropped the more battered-looking overnight bag on the floor to stake his claim. 'I insist the lady takes the bed. Even if I'm the guest and it would really be more polite to let me have it but still, beggars can't be choosers.'

'Beggars can still get a kick in the nuts,' I replied as he made himself at home. 'Why can't he sleep in the house?'

'Because the sofa in the house doesn't pull out into a bed and we've filled all the other bedrooms. Come on, Soph, it's only Joseph. You've known him since you were kids.'

'You know what the problem is,' Gregory said with a snicker. 'Your girl's worried she won't be able to keep her hands off him.'

It was official. They were the two most awful men

on the face of the planet. Once again, I'd fallen into Joe's trap, I'd let him get to me and he knew it.

'Look, if Sophie's *that* against it—' Joe started but I cut him off before he could make another asinine suggestion.

'Sophie is that against it because Sophie doesn't like you,' I confirmed, whirling around to jab him in the chest with a very pointy finger. 'If you absolutely, positively must sleep on the sofa bed, knock yourself out. Just don't talk to me, don't look at me and don't be surprised if you find yourself accidentally smothered by a pillow in the middle of the night.'

'I think we all need a cup of tea,' Dad said, walking very quickly towards the front door before I could change my mind again. 'Joseph and Gregory have had a long drive, and Sophie, I'm sure you want to get your things from the house and, I don't know, get dressed?'

'Maybe a Baileys for Sophie,' Joe suggested before lowering his voice and leaning in so only I could hear. 'But you should keep the PJs on, they really are sexy.'

Slapping each other on the back as they went, the three men strolled out the front door laughing, leaving me all alone in the cottage, marvelling at how quickly a dream could turn into a nightmare.

'They really couldn't find it? No one handed it in, not even the bag?'

William shook his head, watching on while I unpacked my things in the cottage. I'd chucked everything back in my suitcase and bolted down the garden as fast as humanly possible to stake my claim on the bed before Joe could come up with any fun new schemes to ruin my weekend.

'No one's handed anything in,' he replied, giving his beard a scratch. 'Man at the depot said the most likely scenario is someone found it, nicked the laptop and chucked the rest in the bin. There's no reason for you to panic.'

'There isn't? Gosh, thanks for letting me know, I was just about to start but now I won't.'

'You sound exactly like Mum when you attempt sarcasm,' William said as I lined up my skincare products on the bedside table with aggressive precision. 'And that's not a compliment.'

'You don't understand how bad it is,' I replied with a whine. 'That draft is a mess. If anyone reads it—'

'If anyone reads it and knows what it is, they'll think they've won the lottery,' he finished for me. 'Authors always think their first draft is a crime against god and man and nine times out of ten that's not true.'

'That might be the biggest lie you've ever told.'

'Seven times out of ten,' he amended.

'William.'

'Fine, five and a half. Bottom line is, the bag is gone. There's nothing else we can do, time to move on.'

The tote bag was gone. My manuscript, the book, all the evidence of my identity. The thought of someone reading my work in progress gave me chills. I felt so vulnerable, like I'd been locked out the house in my underwear and not nice underwear at that.

'Dad's done a good job with this place, hasn't he?' William looked around with admiration, changing the subject before I could spiral any further. 'Who knew he had such a knack for interior design?'

'Me. They use my Netflix password and he's been watching all the back seasons of *Queer Eye*.'

'Seems sturdy.' He knocked on the wall and nodded as though he had any idea what a sturdy construction was supposed to sound like. 'Soph, if I say something do you promise not to take it the wrong way?'

Whatever he was going to say it seemed there was only one possible way I was going to take it. I busied myself by opening up my suitcase and unrolling my outfits, still unsure as to why I'd bothered to bring so many clothes when I would almost certainly spend all weekend in jeans as usual.

'Whatever it is, spit it out,' I said, preparing for the worst.

'It's just . . . you seem a bit down,' he said carefully. 'For someone whose lifelong dream has always been to write a book, I thought you'd be a bit more excited about everything that's going on.'

I shook out a slinky black dress I bought three years ago but still hadn't worn despite packing it for three different weddings, two hen dos and a girls' trip to Amsterdam. It was a beautiful dress but I'd never felt beautiful enough to wear it.

'I am excited,' I replied. 'I'm ecstatic. I'm cock-a-bloody-hoop.'

William frowned doubtfully as I hung the dress on the front of the wardrobe where I could stare at it all weekend and once again, not wear it.

'I'm being serious, I'm worried about you. No one's saying you have to throw yourself a parade but if anything you've been even more withdrawn than usual since the book came out.'

Withdrawn? I'm not withdrawn,' I replied, checking and checking his allegation in my head.

'Tense then,' he suggested but I shook my head to refute that too.

'Everything is absolutely grand. I've just been—'

Looping an imaginary noose around his neck, he cut me off with a deeply unattractive choking noise.

'So help me god, if you say you've been busy, I'm going to come over there and give you a dead arm. Yes, you're busy, everyone's busy, but not everyone has a bestselling book, a movie deal and I know the royalties haven't started coming in yet but, sister of mine, I'm your agent. I've seen the numbers. You're about to be hanging-out-on-a-yacht-with-Leo rich and we both know it. That's not enough to raise a smile?'

I tossed five times the number of pairs of knickers I could possibly need in one weekend into the bottom of the wardrobe and shrugged.

'Boats make me seasick and we both know I'm way too old for Leo.'

'Well, something's wrong,' he replied, not settling for my answer. 'Are you being bullied at school?'

'William, I'm the teacher.'

'And I'm assuming there's nothing to report on the romantic front?'

The closeness of Joe's lips to mine flickered through my mind.

'Nope.'

'But you're getting out, seeing your friends?'

'Yes, I'm getting out and seeing my friends,' I replied with an indignant sigh borrowed directly from my sister. 'Not as much as usual, admittedly, but with the head of year thing at work and writing the sequel, I can't do everything. And I'm the only single one in the group at the moment. It's not always the most fun thing in the world to hang out with a load of loved-up, sprogged-up women when the closest you've come to an erect penis in the last six months is writing about one.'

'To be filed under "Things I never needed to hear my sister say",' he grumbled. 'Fine, I won't mention it again. As long as you're not turning into a hermit just to keep your secret.'

'Your concerns have been noted,' I assured him while wrestling a coat hanger off the rail. It was nice to know he cared. He dipped into my suitcase and pulled out my most comfortable bra with a look of horror.

'As long as you know you won't be able to keep this under your hat forever,' William said, holding it up to the light to examine the bra in all its washed-out beige glory. 'One way or another, the whole Este Cox thing is going to come out and also, please will you go under-wear shopping immediately.'

Yanking my bra out of his hands, I shoved it in the wardrobe along with my socks and knickers. 'What if I want to be one of those eccentric weirdos who sits on millions their whole lives then leaves it all to a cat sanctuary?'

'It could never be me,' he replied aghast. 'And it won't be you either. As your agent, I'm very much expecting you to shower me with extravagant gifts and luxury holidays.'

'All you did was give the contract a once-over after I negotiated it myself.'

'It was a very thorough once-over.'

'You sent it back with a thumbs up emoji in less time than it took me to make a cup of tea.'

'I'm very efficient.'

Zipping up my empty suitcase, I slid it under the bed, disproportionately pleased with how neatly it fit. Across the room, nestled against the sofa, was Joe's overnight bag. Even though it was half the size of my suitcase, it filled the entire cottage with his presence, the worn, masculine leather quietly confident amongst all the soft, feminine furnishing, and it took every ounce of strength I had in me not to hurl it away into the field, like Miss Trunchbull hammer-tossing that little girl by the pigtails in *Matilda*.

'What's the deal with this one?' William asked, crossing the room to inspect the bag for himself. 'I haven't had the pleasure yet.'

'I wouldn't to call it a pleasure,' I replied. 'Tall, dark and twattish.'

'Genuinely hot or publishing hot?'

'Genuinely,' I admitted through gritted teeth. 'And he knows it.'

It was an important distinction. Meeting an eligible man who worked in publishing was like finding the last bottle of water on a desert island, only the island was an office building in London Bridge and the bottle of water was an incredibly average-looking man called Tom. Single men had an unfair advantage over single women simply because they were a rarity. There was no getting away from it, Joe Walsh was a unicorn. Undeniably, earth-shatteringly, brain-meltingly good-looking.

Not that I cared.

'I'd say come and stay with us but we've got Sanjit's family and they're already using all the hot water before I even get in the shower,' William said, plopping down on the arm of the sofa, prodding the cushions with the same expertise he'd shown when examining the walls. 'I vaguely remember Joe from when we were kids. Awkward bugger as I recall. Didn't he move to America with his mum?'

I nodded.

'Moved to America, went to Harvard, worked in publishing in New York after uni, came back to London a few months ago and now he's blagging it at MullinsParker as some sort of incredibly self-important creative director. Lives in King's Cross like a wanker.'

My brother folded his arms across his chest, head cocked to one side.

'What?' I asked, embarrassed to realise I'd been talking so fast, I was out of breath.

'Thanks for the bio, Wikipedia.'

'Know thy enemy,' I replied hotly. 'I'm an adult woman with access to the internet, took me two minutes to find that out. His Instagram isn't private and the weirdo updates his LinkedIn *constantly*.'

In the two minutes I had to myself between moving my stuff to the cottage and William's visit, I conducted my search, certain there had to be something in his digital footprint that would give me a good, strong case of the ick. But no. He only used his Instagram to show-case his annoyingly impressive work and, as far as I could tell, he didn't have any other social media accounts. His enthusiasm for LinkedIn should've been a turn-off but it somehow managed to have the opposite effect. Aside from the fact he clearly had a strong work ethic, having kept himself busy with part-time jobs all through university, he was still listed as a board member of a volunteer organisation that helped underprivileged kids get involved in the arts in New York. If that wasn't bad enough, in between all the usual boy music, his public Spotify playlists were littered with Beyoncé and Taylor Swift tracks, *and* he only listened to Taylor's Versions.

The man was too good to be true.

Given a little more time, I was certain I could find something incriminating, something unforgivable, like a video of him kicking puppies or throwing up a peace sign next to a tiger in Thailand or, even worse, drinking Logan Paul's energy drink. There had to be something. There was always something.

'Poor Joseph,' William laughed. 'He's met his match, hasn't he?'

'He prefers Joe,' I replied adding; 'Not that it matters.'

'Not that it matters,' my brother agreed gleefully. 'Shall we have a look in his bag?'

I pasted on a look of shock, as though I hadn't spent every single second between Joe's departure and William's arrival fighting the urge to do exactly that.

'William Leo Taylor, I am disappointed,' I said, dashing over to the window to peek out the curtain. The coast was clear. 'That you didn't suggest it earlier. Get it open.'

He hoisted the bag onto the sofa and unfastened a tarnished brass buckle before opening the zip, each soft click-clack of the teeth parting ways tickling my eardrums. The cottage suddenly seemed very, very quiet.

'Looks pretty standard. Shirts, socks, deodorant,' he said as he poked around inside. Then he stopped and looked me dead in the eye. 'Oh my.'

'What?' I asked, my heart racing as I dashed to his side.

'Your man is packing some very fancy pants,' he

fished through the neatly folded fabric to produce a pair of silky-looking black trunks. 'Calvins. Nice.'

'Put them down!' I ordered. 'I don't want to see his underwear.'

'Really?' William waggled his eyebrows up and down. 'Tall, dark and twattish used to be your type.'

'I'm in recovery,' I said as I slapped the underwear out of his hand and watched it float to the ground. 'What else is in there?'

'What else is in where?'

The two of us spun around at once, standing shoulder to shoulder in front of the open overnight bag, so close together a draught couldn't have got between us. Charlotte glared at us from the doorway, peach hair backlit by the sunny morning, her oversized blue hoodie and grey jogging bottoms swamping her tiny frame. All my sister's clothes were either five sizes too big or practically non-existent, there was no in between.

'What are you two doing?' she asked, suspicion narrowing her brown eyes. She wouldn't appreciate me saying it but she really was growing up to be a pure clone of our mother.

'Nothing,' I replied. 'We weren't doing anything.'

'Well, not nothing,' William corrected. 'We were just saying how amazing it is that you're going to open a bookshop and wondering what your favourite reads of the year are so far?'

I felt a sharp elbow in my ribs as Charlotte's face lit up.

'Yes, that's right!' I exclaimed. 'I was telling William how much you loved *Iron Flame* and how I couldn't imagine you'd loved anything else quite as much then he said he'd love to hear your current top ten and—'

'I *did* love *Iron Flame*,' she replied, so thrilled to be talking about her two favourite subjects – books and herself – that she immediately forgot to be suspicious. 'But there has been a lot of great stuff this year. *Fate Breaker* killed me if we're still talking fantasy and you know I'm an EmHen girlie, so you've got to read her latest if you haven't already, but aside from romance I'm mostly into dark academia right now . . .'

'Is that right?' William stepped forward and put his arm around Charlotte's shoulders, pushing her out of the cottage. 'Tell me, in your professional opinion, Colleen Hoover, is she overrated?'

William turned to give me a wink as they started back down the path. He really was the best brother in the world.

As soon as they were a safe distance away, I stuffed Joe's belongings back into his bag, the silky black trunks and soft cotton T-shirts falling over each other in their bid to escape. It was wrong for a man to have such lovely things. CJ's underwear had all been from M&S, all washed to within an inch of its life and in no way, shape or form could it ever be considered sexy. Exactly the way things were supposed to be. How could a woman trust a man who spent more money on his pants than she did?

'Call me cynical,' a voice said, right as I fastened the brass clasp with a satisfying click. 'But if you came in here to find me going through your things, I don't think you'd be very happy about it.'

'Someone needs to put a bloody bell on that bloody door,' I muttered, pressing a hand against my pounding heart. Joe stood in the doorway in silence, arms crossed, waiting for me to defend myself.

'I wasn't going through your things,' I told him, obliging against my better judgement. 'I was . . . putting your bag on the sofa. You left it on the floor. I was protecting it, in case there are mice.'

'Get a lot of leather-eating mice in here, do you?' he asked, leaning against the doorframe.

'Yes,' I replied. 'Loads.'

'Then I owe you my eternal gratitude.'

Joe swept his dark, wavy hair out of his face with a careless hand and every muscle in my body clenched at once. 'I'll have to think of a way to thank you properly on the way.'

I blinked back at him, confused.

'On the way to where?'

'So many questions,' he sighed. 'All you need to know is, I volunteered us for a mission and we're already late, so get your hands out my pants and let's go.'

With that, he turned and strolled off up the garden, whistling a tune I vaguely recognised from our two-man karaoke party.

'He's an arsehole,' I said out loud, disbelief tempering the volume of my voice. 'A complete and utter arsehole.'

But that fact didn't stop my traitorous stomach flipping with anticipation as I grabbed my phone and followed him out of the cottage.

CHAPTER ELEVEN

It made perfect sense that central London resident, Gregory Brent drove a brand-new Range Rover.

'He used to have a Porsche which was much worse,' Joe told me as we pulled it out the driveway and onto the country lane that led from my parents' house. 'Swapped to this last year, thank god. He wanted something with a bit more space.'

'For his ego or his aftershave collection?' I asked, winding down the window.

'Subtlety has never been my father's strong point,' he replied with a small smile.

'And yet you decided to drag yourself all the way up here to spend a last-minute weekend away with him.' I tapped my nails against the cream leather interior. Soft as a baby's bum. 'Such a good son.'

He turned the steering wheel and the car rolled smoothly onto the main road.

'Between you and me, I might've had an ulterior motive.'

'Such as?' I looked over at him, his profile strong

against the colours outside the window, a blur of leafy trees and stone walls and endless golden fields of wheat.

He didn't reply, not right away, instead he stared straight ahead and put his foot down, the speed of the car pushing me back into my seat. Pinching my lips together, I kept my eyes forward and my mouth closed. I certainly wasn't going to be the one to speak next. If he had something he wanted to say, he could say it. I was perfectly happy to sit in silence and watch the world pass by, ramblers waiting to cross the road with their rucksacks and walking sticks, flocks of fluffy sheep, a cherry red stop sign, his lightly tanned forearm that drew a straight line from his muscular shoulder down to his wrist, his huge hand that palmed the gear stick and the fingers splayed across the leather-covered steering wheel, as his thumb rubbed rhythmically against the buttery fabric and—

'So where are we going anyway?' I asked, clearing my throat and crossing my legs. 'You said you'd volunteered us for a mission.'

He glanced over at me, wearing the look of a man who knew he'd just won a point.

'Your mum needed someone to pick up her order from the butcher and I needed to get away from my dad.'

'And I need to be here because?'

'You're my glamorous assistant. You're going to help me carry two dozen pork sausages, a dozen beef burgers and a fuck load of chicken.'

'A fuck load?' I repeated with concern. 'Is that metric or imperial?'

'It's exactly what your mum told me,' he said, still

110

grinning. 'She said something about better to have too much than not enough but unless they've invited Joey Chestnut, I'd say they've likely overdone it.'

'Joey Chestnut?'

'Competitive eater. Have you ever seen a hotdog-eating contest?'

'Relieved to say I have not.'

'Don't look it up. At least not until after the barbecue. It's intense, I was there when he broke the world record, seventy-six hotdogs and buns in ten minutes.'

'I'm guessing this was when you lived in America?' I said, momentarily wondering if I'd missed my calling in life. My personal record was only four hotdogs and three buns after a particularly stressful IKEA visit but I was sure I could do better with the right training.

'Land of the free, home of the brave,' he said with a nod.

Two cars ahead of us, a set of traffic lights turned red and we slowed to a stop. The car hummed, desperate for Joe to lift his foot up off the brake and I understood its yearning. I felt safer when the car was moving. Sitting here in a heavy silence, waiting, impatient, was too much. Unable to resist one moment longer, I looked at Joe. He was looking right back at me, those blue eyes holding me still in space and time. Why did the worst men have the most beautiful eyes? If there was any justice in the world he'd be made to trade with a nice accountant called Gareth, who always called when he said he would and took the bins out without asking. Joe didn't need another weapon in his arsenal. If he walked out into a sunlit meadow and sparkled from head to toe, I wouldn't even be surprised.

'These must be some impressive sausages if they're

sending us all the way out to the butcher,' I said when we arrived at our destination, opening my door and hopping out the car before Joe could turn off the engine. 'My parents aren't exactly known for their discerning culinary tastes. Dad's favourite food is Butterscotch Angel Delight and my mum doesn't even bother to heat up the tin of rice pudding before she digs in.'

'Pulling out the good stuff for guests maybe?' he suggested, quickly positioning himself to walk on the outside of me, closer to the busy road.

'Two years ago, they had Stephen King come to visit and ordered him a Domino's.'

Joe whistled, long, loud and clear. 'Then these must be some pretty impressive sausages.'

The butcher's shop was in Baslow, much further away than the supermarket or even the butcher in Harford, so I knew there had to be a reason Mum had insisted on buying her meat here. It was a traditional Peak District 'ye olde shoppe' limestone affair with a huge glass window displaying its wares and a sign above the window that read 'McIntyre's Meats'. Inside, I saw a solid brick wall of a man expertly handling a shiny silver cleaver.

'I think I see why Mum likes this butcher more than the other,' I said, the puzzle pieces falling into place as I watched him effortlessly hack a rack of lamb in two.

'She did say something about him having a lot of followers on Instagram,' Joe replied. 'She didn't mention the fact he competed in the Mr Universe competition on his days off.'

The butcher raised his head, presumably alerted by the extra testosterone in the air, but if Joe was threatened by the appearance of another super-hot man, you couldn't tell. Probably too dangerous to show fear in his presence, especially when he was armed.

'Sophie, before we go in to collect a fuck tonne of chicken, I want to clear the air.'

I tore my eyes away from the human beefcake and allowed them to rest on Joe. He stood right in front of me, both hands clasped around the back of his neck, chin jutting out slightly. Defensive with just a touch of irritation.

'I know you don't want me here—'

'Oh no, what gives you that idea?' I asked, setting foot on the stone step that led up to the butcher's front door, but before I could open it, he gripped my arm gently and pulled me back down to the street.

'It's impossible for you to let me finish a single sentence, isn't it?' he said, his thumb and forefinger almost meeting in a perfect circle around my bicep. His hands were huge. 'I was going to say, I know you don't want me here but I don't want to ruin the weekend.'

'It's a bit late for that,' I replied. The warmth of his skin scorched through the thin sleeve of my T-shirt. 'Honestly, Joe, I don't know why you're here unless it's to torture me. After everything you said to me yesterday, it doesn't make any sense.'

'I was an idiot and I was drunk. I didn't mean any of it.' He threw up his hands with evident frustration. 'I've already apologised, what more do you want from me?'

I didn't dare confess the answer to that question changed every other minute.

'Then why say it in the first place?' I asked instead, wrapping my arms protectively around my body. 'You

113

absolutely meant all of it and that's fine, it doesn't matter, I don't care what you think about me.' Or my book, I added silently.

'Well, I care what you think about me.'

He looked so genuine, so contrite, I almost believed him. And I wanted to, I really did. But where would that get me? Joe Walsh was a subplot, an annoyance sent to distract me from the main storyline. I still had a book to rewrite, a laptop to find, the imminent arrival of my ex-boyfriend to worry about and how many days did I have left to return my ASOS parcel before I was stuck with three pairs of jeans that didn't fit? The only thing I did know was I had no spare brain cells left over to waste on Joe Walsh.

He stood staring at me, waiting for a response. So I gave him one.

'Would you mind going in to pick up the order?' I asked politely.

Inside the shop, the keen edge of the butcher's cleaver sparkled in the sun before he brought it down, slicing through bone like butter.

'No problem,' Joe said. 'Don't like being around raw meat?'

'Don't trust myself around sharp knives,' I replied.

'Then I'll be right back,' he said, his shoulders slumping in defeat.

Once Joe was safely inside, I took out my phone and did something I never allowed myself to do in the cold, sober light of day. I looked at my ex-boyfriend's Instagram. Usually, I managed to keep my social media self-harm to sleepless nights and drunk Uber rides but this wasn't emotional masochism, this was self-preservation. I needed a reminder of how badly it hurt when another pretty literary user broke my heart.

Colin and I met at the Chimamanda Ngozi Adichie event during the Edinburgh Book Festival, both of us awkwardly avoiding the crowds, sitting in the safety of the back row. From the very first day, it was so easy. No drama, just comfortable fun. I was getting ready to start my first term at Abbey Hill school, he was applying for publishing jobs all over London and the two of us sat up late every night, talking about all the books we'd read and all the books we wanted to write. He dreamed of creating something profound and meaningful, I wanted to write a book that made people smile, and at the time, we agreed that both ambitions were equally valid. We were so in love, it only made sense for us to move in together right away to save money. Once my teaching career kicked in, my book went on the back burner, but Colin only worked three days a week as an agent's assistant which gave him plenty of time to hammer out his debut, a book based on one of my ideas that I didn't have time to dig into. He wasn't making a lot of money but that wasn't a problem because I was happy to pay the rent, at least until he landed a big book deal, then we agreed I could finish work and concentrate on my writing too.

When he got an agent, everything changed. Overnight, Colin wrapped himself up in a chrysalis of hype and, out of the cosy cocoon I thought I knew, crawled too-cool, CJ Simmons. CJ didn't want me to read his drafts, CJ had no use for my notes, and after he sold his book, CJ claimed his publicist wanted him to pretend he was single to keep the female readers interested, like he was some kind of literary Harry Styles. A year later, on the same day his book was published – an instant critical, if not commercial, success – he dumped me. After five years together, we'd allegedly outgrown each other. Better off as friends, he said.

Colin needed me until CJ didn't. It was that simple.

CJ's Instagram was all moody black and white images, everyday objects shot at weird angles and endless teasing about his next novel, although when it might actually come out remained a mystery, much like why I put up with him for so long. The man wore a leather thong around his neck with Chris Martin's plectrum hanging from it for god's sake. What was I thinking? No. I promised myself it would be nice guys only after CJ which was why I'd been single for two years. I would not fall for it again.

'A little help?'

I looked up from my phone as Joe staggered down the single step to the street, straining under the weight of several trays of meat. I grabbed the top tray and my spaghetti arms quivered under the weight.

'At least now we know the exact weight of a fuck load of chicken,' he joked but when he smiled at me, I saw CJ, even if I couldn't imagine Joe wearing a leather thong necklace, and I couldn't smile back.

'We should get back,' I said, turning away from him and pouring every ounce of energy I'd ever had into my non-existent muscles. 'It's too hot for these to be out the fridge for long.'

'Fine.'

He strode out in front of me, not bothering to keep to my side this time which was, like he said, fine. It wasn't the traffic I needed protecting from.

We marched to the car in silence, Joe fumbling for

his keys, holding them up but not pressing the button to open the boot. The man was a masochist.

'Right, I've got something to say and this time you're going to let me say it,' he said as my sad little biceps and triceps screamed in protest. 'You've decided you don't like me and I can't make you change your mind.'

'Please can we do this when I've put the chicken down?' I asked, searching for a safe place to put the tray as my arms started to shake uncontrollably.

'No, I want to say this while I've got your attention,' he insisted. 'You might think I'm some super creep who stalked you up here—'

'Because you are.'

'—but I wasn't stalking you,' he went on, talking over me this time. 'I came up because my dad invited me, I didn't have any other plans and, like an idiot, I thought it might be fun. And because I have something for you.'

He pressed the magic button on his key fob and the hatch opened impossibly slowly, almost as though it was in on the drama. The boot of the car was spotless and completely empty apart from one thing. A slightly grubby, well-used canvas tote bag.

My slightly grubby, well-used canvas tote bag.

'Oh my god!' I screamed, reaching forwards. The tray of chicken slipped from my grasp and dozens of drumsticks tumbled off into the road.

'Fuck!' Joe exclaimed. 'The chicken!'

'Fuck the chicken!' I yelled with delight. 'You found my bag!'

'I didn't find it, you left it in the karaoke bar,' he said, sliding his trays of burgers and hotdogs into the boot as I grabbed my bag and clutched it tightly to my chest, chicken drumsticks be damned.

'I was going to give it to you earlier but after that scene with your sister and the "fake" handbag, I got the feeling I should wait until we were alone.'

I nodded, only half listening as I pawed at the contents. It was all there, the laptop, the manuscript, the copy of *Butterflies*, and all the incriminating post with my name and address.

'Your family don't know, do they?' Joe said.

'Know what?' I asked in a painfully squeaky voice, the worst liar in the world.

'That you're Este Cox.'

It was too strange to hear him say it, a statement and an accusation.

'What are you talking about?' I half-laughed, shaking my head as I thumbed through the pages, certain words and phrases catching my eye against my will. Why did I have to write even more spice into the sequel? So help me god, if he'd read it . . . 'Mal told you, I'm a big fan and, um, that's all.'

'A big fan who writes a sequel to *Butterflies* for a laugh?' He cocked his head to one side and raised an eyebrow. 'It's all right, Sophie, I won't tell anyone. Firstly, I work for your publisher and secondly, I'm not as big an arsehole as you think.'

It wasn't as though I had much of a choice. He knew the bag was mine, he'd seen what was inside and as much as it pained me to admit it, he wasn't stupid.

'No one knows except Mal and my brother,' I said, before chewing on my bottom lip. Then another thought occurred to me and I felt faint. 'Please tell me you didn't tell your dad?'

Joe scoffed then smirked. 'I've learned the hard way not to tell my dad anything if I can help it.'

Gripping my tote bag like it was the last life jacket on *The Titanic*, I looked at him with wet eyes, unexpectedly overwhelmed.

'I know how stressed I'd be if I lost something like that,' he added. 'I wanted to make sure you got it back safely.'

'Thank you.' I was desperately trying not to cry. Trying and failing. 'This is the most incredible thing, I really thought it was gone forever. I owe you one.'

Then Joe smiled. It was the same smile I'd seen the day before, the one that hesitated halfway, like it wanted to make sure he was truly happy before it committed, then lit up his face, my face and the whole world.

'Happy to be of service,' he said. 'But we've got a real problem now, haven't we?'

I squeezed my tote bag even tighter.

'We have?'

'Yes.' He squatted to pick up my empty butcher's tray and held it aloft. 'Where are we going to find another fuck load of chicken at such short notice?'

119

CHAPTER TWELVE

'Give me an hour,' said the hot butcher in a low Scottish burr as I sheepishly handed the empty tray back across the counter. 'I've got an order coming in, there should be enough to pull together the same again, give or take.'

'Amazing. Thanks, mate, you're a life-saver,' Joe replied, handing him the other trays of meat to go back in the fridge while I hovered behind him, an anxious mess of deep bows and prayer hands.

'Mostly scared of her mother,' the butcher countered. 'She's a very exacting woman. Last month, she returned a chicken because the legs were different sizes.'

They both gave me a look, as though I was the one who went around judging chickens on their appearance.

'He shouldn't have skipped leg day?' I offered.

Neither of them laughed. Harsh but fair.

'We'll leave you to it,' Joe said, catching my wrist in his massive hand and leading me back out of the shop.

*   *   *

'What are we supposed to do for the next hour?'

Joe flashed his eyebrows and I exhaled an unimpressed huff.

'All right then, we've got two other options,' he replied. 'We can either stand here and argue for another sixty minutes or we can go for a walk. Lady's choice.'

'Walk where?' I asked, turning in a circle and seeing nothing but green. 'The pub is too far away and I don't think we'd be able to kill much time at the post office.'

'You know you can put that back in the car,' he said, nodding at the tote bag on my shoulder. 'It's not going to disappear again.'

'No way. It doesn't leave my sight.' I was holding onto it so tightly, the sharp edges of the hardback book dug deep into my ribs. 'What if I leave it in the car and the car gets stolen? Or it gets so hot in there, my computer explodes? Or—'

'Sixty minutes of arguing it is,' Joe declared happily. 'Not what I would've chosen but—'

'Fine, we'll walk!' I muttered. 'Even though there's nothing to walk to.'

'Are you joking?' He strolled ahead of me on the narrow footpath and waved his hands around at my alleged nothingness. 'Maybe I've spent too long living in cities but this is beautiful. It's called the countryside, Sophie, you don't have to do anything, you just exist in it. Appreciate it for what it is.'

'Oh, god, you're one of them,' I groaned, clutching the straps of my bag.

'One of who?'

'One of those awful city people who only leave London twice a year and think it's hilarious to say things like "Ahh, fresh country air" every time they smell manure.'

'There's nothing like a bit of cow shit to clear out the lungs,' Joe said, inhaling deeply until the buttons on his shirt began to strain across the chest. 'Like it or not, you're stuck with me until Braveheart back there can replace the chicken you dropped, and unless I'm very much mistaken, *you* owe *me* a favour.'

'And this is how you want to cash it in?' I looked out across the patchwork quilt of fields that rolled off into the horizon. 'On an unplanned rambling expedition?'

'You say unplanned rambling expedition, I say spontaneous outdoor adventure.'

'And what if I don't want to go on a spontaneous outdoor adventure?'

'It's too hot to sit in the car but you're welcome to wait outside the butcher's like a badly behaved Labrador,' he replied helpfully. 'Or you can stop being a brat, get your arse over here and come with me.'

'I'm not being a brat,' I argued, even though I definitely was. I couldn't help it, he had an uncanny ability to bring out the absolute worst in me. In fact, he seemed to have a direct line to all my baser instincts, something that became painfully clear as I watched him hop up onto the wall, his khaki-coloured trousers pulling taut across his backside as he went. And on top of that, he was impossible to read. One minute he was all slick charm and double entendres, the next he could almost pass for a decent human being. There was no way to know which one was the real Joe and I wasn't about to risk my sanity to find out simply because he had a spectacular arse.

Objectively speaking.

'There's an ice cream van parked over there,' he called, pointing off down the field as I ventured over towards the wall. 'Hurry up if you're coming, I want a Mr Whippy.'

'It better be proper ice cream or we're not having it,' I shouted back. 'Those soft serve machines are full of bacteria.'

'That must be what makes it so tasty.'

My legs wobbled as I clambered up the wall, tote bag banging against my hip, old stone scratching against my jeans. Once I was positioned on top, one leg dangling on either side, I saw that the drop down to the field was far greater than from the street.

'Need some help?' Joe asked, balancing on top of an old tree stump.

'No, thank you,' I replied, hoisting my other leg over until I was balanced right on the edge of the wall.

'Want me to hold your bag?'

'I've got it.'

He hopped off the stump and leaned casually against a tree.

'Looks like it.'

It wasn't the longest drop of all time, only about three and a half feet, but I'd never been a fan of heights and, as far as I was concerned, heights meant any time my feet were an uncomfortable distance off the ground. If human beings were meant to be up high, our bones would be made from a much more forgiving material. I shuffled as close to the edge as I could before launching myself into a slow-motion slide down, scuffing my trainers and destroying my dignity as I went. Graceful, it was not.

'Impressive,' Joe said as I swiped the muck and moss off my backside. 'Are you a professional climber, by any chance?'

'No,' I answered. 'I'm retaining my amateur status so I can climb down walls in the Olympics. Now where's this bloody ice cream van?'

The thought of a man eating soft-serve was a definite ick. Holding the cone, poking the ice cream with a little pink tongue and lapping at it like a Pomeranian with a Puppuccino. Like all great icks, I couldn't say why but it was one of those weird things that turned my vagina into the Sahara Desert.

Or at least it usually did.

'With this ice cream, I call an official truce,' Joe said, holding his cone up high. 'Deal?'

'Deal,' I replied as I tapped my phone against the card machine. ApplePay at the ice cream van, it just felt wrong. 'At least until you do something to piss me off again.'

He laughed as he turned to walk away. 'I think that's exactly what they wrote in the Treaty of Versailles.'

'Word for word,' I replied, giving the ice cream man an appreciative smile.

'What did you get?' Joe asked. He marvelled at the Franken-Cone in his hand. One scoop of strawberry ice cream, one scoop of salted caramel, multiple flakes, rainbow sprinkles, a bubble-gum ball in the bottom, and strawberry *and* chocolate syrup on top. It was a crime against god and man.

I held up my regular 99, one scoop of vanilla and one chocolate flake in a cone, and he let out a long, disappointed sigh.

'Sophie, you didn't even try.'

'Can't beat a classic,' I argued. I was thrilled with my choice.

'Not very adventurous, are you?'

'I'm adventurous when I want to be.'

He wrapped his full lips around the peak of his strawberry scoop then licked them clean. 'Really?'

Definitely no trace of the ick.

'Really,' I replied, looking away. 'But I also prefer to avoid disappointment and I can't think of many things more disappointing than ordering the wrong ice cream. What if I ended up with something I didn't like?'

'How do you know what you like if you never try new things?' he countered.

'There are lots of things I've never tried and I already know I don't like them.'

The ice cream van's engine revved into life behind us, a tinkling piano rendition of 'Pop Goes the Weasel' filling the silence.

'We don't always know as much as we think we do,' Joe said with a wicked grin before marching off down the lane. 'You should be a bit more open-minded. You might surprise yourself.'

'I can't believe you said there was nothing around here,' he declared as we strolled along the lane that ran between two fields, waist-high hedgerows on either side.

'There isn't?' I replied. 'All I see is sky, dirt and an idiot with an ice cream. That's it.'

'Don't call yourself an idiot,' Joe admonished and I heard myself laugh. 'Look around, it's beautiful. Fields of wheat, wildflowers, adorable sheep. There are many fucking sheep, Sophie, tell me that's not amazing? There's nowhere else in the world like the English countryside in the middle of summer.'

I rolled my eyes and took a bite of my ice cream. 'You were in New York too long.'

'Truce or no truce, I'm afraid I will have to fight you on this. Stand still and tell me what you see.'

'Other than sky, dirt and an idiot with an ice cream?' Scanning our surroundings, I hitched up my shoulders into a shrug. 'I give up. Lots of reminders that I forgot my hay fever tablets?'

'Now sit down,' he instructed, nodding at a fallen tree that rested by the side of the lane, a kind of make-shift bench. 'I'll tell you what I see.'

We both sat, him moving closer to me than was necessary, and I could smell the synthetic strawberry and sugary sweetness of his ice cream fighting with the light woody touch of his cologne. The true quiet of the countryside had always unnerved me. I'd always been a city mouse, or more like a mid-sized town guinea pig. Tring wasn't exactly the epicentre of the world but I liked to know there were people around me, relatively reliable public transport and a twenty-four hour shop with milk, teabags and that one out of date can of chickpeas that had been on the bottom shelf as long as I could remember. Sitting here beside Joe, I quickly developed a new appreciation for the middle of nowhere. The air was already heavy and hot but the tall grass behind us rustled as we sat, a soothing, fluttering sound that almost made me want to lie down and feel them brush against my skin.

'Look at that sky, crystal clear and cornflower blue,' Joe said, seemingly awestruck by a perfectly normal day. 'Then you've got the fields, all those merging shades of gold and green.'

'I thought I was supposed to be the romance writer,' I replied. 'Sounds like you're describing a leprechaun orgy.'

'And I thought you were a primary school teacher.'

I took a big bite of my 99. 'You should eat that monstrosity before it melts,' I told him, fighting through the brain freeze. 'It wasn't cheap, you know.'

'Got it. We're changing the subject. No problem.'

He did as he was told but he couldn't just eat an ice cream like a normal person, oh no, that would be too easy. Joe concentrated on the task at hand with a passion that made me weak. Every time his tongue darted out of his mouth and wrapped itself around the ice cream, his eyes closed with pleasure and involuntary groans of ecstasy escaped his throat. It was obscene.

I'd never been so turned on in my life.

'I have a confession to make,' he said, licking his fingers one at a time when the ice cream was gone.

'A confession?' I replied, thick, creamy vanilla dripping down my fingers, melting almost as fast as I was. He reached his hand out towards my face and I held my breath, his thumb grazing my chin as he slipped my bag off my shoulder and reached inside to pull out the hardback edition of *Butterflies*.

'It's about your book—'

'As *if* that's the Spice Rack special edition of *Butterflies*?'

Appearing out of nowhere, a girl somewhere around my sister's age came running towards us, arms outstretched, her hands making desperate grabby motions. 'It is! How do you have this? No one on earth has this!'

'Where the fuck did she come from?' I asked Joe, looking over both shoulders and seeing no one else for miles.

'I was out running,' she replied, doubled over as she caught her breath. 'I saw the book, I ran faster.'

127

Joe turned the book over in his hands to check the back cover and there it was, the little gold Spice Rack book of the month logo. The girl gasped, pressing multicoloured fingernails against her red lipsticked mouth. Out for a run in a full beat wearing gold lamé leggings and a lilac lace bralette. First two ice creams cost me the best part of twenty pounds and now this? I swear I aged a decade every day.

'There were teasers on TikTok but it hasn't even been confirmed yet. This is the most exciting thing that has ever happened to me, you've got to tell me how you got it,' the girl babbled, then she turned her gaze on me, eyes opening wide, defying the weight of her false lashes. 'You,' she whispered. 'Are you—'

'I work for the publisher,' Joe interrupted, casually waving the book back and forth to get her attention. It worked, she couldn't take her eyes off it. She was Gollum and *Butterflies* was her precious. 'It hasn't been announced yet, I managed to get an early copy for my friend.'

'Please,' she said with complete reverence, hands clasped together in prayer. 'Can I touch it? I promise I won't run off with it, I just want to see it.'

Joe looked at me, I looked at her then back at him.

'Of course you can,' I said, taking it from Joe and handing it over. 'It's just a book.'

She took it carefully in her hands, grasping it only at the very edges. People held newborn babies with less care.

'It's stunning. The foiled boards, the spredges, the printed endpapers . . .'

Even though I knew my book inside out, I suddenly got the feeling we were intruding on something extremely personal. She had a relationship with *Butterflies* that existed well beyond me, a completely different connection. I might be its mother but she was its lover and watching her fondle the book with her mouth hanging half open felt deeply inappropriate.

'Can I ask you a question?' Joe asked as I dropped the remains of my ice cream behind the tree trunk, too anxious to eat it now. 'What is it that you love about *Butterflies*?'

He held out his hand for the book and she stared back at him, confused, before slowly realising what he wanted. Heartbreak etched itself onto her face and, with the greatest reluctance, she gave it back.

'Everything,' she told him, whimpering as the book passed out of her grasp. Her whole body lurched with it like the two of them were physically linked. 'The story, the characters.' She paused, her cheeks turning scarlet. 'The spice.'

The way I sucked my cheeks was so violent, it was a wonder my entire face didn't collapse in on itself.

'It's the connection,' she expanded. 'When Jenna meets Eric, it's electric. I want that. All that passion and emotion. He really sees her, you know? That's so sexy.'

'Interesting, OK,' Joe replied, rubbing the underneath of his chin with the back of his hand. 'You don't think books like this give women unrealistic expectations?'

She glared down at him, appalled.

'Only if you don't think you deserve love.'

'Ouch,' I said through gritted teeth as he winced. 'I felt that one.'

'I do deserve it,' she stated as I silently cheered her on from the sidelines. 'I deserve someone who supports me, believes in me *and* knows how to hit it. We all do. You probably don't understand.'

'What makes you say that?' he asked.

'Because you're, like, a conventionally attractive straight man,' she replied. 'So, you know, you're limited.'

Joe quirked an eyebrow. 'What makes you think I'm straight?'

'Your aftershave, your haircut, your trousers, your shoes, the way you're sitting and the fact you asked that question.'

He bowed his head as I smothered a laugh.

'Guilty as charged.'

'Then it's probably too hard for you to understand,' she said, altering her tone to address him the same way I talked to the kids in Year One when they didn't want to share the colouring pencils. 'But Este Cox gets it. That's why I love romance novels. When I read a really good one, I see how the world could be. *Should be.* I'm only twenty-three and I've already been through, like, more than enough. Books like *Butterflies* let me take a time-out from reality.'

'Then it's escapism,' Joe said, trying to summarise her explanation. 'Romance novels are popular because they're escapist.'

'And what's wrong with that?' she challenged.

'Nothing,' he replied quickly before she could shred him into another thousand pieces. 'I didn't say there was—'

'Good, because anything that lets you take a much-needed step back from everything going on in the world today seems very fucking important to me.'

She snatched the book back from his undeserving hands and cradled it defensively, covering its ears so it wouldn't have to hear his ignorant comments. I didn't move, couldn't speak, but somewhere in my chest, I felt a spark of pride. She really, truly loved the book. My book.

'You should keep it,' I heard myself say. 'We can get another one.'

She looked at me like I'd offered her front row Taylor Swift tickets and not a slightly fancier copy of a book she already owned. It wouldn't have even taken a feather to knock her down, the slightest sigh would've done the trick.

'Are you serious?' she said. 'I can really keep it? It's my favourite book of all time, I'll take such good care of it.'

'Just promise you'll keep it under wraps for now. And leave a positive review on Goodreads,' Joe said as I forced myself to sit in the unfamiliar glow of her adoration.

'Already done,' she gushed, hugging her book to her chest. 'I'm counting down the days to the sequel. Literally, I've got a countdown on my phone. Only two hundred and eighty-five to go.'

'That's not terrifying at all,' I whispered, holding on to my tote bag extra tightly in case she had X-ray vision and could somehow see inside. If she knew what was inside, there was every chance I'd lose a limb trying to protect it.

'I know, how am I supposed to wait so long?' she laughed before cutting herself off, dead serious. 'Like, Este, write faster, babes.'

'You probably want to get on,' Joe said as I tried to remember to breathe. Two hundred and eighty-five days. 'Nice to meet you . . . ?'

'Chloe,' she replied, snapping back to her senses. 'Chloe Khan. ChloeKhanReadsItAll on TikTok, add me. And thank you so much!'

She took off down the hill, running so fast I couldn't have caught up with her if I'd tried, vanishing into the distance almost as quickly as she'd appeared.

'OK that was mad even from my perspective,' Joe said, watching as I slid off the trunk and deposited myself onto the ground, pressing my palms flat against the cool grass on either side of me. 'What was it like for you?'

My fingers curled around the long blades of grass and yanked them out of the ground.

'It was very, very weird.'

'Good weird?'

'Weird weird.'

I rubbed the grass between my palms, bringing my hands up to my face so I could breathe in the fresh scent, something natural and grounding to calm me down but it didn't work. I was too high on sugar, sun and Chloe Khan to know how I felt about anything.

'But she loves the book,' Joe pointed out, joining me on the ground. 'There are hundreds of thousands of Chloe Khans out there, hanging on your every word. How are you not screaming from the rooftops and celebrating every second of the day? I would be.'

'Because for every one of her, there's ten Joe Walshes,' I replied, dumping the grass and wiping my palms against my already mucky jeans 'Someone who thinks romance novels are unrealistic and stupid and wants all the Chloe Khans to justify why they read them in the first place.'

'You don't listen to them, do you?' he asked with a

faint laugh. 'What do the Joe Walshes of this world know?'

I gazed out across the rolling fields and tried to count all the different shades of green. It was impossible. There were so many and every single one was beautiful. So Joe had been right about one thing at least. Also the sheep. There really were a lot of sheep.

'The truth is, I could read a thousand positive reviews about my book and I would only remember the one negative one,' I admitted. 'The bad stuff is so much easier to believe than the good. I want to be proud of it but deep down, if I'm totally honest, I think the people who say it's bad and worthless might be right.'

Joe didn't answer right away, instead he sat with my words, thinking them through, and I let him, resisting my perma-urge to fill the empty space with a joke or a change of subject. Eventually, his forehead creased in a troubled frown, dark eyebrows drawing together over his blue eyes.

'Before we were interrupted, I was about to make a confession,' he said, nudging me softly. 'When I said all those stupid things yesterday that you very clearly and understandably took to heart, I hadn't read *Butterflies*.'

'You hadn't read it?' I replied, not even slightly able to conceal my surprise. 'But you're king of the brand team? You're in charge of the message of the book, isn't that what you said?'

'Yes,' he admitted. 'But I only skimmed it.'

'You mean you read the dirty bits?'

'I read the whole first chapter!' He paused for a moment. 'Then the dirty bits. Someone else on my team read it and gave me the overall gist. I suppose I thought I didn't need to read it to understand it.'

A self-deprecating laugh forced its way out of my throat.

'Wow. Thanks for proving my point.'

'Actually, I proved myself wrong. And when I'm wrong, I say I'm wrong.'

'Thanks, Dr Houseman,' I mumbled, furious at the tears I felt burning the backs of my eyes. There was no need to be upset, it was hardly a shock. Plenty of people made assumptions about my book, about all romance novels, without reading them. My parents. My head teacher. Half the internet. Every single media outlet that chose to act as though the entire genre didn't exist.

'But,' Joe continued. 'I stayed up half the night reading it and I loved it.'

'Course you did,' I told him, one treacherous tear clinging to my lower lashes. 'You don't have to lie, Joe. I meant what I said before, I really don't care what you think.'

'Then you won't care that I thought it was funny, sexy, emotionally intelligent and that I shouted at Jenna when she refused to admit how she really felt when Eric asked her.'

'Liar.'

'One hundred percent the god's honest truth,' he declared. 'She might have questionable taste in running gear but Chloe was right about your book. The whole time I was reading, everything else just went away. When I got to the end, I was in pieces. It felt so real.'

'Well, bugger me,' I muttered, flicking away the solitary tear when no others came to join it. 'Joe Walsh embraces a happily ever after.'

'Something like that,' he said with a crooked smile. 'She was right about the rest of it too. You put something into words I didn't know how to express. I want what Jenna and Eric have.'

'Or you don't want me to tell Mal all the shitty things you said and get you sacked?'

My eyes met his, chocolate brown and ocean blue, and I searched for the lie. The smirk behind the smile. But there was nothing there. As far as I could tell, he was completely genuine. As far as I could tell. He turned his body towards me, brushing my hair over my shoulder and whispering right into my ear.

'I want to be consumed,' he said, his words a soft growl as he leaned in. 'I want the thought of her to set me on fire. I want to surrender to the flames and burn until there is nothing left but my love.'

A violent thrill shot through me, as though someone had shocked my spine with a cattle prod. I couldn't believe it. He was quoting my book at me, word for word.

'You read it,' I replied with wonder. 'You actually read it.'

'Every chapter, every page. Some chapters more than once.'

I wrapped my hands around my legs and squeezed tight to stop myself from shaking. 'Chapter five?'

'I liked chapter five,' he confirmed. 'But not as much as chapter seventeen.'

When I gulped and I knew he was close enough to hear it.

'Chapter seventeen kept me awake all night,' Joe said, moving as close as it was humanly possible to be without making contact. I could feel his lips on my ear even though we weren't quite touching. 'Chapter seventeen might keep me awake forever.'

The world around us, the trees, the grass, the sun and sky, all disappeared. There was nothing above and nothing below, just us. His face was too close to see clearly, an Impressionist blur, and it drew me in, proximity clouding my mind and my judgement. It was too much and not enough but no matter how badly I wanted to, I couldn't do it.

'Would you look at the time!' I exclaimed, leaping to my feet and accidentally clobbering Joe in the face with the corner of my tote bag. 'The barbecue is supposed to start soon, isn't it? Mum must be wondering where we are. We'd better get back to the butcher's, a fuck load of chicken waits for no man.'

'You can ask if he's got a steak for my eye while we're there,' Joe grunted, his right eye tearing up as he stood. 'What are you trying to do, blind me?'

'Don't be such a wimp,' I replied, marching on the spot. 'I barely touched you.'

'I know,' he murmured. 'And look at the state of me.'

He took a step back, eyeing me warily as though I was the dangerous one, and I clucked out a laugh in a vain attempt to dispel the tension.

'It hasn't even left a mark,' I told him shakily. 'You'll live.'

'As long as I stay away from you,' he replied, grim and determined. 'You're a menace, Sophie Taylor. Just keep your distance, yeah?'

Speechless, I watched him stalk off down the lane, leaving me in his dust.

CHAPTER THIRTEEN

For the rest of the afternoon, I did exactly as he asked.

We walked back to the butcher's in silence, picked up Mum's meat order and, as soon as it was safely in the car, I asked Joe to drop me off on the way home.

'Drop you where?' he asked stiffly.

'Here is fine,' I replied, checking the address on my phone. 'I'll walk the rest of the way.'

'I don't mind taking you all the way,' he said, the corner of his mouth twitching. 'Wherever it is you're running off to.'

'Here is fine,' I repeated. 'Thanks.'

He stared straight ahead as I unbuckled my seatbelt and climbed down from my seat. 'Do you want me to take your bag?'

'No, thanks.' I shook my head. 'The bag—'

'Stays with you,' Joe finished for me. 'Got it.'

The car door wasn't even closed when he restarted the engine and pulled away, tyres squealing in protest.

* * *

The café on the high street was new, and it looked nice. Modern but inviting, cosy but not stuffy. There were quite a few people inside but I didn't recognise any of them so I stood by the door, basking in the sunshine, and waited patiently. My patience was rewarded ten seconds later.

'Penny for your thoughts?'

'I couldn't even charge you that in good conscience,' I said, turning to see one of my favourite people in the entire world racing towards me with her arms open.

'Good because I haven't got any cash on me anyway,' Sarah replied as she pulled me into the biggest, warmest hug in the world. 'Oh, it's good to see you, Taylor. Look at me coming in on my afternoon off, I must really love you.'

It was exactly what I needed. A quick break with my best friend, someone who didn't run hot then cold, or rather scorching then arctic. I always knew exactly what Sarah Nixon was thinking. Everyone did, it was both a blessing and a curse.

'Shall we get a coffee?' she suggested. 'My treat.'

'Does it really count as a treat if you own the coffee shop?'

'Oh, so you want to pay double?' Sarah replied cheerfully. 'Works for me.'

'Your treat it is,' I said, following her inside.

Sarah Nixon wasn't just my oldest friend. Sarah was my childhood *pen pal*. Our love ran real-handwritten-letters-sent-to-each-other-in-the-post deep. When we were little, her parents lived in Bakewell, next door to my grandparents. Every time we came to visit, I'd put in a ten-minute shift with the family then race around to Sarah's house to play in her massive only-child bedroom or, even better, in her treehouse. Proof enough that her parents loved her way more than mine loved me as far as I was concerned.

In between visits, we wrote each other essays on Groovy Chick writing paper in multicoloured glitter gel pens, disclosing every last little detail of our lives. Sarah knew things about me I'd never told anyone else; I'd always found it easier to express myself in writing than in real life. Eventually, we abandoned letters and graduated to emails, then when we got our own phones, pages long emails turned into a barrage of texts and DMs, until we arrived at our current destination of infrequent three-hour phone calls supplemented by a daily exchange of gifs and heatless curler hacks. We left memes in each other's DMs the way cats left dead birds on the doorstep, a silent but meaningful offering. Friendships like ours didn't need to be coddled with never-ending deep conversations, a crying laughing emoji response to a photo of a cat that bore a passing resemblance to Timothée Chalamet was more than enough to keep our love alive.

'Go on then, what do you think?'

Standing behind the bar, Sarah opened out her arms wide, presenting the coffee shop to me like I'd just won a game show and this was my prize. As far as I was concerned, I had. Free coffee whenever I wanted? It was better than winning the lottery.

'I don't think anything, I know for a fact this is the greatest coffee shop I have ever seen,' I told her as she fiddled with a very large, very shiny silver machine. 'Can I have a go? I've always wanted to play barista.'

'Touch my Gaggia and I'll chop your hands off.'

I gave her a thumbs up and kept my mitts to myself. Sarah did not tell lies.

'Still can't believe you did it,' I said while she busied herself cranking handles and pouring milk into little silver jugs. 'From accountant to coffee shop owner in five easy steps.'

'There were more than five and none of them were easy. But they were necessary. You're not going to believe this, Soph, but it turns out bookkeeping is really boring.'

'No!' I exclaimed, slamming my hand down on the counter. 'I refuse to accept it.'

She gave me the kind of look you could only exchange with a person who still remembered when you thought you might be pregnant because you let Assad from the sixth form finger you at your sixteenth birthday party. Her not me, obviously. No one from the sixth form wanted to finger me, not even when I was in the sixth form. I was, to put it kindly, a late bloomer when it came to romance.

'It was a bit of a left turn,' she admitted. 'You must have thought I'd lost it.'

'That implies I thought you ever had it in the first place. Honestly I was more surprised when you told me you wanted to be an accountant.'

I spun around on my stool to get another look at the place. It was welcoming and warm, but still felt fresh and fun, a far cry from the traditional tearooms of Bakewell and the copy-and-paste coffee shop chains that seemed to pop up everywhere these days. Everyone who came in left smiling and even the other girl behind the counter looked happy to be going about her day.

Couldn't say the same for the staff in my local Starbucks. They always seemed to be one non-fat, no-whip, triple-shot Frappuccino away from an emotional breakdown. Sarah's coffee shop truly felt like a one-of-a-kind place and I loved it.

'Fair point.' She held a stainless steel jug to the steamer with easy confidence, effortlessly frothing up the milk for my latte as she spoke. 'I can't even tell you what brought it on. I woke up one morning and knew I could not stand to sit in the office staring at a screen full of numbers for one more day.'

'I'm still impressed you were ever able to do it,' I replied. 'You know how I feel about maths.'

'Numbers are not your friend,' she acknowledged with a smile. 'It was time for a change. I understand how to run a business, I've never met a cup of coffee I didn't have a very informed opinion on, and not that I'm advocating for divorce in general, but it helps that Dave takes the kids three nights a week.'

'The two of you make divorce look so good, I almost want to get married just so I can split up,' I remarked, breathing in the deep, rich coffee aroma as she ground a fresh espresso shot. 'I've never seen two people more thrilled to get their decree nisi and, to the best of my knowledge, you're the only couple I know who had a joint party to celebrate.'

'At least you won't have to murder him in his sleep,' Sarah said, misty-eyed with nostalgia. 'Again, Taylor, best maid of honour speech ever.'

'You know I would kill for you in a heartbeat,' I replied. 'Please ask me to kill for you.'

She looked at me from underneath her blunt blonde fringe. 'Anyone in particular?'

Tell her about Joe, whispered the little voice in my head that loved to get me into trouble. But I knew if I told Sarah about Joe, she wouldn't want to talk about anything else and I was there to catch up with her, not to describe his tropical-beach-blue eyes and thick black eyelashes and the way I thought the lower half of my body had been struck by lightning when he quoted my book back at me. I was literally here not to think about any of those things for as long as possible.

'Taylor?' Sarah said, stretching my last name. 'Out with it. Is there something you want to tell me?'

'Nope,' I replied, stomping down all my thoughts of Joe as far as they would go.

'Because if I learned anything over the last two years it's that talking is better than keeping things bottled up and change is good.' She took out a large powder blue mug from underneath the counter and carefully crafted my triple-shot vanilla latte with an added flourish of freshly shaved chocolate. 'Turns out you don't have to stick with something if it's making you unhappy just because you're already doing it. Or him. Or her, as the case may be.'

I sucked my bottom lip under my top teeth and looked down, flooded with guilt. It wasn't only Joe that I was keeping from her. For almost thirty years, we'd told each other everything, even things we didn't want to know, like the time she told me how Dave liked a finger up the bum during sex. Right before she walked down the aisle. But I hadn't told her about *Butterflies*. When I started writing it, I didn't say anything because she was due to give birth to my second godson, and I really didn't think I'd even finish it. When I found the courage to send it to Malcolm, Sarah was in the middle of her divorce, and as much as we joked about it now, those things were never fun and I didn't want to burden her with my silly little side project. By the time the book blew up, I simply didn't know how to start the conversation and now it had been too long. What was I supposed to say? What's that, Sarah? You're leaving your reliable career as an accountant and taking a massive risk on a little local coffee shop while financially supporting two kids more or less alone because your well-meaning but ultimately useless ex-husband, who still wears Lynx Africa even though he's thirty-four years old, can't keep a job for more than six months at a time? Well, yes, that does sound quite stressful but please sit down and let me tell you about my movie deal, they're looking at Ryan Gosling for the lead.

It hardly rolled off the tongue.

'How's that coffee?' she asked when I'd been altogether too quiet for altogether too long.

'Incredible,' I answered automatically before I'd even tasted it. 'Please can I get seventy-four more to help me get through this weekend?'

Sarah laughed as she poured herself a glass of water. 'The visit is going well already then?'

'As well as can be expected.' As expected, my latte was delicious. I took a sip and transcended to the next level of existence. It was strong and it was delicious. 'Dad's being a weirdo, Mum's stress vein has been out since I got in, Charlotte's, well, Charlotte, and guess what? They've invited CJ.'

'He's not coming though, is he?' She groaned when I nodded. 'Oh, fuck off. I thought I'd seen the last of that gremlin. Imagine getting a pity invite to your ex's dad's birthday and actually showing up. He's shameless.'

'Even better, he's staying at the house,' I told her, attempting to laugh but failing miserably. It really wasn't funny but Sarah seemed to disagree.

'Sophie!' she exclaimed. 'That's the best news I've heard so far!'

'It is?'

'Yes! It's so much easier to kill someone when they come to you. Less lurking, more unaliving. Please let me do it. Please, please, please?'

'OK but only because you asked nicely,' I replied before turning an inquisitive eye on my best friend. 'Speaking of the curse of heterosexuality, how's that going? You're not seeing anyone?'

'Have you seen pink smoke coming out the Vatican?' she asked. 'My romantic life is made of silicone and takes three AA batteries that need replacing weekly. Who am I supposed to meet around here? You're the one who is young, free and single, living it up in—'

'Tring?' I finished for her. 'Nixon, the average age of a man in Tring is eighty-two and I'm not talking a Harrison Ford eighty-two, I mean soft foods only, bed by half-past seven and lucky if you wake up again in the morning eighty-two.'

She looked off into the dreamy middle distance and sighed. 'Sounds like a dream come true. Whatever, Taylor, no one's saying you've got to meet the love of your life at the pension office. Tring is what, half an hour out of London? You're practically living with the pigeons in Trafalgar Square compared to me.'

'The pigeons would make better boyfriends,' I said as she chugged her water. 'Trust me, the men of London are not better than the men of Harford. The men of London are human bin bags. Cheap black bin bags full of hair and bin juice just waiting to split open in the middle of the kitchen. I'd rather go out with three raccoons in a trench coat.'

The two of us sat quietly for a moment, silently commiserating with each other and every other human unlucky enough to be looking for love.

'I don't know what's wrong with them,' Sarah said, leaning over the counter and resting her chin in her hand. 'Imagine being a man with a penis and not wanting to put it in one of us.'

'All we're looking for are two decent humans with no baggage, some emotional intelligence, a good heart, the right stance on all political issues and preferably their own teeth, who won't mess us around and break our hearts,' I replied. 'Is that too much to ask for?'

She lifted a glass cloche that covered a stack of chocolate chip cookies and handed one to me before taking another for herself. 'I can be flexible on the teeth to be honest with you. And the decency. And I don't mind a bit of messing.'

I broke the cookie in two then took a big bite. Heaven.

'We're buggered, aren't we?' Sarah said before taking a bite of her own biscuit.

'Yep,' I replied, unable to keep the image of Joe's smile from sliding, unbidden, into my head. 'Completely buggered.'

CHAPTER FOURTEEN

When I got back home, Joe wasn't in the cottage, but that didn't mean it was empty.

'What are you doing?' I demanded when I opened the door to find my sister pillaging my belongings, all the clothes I'd just put away strewn across the double bed, shoes on the floor, make-up dumped on the sofa, all of it open, unfastened or pawed through. 'Didn't I tell you to stay out my stuff?'

'I'm in here because I live here,' she replied, my favourite cream silk shirt thrown over her cocoa-coloured bike shorts and sports bra. 'And I'm not going through *your* stuff, I'm looking for the dust bag for *my* Chanel. It was in your suitcase earlier.'

'You mean the last time you were in my room when you shouldn't have been?'

I walked over to the bed, pulled out my suitcase and unzipped the front pocket to extract the little black and white bag. There wasn't an awful lot of point in holding onto it now.

'Is there anything else I can get you while I'm here?' I offered. 'My dress? Pair of shoes? Couple of kidneys?'

'You can only donate one kidney or you'd die,' Charlotte said, disgusted with my stupidity in a way only an eighteen-year-old can be.

'I still wouldn't put it past you,' I replied. 'Now piss off so I can get ready for this barbecue, and please stop going through my things.'

'Don't worry, there's nothing else worth having.' She blew a kiss as she flounced past me, waving the dust bag over her head like a victory flag, then shrugging off my shirt and letting it fall to the floor.

'Don't worry about closing the door or anything,' I shouted as I surveyed her wreckage. The beautiful tiny cottage was a mess. How could one person cause so much carnage in such a short time? Charlotte was part-human and part-Tasmanian devil and, if I was being honest, I'd have taken a full-blooded Tasmanian devil over my sister in that moment.

'What happened, have we been robbed?'

Joe stood in the open door, scanning the disaster area in front of him.

'We've been Charlotte-d,' I replied, allowing my tote bag to slip off my shoulder onto the bed, the soft mattress accepting the weight with a sigh. 'Don't worry, I don't think she touched your stuff.'

'Looks like someone did.' He stooped to pick up my abandoned shirt, laying it over the back of the sofa as he eyed his weekend bag. 'Oh right, that was you.'

'I told you, I wasn't going through it,' I said, covering my red face with a pile of my clothes. 'I was moving it.'

'To save it from the mysterious leather-eating mice, I remember.'

The atmosphere between us was just as strained as it had been on the way to the butcher's and I was starting to think I preferred smarmy sleazebag Joe to stiff and snippy Joe. At least that version gave me something to work with, a chance to practise my banter. This one gave me nothing at all and I wasn't about to apologise when I hadn't done anything wrong. Well, apart from conk him in the face with my laptop and that wasn't on purpose.

Concentrating very hard on looking at anything other than me, Joe unclipped and unzipped his bag and pulled out a matching leather washbag. 'If it's all right with you, I'd like to shower before the party kicks off. Unless you want to go first?'

'You want a shower?' I replied. 'In here?'

'I was thinking I'd use the bathroom specifically but yes, I want to shower here at this cottage.'

Apparently his need was so great that he started stripping down right in front of me, his shirt already balled up in his hand as he unfastened the top button of his trousers. Joe had the kind of body that looked like he worked on sailing ships in days of yore and tossed around barrels full of ale as a workout. Strong arms ran up to meet broad shoulders and a barrel chest, and yes, there was hair on that chest and no, I didn't hate it. There were no carefully sculpted abs but his stomach was flat, with exactly the right amount of soft-ness to let you know he wasn't afraid of carbs. Combined with his charm, charisma and stupidly handsome face, it was truly irresponsible of him to walk around like that. Only he wasn't trying to be charming right now, just irritating.

'You've got to be kidding me,' I breathed before I could stop myself. 'I mean, no, you're not using my bathroom. And put your bloody shirt back on.'

'What do you want me to do?' he asked, shirt still decidedly off. 'Hose myself down in the middle of the garden?'

There was another mental image I wouldn't be able to escape for the rest of eternity.

'You're being ridiculous,' he said, dismissing my protestations and tucking the washbag under his arm. 'You can't call the bathroom off limits when we're sharing the cottage. What happened to "you owe me"?'

'What happened to me keeping my distance?' I asked. 'That was your request, wasn't it?'

There was no air conditioning in the cottage but despite the humid day outside, the atmosphere was positively frosty. We glared at each other from opposite sides of the room, neither one about to back down.

'Sorry, I assumed you'd be capable of basic human decency,' he said, blinking first, much to my delight. 'I wasn't asking for your permission to use the shower, I was being polite and asking if you wanted to use it first. Why does everything have to be a fight with you? You're so fucking defensive.'

'I wouldn't have to be defensive if you weren't so unpredictable,' I volleyed back.

'I'm not unpredictable.' Joe frowned, looking surprised by the accusation.

'Inconsistent then,' I amended, picking up a pair of leggings and attempting to fold them, black Lycra slapping me in the face and wrapping around my neck. Leggings were really hard to fold when you were annoyed. 'You're inconsistent. And antagonistic. And flighty.'

'Flighty?' he scoffed, popping the rest of the buttons on his fly to reveal a flash of the same kind of black boxers I'd seen in his bag. 'All right, Nana. I'm going for a shower. Something I do every day. *Consistently.*'

When I heard the water start running, I was still standing by the wardrobe, wrapped up in my leggings-slash-scarf-slash-straitjacket, bristling with anger.

'Forty-eight hours to go,' I muttered to myself as I yanked the leggings from around my neck. 'Then you never have to see him again.'

'I just think it must be such a shallow existence,' I said to Sanjit, gesticulating wildly with my second drink and eyeing Joe across the garden. He was laughing uproariously at something one of Mum's aqua aerobics friends said and pretending not to notice her subtly squeezing his bicep. 'Look at him. All that flirting. It must be exhausting, he looks exhausted. Don't you think he looks exhausted?'

'I don't know, he looks pretty good to me,' Sanjit replied. 'Sophie, have you had anything to eat today?'

'Percy Pigs and a biscuit.'

'All the major food groups covered then,' William commented.

The barbecue was a small gathering, just like Mum said it would be, a couple of close friends who were staying the weekend and our unfortunate family, but the limited number of people only made Joe's massive presence stick out like a sore thumb. A great big massive unbearably attractive sore thumb.

'That man is an Adonis,' my brother disagreed, all three of us openly staring now. 'He hasn't missed leg day since birth, has he? Must've been doing squats in the womb.'

'Yes, but it's not about looks,' I insisted, tapping one finger against my temple a little too hard, a little too fast. 'He's fake. He tells everyone whatever he thinks they want to hear, whatever it takes for him to get what he wants out of them, and if that doesn't work he sulks like a baby.'

'And what exactly is it he wants out of seventy-three-year-old Lesley over there?'

The two of them clinked their glasses together in a toast that I couldn't quite hear but from the laughter that followed was the funniest thing anyone had ever heard.

'He wants to make me jealous,' I replied, throwing back a gulp of my drink. 'He wants me to see him having an amazing time because he doesn't care what I think. Except he does, he totally cares.'

William flashed an 'unlikely' look at his husband. 'Nice to see a girl with confidence.'

'Not because I'm so incredibly fit he can't help himself,' I replied, stumbling only very slightly over my words. 'Men like him only want what they can't have. He knows he can't have me. It's all a game to him.'

That was the conclusion I'd come to while he took such a long shower there was no hot water left for me and I was sticking to it. Not that a cold shower was such a bad thing. I probably would've dialled the temperature down on myself anyway after he came strolling through the cottage, dripping wet and wearing nothing but a towel.

Lindsey Kelk

'He can have me if he wants,' Sanjit said. 'No offence, William, but given half the chance I would climb that man like a tree.'

'None taken,' my brother, his husband, replied. 'I'd hold the ladder for you.'

But I was unmoved.

'You both need your heads checked. Did I tell you Mal said he's a cad? And a bouncer. I mean, a bounder. He could be a bouncer though, couldn't he? He's big enough.'

'Soph, seriously, how much have you had to drink?' William plucked the glass out of my hand and gave it a desultory sniff. 'And what the fuck is in here in the first place?'

'It's only my second,' I hiccupped defensively as he took a sip. 'It's just Pimm's. With a dash of Malibu. And a shot of vodka. Pimm's is hardly even booze, is it? More like pop.'

'This tastes like something I would've knocked back in the student union on a bet,' he replied, pulling a face before passing it to his husband. 'You need something that isn't ninety-seven percent sugar.'

'And something to drink that isn't ninety-seven percent proof,' Sanjit added, screwing up his face as he swallowed. 'Are you sure this isn't paint stripper?'

'It's one match away from being a Molotov cocktail. If we need something to get the bonfire going later, I'll know where to go,' William said, dumping it out onto the grass before the pair of them led me away, one on either side, like they were escorting me from a very shit club. 'Now what are you having: chicken, hotdog or a burger? Don't get too close to the barbecue, you'll go up like a nuclear bomb.'

Behind the grill, I saw my dad, resplendent in a chef's hat and a black apron that said 'Mario Puzo's The Grillfather', a bookish-barbecue pun I might've found funnier if I'd been allowed to finish my cocktail but it was still nice to see him looking so happy.

Or at least it was until I saw who was standing beside him.

CJ.

One look at him and I was stone-cold sober.

'Shall we get this over with?' William asked. 'Or do you need to pop inside first and find a suitable weapon?'

'I don't need a weapon,' I replied as my ex grabbed the barbecue tongs and pretended to snap them at my mother's arse. 'If I wanted to, I could dismantle that man in under thirty seconds, handsfree.'

Sanjit turned away, unable to watch. 'It's still beyond me why you let him take all the credit for that book when we both know it was your idea in the first place.'

'Because it's such a bag of pretentious shite, I don't want people to know I was on the same continent as CJ when it was being written?'

'There is that,' he conceded.

For months, CJ's book, *Deckled Edges*, had haunted me. The matte black dust jacket followed me everywhere I went, bookshops, supermarkets, the staffroom at work. Someone I met on Hinge even brought it with him on what turned out to be a very short first date. Sadly, the obnoxious cover wasn't the worst of it. There was the dedication (to himself) then acknowledgements (noting all the support from my mum and my dad but never once mentioning me) and his insistence on constantly referring to himself as the 'voice of the voiceless', a term I knew for a fact he'd stolen from the wrestling show he watched religiously every week, even though he would never admit it now. Not to mention the self-important, naval-gazing writing itself.

'If I were you, I'd have shoved his MacBook so far up his arse he'd have to swallow his hands to type,' Sanjit said through gritted teeth. 'Was he always such a little shithead?'

'Not at the beginning,' I admitted as CJ rolled up his sleeve to show off a giant gold watch that would've even looked a bit tacky on Liberace. 'He was sweet when we first met.'

'Everyone's sweet when you first meet,' William commented.

I looked over to the crowd of women that had amassed around Joe and shook my head.

'No. Not everyone.'

On the surface, the two men couldn't have been more different. There was CJ in his Zara dupe of a Hedi Slimane suit and please-take-me-seriously wire-frame glasses, then there was Joe, a solid chunk of man, dressed in perfectly fitting straight leg jeans and a white linen shirt, the cuffs loosely rolled up to the elbow to weaponise his dangerously erotic forearms. CJ was intense and engaging, Joe was easy charm personified. CJ was Tom Hiddleston, Joe was Chris Hemsworth, looks-wise, anyway, when it came to personality the comparison was an insult to both Loki and Thor. But for all their differences, underneath the surface, I knew they were the same. Two smug men who thought they knew better than silly little me.

'Oh, fucking hell, he's waving,' William groaned as all three of us caught CJ's eye at the same time.

'You're the one who said let's get it over with.' I

reversed the grip on my brother's arm to stop him from bolting. 'You can't make me go through this alone.'

Sanjit turned his bottle of beer upside down, allowing the last dregs to fall onto the lawn. 'Oh no, what a shame, I must go and get another. Do give him my best.'

'Get the divorce papers while you're at it,' William suggested when he tapped his fingers to his forehead in a mock salute and scuttled away. 'Never marry a lawyer. That's the best romantic advice I could ever give you. They're always weaselling in or out of something.'

I looked up at him with one raised eyebrow.

'You said the best romantic advice you could ever give me was to shag as many men as humanly possible because they're all so terrible, you might as well go with the one who knows how to bang?'

'When did I share that nugget of wisdom?'

'On my sixteenth birthday.'

'I clearly left it too late because you didn't bloody listen, did you?'

Barging through the crowd and dragging me behind him, William slapped CJ on the back so hard, he spat out his sausage. 'Colin, you hateful little wankshaft,' he boomed. 'How the devil are you?'

It was one of my brother's greatest skills, delivering the most damning insults on earth with such a big, friendly smile, people never knew if he was joking or not.

'Evening, William,' CJ said, clearing his throat. CJ knew. 'Sophie.'

'CJ,' I replied, staring straight through him.

'How are you doing?'

'Not too bad, you lanky streak of piss,' my brother replied, even though the question was directed at me.

'How's the new book coming? Wasn't it scheduled for this summer?'

'Originally.'

His green eyes found mine before I could look away. Five years together and now I couldn't for the life of me remember what I'd seen in him. 'Hugh decided to move it. You can't rush these things, can you?'

'Certainly not,' my dad chimed in, joining our group and throwing his arm around CJ's shoulders. 'Art takes time, we all understand that here.'

'We definitely do,' William replied 'With a talent like CJ's, there's no way he could be a one book wonder. Unless, I don't know, you lost your inspiration? Your muse? The person who actually came up with all your good ideas?'

'Can I get anyone a drink?' I asked, pasting on a meaningless smile as CJ opened his mouth to reply. 'No? Great. If anyone needs me, I'll be anywhere else but here. William?'

The pair of us turned and walked briskly away, the soles of my sandals bouncing over the freshly mown grass, CJ still defending his creative block to my dad, rambling about the myopic lens of an alienated society, and I was extremely relieved not to be the one who had to listen to it any more.

'Well done,' my brother said as we slowed our pace. 'I can't even look at his rodent face without wanting to slap the taste out of his mouth.'

'I had many more years of practice than you,' I reminded him. 'Every time I feel the urge to bludgeon him to death with his Critics' Circle Debut Novel trophy, I remind myself how few copies of *Deckled Edges* sold, awards or no awards.'

He laughed and held up his hand for a high five which I gladly met. 'Publishing loves books about publishing. We both know it's a piece of overwritten shit. Scathing satire addressing the perils of a young female editorial assistant in a London publishing house my arse.'

'Might've been helpful if he'd ever been an editorial assistant, or a young female,' I suggested. 'Or you know, even spoke to one.'

'I saw it on a list of worst male-written female characters a few weeks ago but I didn't send it on. I know you'd rather be the bigger person.'

'Oh, god, no. Send it to me, I can always use something calming to read before bed.'

'If you'd only let me scream from the rooftops you're the bestselling author in the world,' he grumbled. 'Go on, you know you want to. This would be the perfect place to do it.'

'Only if your plan is to give Mum and Dad his and hers heart attacks for his birthday.' I inhaled deeply and blew out as much stress as I could. 'You're right though, I can be the bigger person. At least until I get the chance to spit in CJ's drink or push him down some stairs.'

'That's my sister.' Slowing almost to a stop, William looked around at the over-sixties crowd. 'Where's Sarah tonight?' he asked. 'I thought Nixon might've graced us with her presence.'

'She'll be here tomorrow,' I replied, smiling at the thought. 'She has the kids Friday, Dave has them Saturday.'

'He couldn't take them tonight as well?'

'Dave couldn't take his own temperature without step-by-step instructions from Sarah.'

'Pretty but stupid,' William assessed, not incorrectly. 'OK, this is my official, updated best romantic advice: find something nice to look at that's still mentally competent. I'm not saying everyone's husband needs to be able to explain how the Hadron Collider works but at least find a partner who knows *Lord of the Rings* is fiction and not something that happened a very long time ago.'

'In his defence,' I started, wincing at the memory of my brother's first conversation with Sarah's ex-husband, William looking at me expectantly. 'No, I haven't got anything, you're right.'

'It wouldn't have been so bad if he hadn't been so determined to convince us he knew a Hobbit.' He glanced over at the grill where Sanjit stood empty plate in hand and a blank expression on his face. 'If you're all right on your own for a minute, I should go stop Sanjit before he eats himself into gout. The man has no self-control when it comes to a barbecue.'

'No worries,' I said even though there were in fact worries. Many, many worries. Outside my brother, my options for company at the barbeque were limited. Mum was locked in an animated discussion with her best friend, Jericka, another critic, a very intense woman who couldn't have a conversation with anyone about anything without bringing up Russian literature. Dad's pub friends only knew how to talk about politics, war novels and actual war, three things I had no interest in debating with a group of old men on a Friday night or ever. I'd sent William away, Charlotte was nowhere to be seen, CJ made me want to poke out my own eyes with a chicken kebab and I would happily chew off my left leg to avoid talking to Aunt Carole and Uncle Bryan, who were dressed for an arctic expedition despite the fact I was sweltering in jeans and a T-shirt, which left only one other person and I was, as had been requested, keeping my distance from him.

Artfully dodging all potential social interactions, I sloped off to the back bar, or to describe it more accurately, a pasting table under a tablecloth, and poured a full-to-the-brim glass of rosé. I didn't even want it but I needed a prop, something to do with my hands and, if necessary, throw at someone.

'You always did like your pink wine.'

'And you always liked bothering me when I wanted to be left alone,' I said with a sigh when CJ sidled up beside me at the bar, a self-satisfied smirk on his face. 'So I see neither of us have changed.'

'Oh, Sophie, Sophie, Sophie. You and your sense of humour.'

He laughed and brushed his dark blond hair back behind his ears, something I used to find boyish and endearing but with the way it was beginning to thin at the temples, I couldn't help but think he ought to leave as much of it forward as possible. 'How have you been?'

'Fine until I found out you were coming,' I replied sweetly.

'Just because we're not together any more doesn't mean I'm not part of the family,' CJ said, flashing huge puppy dog eyes.

'Colin, that's exactly what it means.' I took a long, unhappy chug of my wine. It would be a waste to throw it. 'They're my family, not yours.'

He swirled the whisky in his glass, bringing it to his lips but barely taking a taste. I was probably the only person here who knew he'd much rather have what I was drinking. Colin loved rosé and hated whisky. CJ, it seemed, had learned to tolerate it.

'Sophie, I want you to know, I do empathise,' he said, one hand in his pocket, shoulders drawn back straight. 'It must be difficult for you, watching me live my dreams from afar while you're stuck in a dead-end teaching job, but you need to move on.'

I turned to stare at him.

'What did you just say?'

'It's time you got over me,' he said, pressing the whisky glass against his chest. 'For your own sake.'

'Colin, you're the one at my dad's party. Believe me, I'm over you. I'm Taylor Swift, Joe Alwyn, entire break-up album over you.'

He sniffed, tipped the whisky to his lips again and shrugged.

'If you say so.'

'I do say so!' I exclaimed, fighting every urge to dump my whole glass of wine over his head. 'You're the moon and I'm the cow. This is me, jumping over you.'

'Don't listen to those intrusive thoughts, you're not a cow. That's the internalised misogyny talking.' He leaned to one side and craned his neck to check out my rear view. 'Might be worth going up a size though. Your jeans are a bit tight and not in a good way.'

'So much for my promise to Sarah,' I muttered, looking for a hard surface to break my glass on. Throwing wine on him wouldn't be enough. The man had to die and it could not wait until tomorrow.

'Oh, wow, aren't you JC Simons?'

'It's CJ Simmons.' CJ pulled himself up to his full height to reply to the voice that had interrupted my violent fantasies. 'And you are?'

'Joe, Joe Walsh.'

Also known as the last person I would've asked to come to my rescue but as he'd correctly stated earlier beggars could not be choosers, and I was begging for someone to save me from a life sentence. Although I was fairly sure there wasn't a jury in the land that would put me away for relieving the planet of the curse of Colin. All I'd have to do was show them a photo of his black on black Tesla and I'd probably get some kind of medal instead.

'Forgive me, I can't remember the title but didn't you write that book?' Joe clinked his beer bottle against CJ's whisky-filled tumbler, ignoring me completely. 'The one about the editorial assistant who accidentally offed her boss and ended up taking over the company. What was it, *Speckled Eggs*?'

'*Deckled Edges*,' CJ corrected, his left eye twitching. 'Yes, that was me. Have you read it?'

'Oh, fuck no,' Joe laughed. 'I flicked through it in a charity shop but seriously, what a pretentious bag of wank. If you're short on copies, they've got a whole boxful at the Oxfam in Kentish Town. You look like the kind of person who gives out all your author copies. Whether people want them or not.'

The shoulders of CJ's jacket rose as his neck retracted into the crumpled white collar of his shirt, part hipster, part tortoise, all tit.

'Not to be rude but, mate,' Joe carried on as CJ blinked at him from behind his non-prescription glasses. 'Have you ever even had a conversation with a woman? Have you met one? Because that main character made your average manic pixie dream girl look like Margaret Thatcher.'

'I think one review called her a vacant projection of the male gaze,' I interjected, tilting my head to the side as Joe snapped his fingers.

'Nailed it. Of course, I'm sure that's exactly what JC was going for.'

'I'm sorry, what did you say your name was?' CJ's hand was shaking so violently, whisky spilled over his fingers, staining the cuff of his stiff white shirt.

'Joe Walsh,' replied my new favourite person. 'Creative director at MullinsParker. I'm told I'll be working on your next book. If it ever turns up.'

'I heard they're raising the retirement age to seventy-five so there's a chance,' I added. 'A tiny little whisper of a chance.'

'You two are hilarious. Do let me know when you've written your novels so I can offer you the same support,' CJ snapped. 'Sorry, is that Salman over there? I must go and say goodbye before he leaves. Excuse me.'

'Is it Salman?' Joe asked, turning to watch him sprint across the garden as quickly as his pointy ankle boots could carry him.

'It's my dad's friend Gordon from the garden centre,' I said, grinning. 'Easy mistake to make except for how he looks literally nothing like him.'

'That book of his really was a piece of shit. How do you know him?'

I sipped my wine and shook my head.

'We went out. For five years.'

Joe coughed, choking on a mouthful of beer, and banged his fist against his chest.

'Understandable reaction,' I said, lifting my glass in acknowledgement. 'But it was a long time ago.'

His eyebrows slowly crept back down his forehead

but he couldn't seem to completely wipe the look of surprise from his face.

'I can't lie, I wasn't expecting that,' he replied. 'You don't seem the type to suffer fools gladly.'

I fixed him with a level stare and sipped my wine. 'And now you know why.'

The round bulbs strung up and down the garden glowed softly against the dimming sky. We still had another hour or so of soft summer daylight but there was a whisper of evening in the air that smoothed away the harsh edges of the day and opened up all kinds of possibilities. Things you could say or do at night that couldn't be said or done in the day. Joe's hair was still damp from his shower, wavier than usual, and his white shirt set off his light tan. He had the kind of skin that turned golden from two minutes out in the sun and our countryside walk had given him a healthy, sexy glow. All it had gifted me were salmon pink cheeks and a Rudolph nose that had challenged my makeup skills to their very limit.

'I haven't seen your dad all night,' I said, searching for someone who should've been easy to find.

'Taken to his bed with an alleged migraine. Although last time I looked in on him, he was watching the cricket on his phone. He can only stomach not being centre of attention for so long.'

We stood by the bar, watching the gathering, not quite together but not quite apart. I was only being polite I told myself, I owed him for the CJ save. That was the only reason I hadn't walked away. It would've been rude.

'Are you having fun?' I asked, again only out of politeness.

Joe bounced the mouth of his bottle against his lips and nodded.

'I am. Your parents are very kind people. I've already been invited to join your mother's aquaerobics class, she and her friend Lesley were very insistent.'

'They say it's good for the joints,' I replied, fighting a smile. 'Low impact, excellent cardio.'

'Bit too far for me to come up from London every Wednesday,' he said. 'I'll have to find something else to keep my heart rate up. Any recommendations?'

'Maybe you should get a Peloton, that would keep you off the streets,' I suggested when he smirked, reminding me exactly why I was avoiding him in the first place. 'Anyway, I'd better get back to keeping my distance.'

'Please don't go.' He reached out to grasp my wrist, lowering his voice to a soft rumble that curled around my ears like a caress. 'There's a vague possibility I wasn't thinking straight when I said that.'

'Too much ice cream?' I suggested with an anxious laugh. 'I did tell you salted caramel and strawberry did not belong together.'

He tightened his grip gently but firmly around my wrist.

'It's not the ice cream,' he said. 'The thing is, I can't get a handle on you and that makes me feel . . . I don't know. Nervous.'

Now it was my turn to look surprised.

'I make you feel nervous?'

'You make me feel a lot of things.' He leaned in towards me, his eyes glassy and dark. 'Maybe we should go back to the cottage and discuss them further?'

'That would not be a very good idea,' I said, stuttering

out the words as my body attempted to cut my brain off from my mouth. My thoughts and feelings were no longer in sync. Joe rubbed his thumb against the thin skin inside my wrist, and he smiled as goosebumps prickled into life along my arm.

'It would be an exceptional idea,' he promised. 'I've got some very pressing questions about the scene in your book where Jenna and Eric get trapped on the roof of the hotel that really can't wait. Pressing professional questions.'

A civil war was being waged throughout my body. Everything between my knees and my neck wanted to go but my feet remained firmly connected to my brain and my brain said no. At least it did until he pushed my hair away from my face, his lips making contact with my ear, and my whole body shivered.

'Fuck all the games. I want you, Sophie,' he whispered. 'Now.'

That was it, the moment I lost the fight. All my control, my better judgement, everything I'd spent the entire day reminding myself, went out the window. He wanted me, I wanted him and nothing else mattered. The man was quicksand and I was already up to my neck.

'Let's go back.' Joe pulled on my arm, drawing me away from the party, away from the lights. 'No one's going to miss us and I can be quiet if you can.'

Stumbling along, I followed him, everything that wasn't Joe blurring out of focus. I fumbled in my pocket for the keys, his body pressed against my back, when the cottage door opened from the inside.

It was Charlotte.

And in her hand, she clutched a stack of paper.

'You!' she boomed as she waved it at me.

I dropped Joe's hand like it was on fire and took several steps away from him, walking directly into a rosebush.

'What about me?' I asked, fighting my way out of the all-consuming Joe Walsh haze.

'You know full well what I'm talking about!'

Everyone turned to see why Charlotte was yelling right as I realised exactly what was in her hand. Oh no. Oh no no no no no.

'Why was the manuscript for the next Este Cox book on your bed?' she demanded, the crumpled pages in her hand covered in recognisable scribbles and scrawl.

'It wasn't on my bed,' I replied, one foot in the flower-bed, one foot out. 'It was in a bag, beside the bed.'

'It was on your bed,' Joe corrected very quietly. 'I might have taken it out the bag when you were in the shower and forgot to put it back.'

Mum crossed the garden at lightning speed, wearing her 'not in front of company' frown as I attempted to end his life with a glare. 'Sophie, Lottie, what's going on?'

'I have no idea,' I said, eyeing the stack of A4 in Charlotte's hands and still waiting for my brain to come back online but it was taking far too long to reboot.

'There's only one explanation I can think of,' my sister challenged, ignoring our mother and stepping forward to flap the manuscript at me, cooling my red face with an accusatory breeze. 'Are you going to make me say it?'

It was right there, the truth, on the very tip of my tongue. But I couldn't speak the words, I wasn't ready.

'Lottie, please don't,' I pleaded softly as Bryan,

Carole, CJ and all the rest started to drift down towards us. 'You've got the wrong end of the stick.'

'Both ends of a stick are the same, Sophie,' she snipped back. 'It's a stick.'

'What Sophie means is, it's not her manuscript.'

Joe took a defensive step in front of me, blocking out my irate sister. He glanced over his shoulder to give me a meaningful look but I had no idea what the meaning might be.

'Then why was it in the cottage?' Charlotte asked, switching her suspicious stare from me to Joe.

'Because it's mine,' he declared. 'I'm Este Cox.'

CHAPTER FIFTEEN

'I have the manuscript because I'm Este Cox,' Joe said again, chin lifted high and proud. 'That's why it's in the cottage. It has nothing to do with Sophie.'

The very large, open garden suddenly became very small and very closed in, and I couldn't seem to fill my lungs with enough air to keep me upright. Joe held out a steadying hand, eyeing me with concern.

'Are you all right?' he asked.

'No,' I replied. 'What are you doing?'

'You're Este Cox?' Charlotte asked before he could reply, big brown eyes bulging out of her head.

Joe pulled back his shoulders to emphasise his majestic stance. 'That's right. And I'd appreciate it if you kept it to yourself. As you know, I have chosen to remain anonymous for a reason.'

'This isn't happening,' I muttered, looking for somewhere to put down my wine glass and also myself. My legs weren't going to hold me up much longer.

'You wrote *Butterflies*?' Mum asked as she gently pulled the messy manuscript out of Charlotte's frozen fingers. I held my breath as she scanned the pages. Surely she would recognise my notes in the margins? Surely she would hear my voice on the page?

'Yes?' Joe looked over at me again, sounding slightly less sure of himself this time.

'And this is the sequel?

'That's right.'

She shuffled the pile back into a neat stack and handed it to him. 'Then this is yours.'

'But Mum—' Charlotte protested.

'But nothing,' she replied sharply. 'You shouldn't have been going through Joe's things. Or should I say Este's.'

My heart sank. There was no reason for her to recognise my barely legible notes when I could hardly make sense of them myself and why would she hear my voice when she wasn't listening for a different tune?

'There's no way you wrote that book,' CJ said, poking his nose at the manuscript until Joe snatched it away. 'You're a man.'

'Which disqualifies me how?'

'Because it was obviously written by a woman,' my ex spluttered. 'It's for women. It's about women.'

'It almost sounds as though you're saying you don't believe a man could write a convincing female experience,' Joe replied, clutching the stack of papers under his arm. 'Ironic, considering.'

In the five years we were together, Colin often got annoyed or frustrated but he didn't get angry, not really. CJ, it seemed, did. It wasn't a good look on him. His lips curled back until he was all tooth and gum, his features soured and a blotchy red rash coloured his throat.

'It's mindless shit is what it is,' he announced, squaring up to Joe in a not at all flattering stand-off.

'It's not shit!' Charlotte all but screamed as she forced her way in between them. 'How many times do I have to tell people? It's a feminist masterpiece. It's—'

'A book about the frustrations women have to put up with every day and how they deserve to have their needs met,' Joe said, parroting back exactly what I'd told him as CJ backed away.

'It's porn,' Aunt Carole said, clutching at her padded gilet in horror. 'Filth. Plain and simple. No one is reading something like that for the story, they're reading it to, well, I don't think I need to say any more.'

'So what if they are?' Charlotte answered. 'Show me a society in the history of humankind that hasn't had porn? Just because you all had to hide your grotty magazines under the mattress, don't come for my books. *Butterflies* is healthier than Big Butts Monthly.'

'Is that a real magazine?' Bryan asked, too enthusiastically.

Before that moment, my worst recurring nightmare always involved having to resit my A Level history exam completely naked but this was so much worse. Standing in my parents' garden while my family argued about my book and the societal impact of porn would haunt me for the rest of my life.

'You could make the argument,' my mother inserted, commandeering the conversation with her calm, quiet voice. 'That reading erotica, or romance if that's what we're calling it, is a feminist act.'

'You could?' My head sprang up like a jack-in-a-box. 'You specifically?'

'If you subscribe to the theory that feminism is about choice,' she replied. 'Women, everyone, should have the choice to read, write and be whatever they want. In that sense, these books could, I suppose, be considered a radical act.'

'And not frivolous, predictable, badly written, misogynistic nonsense?'

She blinked a couple of times, her huge eyes owlish behind her glasses, but wasn't fazed by my reminder of her own earlier review.

'As you know, I haven't read it. But from what I can gather, the overall message of this book in particular doesn't seem to be harmful in any way.'

'It's not harmful, it's empowering,' Charlotte said, now fully wrapped around Joe's arm. 'Writing misery in this century should be illegal, things are shit enough. Do we really need another *Deckled Edges*?'

'*Deckled Edges* is a satire,' CJ blustered. 'It's a dark comedy.'

Charlotte wrinkled her nose in disgust. 'So dark I couldn't see the laughs.'

'What exactly is going on here?' My dad elbowed his way to the front of the group, looking from guest to guest for an answer. 'I go inside to use the loo and five minutes later all hell's broken loose?'

'Dad, it's the most amazing thing ever. Joe is Este Cox!' Charlotte said, welded to his side so tightly it would've taken a crowbar to get her off him.

'Este, is it?' Dad looked Joe up and down and nodded. 'Perfectly fine with me, son, happy to call you whatever you like but I don't know if you'll have such an easy go of it with Gregory.'

'Hugh, darling, no,' Mum pressed two fingers to

171

her forehead, right between her eyebrows, and closed her eyes as she took a breath in. 'He isn't changing his name to Este. It appears that Joseph here has been writing under a *nom de plume.* He's the author of your daughter's latest literary obsession, *Butterflies.*'

'Is that right?'

I couldn't believe it. Dad looked thrilled. England winning the World Cup, bacon being declared a health food, Gillian Anderson asking him out for tea thrilled. 'Then congratulations are in order, Joseph. You must tell us everything.'

'No, really, it's your birthday,' Joe said as he desperately tried to wrangle his arm away from my limpet-like sister. 'Like I said, I used a pseudonym for a reason. No one knows I'm the author and no one can know I'm the author so please, I really need you to keep it under your hats.'

'They will,' Charlotte promised, skewering everyone with a threatening look. 'On one condition. You do a signing at my bookshop.'

'I'd love to but I don't see how it could work with me staying anonymous?' he replied as I managed to gather my senses just enough to tip back half my glass of wine in one gulp.

Charlotte beamed up at Joe, still hanging on his arm like a nineteenth-century heroine caught mid-swoon, and he smiled awkwardly back, manuscript held securely to his chest. Then she pulled out her phone from her pocket and snapped a photo of him, stack of papers in hand.

'You can't expect to stay anonymous forever,' she reasoned, releasing him from her vice-like grip as she reviewed the incriminating image. 'Either you do an in-person live event at my bookshop or I post this to TikTok tomorrow night. It's totally up to you.'

Joe's eyes opened so wide it was a wonder they stayed in his head. 'Call me cynical but that sounds a lot like blackmail.'

She turned her phone around to show him the photo. It wasn't his best. Deer in the headlights fear didn't look good on anyone.

'It does, doesn't it? You have twenty-four hours to decide.'

'I'm going to go out on a limb and say you're not entirely pleased with me.'

'Whatever gives you that idea?' I asked Joe when he found me alone at the back door of the cottage after the fuss died down and the gathering dispersed.

'Couldn't really say. Just a hunch.'

I smiled pleasantly as I continued to hurl his belongings, one by one, off the little porch over the wall and into the field behind the cottage.

'I was trying to help,' he said. 'But given the fact you've just chucked my pants into a pile of cow shit, I'm going to guess that wasn't obvious?'

'Help?' I paused, his overnight bag in one hand, a very nice pale blue cashmere sweater in the other. 'You were trying to help?'

It was finally dark outside, but the moon was full, casting a milky luminance across Joe's face, highlighting the high planes of his cheekbones and the downward curve of his mouth.

'You didn't want your family to know you're Este Cox,' he replied, nervously eyeing the sweater as I pulled back my arm.

173

'And you couldn't think of a better reason why you might have the manuscript?'

'Such as?'

'Such as you're the creative director at Este Cox's publishing house and you have the manuscript because you're working on the cover?'

He barely flinched when I balled up the lovely sweater and threw it as far as I could.

'Fuck,' he muttered. 'That would've made more sense.'

'Yes,' I said, the sweater sailing through the air before catching on the willow tree behind the cottage and waving back and forth like a fancy flag of surrender. 'It would.'

'Sophie, I'm sorry, I really am, but you looked so freaked out, I had to do something.' Joe took a speculative step forward and I retaliated by pulling a black leather sunglasses case out of the bag. He retreated at once. 'Telling them I'm Este was the first thought that came into my head and please don't throw those, they were very expensive.'

'Obviously there were very few obstacles blocking its way,' I said through gritted teeth as I chucked the glasses case. 'Do you have any idea what you've done?'

'Aside from save your arse?'

I'd crossed a line with the sunglasses. He crossed the porch in two long strides and grabbed one handle of his overnight bag.

'It was a stupid thing to say, I see that now, but I can fix it. First thing tomorrow morning, I'll explain it was all a joke and, like you said, I only have the manuscript because I'm working on the book. They'll believe me.'

'Why wouldn't they?' I agreed, refusing to let go of the bag. 'People will believe anything that comes out your mouth.'

We stood face to face, each holding onto one handle of his open and half-empty bag until Joe yanked it out of my grasp. He let it fall to the floor, the rest of his belongings spilling out onto the ground.

'Everyone except for you.'

I wasn't prepared for his voice to be so soft.

'I'm sorry,' he said again as I rubbed a sore spot on my palm where I'd been holding on to his bag too tightly. 'I am genuinely sorry. I should've known better. Every time I try to help someone, it only makes things more complicated.'

My head swam as I held my breath to protect myself from the warm scent of Joe's skin and when placed his hand in my open palm, my fingers automatically curled around his.

'Why is it that every time I'm with you, I'm apologising?' Joe asked. His huge hand swallowed up mine, strong and warm.

'Because you know when you're beaten?' I suggested, tiptoeing precariously close to the edge. This was it. This was our moment.

'Can I ask you something?'

'Yes,' I tried to say. The air that left my lungs passed over my lips too softly to make a sound.

'Are you more upset that I said I wrote the book or that your family were so impressed by it?'

The moment passed.

With a feeble shove, I pushed him out of my way and stormed back inside. 'You might want to get your stuff back before the foxes run off with it,' I said, leaving him out on the porch. 'Some of it looked expensive. Tacky but expensive.'

'Are you going to help me?' he asked.

'No,' I replied, grabbing my phone and the cottage keys from the bedside table, just in case he had the bright idea to lock me out. 'I'm going to clear up your mess. Don't wait up.'

The door closed behind me with a satisfying slam.

Most of the house lights were out and all the curtains were drawn, only my sister's room, the landing and the kitchen still showed signs of life when I found myself standing at the back door. I had no more idea of what I wanted to say than I had when Charlotte marched out of the cottage brandishing my manuscript but I knew I had to say something. It didn't have to be difficult. All I needed to do was stick to the facts.

Joe isn't Este Cox, I am.

He didn't write *Butterflies*, I did.

Then I would remind them it's a feminist masterpiece with absolutely no pegging and all of this nonsense would be behind me forever.

With my hand on the doorknob, I took a moment to visualise a happy outcome with proud parents and an adoring sister rather than an angry mob waving pitch-forks, then I stopped. Two blurred figures walked into the kitchen, their features obscured by the pebbled glass, both speaking softly but still loud enough to carry out the latched open window.

'It's very interesting, I can't think of another example,' Mum said in between the opening and closing of cup-board doors. 'I've only flicked through it but, I have to say, men rarely write so sensitively about female desire.'

'Men rarely do anything sensitively when it comes to female desire,' a second voice said. Jericka, mum's friend, the overly intense critic. 'That's why these books do so well in the first place.'

'And the things he writes about,' added a third voice. 'I've never read anything like it. Not that I usually read those sorts of things, you understand.'

'Yes, Carole, we know,' Mum replied. 'You only read it on behalf of your church group.'

'Know thy enemy,' she confirmed.

'I don't remember that line from the Bible,' Jericka said. 'Which book is that exactly?'

I pulled my hand away from the door and pressed myself up against the wall beside instead. Explaining the truth to my mother was one thing, confessing in front of Jericka and Auntie Carole was another.

'It does demand a re-evaluation of the text,' Mum said, the dishwasher creaking open as she spoke. 'Joseph has obviously connected to something in a lot of women.'

'Sometimes it takes an outsider to see us more clearly,' Jericka offered. 'One might even say there's something almost satirical about it. Not only has he believably aped the genre, he's excelled in it.'

'Goes to show most of these books aren't worth the paper they're written on when a first-time male author can wipe the floor with the lot of them,' my mother agreed. 'Shame he doesn't want to come forward, he's a good-looking boy. The PR team would have a field day with him.'

The dishwasher slammed shut, smothering murmurings of agreement.

'Didn't Sophie used to talk about writing a book?'

Carole said as I crouched down underneath the window to hear them more clearly.

'She did. And then she went into teaching.'

Maybe I didn't need to hear more clearly after all.

'It's a noble profession,' Jericka said, earning her several thousand brownie points with me. 'Encouraging the next generation, inspiring young minds.'

'Yes, that's very true and I'm proud of her for it,' Mum replied. I leaned against the cold stone, steeling myself for the inevitable 'but' that hung in the air.

'I know it's a terrible thing to say but I expected something more from her. She's such a bright girl, could've gone into any industry really but I always assumed she'd follow us into the publishing world. I'm not ecstatic about Charlotte deferring her education but you can't help but be impressed by her determination. Where's that ambition in Sophie? She's too soft to be a killer agent like William but she would've made a marvellous editor and she did, like you say, always *always* want to be a writer.'

My thighs were already screaming from the deeply uncomfortable position I found myself in, physically and emotionally, and I very much wanted to leave. But how could I?

'She's still young, there's time for her yet.' Jericka sounded like she was trying to convince my mother I could still turn back from a life of crime. 'Toni Morrison didn't publish *The Bluest Eye* until she was thirty-nine.'

'But she was already working in publishing then,' Mum reminded her. 'Not coddling toddlers and wasting her potential.'

'And don't forget,' Carole added. 'Those who can do, those who can't teach.'

'Carole, that's a terrible thing to say,' Mum replied, only waiting a second before adding, 'but you're not the first to say it.'

'Could be worse,' Jerick clucked. 'At least she's not a romance writer.'

Lowering myself to my hands and knees, I crawled away from the house and crawled back down the garden like a dog. As well as being thematically on point, it was the only way to make sure they wouldn't see me and I was not in the mood to make my confession now.

I hid *Butterflies* from my parents because I couldn't stand the thought of disappointing them. What I hadn't realised until tonight was how disappointed my mother already was. As a lifetime romance reader, I was used to snobbery. Ever since my fated meet-cute with the copy of *Bridget Jones's Diary* someone left behind on a bus when I was fourteen, and I knew from the very first 'fuckwit', there was no turning back. Mum dismissed it all as 'chicklit' back then and I hid my ever-growing collection under my bed, pristine and treasured, while I distracted my parents with the dog-eared copies of Ayn Rand and Hemingway bought from second-hand shops. After a while, chicklit fell out of fashion and people started calling it 'women's fiction' which I never really understood. The gender label made no sense. There was no 'men's fiction' section in the bookshop, why were we the ones who had to be othered? In fact, if a man wrote a love story, or any kind of book with a romantic storyline at its heart, it went right in the window and won all the prizes, while my beloved books, the ones that talked about the lives of women, all the things that mattered to us, large and small, were tucked away on a shelf or squeezed together on one very pink table. Now things were different. Romance ruled, and younger and braver women than me shouted their fandom from the TikTok rooftops. There were still plenty of snobs around to judge them, but they didn't care. That was the one thing my mum was right about. They loved what they loved, regardless of what other people thought, and that kind of love is a radical, rebellious act. But it didn't make up for knowing your parents were disappointed in you.

'She returns,' Joe declared as I opened the door and skulked inside, head hanging low. 'When you said don't wait up I thought that meant you weren't coming back. And by "thought", I mean, hoped.'

'I'm really not in the mood for this,' I replied, keeping my chin down and my hair in front of my face. 'Can I just brush my teeth and go to bed please?'

'No one's stopping you.'

I moved past him without looking up, one foot in front of the other, the bathroom was so close. Three more steps and I could lock the door, turn on the taps and wash the whole day away. But Joe stepped in front of me, blocking my path, his non-committal sarcasm replaced by concern.

'What happened? Are you OK?'

'More than.'

I ducked past him, closing the bathroom door and turning the lock before he could get a good look at my tear-stained face.

My disappointing, unambitious tear-stained face.

'Sophie?' he called my name doubtfully through the door.

'I'm perfectly fine,' I replied, hating how weak and shaky my voice sounded.

'You're sure?'

'Sure I'm sure.'

He was still outside the door, I could feel him hovering and I stayed stock still until his footsteps petered away. I didn't realise I was shaking until I stopped.

The sight I saw reflected in the mirror was not a pretty one. My eyes and nose were red raw, my hair needed a good brush and what mascara had survived the walk back from the house had stained my under eyes a sickly, patchy grey. I looked disgusting but then I felt disgusting so it all worked out perfectly. Meeting myself in the eye, I gave Mirror Sophie a fierce look. A woman I followed on Instagram, who loved dispensing advice while contorting herself into a variety of advanced yoga poses, said no matter what, you should always be able to find one good thing about your day and I was determined to do it. There was Sarah, as always, but seeing her so happy and fulfilled by her new job only reminded me how confused I was. Her vanilla latte was definitely a highlight but if that was the best I could do, I really was in trouble.

The girl we met on our walk. *Butterflies'* biggest fan. That should've been something I could cling to, someone who willingly went to bat for me and my book simply because she loved it. But what good was the adoration of strangers when the people you loved most didn't respect you? Even CJ, who had to be one of the top five most annoying people in the world, had dumped me. I wasn't sad about the end of our relationship and I definitely wasn't still hung up on him, no matter what he wanted to believe, but what did it say about me if even a man like that ditched me at the first opportunity?

After ten minutes on the side of the bath with wads of cold, wet tissue paper pressed against my eyes, I opened the bathroom door. Facing me was a semi-transparent white wall suddenly erected in the middle of the cottage, dividing the room in two. My bed on one side, his sofa on the other. Shoelaces, four of them tied together in one long line, stretched from one end of the room to the other, the fabric that separated us draped over the top.

'What's going on?' I asked.

'I like privacy when I retire,' Joe quoted from his side of the partition. 'I'm very delicate in that respect. Behold the walls of Jericho!'

'You've seen *It Happened One Night*?'

His head peeked around the sheet wall and he smiled, his best Clark Gable impression. 'Only about a thousand times.'

He disappeared back behind the thin white partition, the light of the moon shining through the window and outlining his body against the fabric. Broad shoulders, narrow waist, thick thighs. It was almost as though he was putting on a show.

'You took down the curtains,' I realised, looking away. 'But the moon's so bright tonight, how are you going to sleep?'

'I could sleep on the surface of the sun, don't you worry about me,' he replied. 'Are you OK?'

'I'm OK.'

Slowly, I peeled back the covers on the huge bed and slipped underneath. It had been a warm day but the night was cooler and I was grateful not to have to toss aside the comforting weight of the duvet. Almost as grateful as I was for his gesture.

'Joe?' I said, pulling up the sheets to my chin.

'Sophie?' he replied.

'I'm sorry.'

'You are?' His voice was rich with pleasant surprise. 'What for?'

'For throwing your things outside. Did you manage to find everything?'

'Yes. I had to tangle with a very dapper badger to get my boxers back but aside from that there was no harm done.'

In spite of everything, a small smile forced its way onto my face.

'I suppose you think that's funny.'

'Not really. I could've got TB, Sophie, badgers are riddled. But then he drove off in a Ford Model T with a toad and a mole, muttering something about weasels. It was all very dramatic.'

The pale moonlight streamed through the undressed windows, illuminating the fabric that separated us like a cinema screen. Joe's silhouette moved slowly but surely, unbuttoning his shirt, starting with the cuffs then moving down his body, one button at a time. It wasn't a silent movie and I held my breath to better hear his sound effects, the unexpected thrill of a zip followed by the schlump of his jeans hitting the floor. He bent down to pick them up and the fabric rippled as his angles changed, now wearing nothing but those silky black boxers. I waited for him to get into bed but he didn't move. Instead he stood right by the sheet, the only thing that separated us, the fluttering, flimsy fabric.

'Sophie?' he said, the soft sound of my name filling the cottage.

'Joe?'

'Nothing.'

He climbed into bed, the sofa creaking happily as his weight tested the new springs and I stared up at the ceiling, wide awake.

'Get some sleep,' I said, not quite ready to let go of the connection.

'You too.'

There were more rustling sounds, sheets moving across skin, the mattress yielding to the weight of his body.

'Sweet dreams,' I added.

'I hope I have the same dream I had last night,' he replied.

I moistened my dry lips and, even though I knew I'd regret it, cleared my throat to ask the question.

'What did you dream about last night?'

'You.'

It hung in the air, a statement, a confession. An invitation.

'Goodnight, Sophie,' he said, the springs creaking one more time as he settled himself.

'Goodnight, Joe,' I whispered back, rolling onto my side and closing my eyes with a smile.

CHAPTER SIXTEEN

Joe was a heavy sleeper.

He didn't even stir when I climbed out of bed the next morning, dressing quickly and quietly, and edging past the sofa-bed to let myself out the cottage before he could wake. It had been a restless night, sleep hovering just out of reach from the moment I closed my eyes. Every time I felt myself slipping towards blissful oblivion, my brain decided to scroll through some of our greatest hits, all the classics with some new trauma thrown in for good measure. Everything I had to lose if people found out I was Este Cox, my mother's disappointment, the fact I'd wasted five years of my life with an arse like CJ and even he didn't want me, and the conversation I was going to have at some point in the near future with the man next door, who kept parking so close to my driveway, it was almost impossible for me to back out without hitting him. How difficult was it to pull up two more feet? He was definitely doing it on purpose.

And if that wasn't enough, each time I rolled over,

I heard Joe Walsh. The whisper of sheets against skin, the soft sighs and quiet murmurs, and every other barely audible exhalation that might as well have been a twenty-piece brass band. I couldn't possibly relax with him so close to me. How could he lie there sleeping peacefully when I couldn't keep my eyes closed for five minutes at a time? The audacity of the man. So, it was safe to say I didn't look my best when I jogged down the side of the house, bypassing breakfast with the family, in favour of a walk to visit the best coffee shop in town.

Even though it was early, Sarah was already busy, most of the tables full and a short queue forming out the door. I recognised the tetchy expressions on their faces. You simply did not come between a person and their coffee before nine a.m. if you wanted to live to see lunchtime.

'Taylor!' she cried happily when she saw me hanging around the doorway. 'Get in here. What are you drinking?'

Several pairs of eyes burned into my back. If looks could kill, I'd have been six feet under.

'No, you're busy,' I said, loud enough for them all to hear. 'I'll come back later.'

'You certainly will not. Get your arse back in here immediately.'

There was one thing scarier than an early morning coffee shop customer and that was Sarah Nixon. I knew better than to argue, shuffling through the tables with murmured apologies to anyone and everyone.

Ignoring the outrage with two large pink takeout cups in her hands and a paper bag of pastries hanging from her mouth, Sarah left her colleague in charge and beckoned me to follow her down the little hallway and out a back door to an alley. Two plastic chairs sat at a small table, the York stone walls of the shops on one side of us, a row of trees on the other, early morning dappled sunlight shining through their branches.

'It's not a vanilla latte but you'll like it,' she promised, pushing one of the coffees towards me when I sat down.

'What is it?' I asked with a cautious sniff.

'Mr Atkinson's coconut flat white. Orders the same thing every day because he doesn't like coffee.'

I took a tiny sip as she sat opposite me.

'But it is coffee?'

'I know.' Sarah tore open the paper bag that contained two chocolate croissants. 'But don't tell him that. Now, tell me what's going on and why you look like something the dog dragged in, ate up, threw up, ate again and shat out?'

And to think of the two of us, I was the romance writer.

'It's a lot of stuff.' I crumbled a bit off the pastry, unsure where to start. 'And it's complicated.'

'Have you forgot who you're talking to?' she laughed. 'Don't "it's complicated" me. Is it CJ? Was he there last night?'

'Yes, he was but no, it's not him.'

It wasn't. If CJ were a book boyfriend, he wouldn't even get Daniel Cleaver status in my story. More like I was Elizabeth Bennet and I'd accidentally gone out with Mr Collins for five whole years.

Sarah studied me carefully and I kept my face busy, eating and drinking and not thinking about Joe or my mum or Joe or *Butterflies* or Joe. Eventually, she sat back in her chair and glared at me with accusatory eyes.

'What?' I asked, heating up under her gaze.

'You said you weren't seeing anyone but you've got romantic drama face.'

I tore off a huge piece of flaky pastry and stuffed it in my mouth. 'I do not have romantic drama face. There's no such thing as romantic drama face.'

But it was too late, she already smelled blood in the water.

'Taylor, don't be a dick. There are circles under your eyes darker than a black hole, you've got a mouth like a cat's arse and you are inhaling that croissant like someone's going to take it away from you. You're an anxious eater and you're never more anxious than when you have romantic drama. You didn't come running in looking like the girl from *The Ring* just to say hello, you came because you needed to talk to me, so go on, talk.'

'Anyone who doesn't inhale a croissant this good wants their head checking,' I muttered, savouring a speck of the buttery goodness before relenting with a very big sigh. 'I came because seeing you always makes me feel better.'

'Thank you, of course it does, and why do you need to feel better?'

'All right, I'm stressed out,' I admitted. 'But I'm stressed out about a lot of things, not only romantic drama. Work stuff, family stuff and—'

'But there is romantic drama!' Sarah held up a triumphant finger and I kicked myself at the slip up. 'Out with it, what's their name?'

'He doesn't deserve a name, he's an idiot,' I mumbled, not at all picturing the way the thin white sheet had been draped over his gorgeous body when I snuck out this morning, arms raised over his head to show off the line of his shoulders, the cut of his collarbone, head tilted to one side, full lips slightly parted. 'Except my body hasn't quite caught on to that yet.'

'Look at your face.' Sarah clapped, delighted, as my cheeks turned a deep shade of scarlet. 'Hate to be the one to break it to you but whoever this idiot is, you're totally into him.'

'Am not.'

'Are too.'

'I am not.'

'You're so in love with him, you couldn't be any more in love with him if you tried,' she said back in a sing-song voice. 'You love him more than I love espresso martinis, Cadbury's I Eggs and Alexander Skarsgård, not all at the same time. Although . . .'

'You're wrong. I could not be less in love with this man,' I announced, an agitated snip clipping off the edges of my words. 'Just because someone is handsome and funny, works with books, likes the same films as you and is big and strong enough to toss you over his shoulder and carry you out of a burning building does not mean you should automatically throw your under-wear at him.'

'Yes, it does.'

In her defence, I'd set myself up there. Crossing my arms and legs at the same time, I looked away, shaking my head more at myself than anyone else. 'Not when he's also so full of shit he could supply manure to every farm between Land's End and John O'Groats.'

But was he? A knot tied itself in my stomach when I thought of his lips against my ear and pulled tightly at the memory of the look on his face when I came back to the cottage, so sad and tearful. It was possible there was a very, very, very small chance I might have misjudged him. I'd been wrong in the past but only on extremely rare occasions, like the time I momentarily doubted Beyoncé's ability to pull off a country record. Shame on me. But what about the things Mal said, the cadding and the bounderesness? Mal wasn't a liar, that had to come from somewhere.

'If you say you're not interested in this man I believe you but humour me for one minute,' Sarah suggested. 'What's the future Mr Sophie Taylor's name?'

'The future Mr Sophie Taylor is a clone of Ryan Reynolds that hasn't been created yet, as you well know,' I replied. 'The man sent to punish me for terrible crimes I must have committed in a past life is called Joe Walsh.'

'Then tell me about Joe Walsh.'

The incriminating wash of scarlet crept down my throat and mottled my chest.

'His dad is friends with my dad. They're both up here for the party.'

'His dad is friends with your dad? If this were a Jane Austen novel, that would be enough to see the two of you married off.'

'Thankfully, times have changed,' I said. 'But if it was an Austen novel, he'd be a Wickham, not a Darcy. Pretty, sneaky and completely full of it.'

I swirled my cup, blending the coffee and the coconut milk, as she tucked into the middle chunk of her croissant, the best bit according to Sarah and, according to Sarah logic, you should always eat the best bit first. 'I'm not in love with him, it's purely physical and I don't do purely physical. There's something about him that makes me want to climb the man. It's pheromones, right? Tell me it's pheromones so I don't have to have myself committed.'

'Sounds like a crush to me,' she replied, picking each layer of pastry apart, starting with the crunchiest. 'I will admit it's not like you to lose your mind over strong thighs and a sleazy smile but there's a first time for everything, which leads me to my next question: does he feel the same? Has he expressed an interest in climbing you also?'

Resting my arms on the table and my head on my arms, I catalogued all our almost moments, the knot in my belly squeezing even tighter. 'This feels so weird to say but I actually think he does.'

'And that's weird because?'

'Because no one in the history of ever has been interested in me for purely physical reasons and don't start with all that "but you're so pretty" stuff because a), it doesn't count coming from you, and b), I've got many years of precedent to back me up. It's just not me.'

'That's because I've never met anyone with a stronger "touch me and die" vibe,' Sarah replied. 'Call it boundaries, call it self-respect, either way I wouldn't know, but that's not the point. The point is, I think you should probably have sex with this man. Immediately if not sooner.'

I raised a single questioning eyebrow in her direction.

'For science,' she added.

A second eyebrow joined the first.

'It's an important experiment!' she exclaimed. 'If your interest in him is purely physical then you need to get it out your system before you spontaneously combust, and it sounds like he'd be a willing participant. Once you've banged, the feelings should go away. He likes the look of you, you like the look of him, I'm really not seeing the bigger problem.'

'I can think of one,' I said. 'I don't trust him.'

'Why not?'

'Because one minute he's trying to charm the knickers off everyone in the room, the next he wants to sit down for a deep and meaningful then he's storming off in a huff like he's the one who's being messed around.' I picked at a loose thread in the cuff of my old cardigan until it pulled the fabric, annoyed at Joe then annoyed at myself for picking at the loose thread in the cuff of my cardigan. 'How can someone be so nice one minute and such an arsehole the next? And he's too handsome to be trustworthy. No man that attractive has ever in the entire history of the world been referred to as "nice".'

'What if he's a good guy trapped in a shagger's body?' Sarah suggested. 'Maybe he wants to be a decent human but he's cursed with such hotness, women keep flinging their knickers at him like kryptonite and dragging him back down to their sordid level.'

'Must be so hard for him,' I replied drily. 'Imagine the suffering he has endured.'

'Or maybe he's running hot and cold because he's trying to crack on to a woman he really likes and she's treating him like a complete psychopath simply because he's interested in her.'

'You're absurd.'

'And you're finding excuses to keep your distance. I'm suggesting you sleep with the man not give him your online banking password. Although I'm assuming it's still the same password you've been using for everything since 2009 because you're practically begging to get your identity stolen.'

'OK, you shut up now,' I replied.

'OK, SophieMelark4Eva009?'

'I said shut it, MrsSarahCullen69.'

We both picked up our croissants at the same time, Sarah with a smile on her face, me very much sulking.

'I'd like to raise a hypothesis,' she proposed as I took the last bite of my pastry. God, they were good. Covering my mouth with my hand, I eyed her across the table.

'Which is?'

'What if it's yourself you don't trust and not this Joe character?'

'Yes, it's definitely him,' I answered right away.

She wrapped her ponytail round on itself, curled her blonde ringlets into a huge bun, let it fall, then repeated the process.

'Feel free to disregard this if it does nothing for you,' she said after securing her third go with a hair stick she produced from her pocket. 'But as your friend, I have observed the fact you haven't exactly put yourself out there since you and CJ ended it. Maybe you're a bit gun shy. It would make sense for you to be a bit nervous.'

'It would but I'm not,' I insisted. 'Cautious, yes. Nervous, I don't think so.'

'Well, what do I know?' she said lightly, wiping her hands on the legs of her jeans. 'Just seems a bit odd that you're so dead against having a go on this supposedly handsome, funny, book-loving hunk. You haven't even kissed the man, so I can't imagine what he could have done to have your guard up like this?'

It was cool in the alley behind the coffee shop but I could tell the day was going to be a scorcher. You could smell it in the air. I tugged the newly pulled sleeves of my cardigan over my hands and looked back at my friend as she drank her coffee with a pleasant, innocent expression, just waiting for me to break.

'There's something else going on here and you don't want to tell me, which is fine,' Sarah said, setting aside her pink cup. 'But you know I'll get it out of you. Wouldn't it be easier to give in now?'

There wasn't a person alive who would be able to keep a secret from Sarah Nixon for more than half an hour. Not even the best-trained intelligence operatives would be a match for her nonchalant approach to forcing the truth out of you. She really had missed her calling as an interrogator.

She dipped what was left of her croissant into her coffee and took a bite. 'In about ten hours, you, me and this stud are going to be at the same party. I will be child-free for the whole evening and I will have unfettered access to wine. I will be unstoppable.'

Puffing out my cheeks as far as they would go, I blew out the air slowly. Once again, Sarah never lied.

'Maybe you shouldn't come to the party,' I suggested, only half-kidding. 'It's going to be terrible. Incredibly boring, lots of old people, average age of ninety-seven, I think.'

'Your brother told me there's an open bar, it's no kids allowed and your dad hired a bouncy castle I'm coming.'

'Dad hired a bouncy castle?' I repeated as she finished her breakfast and wiped her mouth with the back of her hand. 'What is he thinking? Someone's going to break a hip.'

'One way or another. If Joe's thighs really are as big as you say.'

I frowned.

'I don't specifically remember mentioning his thighs.'

'Are they massive though?'

'They're average,' I replied. 'Completely ordinary thighs. You're projecting.'

Only she wasn't. His thighs were incredible.

'Final offer. Tell me what's going on, and I'll give you a cookie,' Sarah said, leaning across the table to stare right into my eyes.

'Give me a cookie and I'll tell you,' I replied, calling her bluff.

'On the way out,' she bartered. 'Now let's hear it, Taylor. All of it.'

I felt so stupid. This was Sarah, I could tell her anything and everything and she would never judge me, but I couldn't properly explain the Joe situation without explaining the *Butterflies* situation, and it wasn't that I didn't trust her but it seemed so unfair to expect another person to keep my secret. That said, I really needed to talk to someone and there was no one on the planet who knew me better, not even William. Big brothers had very clear limits when it came to their little sisters.

'Right, I will tell you and I don't want to be overdramatic, but,' I said, checking over both shoulders to make sure we were alone as she squealed with glee. 'If I do, you have to swear you'll keep it to yourself.'

'Unless you're about to tell me you're the princess of Genovia, I guarantee you're overreacting,' she replied with mock offence. 'Who am I going to tell, my kids? If it's not Minecraft or WWE, they couldn't give a shit.'

I took a final sip of Mr Atkinson's coffee to prepare myself. The look on William's face when he FaceTimed me after reading the first sex scene was something I'd never forget. He demanded he got twenty percent to represent me as my agent instead of the usual fifteen, then broke down in tears sobbing 'but you're my baby sister' over and over and over.

'Have you heard of a book called *Butterflies*?' I asked, shifting nervously in my seat.

'Heard of it?'

Sarah's expression changed immediately, rabid excitement replacing her curiosity as she patted herself down for her phone. 'How have we not talked about this? That book is basically my whole personality. See? I'm halfway through the audiobook.' She swiped into Audible and held it up as evidence. 'I've already got the paperback but one of the mums at school said I had to get the audiobook and I'm glad she did. It's good to have both your hands free while you're listening, if you know what I mean.'

'I really wish you hadn't said that,' I groaned. '*You're* going to wish you hadn't said that.'

'What has *Butterflies* got to do with anything?' She still kept one loving, protective hand on her phone as she barked out a laugh. 'Joe isn't Este Cox, is he?'

'Nope.' I covered my face with my hands, breathing in the scent of my fabric softener, peeking at my friend from between my fingers. 'I am.'

Across the table, she stared at me with her mouth hanging open, speechless. Sarah Nixon, lost for words.

'Well, you were right as always,' I said. 'There really is a first time for everything.'

CHAPTER SEVENTEEN

Harford was separated from the real world by an arched sandstone bridge that crossed a pretty stream and elicited polite little paps from car horns as all the happy drivers encouraged one another to go first. There was an old mill and an even older church, as well as lots of adorable limestone houses and gardens full of colourful summer flowers, hollyhocks and delphiniums, which towered over garden walls, almost as tall as me. Even though it had been part of my life ever since I was a little girl visiting grandparents, it still felt unreal to me, the kind of place you might expect to see on an early Sunday evening BBC drama where members of the clergy solved gentle, quirky crimes. And after my conversation with Sarah, I suspected I might be the next victim of said crimes.

She took the news incredibly well and naturally, she was super cool about it. Or at least she was after she'd finished screaming and throwing things at me, demanding to know how I'd dared keep my secret for so long. By the time we got to the end of the whole drama, even she had to admit the Joe situation was a little more complicated than she'd first assumed but there hadn't been enough time to dig in any deeper. The morning rush reached fever pitch just as I was telling her how he hung the sheet across the cottage and Sarah's skills were needed at the espresso machine.

'The most obvious answer here is that you never should've lied in the first place,' she said as she wrapped the strings of her apron around her waist. 'How many times do I have to tell you, it doesn't matter what other people think.'

'At least once more,' I replied, tying them in a big bow behind her back. 'And that might be the most obvious but it's also impossible unless you have a time machine. Any other bright ideas?'

'Not yet but I'm sure I'll have it all worked out by this evening. You know me, I'm a problem solver.'

'You're amazing is what you are,' I replied, meaning every word.

'It's the only way I know how to be.' She handed me my promised cookie then slapped me on the backside. 'All right, Este, on your way. Text me if you need me, otherwise I'll see you tonight.'

As I stepped out onto the high street, the world felt a little bit lighter. Sarah was ecstatic for me, even if it did mean she couldn't read *Butterflies* ever again (her words, not mine) and she completely understood why it might make things difficult at school if the truth came out. She was also ready to fight my mother to the death, which would've worried me more if she hadn't hero-worshipped my mum ever since she caught us pouring vodka into our orange juice at a New Year's

Eve party when we were fifteen and, appalled with our choice of amateur screwdrivers, took us into the kitchen to teach us how to make dirty martinis. My mother was a big believer in learning all the essential life skills early.

In the sunshine, picture perfect Harford looked especially camera-ready. Not only was it steeped in the usual old English charm, but brightly coloured bunting stretched across the street, hundreds of red, yellow, pink and blue triangles of fabric zigging and zagging along, barely even fluttering in the still morning air, and drawing me down to the green where people were setting up for the summer fête. My heart lifted at the sight of pasting tables and folding chairs and sky-rocketed when I spotted the candyfloss machine. When I was little, the fête was my favourite part of the summer holidays, running around with five pounds in my pocket and a bellyful of sugar. Just being in close proximity to a game of hook-a-duck made me feel like I could run through a brick wall. I scoured the scene for a fudge stall, suddenly overcome with the desire to put my pancreas to the test, but it was too early to tell what anything would be, no one had their signs up yet. All these tents and booths could be for anything – home-baked biscuits, guess how many sweets in the jar, bric-a-brac, white elephant, which was basically the same as bric-a-brac but the fête organisers had a 'no two stalls alike' rule, unless that stall sold cake. You couldn't have enough cake.

No matter how muddled I'd felt when I left the cottage, it was impossible to be miserable when the world was sunshine, blue skies and strawberries and cream. The air smelled sweet and full, the taste of

summertime tangible on my tongue and there was something about the green grass under my feet that made
me smile. Well, the grass and the tremendous amount
of coffee I'd consumed at Sarah's. There had to have
been at least three shots in Mr Atkinson's coconut flat
white because I was pretty sure no one else around me
could hear the buzzing sound that echoed in my ears.

I skirted around the edge of the green for fear of being
drafted into helping to set up the best vegetable competition, and without planning on it, found myself in front
of another new addition to Harford's high street. There
it was, right where the greengrocer's once stood. The
flaking green paint had been replaced by a fresh vivid
blue and there was a neon sign in the window, and
another hand-painted above the door, both of them
declaring this to be 'Charlotte's Bookshop'.

'Wow,' I said softly. 'It's really real.'

I wasn't sure what I'd been expecting but it wasn't
this. *This* looked like a proper bookshop. Not all the
way finished yet but even from the outside I could see
how great it was going to be: the open shelves, the cute
little reading nooks and even a branded 'Charlotte's
Bookshop' mirror for selfies. My sister had done all this
and passed her exams? The results weren't in yet but
she had never achieved anything less than top marks
for as long as she had lived. She was even in the top
percentile for growth and weight when she was a baby
so I had no doubts.

It wasn't much after ten a.m. and, aside from the
flurry of activity around the fête, our sleepy town was
still quiet, save the odd woollen-socked rambler beginning or returning from an adventure in the peaks. I was
still staring in Charlotte's shop window when a car

trundled up the road, slow enough to suggest it was looking for something. When it rolled to a stop, I realised it was a car I recognised.

A Range Rover.

'Not the sister I was expecting to see here,' Joe said as he opened the door and hopped down to the pavement, phone in one hand, cup of coffee in the other. A not particularly pleasant mix of anxiety, arousal and caffeine spiked in my bloodstream, and I shrank back a step. Somewhere in the evolutionary mess, my fight-or-flight reactions had both been accidentally set to 'curl up into a ball and hope it goes away', which I was fairly sure only worked on bears. Or was it wolves? Either way, it definitely wasn't going to work on Joe Walsh.

'You're meeting Charlotte?' I combed my hair through with my fingers, all too aware there was nothing I could do about my creased-up dress and comfy old cardigan. He looked fresh and crisp, I looked like I'd got dressed in the dark.

Which I had.

But Joe didn't seem to notice. He never once took his eyes off mine.

'She wanted to show "Este" the shop where she'll be making her first-ever public appearance.'

I looked away first, turning my gaze to the unfinished window display.

'What happened to telling everyone it was a mistake?' I asked, fingertips lightly touching the glass. 'I thought it was all going to be straightened out by now.'

'Small bump in the road with that plan,' he replied, screwing up his face with evident frustration. 'Your sister doesn't believe me. She says—' He paused and pulled out his phone to accurately quote her message.

'I'm eighteen not an idiot, see you at the shop, Este, then there's about five thousand kisses and a gif of Lisa Simpson dancing.'

'Mad to think we're living in a time when we don't believe someone, even when they're trying to tell you the truth.' I rubbed my temples as he turned the phone around to show me the message, Lisa Simpson undulating underneath a row of X's and O's.

'Perhaps if we were telling her the whole truth, she might be more inclined to believe it.'

'And perhaps if you hadn't said you were Este Cox last night—'

'Hey, Sophie, here's an idea. Do you want to continue this pointless fight inside?' Joe interrupted with a glorious and unbothered smile. 'Charlotte's running late, she gave me the keycode to let myself in. Although how she got my number in the first place is a mystery.'

'My sister could find Amelia Earhart's contact details if she put her mind to it. I'm sure your phone number was no trouble whatsoever,' I replied, declining to acknowledge his comment about the pointless argument, even though he was right. Especially because he was right. Why *would* Charlotte believe he'd made something like this up? Even I wasn't really sure and in theory he'd explained it more than once.

Concentrating, he tapped a six digit number into the silver keypad on the blue door and I noticed the distinctive pink shade of his cardboard coffee cup as he brought it up to his lips.

'Where did you get the coffee?' I asked.

'Coffee shop,' he replied smartly. 'Down the street.'

We must have just missed each other. The thought

of Joe buying coffee from Sarah without either of them knowing who the other was gave me an unexpected thrill I hadn't felt since she worked weekends at the big Tesco when she was sixteen, and texted to tell me Dev Jones, my unrequited sixth form crush, was looking at condoms in the personal care aisle.

'It's pretty good for outside London,' he added.

'Wild that something as rare as coffee exists outside a capital city,' I replied, leaping to Sarah's defence. 'There are other places in the country, don't be such a snob.'

Biting his lip to restrain a grin, he held the door open with his body, forcing me to sidle past him to pass through the old narrow entrance, coffee and pastry held up above his head. The smell of last night's barbecue clung to his hair, the smoky aroma blending beautifully with his warm skin and fresh deodorant. I breathed in as I passed, my back brushing against his front, and my head swam.

This man was going to be the death of me.

The shop was even more impressive on the inside than it was from the street. I inhaled the fresh paint, wood-stain and boxes and boxes of brand-new, unread books. To me it was even better than new car, cut grass or freshly washed sheets. I wished there was a way to bottle it and keep it forever, but I must've bought at least a dozen different 'bookshop-scented' candles and was still searching for the perfect blend. No one could capture this magic.

As Joe closed the door behind us, I found myself in front of a table full of contemporary romance. These were the books I'd turned to when things fell apart with

CJ, the stories that helped me believe life wouldn't always be so miserable and imagine a time I might feel good again. Emily Henry, Mhairi McFarlane, Elena Armas, Tessa Bailey, Tia Williams, Lucy Vine, Rebecca Serle, Sophie Cousens, Kennedy Ryan, Jasmine Guillory, Sarah MacLean, Beth O'Leary, Fallon Ballard, Ali Hazelwood, Sarah Adams, Hannah Grace, Lucy Score, Lia Louis, the list went on, the list was endless. So many women writing so many words and every single story essential. Charlotte had covered all her bases, historical, fantasy, sci-fi, classics, graphic novels and even a few select thrillers even though I knew they were not her thing at all. The other side of the shop was dominated by her immense YA section and the thrill of seeing so many different books from so many different authors was overwhelming, every kind of person seen, heard and represented. I turned in a slow circle and breathed in deeply. Paper and ink and binding glue. Perfection.

'I've always loved the smell of books,' Joe said, reading my mind. He picked up a beautiful hardback edition of *Wuthering Heights*, one I hadn't seen before, opened it up and sniffed. I turned away from the rapturous look on his face and wandered over to the small collection of second-hand books on the back wall.

'Don't you think there's something fascinating about used books?' he asked. 'Right this second, you're looking at a book that's been read a dozen times by a dozen different people over more years than you've been alive. I can never get over it, the thought of one person sitting down to write a story and all the different people who pick it up over the years and read it. The same words taking on a completely different meaning every time.'

'Joe Walsh, you're a secret romantic,' I teased. 'I never would've guessed.'

A small smile played on his face and he looked over at me, Emily Brontë in hand.

'Never said it was a secret.'

As usual, Sarah was correct. I barely knew him. Surrounded by books, I felt safer than before, like I was on home ground, like I could be brave.

'What's the most romantic thing you've ever done?' I asked.

The smile faded into something more complicated and he shook his head very gently. 'Depends who you ask.'

Turning his back, he took himself off to inspect the historical fiction shelves, leaving me behind.

The bookcases opened up to a space around the till, a beautiful bookish mural of women writers painted on the back wall and a narrow corridor off to one side leading away to the back of the building. I wandered down the corridor, running my fingertips over the walls. Maybe, when he wasn't being impossibly frustrating, Joe was a romantic. Not the breezing-into-a-fancy-restaurant-with-a-dozen-red-roses kind but personally I'd never been interested in those kind of generic gestures anyway. Everyone's definition of romance was different. One woman's rose petals scattered through the house was another woman's hiding a bag of Mini Eggs in your handbag and I for one was definitely a Mini Eggs girl. Imagine trying to feel sexy when you knew you were going to have to vacuum up those petals in the morning. Dried me up faster than salt on a slug.

Charlotte's small back office-slash-stockroom was already full to overflowing, organised chaos compared to the bright and airy front of the shop. Ancient wooden beams supported the low ceiling and there were dozens of cardboard boxes stacked up against whitewashed walls, a heavy-looking desk tucked away in the corner with a computer on top and my dad's old laser printer hidden underneath. The room was dimly lit with only one small window, perfect for protecting delicate books and softening the edges of everything it touched. Aside from the addition of electricity, I could easily believe nothing had changed about this room since the place was built, hundreds of years ago. It smelled old but in a warm, reassuring way. Nothing bad could happen to you in here. Where the shop was all shelfies, selfies, loud debates and sweet cream nitro cold brew, this room was made for cups of tea and curling up with a good book that left you full of feeling, long after the tea went cold. Flicking through a pile of glittery stickers on the desk, I smiled. I was so proud of Charlotte.

'I've got to hand it to her, your sister has done a good job with this place.'

Joe appeared at the end of the hallway, his shoulders barely squeezing through the door. He stooped to dodge one of the beams, marvelling at his surroundings as he came closer and dominating the enclosed space with his physicality.

'She really has,' I agreed, wrapping my cardigan tightly around me, my last line of defence. 'You forget so quickly, don't you? I should've known she'd ace this, she's so sure of herself. I definitely had more faith in myself when I was eighteen.'

'When I was eighteen, I didn't have a clue.' He followed up with a rich, deep chuckle that echoed off the low ceiling and reverberated through me. 'I was human chaos back then. Always acting on impulse, no concern for what might come next.'

'Do you act on impulse now?' I asked before I could bite back the words.

He looked down at the copy of *Wuthering Heights* still in his hands, opened the cover and flicked through the pages before setting it down carefully.

'Sometimes.'

I backed into the edge of the desk, feeling my way around until I was safely behind it, and dropped my bag on the surface with a dull thud. There was a single box of books next to the computer and I feigned interest in its contents, afraid that if he caught me in his gaze again I wouldn't be able to move. Inside was an untouched stack of freshly printed pink books. What else but *Butterflies*? My own book was now officially stalking me.

'A chaotic romantic with impulse control,' I replied with a hitch in my voice as I closed up the box. 'Sounds dangerous.'

'Mmm. If I were you, I'd stay away from a man like that.'

'I'm trying.'

It was so quiet. No whirr of air conditioning, no rumble of traffic, only the muffled sound of footsteps on the concrete floor and my own erratic breathing.

Joe reached his arms up over his head and grabbed hold of one of the wooden beams, testing its hold before leaning into it. His body blocked out almost all the light from the little window, casting him in shadows and making it impossible to read his expression. I ran my hand across the smooth surface of the desk. It felt solid.

'What changed?' I asked, running his words back to myself.

'What do you mean?' Joe replied without moving.

'You said you *were* human chaos. What changed?'

He didn't reply right away, waiting until he knew what he wanted to say before he said it.

'It wasn't one thing,' he said with a tilt of his head. 'My mum left Boston, moved back here, up to Scotland, a couple of years earlier and she wasn't in the best health. I wasn't enjoying my job, and there were, I don't know, other things.'

'Romantic things?' An undeniable stab of jealousy stuck in my side.

'Lots of things,' he said vaguely. 'I needed a change. I needed to change.'

'So you moved back to London.'

He nodded. 'New York is an incredible place but it's very easy to play Peter Pan for way too long. As long as you take your career seriously, you don't really have to take life seriously, and my New York decisions were not always that smart.'

'But you're different now?' I said. I hoped.

'How come you went into teaching?' Joe asked, deflecting my question with a question. 'Your whole family is in publishing one way or another but you're a teacher. Why?'

Sinking into the chair behind the desk, I rested my chin on my clasped hands. If he didn't want to answer my question properly, I didn't have to answer his properly either.

'Because I'm only teaching kids until I find a rich husband,' I reminded him. 'I must still be looking.'

Maybe I was imagining it but even in the low light

of the stockroom, I thought I could see a pink tint take to his complexion. 'I might have been wrong,' he replied. 'But you aren't easy to read, Sophie Taylor.'

The chair behind the desk was very comfortable, a heavy wooden frame with old, soft leather cushions. Once upon a time, I imagined it might've been too firm, too overstuffed to stay in for long, but now, when I sat back, the cushions gave and I sank into them with ease.

'The truth is, I don't really know why,' I confessed, meeting honesty with honesty. 'When I was younger, I really wanted to be a writer. You should see the *Twilight* fanfic I wrote when I was a teenager, actually, no you shouldn't. No one can read that ever.'

Joe laughed softly but let me carry on speaking.

'You're right though, it should've been easy. Both of my parents, my godfather and my brother were already in the industry, any of them would've helped me find a job.'

'You wouldn't have been the first publishing nepo baby,' he agreed. 'What stopped you?'

I traced the patterns in the surface of the desk. The grain of the wood had been smoothed out over who knew how many years by people sitting here doing who knew what. Maybe great novels had been written at this desk. Or love letters. Or maybe it had only been used to do the accounts and play snakes and ladders. There was no way to know.

'I was scared,' I told him, surprised at how easy it was to say out loud in front of him. 'Everyone thought I would graduate with a great literary novel in my back pocket. Mum was convinced I was going to be the next Donna Tartt, Dad was always bragging to everyone at work about how talented I was, but all I had were a dozen first chapters of a dozen different books and they were all terrible.'

'I bet they weren't, I bet they were good.'

'They weren't good enough for Hugh and Pandora Taylor's daughter.'

I thought back to all those nights I spent in front of a laptop, trying to construct clever sentences and create bold imagery, always imagining my parents reading over my shoulder. I desperately wanted to write something important and literary but my heart just wasn't in it.

'When I gave up trying to write something they would approve of, the thought of taking a job in publishing felt like punishment. I didn't want to move home so there wasn't a lot of time to come up with an alternative career path.'

'Sophie, no one expects a twenty-one-year-old to have it all figured out,' Joe said. 'You're being incredibly hard on yourself.'

I shook my head and looked around the room. 'Charlotte is only eighteen and look at this. If I didn't have something else, I would've been dragged into one of their offices by the scruff of my neck and I couldn't stomach the thought. Teaching seemed like a good back-up plan.'

An unseeable cloud passed over the sun somewhere high above us and filled the whole room with shadows. I rested my chin on the boxful of *Butterflies* and sighed.

'I thought it would be easy but it isn't. All those people who think teaching is a cop-out ought to spend one week dealing with a bunch of ten-year-olds, prefer-ably two weeks before the summer holidays,' I said, opening the door to happier memories. 'But I love it. Obviously not the admin or the bureaucracy, and I swear, some of the parents were put on this earth to test my will to live, but every day is different. I like the creativity and yes, I know it's a cliché but the kids are so great. Mostly because they leave our school before they've been ruined by hormones and social media – but that's a secondary school problem, not mine.'

'But do you love teaching more than writing?' Joe asked, still holding his position. His face was completely blotted out now, his body outlined by what little light made it through the window.

'I don't have an answer to that yet,' I admitted. 'They're so different. With teaching, I'm surrounded by people all day. When I'm writing, it's just me. I don't know if I would like that all the time.'

'It can be a lonely career,' he acknowledged. 'Most writers I know are introverts, they prefer their own company.'

'Maybe most writers you know are psychopaths,' I suggested and he smiled.

Outside, the clouds passed and Joe's features slowly emerged from the shadows. He was staring intently, not at me but at my book.

'When I was younger, I wanted to be a writer too.' He let go of the ceiling beam and came closer to the desk to pick up his own copy of *Butterflies*, tapping it against his open palm like he was trying to shake something loose.

'Really?' It was difficult to imagine. CJ fit the stereotype, Joe didn't. I couldn't imagine him tearing back into his dorm room, hanging up his lacrosse boots and settling down to pour his thoughts into a Moleskine journal. If there was such a thing as lacrosse boots. I needed to read more sports romances.

211

Thumbing his way through the pages, Joe's eyes scanned my words before settling somewhere in the middle of the book. Somewhere that looked dangerously close to chapter seventeen.

'I did, but I wasn't very good at it. Not like you.'

'There are plenty of people who don't think I'm very good at it,' I replied with a laugh.

I watched his eyes scan the pages until he found what he was looking for. Clearing his throat, Joe moved until the light from the window shone directly on the book.

'*When his eyes find mine, everything I've been fighting against falls away,*' he read in a measured, certain voice.

Oh no.

It was chapter seventeen.

'*He comes closer until he is all I can see or breathe, the sound of his voice rumbling like thunder in my ears. "Why did you dance with him?" Eric demands to know. I don't have an answer ready and he doesn't give me a chance to think of one. "I've never been so mad at you," he whispers as his hand clamps my upper arm, tight enough to leave fingerprints. "You're the one who left," I tell him, furious at his reaction but at the same time, I felt myself melting at my core, "what did you want me to do?" I wanted him angry, I wanted him mine. Jealousy tightens his grip on my arm and his gaze sears my soul. "I want you to get on your knees," he breathes. "And I want you to show me you're sorry—"*'

'You're not going to believe this but I'm familiar with the story,' I said, curling the sleeves of my cardigan around my fingers to stop my nails from cutting into the flesh of my palms. 'I don't need a DIY audiobook.'

What I did need was a glass of cold water, a fan and

maybe a chastity belt. I felt like a swan, gliding elegantly on the surface for all to see while my legs kicked wildly under the surface, struggling to keep up the pretence. Only I couldn't feel my legs, just the swirling heat between them.

'It's difficult for me to believe someone as odious as your ex-boyfriend could inspire something as hot as this.' Joe perched on the edge of the desk, still holding the book, his forefinger saving the page. I crossed my legs at the ankles and squeezed my thighs as tightly as possible, hoping to weld them together under my dress. 'I wish I could understand what you saw in him?'

'He did inspire it but not in the way you think,' I told him. 'I was bored and lonely, CJ was what I had, the relationship between Eric and Jenna was what I wanted.'

I shrugged off my cardigan before I could overheat. It was stuffy in the stockroom. Stuffy and close and so hot and why did the smell of old books blend so beautifully with the smell of Joe's skin?

'So it's your fantasy.'

Questions like that were why I didn't want to do interviews. If there had been any more fire in my cheeks, they could've used me to power a nuclear reactor.

'Only it doesn't read like a fantasy.' Joe opened the book again, reading on in his head. 'It reads like someone who knows exactly what she wants.'

He slid his finger down the page until he found what he was looking for and spoke my own words back to me, speaking so soft and low I had to strain to listen, even though I knew every single word backwards.

'"*That sorry excuse for a man could never touch you*

the way I can," Eric says as his hand moves down my arm, slowly stroking the back of my hand before passing over my bare thighs and slipping between my legs.'" Joe paused, his voice cracking, and I heard a sharp intake of breath before he started the next sentence. *'"He could never make you groan the way I can, he could never make you beg for more. He could never make you come the way I can, until all you see are stars and your body lies limp and breathless—'"*

'I've heard enough,' I said although when I heard the tremor in my voice I didn't even believe myself.

Leaving *Butterflies* on the desk, Joe stood up, effortlessly shoved the heavy antique to the side, and slowly, never once taking his eyes off mine, knelt down in front of me. He rested one palm on each of my knees and gently pushed my legs apart, moving closer until I could feel his breath, warm against my thighs.

'You can stop now,' I think I said. 'I've read *Iron Flame*, this is not your bookshop, this is not the throne of Tyrrendor and I'm not—'

'Not what?'

My eyes locked on his.

'Yours.'

A soft gasp escaped my lips as he let his hands glide over my skin, moving unbearably slowly, until they slid behind my hips, his fingers pressing into the soft curves of my body. He paused for one long heartbeat then yanked me forward until our bodies were flush, my arms instinctively circling his neck, his face tilted up towards mine and mine angled down towards his, drawn to him like a magnet. I couldn't read his mind but I didn't need to. His intentions were very clear and my body throbbed with anticipation.

'Do you really want me to stop?' he asked. 'Because I will if you ask me to.'

'I don't know what I want,' I said, a gentle moan escaping as his lips grazed my jaw.

'Yes, you do.' He teased the shoulder strap of my dress with one hand, the other still firmly grasping my hip, holding me in place. 'You want me to make you feel the way Eric makes Jenna feel in your book. You want me to make you come so hard you see stars.'

'And what do you want?' I asked when the heat of his mouth moved to my throat, his full lips and velvet tongue flicking against the tender skin. Between my thighs, I felt his fingers test the edge of my underwear and my back arched to bring him closer, unable to wait one second longer for what came next.

'You. More than I've ever wanted anything.'

'Hello?' a high-pitched voice called out from the other room. 'Este, are you in here?'

'Fuck!' The word came out through gritted teeth. 'Charlotte!'

My thighs slammed shut and I shot upright, pulling Joe to his feet then thrusting him into the chair. If it was even vaguely possible, he looked even more stunned than I felt. He shook his head sharply, blinking again and again as I hurled a copy of *Butterflies* into his lap to cover his raging erection.

'OK, that hurt,' he croaked with tears in his eyes.

'I hope it's you,' Charlotte yelled. 'Otherwise I'll assume it's burglars and you should know I'm a black belt in Krav Maga. I will kick your arse if I have to.'

As her footsteps echoed down the corridor that connected the shop to the stockroom, I positioned myself on the edge of the desk, but I was still far too close to Joe to be capable of rational thought. Grabbing my bag and cardigan, I bolted all the way across the tiny room, assuming what I hoped was a completely natural position, right as Charlotte burst in. Her grin faltered as she looked at Joe, shellshocked and swiping at his already perfect hair, then over to me, buttoning my cardigan, grinning like a maniac and leaning against a recycling bin with my legs tightly crossed.

'What's happening?' Her tiny pixie face was furious. 'What are you two doing?'

'Nothing,' we chorused in unison.

'You're both terrible liars,' she replied. 'Why are you so red? And why is he crying?'

'We were arguing,' Joe managed to say, still a little more high-pitched than usual.

Somehow, I managed to reset my face, raising my chin and pursing my lips to dispel any trace of desire. According to the dusty mirror on the opposite wall, it worked. I looked more like I'd been taste-testing cat food than preparing to . . . no, no, I would not think about it.

'About what?'

He cleared his throat but his voice still cracked when he spoke. 'About our favourite Elena Armas novel. I like *The Long Game* but Sophie's dead set on *The Spanish Love Deception*.'

'That makes sense because you probably love football and if I'd gone out with CJ as long as she did, I'd be fantasising about Aaron Blackford as well. But you're both wrong. True fans know all about *The American Roommate Experiment*.' Charlotte stood with her fists resting on her skinny hips, a pose I too had inherited from our mother but she definitely pulled it off with more authority. 'Soph, would you mind fucking off? I need to have a proper conversation with Este and you're bringing down the vibe.'

'Happy to,' I said, slinging my bag across my body without another glance in Joe's direction. 'See you both later.'

When I stepped out of the shop and onto the street, I was relieved to discover I hadn't slipped into an alternate dimension where I almost had sex with a man I barely knew on the cold concrete floor of my sister's bookshop stockroom. There were cars and buses and people carrying reusable shopping bags and not a single soul with their hand very nearly in my knickers.

Head rolling all the way back, I rested against the wall of the neighbouring building, a florist owned by a former touring guitarist for Led Zeppelin called Heavy Petal, and waited for all the chemical reactions popping off in my body to dissipate. Why hadn't I paid more attention in biology? Ali Hazelwood would know the scientific reason why my heart rate was sky-high, my pupils were dilated and I could still feel Joe's handprints on my thighs. Imagine writing romance novels and being a literal neuroscientist? English wasn't even her first language, the bloody overachiever. I needed to get a very serious grip on myself.

'Sophie! You're still here!'

And Joe flying out of the shop looking like he'd just seen inside the Ark of the Covenant wasn't going to help matters.

'Shouldn't you be talking to the shopkeeper, Este?' I asked, fussing around inside my handbag, a classic avoidance technique and possibly the only reason why women still carried handbags.

'That's why I need to talk to you.'

He grabbed hold of my forearm and my body betrayed me again, neurons firing, hormones releasing, legs wavering. 'What are we going to do about this situation?'

'Which situation?' I asked with a suddenly dry mouth.

'The situation in which your sister and the rest of your family think I wrote your book.'

He looked almost as annoyed as I used to feel and, I had to admit, I definitely preferred the expression on his face when it was looking up at me from in between my legs.

'Yeah, um, I think we're going to have to go with it for now,' I said, producing a claw clip from my bag to pull back my hair.

'Go with it,' Joe repeated. 'What do you mean, go with it?'

'I mean, you told everyone you're Este Cox so until one of us comes up with a decent explanation as to why that was a lie, guess what? You're Este Cox.'

'But I don't know what to say.'

'Twice in one day. There really is a first time for everything.

For the first time since we'd met, Joe looked completely at a loss. He did this to help you, I reminded myself, still avoiding his piercing blue eyes that had turned large and limpet, a move I was willing to bet he only ever pulled out for truly desperate occasions.

'Say as little as possible,' I instructed. 'I know that's going to be difficult but, if in doubt, keep your mouth shut. Talk about yourself instead, I can't imagine it'll be too difficult for you.'

'Come back in with me,' he begged, ignoring my gentle barb. 'I can't do it on my own, I'll fuck it up.'

'No you won't.' Pushing up onto my tiptoes, I leaned in to whisper in his ear. 'Because if you do, we'll never find out what would've happened if Charlotte hadn't walked in when she did.'

And with that, I walked away.

CHAPTER EIGHTEEN

My attempt to sneak back down to the cottage without being spotted was doomed from the start. I hadn't even made it past the kitchen window when two sharp raps on the glass made me jump, followed by the sound of the catch opening and my mother's voice.

'You asked me for my opinion and my opinion is you look like a dick.'

Why hadn't I tried crawling under the window again?

'Sophie,' Dad said, my back still turned to whatever was going on in there. 'Come in the kitchen, we need your opinion.'

I didn't want to go in the kitchen. I'd spent the entire walk back home trying to decide if I even wanted to go back home at all. I was a mess. Ideally, I wanted to find a nice cave, preferably with internet access so I could still watch TV, and spend the rest of my life as a hermit. They got a bad rap, hermits. You never heard it from their side, it wasn't like they could go around on a speaking tour extolling the values of hermitism otherwise they wouldn't be hermits after all but when I walked into the kitchen, I could really see the appeal.

My mother was standing in front of the fridge, bleeding exasperation, while my dad was, for reasons I was sure were about to be explained, dressed as a clown. Baggy trousers hooped at the waist, striped shirt, yellow tie, rainbow ruff and a big, bold, bright red nose.

'I don't want to know,' I told them both, holding up a hand to shield my eyes. 'What you do in private is up to you.'

'Your father,' Mum replied, ignoring my request as usual. 'Has decided this is how he wants to dress for his party tonight.'

'Because it goes with the theme.' He pulled on his suspenders until a flap on the back of his trousers flopped down to reveal polka dot bloomers. 'Think about it, publishing is a circus, isn't it? And we're all clowns.'

'Speak for yourself.' Mum pressed her forefingers into her temples. 'This is why you wanted a bouncy castle? And the marquee?'

Dad scraped one huge clown shoe back and forth across the slate tiles. 'It's more of a stripy tent.'

She stared at him with a glare so fierce, it was a wonder he was still standing. 'Hugh, have you hired a circus tent?'

'The proper terminology is a big top.'

He turned to face me and I could see his hand pumping away at something in his pocket but whatever was supposed to be happening, wasn't. 'Bugger,' he muttered, pulling out a long clear tube with a blue pump on the end. 'Water is supposed to shoot out of the daisy. I'll have to look at it.'

'There's a reason you've only pulled this out on the day of the party and that's because you knew what I would say,' Mum stated. 'You are not wearing that to your party, Hugh, I have invited Jonathan Franzen.'

'He's a great laugh is Jonathan,' Dad mumbled, still preoccupied with his failed water pump. 'You need to see it with the wig. It doesn't work without the wig.'

'Morning, everybody, how are we, and Dad, what in the utter fuck are you doing?'

My brother stood in the kitchen doorway, a look of abject horror on his face. Behind him was Sanjit, Sanjit's mother and Sanjit's father, all three of whom looked even more appalled than William which was no mean feat.

'Come to think of it, I don't want to know,' he said, holding up his hands before anyone could speak. 'Sanj, go and wait in the car, we won't be stopping for a cup of tea after all. I need to go home and wash out my eyeballs.'

'Pandora, Hugh,' Sanjit raised his hand in a hello-slash-goodbye as he hurried his parents out the house as quickly as they'd walked in. 'Can't wait for the party.'

'It's themed!' Dad shouted and Sanjit raised a thumbs up over his head without stopping.

'I only came to drop off the serviettes.' William dumped a square-shaped cardboard box on the kitchen table. 'They say "Happy Sixtieth Hugh" but I think there's still enough time to alter them to "Dad's lost his mind, help yourself to canapés".'

'See?' Mum stood triumphant. 'What did I say?'

'None of you understand the vision,' Dad grumbled as he took himself off upstairs in a huff. 'I'm disappointed in you, Sophie!'

'What did I do?' I asked, as my brother and mother stood around the kitchen table shaking their heads at me.

'He's not wearing it. It'll finish Jeffrey Archer off and that won't help the property value,' Mum said before taking herself off into the conservatory, still muttering away.

'William, can I have a word?' I leapt in front of the open front door and my brother before he could escape.

'Have two, treat yourself,' William replied, holding up one hand to Sanjit in the car. 'What has got into Dad? Do you think he's had a funny turn?'

'There is nothing funny about that outfit. Jeffrey Archer nothing, if Dad drops his drawers in front of me, I won't make it.'

'Don't panic, Mum will talk him out of it,' he said with complete certainty that was, in fairness, well placed.

Mum almost always talked Dad out of his more random decisions including, but not limited to, his obsession with learning to ride a penny farthing, a moustache that made him look exactly like Joseph Stalin and that time he became obsessed with Channing Tatum and wanted to offer him a book deal to write the great American novel 'he just knew he had inside him'. Not to say Magic Mike couldn't pull it out the bag but the obsession was mostly based on the fact my dad watched *Step Up* and *She's the Man* on a constant loop while recovering from back surgery and was on a lot of painkillers. Back surgery he needed because Mum failed to talk him out of the penny farthing well enough.

'Never mind Dad,' William said cheerfully. 'I have to

say I'm very impressed at how you managed to take one great big fucking mess and make it even worse. Incredible work, well done.'

'Thanks,' I replied. 'Wait, are you speaking as my agent or my brother?'

'Agent. As your brother, I still can't even conceive of you having written *Butterflies*. Do you know how many times you used the word "cock" in that book?'

'It was more than once.'

'It was fourteen times.' He slapped the back of one hand against the other palm as he spoke, emphasising each syllable. 'Thank god you had the presence of mind to make the male character American. The thought of an English accent saying the things you put in that book gives me the ick. Ass, sexy. Arse, not sexy. In fact, what is a sexy British word for your backside? Bum? Buttocks? Trouser turnips?'

'Can we concentrate for a minute?' I asked. 'There are more urgent matters to deal with.'

'Like the fact our baby sister is one iced coffee away from telling the world Joe wrote your book?'

'That's one of them,' I agreed gloomily. 'We have terrible parents. Who stands there and watches their child blackmail another human being and does nothing?'

'You tell me, you're the teacher.'

Sanjit honked and William waved to signify we were almost done.

'As your agent, as far as I can see, you've only two options,' he said. 'One, you tell everyone the truth which solves all our problems and makes mine and Mal's lives considerably easier into the bargain.'

'Mal.' I groaned and slapped my hand over my face. 'He's going to lose his mind when he hears about this.'

'Oh yes, he's going to kill you,' William confirmed as though it was a matter of fact. 'Slowly and painfully if you decide on option number two.'

'Which is?'

'You and Mr Walsh come to an agreement in which he acts as the public face of Este Cox and you remain anonymous. I wouldn't advise it but it's been done before.'

I stared off into the middle distance, imagining it for a moment. Could it work? Joe was much happier in the spotlight than me. He could tour, do the interviews, paste his face all over social media, and I could keep my job and keep writing.

'One thing to keep in mind, if you take that route,' William said sternly, cutting into my daydream. 'It would have to be a real business relationship. Contracts, financials, we'd have to NDA him up the wazoo.'

'And that's a legal term, is it?' I asked.

'What I'm saying is, it's bullshit not to claim your own book,' he replied. 'And most importantly, unless you want to be sued to high heavens when it all goes tits up, you definitely won't be able to shag Joe once we've got a contract in place.'

'Shag Joe?' I exclaimed loudly enough for the Bhattas to hear and set off a new flurry of activity in the car. 'What makes you say that? I don't want to shag Joe.'

'Then you're the only one,' he said, switching gears with a frustrated sigh. 'Come on, Soph, tell everyone the truth. All this stuff you're panicking about, it's all in your head. Even if it wasn't, who fucking cares?'

'But Mum and Dad—' I started until he held up a hand to cut me off.

'But Mum and Dad nothing,' he replied. 'That's an

excuse and we both know it. As your agent, I'll go along with whatever you decide but as your brother, I'm begging you, rip off the plaster, tell the truth. It'll only get worse the longer you leave it. The clock is ticking. If you think it's bad now, wait until Charlotte reveals it's Joe, Mal loses his shit because your publisher didn't control the announcement, and next thing you know everyone thinks a man wrote *Butterflies* and Joe's on *Oprah*.'

The image flashed in front of my eyes, the two of them bonding over freshly squeezed orange juice in her back garden in Montecito, a tear in Oprah's eye as Joe detailed his inspiration for the tender love affair between Jenna and Eric.

'Make your decision, I'll back you up,' William promised, walking back to the car. 'But you are going to have to make it.'

A sour feeling turned in my belly as they drove away, Sanjit's dad staring at me out the rear passenger window with terrified eyes, and it had nothing to do with the fact I'd only consumed a croissant, a chocolate chip cookie and a rocket fuel coconut coffee on an empty stomach. William was right.

Joe, Este Cox and I were all running out of time.

CHAPTER NINETEEN

Making sure the front door to the cottage was securely locked, I took the only course of action I could think of and prepared to settle in for some very serious thinking in the best possible place for the task.

The bath.

I sank into the tub like sugar slipped through the foam on a cappuccino, my troubles dissolving away into the water. Daytime baths were better than night-time baths, this was my most fervently held belief in life. They were so much more decadent – who had time to soak in a giant tub full of hot water and bubbles in the middle of the day? Rich people, that's who. People who gave guided tours of their homes on the *Architectural Digest* YouTube channel always had a massive bath next to a window which meant they had too much money and no neighbours. There wasn't a problem on earth that couldn't be fixed with a soak. So many of my best decisions had been made here, the decision to give teaching a shot, finally realising sheet masks were just slimy tissues with holes cut in and the realisation I was allowed to DNF *Infinite Jest* to name but three. Even the initial inspiration for *Butterflies* came to me during a bath.

The memory was so clear. CJ was out again, another literary event he couldn't or wouldn't take me to. It was late and he still wasn't home when he said he would be when I lay back in the bath and closed my eyes to picture my life exactly how I wished it was. Instead of a teacher, I was a writer. Instead of living in the suburbs of London, I was on holiday in America, and instead of an emotionally and physically absent English arsehole, there was a gorgeous, manly cowboy in my bed, one who knew exactly what he was doing with every single part of me and would kill any other man who even dared to look in my direction. When CJ could only manage a five-minute fumble, Eric took his time. When CJ forgot my birthday, Eric celebrated Jenna's with multiple orgasms. I gave Jenna all my problems then created Eric as the solution. The only problem was, I couldn't make my fantasy true.

But what to do now? Decision number one, school. Abbey Hill was notoriously small 'c' conservative in a big 'c' Conservative town. Mrs Hedges, our headteacher, wasn't exactly known for her liberal attitude, and I couldn't see her, the board of governors or the parents' association jumping up and down with joy to find out their new head of year five had been secretly churning out smut on the weekends. I'd been so proud when she offered me the job back in the spring but now I wasn't so sure. I could handle a lot, more than was probably healthy, but writing, teaching and being head of year? It was a lot of responsibility, and you couldn't half-arse teaching. Well, some people did but they were terrible human beings and only made more work for the rest of us.

Writing had always been my dream but would I still love it as much if it was my full-time job? And what if my next book bombed, was I giving up a steady career on a whim? There was no way to know. That was the first decision to be made – was I prepared to sacrifice my teaching career to take a chance on writing?

Decision number two, what to do about Joe. I was still swinging wildly between wishing I'd never met him and wishing he'd bent me over and taken me in the karaoke room, deposit be damned. The man hadn't even kissed me but what had happened in the stockroom had been more erotic than my entire relationship with CJ. Once, when I dared to suggest our love life could be a little spicier, I came home to find him standing naked in the middle of the living room, reading Henry Miller aloud. According to him, it was supposed to be sexy but the only thing it spurred in me was a desire to turn up the heating. He was evidently *very* cold.

Just the thought of Joe's mouth on my neck, his fingers between my thighs, was enough to make me sink lower under the bubbles until the only things above water were my wide, dilated eyes, wallowing like a sex-starved hippo. My nipples puckered as my hand retraced Joe's journey, and I closed my eyes, surrendering to the fantasy and very much hoping an imaginary go on Joe would be enough to clear my mind.

'Sophie?'

There were only two people with keys to the cottage.

I was one of them. The man currently starring in my fantasy was the other.

'Don't come in the bathroom,' I shrieked, pressing

my naked body against the side of the bathtub, water splashing everywhere. In my rush, I'd locked the front door but the door to the bathroom was only pushed to. All Joe had to do was take two steps to the left to see me in all my glory.

'Why, what's wrong?' he asked, taking two steps to the left. 'Oh.'

'Oh,' I agreed, still clinging to the side of the tub, chin hooked over the side. The bubbles were dissipating at a dangerous rate. 'I thought you'd be gone ages. How did you escape Charlotte so quickly?'

He stayed where he was but, in a partial-gentleman move, kept his eyes on the ceiling.

'Your mum texted and said she needed me back at the house.'

'For what?'

'Don't know. Maybe she needs a big strong man to do something big and strong and manly.'

For now at least, I was definitely swinging towards wishing I'd never met him.

'I'm expected in the conservatory in five minutes,' he said, 'or your mum is going to send her minions after me.'

'She'll have a stopwatch going,' I replied, trying to move as little as possible. 'But everything went OK with Charlotte and Este?'

He brushed imaginary fluff off his shoulders.

'Your secret is safe. Turns out I'm a natural at this author business. If you hadn't come on to me in the stockroom like that, I wouldn't have been so mixed up in the first place. You were panicking over nothing.'

'Me come on to you?' The water swirled around my waist and I shifted my position, surging against the sides of the bath. 'You came on to me! All I did was sit in a chair. And you were the one panicking, not me.'

'Recollections may differ,' Joe said with airy dismissal. 'Agree to disagree.'

'I agree to nothing.' I reached for a towel that was just beyond my fingertips, straining over the cold edge of the tub. 'Can you close the door so I can get out please?'

The gentlemanly façade slipped away and Joe's eyes found mine, that crooked smile appearing on his face. He didn't budge.

'Joe, please,' I said with a frustrated groan.

'Oh, I like that. Say it again,' he whispered, unfastening the top two buttons of his shirt.

The water moved against me again, lapping at every inch of my exposed body like soft warm fingertips. 'Joe, I'm serious.'

'So am I,' he replied with darkening eyes. 'I like it when you ask nicely. Makes me wonder what else you might ask for in the right circumstances.'

'You've only got five minutes,' I reminded him, aiming for sarcasm but landing closer to a genuine query. 'Is that enough for you?'

'Not for me but you'd be amazed at what I can do for you in that amount of time.'

He showed no sign of moving, the devilish smile on his face fixed and daring. Still warm in the water, I weighed up my options. Stay where I was, completely at his mercy, or get out the bath and close the door myself.

So many of my best decisions were made in the bath.

If he wanted to play games, we'd play games.

'OK then,' I said. 'I'll get my own towel.'

231

Before I could talk myself out of it, I stood up, warm water running off my body and nothing but judiciously placed bubbles to cover my blushes. A quick check on Joe showed he was still standing but only just. With one hand on the wall, I climbed quickly but carefully out of the tub, reaching for the thick white towel waiting for me on the stand beside the bath. Joe gaped in the doorway, eyes like saucers and a conspicuous bulge straining against his jeans.

'You're testing me, Sophie Taylor,' he breathed as I wrapped the towel around myself.

'And I reckon you're down to about two minutes,' I replied, heart pounding all the way up into my throat. 'Probably wouldn't go back up to the house with a hard on if I were you.'

We both looked at his crotch at the same time, Joe adjusting his trousers. Full of fake confidence, I sashayed past him into the living room where the curtains still separated our sleeping areas to grab the first set of clothes I could lay my hands on.

One thing was for sure. Joe *definitely* didn't need me to turn up the heating.

We didn't share a single word on the way back to the house. I had to double my usual pace to keep up, Joe's long legs striding purposefully as though he were trying to outrun the memory of what had just happened.

'Don't you have better things to do than follow me around?' he said as I skipped around the bench halfway up the garden to get a couple of feet in front of him. 'Surely you could be working on your next book or coming up with new and exciting ways to torture me?'

'I'm not following you,' I replied, tucking his last comment away for later. 'It's lunchtime, I'm hungry. *I'm* going to *my* parents' house to make *myself* a sandwich if that's all right with you.'

He grunted as he hopped over a plaster cast of Horatio's skull, one of Dad's favourite Shakespeare-themed garden ornaments.

'Sophie, I'm begging you,' Joe said with a look of true anguish on his face. 'All I need is a five-minute break where I don't have to think about *Butterflies* or Este Cox or you, naked or otherwise. Is that too much to ask?'

The sleeves of my cardigan hung over my hands and I tucked my fingers into little fists as I stepped aside to let him past.

'I got us into this mess, I'll get us out,' he added. 'Until then, I'll play author.'

'So you're going to carry on pretending to be Este Cox?'

'It's not as though I don't know women,' he replied with a well-timed little snort. It was helpful, I was overdue a reminder of his reputation. 'What I mean is, I have lots of female friends. My best friend is a woman.'

'Course she is.' I nodded even though my expression did not match my words. 'And I'm sure you're very close to your mother.'

'Close enough not to lie to her about writing a best-selling novel,' he retorted, making me snap back with surprise. 'You go and make your sandwich, I'll continue to save your arse. Really, how hard could it be?'

He stormed off into the conservatory, leaving me standing outside without a response. I'd spent an awful lot of time thinking about how all of this was affecting me and not a single second wondering what it might be doing to Joe. He seemed almost as annoyed about the whole thing as I was, so why offer to continue with the charade? This was an interesting development.

'Joseph,' I heard my mother gush. 'Come in, come in, we're so thrilled to have you join us.'

Us? Who else was in there?

Too nosy for my own good, I followed him inside and closed the door behind me. The blinds had been dropped to shade against the sun but there was still plenty of light coming in from the glass roof, more than enough to illuminate the circle of half a dozen or so chairs, each of them occupied by one of my parents' literary luminary friends. Jericka was back, along with several other writers and editors I recognised, every single one of them a prize winner or critical darling or both, and they were all beaming at Joe.

The only person who wasn't smiling was CJ.

'What is this?' I asked on Joe's behalf since he hadn't moved a muscle since he came inside and seemed to have lost the ability to speak.

'Sophie!' Mum looked up at me with surprise as though she'd suddenly remembered I existed. 'Just a small gathering of pals. Every couple of months we throw together something of an informal salon and since everyone was coming for the party anyway I thought it might be fun to have a little lunchtime get-together and chat with Joseph about his beautiful book.'

'His beautiful book . . . you mean *Butterflies*?' I cast an eye around the room to see they were all clutching the same pink paperback. How things had changed in the last twenty-four hours.

'You're welcome to join us,' she replied, searching for a spare chair but finding only a floor cushion that had seen much better days and pointing me towards it.

'But I must ask you not to bring a negative energy to this space. We're all entitled to our opinions and, while I believe artists can only grow from constructive criticism, this is not a critiquing session. Joseph is an invited guest and we want him to feel this is a safe space for him to discuss the work.'

'Discuss the work?'

This time Joe was the echo. Springing into life, diaphanous blue blouse floating around her like a Marks & Spencer's Finest forcefield, Mum directed Joe into the only empty chair left in the room, reaching up to her full five feet of height to push down on his shoulders until he sat, facing the crowd. Not knowing what else to do, I obediently trailed over to the floor cushion, and circled it before settling down, tail between my legs like a bad dog.

'I know it's your first time, so we'll be gentle,' Mum said with a sly smile I did not care for one bit. 'Everyone here has been sworn to secrecy so there's no need to worry about your identity getting out. If only because Charlotte would murder me in my bed if it did.'

The pain I'd seen in Joe's eyes slowly transformed into panic as he realised what was happening.

'Mrs Taylor, I'd love to discuss the book with you but now isn't a great time—'

'Now is a perfect time,' she replied. 'Now, who wants to start us off?'

'But it's Hugh's day.' Joe stood so quickly he bumped his head on the slanted ceiling. 'We should be celebrating him, not banging on about a book. The book. My book. And please call me Joe.'

'Hugh's gone to the train station to pick up that ingrate, Nelson Allen,' Mum said as she coaxed him

235

back into his seat. 'We're all here, we've all read the book and we've all got questions.'

His bottom lip quivered as he took in all the eager faces. 'You've all read it. All of you?'

'Some of us more recently than others.' Jericka made a show of holding up her copy, making sure everyone could see the cracked spine, even though I was fairly sure she hadn't even glanced at it until last night, as she shot CJ and his pristine book a filthy look. 'Writing can be such lonely work, especially when one is operating under a pseudonym. We want you to know we're here for you.'

'That's very kind.'

With woeful surrender, Joe tucked his feet under his chair and slipped his hands between his tightly squeezed thighs as though trying to make himself invisible.

'Shall we start with an easy one?' Mum suggested and Joe nodded readily. 'Your book approaches female sexuality with such vulnerability, always tying the sex to Jenna's emotional growth, even in her most daring and graphic encounters. I would love to get some insight into your process when it comes to putting yourself so squarely in a woman's position.'

A hush fell over the room and I rested my back against the wall, unable to stop a tiny little smirk from appearing. What was it he said? He could play author, how hard could it be? We were about to find out.

'That's an easy one, is it?' He unbuttoned the cuffs of his shirt and slowly, studiously rolled them up to the elbow. Damn a man who knew the power of a nicely turned forearm. 'In all honesty, Mrs Taylor, I don't know. I didn't really think that much about it.'

It was, to be fair, the same answer I would've given.

'An instinctive writer,' Mum breathed. 'The natural-istic approach certainly comes through in the dialogue.'

Incapable of holding her question back a second longer, Jericka jumped in. 'It's such a powerful gift, to be able to translate a woman's desire into words. What made you want to explore the female experience in this way rather than the man's?'

A murmur of approval ran around the room but Joe only stared at them all with his mouth open, a six-foot-five goldfish floundering in the bowl of my mother's conservatory.

'Sophie was telling me, I mean, I was telling Sophie about my inspiration earlier on,' he said, stumbling over his words and looking to me for help I wasn't quite ready to give. 'It was a fantasy. That's right, a fantasy inspired by an ex-boyfriend. I mean ex-girlfriend. I mean, an unfulfilling relationship.'

'No one in this group is here to judge a person's sexual experimentation or identity,' replied a frail older gentleman who had to be ninety if he was a day. 'We're very open-minded. As you must be, considering the content of chapter five.'

'It was a girlfriend,' Joe insisted, deepening his voice and glancing in CJ's general direction. 'A pretentious, boring girlfriend who didn't know a good thing when she had it.'

'Was she the one who gave you such insight into the female orgasm?' asked Jericka, her book falling open easily to the page she was looking for. 'Here, in chapter twenty-nine for example, *I felt dizzy as he filled me up, stretching me to meet his needs, to make me his and claim me as his own. The rhythmic movements of my hips surrendering to his more frenetic pace as that*

237

exquisite sensation, a whisper that started far away began to sing sweet and clear, threatening to overwhelm me as his thick, heavy cock drove—'

'Yes. No. Well, it's very hard to say,' Joe spluttered, cutting her off as everyone else in the room scoured the book for the relevant section. 'I think too many people get caught up in the sex. Don't you think the overall story is more important than the shagg – sorry, the sex?'

Out the corner of my eye, I saw Aunt Carole watching from the door that led to the living room. She looked as though she'd just got back from some kind of strenuous activity, her face damp, cheeks highly coloured and, in her shaking hand, she carried the most battered and well-read copy of my book – of any book – I had ever seen.

'I would argue the sex is the story,' Jericka replied as my aunt crept in, pressed up against the wall like a shadow. 'So often we see the female character's self-actualisation channelled through the male gaze, leaving us with either an underdeveloped naïf awakened to the wonder of ecstatic sex by her lover, or a promiscuous but invariably unhappy woman who cannot connect to her emotions until the hero shows her how. You have presented us with a real, multi-layered, nuanced woman and that's so rare, Joseph—'

'No, it isn't,' I said, the words out my mouth before I could second guess them.

'Sophie.'

My mother said my name like a warning shot across the bow.

'But it isn't,' I insisted, all eyes on me. 'There are hundreds of books out there with "real women" in them, thousands, but you haven't read them because you think they're beneath you.'

It was not a suggestion that went down well.

'Soph, it's not that we consider your opinion invalid,' CJ leaned forwards, condescending as ever, 'but you've said yourself *Bridget Jones's Diary* is your favourite book of all time. A masterpiece, I think, is what you called it when I asked you to defend the position.'

'There's nothing to defend,' I replied as I stood up. I would not take this sitting down, literally, and as usual, he was begging for a slap. 'It *is* a masterpiece. Not one of you would argue if I said *Pride and Prejudice* was my favourite book and the only thing that separates them is two hundred years.'

'Personally, I've always considered the canonical importance of Austen to be overblown,' CJ directed his response to the frail older gentleman who nodded in agreement. '*Northanger Abbey* aside, obviously.'

'Obviously,' the old gent snorted in agreement.

'Sophie, we're not here to debate a genre,' my mother admonished. 'We're here to listen to Joe. Who else has a question?'

'Are you Eric?' Aunt Carole blurted out, the book grasped tightly in her sweaty hands. 'Is he based on you and your. . . physical attributes?'

'Joe, we should get going,' I said before she could cross the room and demand he drop his trousers so she could see for herself. 'I, um, I promised my friend, Sarah, we'd meet her down at the fête and help her . . . do stuff.'

'I think a literary discussion takes precedence over guessing the weight of a fruitcake,' Mum said sharply. 'You go and help Sarah, Joe can stay here with us. I know Maggie wanted to ask something about your background reading.'

Maggie, a bright-eyed woman with canary yellow hair, raised her hand. 'Thank you, Pandora. My question is, would you say you drew more from the writings of Anaïs Nin or Mary Gaitskill for your erotic scenes? There is less overt sadism in your writing, perhaps, but I for one felt it was always hovering at the edges, hidden in the subtext?'

'What are you talking about?' I answered before Joe could. 'There is no sadism, hovering or otherwise. It's good sex, happy sex. Nothing and noone is tortured about any of it. If anything, I'd say it was influenced by Christina Lauren but I doubt you've read them.'

'Darling, please, don't be irrelevant,' Mum said, sounding chippy as I watched Aunt Carole open the Amazon app.

'I'm being entirely relevant,' I argued while my aunt downloaded a sample of *The Unhoneymooners* to her Kindle. 'It's context. *Butterflies* wasn't published in a vacuum, there were hundreds of other brilliant books that paved its way but you're pretending they don't exist and my book is some kind of anomaly when it isn't.'

'Your book?' Carole's head snapped up from her phone. 'What do you mean, your book?'

'My book, our book, the book,' I said quickly. '*Este's* book.'

The whole room sat in silence while they debated whether or not to accept my explanation.

'Joe's book,' I added with weak defeat. The conservatory breathed a sigh of relief and everyone started talking again happily, turning away as if I'd never said a word in the first place. Only CJ continued to stare, as if trying to read some very fine print on my forehead.

'Where is he? Where's my bestselling boy?'

It would have been more helpful if Gregory had chosen to appear ten seconds earlier but I was still unbelievably grateful to see his mutton-dressed-as lamb self stride into the conservatory. He pushed his way through the room looking like a large uncooked sausage in his baby pink tracksuit, and tackled Joe into a bear hug that knocked him out of his seat.

'Look at my son!' he bellowed. 'My brilliant, beautiful, million-copy-selling filth-monger. Giving the ladies what they want, like his old man.'

'Gross,' I muttered, not as quietly as I should have.

'Proud is not the word,' he went on regardless, helping himself to his son's chair. 'Awe. I'm in awe of you, son.'

'You've read the book, Gregory?' Maggie asked politely as he pulled Joe down into his lap like Santa Claus if Santa Claus was halfway through a midlife crisis, dyed his hair an improbable shade of brown and half the breadth of the child on his knee.

'Read it? Fuck no. I thought it was chicklit shit like the rest of you. But I will now. I'm so proud!'

Joe broke his father's grip around his waist and stood, everyone's eyes going with him.

'Anyone would be proud of their kid for achieving something like this,' he said, sending a not at all subtle look my way. 'Isn't that right, Mrs Taylor? If Sophie had written *Butterflies* or something like it, you'd be over the moon.'

The split second it took for my mother to paste on a smile told me all I needed to know.

'We're proud of all our children,' she said. 'But if

Sophie were to write a novel, this wouldn't be her sort of thing, I don't think.'

'I always knew you'd do something great,' Gregory said, the dollar signs in his eyes almost visible. 'You must've made so much fucking money.'

Joe forced his way through the guests to grab my hand. 'Sophie, you're right, we really should go and help . . .'

'Sarah.'

'Sarah,' he finished. 'Thanks for that, everyone, good chat.'

'But I've got more questions!' Carole wailed. 'Have you ever been to Texas? Can you ride a horse? Is it really possible for a woman to have more than one orgasm during coitus?'

'Poor Uncle Bryan,' I said as Joe almost yanked my arm out its socket in his rush.

'Never quote me on this but poor your Aunt Carole,' Joe replied, leading me away and letting the door to the conservatory slam shut behind us.

CHAPTER TWENTY

'Don't deny it, you were enjoying that scene back there,'
Joe commented as we strolled into the thick of the fête,
dozens more children high on fairy cakes and full sugar
squash pinballing across our path. Almost nothing had
changed since I was a little girl. Same stalls, same games,
even mostly the same people. My mouth watered at the
sight of whipped cream and fresh jam sandwiched into
the middle of a Victoria sponge. Some things just
couldn't be improved on.

'What scene?' I replied innocently as we stepped
around a gaggle of little kids, sitting in a circle in the
middle of the green, swapping stickers. Who needed
smartphones? Sticker superiority would always exist.

'Your mother's "literary salon". Don't pretend you
weren't.'

'I wouldn't exactly say enjoying it,' I replied, 'but
you were the one who said it would be easy to play
author. Spoke too soon, didn't we?'

Joe kept his head down so I wouldn't see his face
but I did.

'Possibly fractionally prematurely. And now you're angry with me again.'

'I'm frustrated with the situation,' I corrected before wandering over to the nearest stall.

Joe stayed close behind, attached to me like one of the toddlers I saw leashed to their mothers, only able to toddle so far before they were yanked back onto the bums. The stall held all kinds of homemade treats, anything and everything that could be forced into a jar, from pickled beetroot to pickled blackberries, and a vast colourful array of homemade jams. Joe picked up a jar of damson jam and his eyes lit up like Christmas.

'I haven't had damson jam since I was a little kid,' he said, pulling out his wallet and handing over a fifty, refusing change as he loaded up on jars of jam, much to the delight of the man behind the stall.

'Big fan of damsons, are you?' I asked when he pulled a fold-up tote bag out of his back pocket to carry his purchases. It was a strangely erotic move and I felt a low down flutter at the sight of it. This was bad. No one should be aroused by a reusable shopping bag, not ever.

Joe held one of the jars aloft like it was the Holy Grail, the others weighing down the bag on his shoulder. 'Do you think it'll still taste the same?'

'Can't see why it wouldn't, they haven't changed damsons as far as I know.'

He opened it, his huge hand covering the small lid and twisting it off with ease. Another ordinary move that made my thighs clench when it shouldn't. Then he stuck two fingers into the jam and pulled them out, red and glistening, before sliding them into his mouth, eyes closed. I wasn't sure if it was possible to spontaneously orgasm based on visual stimulation alone, again I was not a neuroscientist, but my field research suggested it might be.

'It tastes exactly the same.'

Joe's eyes opened and found mine straight away, wide and wondrous. I watched as he licked every trace of jam from his skin, unable to move. I couldn't believe how badly I wanted to knock him down to the ground and take the same two fingers between my own lips to find out how good he might taste.

'Want some?' The tart smell of the dark fruit hit me like smelling salts.

'No,' I replied, curt and clipped. Anything more was too much of a risk.

He shook the jar from side to side, my head involuntarily moving with it. 'Sure you don't want a taste?'

I wanted more than just a taste.

'Can you put the lid back on please?' I begged under my uneven breath. 'People are starting to stare.'

Joe turned to take a quick survey of the busy fête. 'Are they?'

'Bloody well put the lid back on,' I ordered as he dug back in for a second taste. 'Who walks around eating jam out the jar?'

He looked down at me, fingers still in his mouth.

'Me.'

There was nothing I could say and my mouth was the only part of me that was dry.

Rolling his eyes, he slowly screwed the lid back onto the jar and placed it safely in his tote bag with the others. Staring intently at the best vegetable contest at the end of the green, I marched towards the enormous turnips with purpose.

'Here's the thing,' Joe said, only ever one step behind at most. 'We're pretty much in the clear now, at least for the weekend. Your mum has sworn everyone to secrecy and your sister has threatened them with grievous bodily harm, and if there's one thing I've learned about the women in your family, it's that their threats hold water.'

'What about your dad?' I asked, pleased to see he was learning.

'My dad can be a lot of things but he won't shoot his mouth off about this if I ask him not to. And bribe him. Although technically, you'll be bribing him since you're the one with all the cash.'

He was probably right. If anyone spoiled her surprise, Charlotte would chop their hands off and I wouldn't want to be on Pandora Taylor's bad side. He'd bought us a little more time at least. The afternoon was warming up and my dress was beginning to stick to my skin. I grabbed a handful of hair and secured a messy bun with my trusty claw clip.

'Might be useful if I had a few stock answers to common questions,' Joe suggested. 'In case there are any insistent fans tonight.'

'What kind of answers?'

'How you came up with the title, what inspired the Texas setting, will there be a sequel,' he replied, listing some of the most hotly debated questions on TikTok. 'And one for me, how did you decide on your pseudonym?'

'You're going to laugh,' I said, colouring up as I spoke.

'Promise I won't.'

'Este is me, S Taylor. S-Tay.'

'And what about Cox?'

I winced, scrunching my entire face up tightly.

'I thought it was funny?'

Joe's jam jars clanked together with the force of his laughter.

'You promised you wouldn't laugh!' I protested as he doubled over.

'And you can't make dick jokes without expecting it to raise a titter,' he replied. 'Sophie, Sophie, Sophie, for shame.'

'It's not like I expected to ever be in a position where I had to explain myself,' I said, not even attempting to defend my incredible immaturity. 'I know it's stupid.'

Wiping a tear away from under his eye, he shook his head. 'It's perfect. I should write a sequel from Eric's perspective under the name Hugh G. Balls.'

'Feel free,' I groaned, the spectre of one of my remaining unsolved problems popping back into view. 'Someone has to deliver a manuscript next week and I'm struggling.'

The side of Joe's hand brushed against mine as we walked, our little fingers almost interlocking before it was gone again.

'Classic second album syndrome,' he said. 'Sometimes talking it through helps a creative block. What's the problem?'

'Wish I knew,' I replied, tucking my hands safely away underneath my armpits. 'I thought I knew exactly what I was going to do but I'm so lost. I've got the plot and I've written a draft, but I can't quite get under the skin of what the book is about, if that makes sense.'

'Makes perfect sense,' he assured me, two little lines appearing between his brows as he concentrated. 'What would you say the first book is about?'

'Trust.'

The word reverberated too loudly around us. Five letters that didn't get the credit they deserved. Whatever Joe was thinking, he kept it well hidden behind a completely impassive face but I felt something change in the air, a subtle shift in the connection between us.

'Obviously there was also a low-key hidden theme of having incredible sex but I don't know if you would've picked that up,' I joked, trying to slice through this new tension but it was stronger than I'd realised and Joe slowed his pace, creating just enough distance between us for me to notice.

'I think the reason the first book resonated with so many people is because you really feel Jenna's journey,' he said, his tone more professional, more considered. I wondered if I was meeting Creative Director Joe for the first time. 'The reader experiences all her thoughts and feelings firsthand. It's very immediate.'

'Thank you.'

'You're welcome.'

The high summer sun beat down on the back of my neck. Every time I took a step closer, he pulled back, either with a snide comment, a sleazy joke or a frosty withdrawal. Each attempt at vulnerability from either of us met an attempt to block. It was the only thing constant with him. Well, maybe not the only constant. His ability to make me feel like I was about to implode was fairly dependable. But if he wanted to swich to strictly professional three seconds after making me watch him lick jam off his fingers, it was no skin off my nose.

'When we meet Jenna, she's completely closed off but by the end of book one, she's opening up,' I said, matching him measured step for measured step. 'She knows what she wants. The sequel is supposed to be about her taking the necessary steps to get it but I can't seem to make it sing. It feels flat.'

'You're likely being far harder on yourself than anyone else would be,' he reasoned. 'What have you got so far?'

Pausing in front of the Brownie friendship bracelet stall, I peeled a stray strand of hair from my damp forehead and shrugged. 'Nothing good.'

'At the end of book one, Jenna had to leave Texas to go home to England,' Joe prompted. 'And Eric went to Alaska to reconnect with his brother.'

I chewed on my bottom lip, flushing with pleasure at how well he knew the book. He really had read it. He really had paid attention.

'Jenna goes back to Austin to profess her love for Eric but, when she arrives, he's still in Alaska,' I said, looking around to make sure no one was listening. 'Nobody's heard from him in months, he isn't answering his phone or replying to emails but all his friends explain to her, this is very standard Eric. But then she meets a hot bartender—'

'Called Joe?'

'Called Elijah.'

'There's still time to change it,' he said, the first crack showing in his newly acquired professional armour. I should've known he couldn't keep it up for long.

'Eventually Eric comes back and Jenna finds herself in a love triangle between the two of them,' I said, flicking my hands out in front of me. 'And then I'm stuck.'

Joe rubbed at the spot underneath his chin, his official 'I'm thinking' move and his head bobbed from side to side as he considered the possibilities.

'Love triangles are hard to pull off when people are already invested in the central relationship. Does Jenna fall in love with Elijah?'

'No, he's just a stand in.'

'But she loves Eric.'

'Yes but she doesn't know if she can trust him.' The jars of jam in Joe's bag clanked together, the only other sound either of us made. 'He's the first person she ever really opened her heart to and he vanished on her.'

'That was their deal though.' There was a defensive edge in his voice I couldn't miss. 'One month together then they both walk away. Isn't she being hard on him?'

'But they fell in love,' I reminded him. 'And that wasn't part of the deal.'

'It never is.'

He left me behind, wandering over to a fruit and vegetable stand and examining a punnet of strawberries without me. I studied his stance, the tight set of his shoulders, tension in his neck, even his feet pointed straight forward as though he was afraid to relax.

'You've got to trust your gut,' he said when I eventually followed to stand beside him. '*Butterflies* works because it was real to you when you were writing. You have to write what's in your heart.'

'Keeping in mind the readers will tear me into pieces if she doesn't end up with Eric?'

'There is that,' he admitted. 'Still, you can't write to order. It has to be true to you, just like the first time.'

'Thank goodness you became such an authority on *Butterflies* so very quickly,' I said, sizing up a basket full of glossy blackberries.

His smile returned slowly, still more removed than before and not quite making it all the way to his eyes.

'I read it again on my Kindle last night when I couldn't sleep.'

'You couldn't sleep?' I replied with surprise.

Joe picked up a blackberry and rested it on his bottom lip, the forced distance in his eyes dissolving into something warmer.

'Did you?'

'How much for these?' I asked the woman behind the stall, swallowing hard and reaching for a punnet of strawberries freshly picked and plump. They smelled so sweet and strong, I could almost taste them.

'Four pounds for one, three for a tenner,' she replied. 'You can mix and match with the raspberries.'

I looked up and down her table, seeing nothing but a sea of strawberries.

'But there aren't any raspberries?'

'No,' she replied. 'They're all gone.'

'Just the strawberries then,' I said politely. 'Thanks.'

Was it any wonder people preferred the self-checkout at the supermarket? Sure, we'd regret it when the robots took over the world but that felt like a small price to pay to avoid interactions like this.

'Let me,' Joe said, cash already in his hand when I tried to stop him.

The woman slid the green cardboard punnet into a brown paper bag before handing it to me, openly gawping at Joe. Another thing you didn't have to worry about at the self-checkout.

'Thank you,' I said as I hurriedly steered him out of danger. Two more seconds and he'd have gone the way of the raspberries. 'I was going to ask if you wanted to play hook-a-duck but I'll take strawberries instead.'

'They've got hook-a-duck?'

I'd never seen someone get so excited so quickly.

'Over there,' I said, pointing past the stalls.

Behind the coconut shy and a truculent-looking pony I wouldn't have gone near even if you paid me, was a round stall surrounded by people already one Pimm's too many into their day, brandishing long sticks with metal hooks on the end, a lawsuit waiting to happen.

'We've got to do it,' Joe insisted, all his walls tumbling down as he grabbed my hand to drag me across the green. 'I'm amazing at hook-a-duck.'

'You're amazing at putting a hook through a loop?' I gasped in mock admiration. 'Someone get me a fainting couch.'

'You wait and see,' he said as we approached the stall, a sea of little plastic ducks, yellow and pink, sailing around him in a circular trough full of water. 'I'm the master.'

'What's the grand prize?' I asked the man behind the ducks, keeping my stick safely below eye level when he handed it over.

'Squishmallow or teddy bear,' he replied before taking a drag off a vape pen. 'Up top.'

I followed his pointing finger to find a half-bald teddy bear and a weepy stuffed walrus gazing down at me. The saddest Squishmallow in all the land.

'I want that walrus,' I said to Joe, a newfound determination in my hook-a-duck game. 'Can you get three ducks?'

'Don't insult me.' He was already leaning over the stall as far as was legally allowed, hook at the ready. 'Whoever gets the most ducks, wins.'

'You want the walrus too?' I replied as I assumed position.

'What I want isn't up on that board.'

He looked over at me and grinned as his hook slipped through the loop on a neon pink duck and he raised it victoriously over his head. 'I'll tell you after I win. One down, two to go.'

'Right,' I replied. 'We'll see about that.'

'The whole thing was rigged,' Joe complained as we crossed the green back towards his dad's car, sad walrus Squishmallow safely under my arm. 'Half the loops on the ducks were too small for anyone to hook them.'

'They weren't too small for me.'

'Man probably gave me a bigger hook,' he sulked. 'Wanted to make me look stupid.'

'That would be a massive waste of his time,' I said with a generous pat on the shoulder. 'You can do that all by yourself.'

I heard him huff quietly through his nose and squeezed my walrus with delight.

'Hang on,' I said as we turned the corner to where he'd parked the car. 'You said first to three ducks wins. What did I win?'

He pulled the key fob out of his trouser pocket and opened the boot, stashing the damson jam and strawberries safely away. 'You've got your walrus, haven't you?'

'And you said the walrus wasn't the prize.' I hugged Walter closer because yes, of course I had named him already. 'So what is?'

'I've been thinking about your sequel,' he said, one hand still hanging onto the top of the raised boot. 'Eric went to Alaska to reunite with his brother, but do you think he might also be running away from his feelings for Jenna?'

'What makes you say that?' I asked, slightly miffed that I hadn't already realised it myself.

Joe left the boot open and leaned against the side of the car.

'From the first night they meet, he keeps telling her he doesn't do relationships, so falling in love the way they do and then her leaving probably made him feel vulnerable. It makes sense to me that he'd want to put some physical space between himself and the place where that happened.'

'Sounds like something you have experience with,' I replied, treading lightly. 'Any chance you're projecting?'

He started to shake his head but the gesture turned into a shrug before he could complete it. 'I don't know. Vulnerability isn't a comfortable emotion for me.'

'I don't think it's comfortable for anyone,' I sat Walter in the boot then closed it carefully. 'I don't think it's supposed to be.'

'Eric doesn't do relationships,' Joe said, looking in my direction but not quite meeting my eyes. Behind him, a wall of weeping willows danced as a car drove by. 'He wasn't looking for anything, he wasn't ready for something so intense.'

'Neither of them were,' I replied, fully aware we were crossing into dangerous territory. 'What's your point?'

'I can understand why his connection to Jenna might make him want to run away. Eric and I are a lot alike.'

It shouldn't have stung but it did.

'Good to know but I'm not sure where that leaves book two.' I teased a loose thread on the cuff of my sleeve, winding it around my forefinger until it pulled tight. 'Sorry, ladies, Eric was only here for a good time, not a long time, it's not going to work out.'

'This is when I remind you your book is a fantasy,' Joe replied. 'And I'm not Eric.'

'You might want to tell Aunt Carole that.' I moved my attention from my cardigan to my pink painted fingernails. I didn't want to look at him.

But I couldn't stop myself.

His eyes were on me now, cautious and wary, as though I might bolt at any second. It was a distinct possibility. I'd rather launch myself into the river than endure another second of this terrible silence. Another car went by, rustling the trees as they bent towards him, straining to make contact, but he was always just out of reach.

'You still want to know what my prize was going to be if I'd won?' he asked.

I combed a loose strand of hair behind my ear and nodded.

'I was going to ask for a kiss.'

My breath hitched in my chest, seizing up, unable to escape even when I parted my lips to respond.

'Maybe you should ask anyway,' I heard myself say. 'You never know your luck.'

Joe moved first, peeling himself away from the car and walking around towards me as I backed up, the hot metal of the Range Rover burning through the thin fabric of my dress. He stopped right in front of me, brown suede desert boots toe-to-toe with my black leather sandals, the car behind me, Joe in front. There was nowhere for me to go.

'I thought it might be a good idea,' he said. 'Get it out of our systems.'

'That sounds like something Eric would say,' I replied as he wrapped my ponytail around his fist and pulled gently, angling my face upwards towards his. 'But you're not Eric.'

'No, I'm not,' Joe murmured against my lips. 'He's just a fantasy. I'm real.'

And then he kissed me.

CHAPTER TWENTY-ONE

'And how was it?' Sarah asked, eyes wild with vicarious excitement. 'The actual kiss?'

I glanced across the party to where Joe was standing in front of the big top-styled marquee that had gone up while Joe and I were at the fete. He was chatting with my mum and a couple I didn't recognise, smiling, nodding, occasionally throwing in a casual laugh. His hair was as carelessly perfect as ever, sleeves pushed up and his trademark white shirt tucked into a pair of soft grey trousers. All his clothes looked like they had been made just for him, tailored to show off his assets, another set of unnecessary weapons in his arsenal, as if the raw materials weren't dangerous enough.

'Oh, you know,' I said. 'Fine.'

But the punch she landed on my upper arm confirmed she knew me better than that.

'That's a lie. You're lying. I want a millisecond-by-millisecond rundown. Where were his hands, where were your hands? Were there tongues, eyes open or closed, did he or did he not get a hard on during? Fine won't do, Taylor, I demand the same level of detail you would've given me when we were fifteen.'

'Firstly, ow.' I rubbed my arm, she was stronger than she knew. 'When we were fifteen, there were no details to share, only me in my room writing *Vampire Diaries* fanfic. I think you're mixing the two of us up.'

'Then pretend you're me at fifteen.' She took a deep drink of the organic prosecco Mum swore they always drank in Umbria, even though she bought it in bulk from Aldi, draining half the glass in one gulp, then set her shoulders, readying herself for battle. 'Hit me with the specifics, I'm ready.'

I hitched up a strap of my dress, fighting off a hot flush when Joe's gaze crossed mine and that crooked smile appeared on his face. The evening was so humid, I could taste the air, but nothing made me sweat like the thought of his lips on mine. 'We were outside, in public, in the middle of the day. How salacious do you think it could be?'

'I don't know but your skin is glowing, your eyes are sparkling and he hasn't taken his eyes off you since I got here, so either you sneaked in a full spa treatment since I saw you this morning or that kiss was more than "fine". You're the romance writer, use your words.'

The only problem was, the words didn't exist. Joe and I had shared the single greatest kiss ever experienced, the kind of kiss that put all others to shame. His hands were in my hair, cradling my face, anchoring us together when the storm rushed in. I fell apart on contact, his mouth, soft and warm and yielding until everything intensified beyond my control and I came apart. The pressure built until a gasp escaped my lips, mine or his, I wasn't sure. It didn't matter. Pinned between the hot hard car and Joe's solid body, I had all but melted away, surrendering everything to the kiss. Who needed to stand? Who needed to breathe? All I could do was loop my arms around his neck and cling on for dear life as his tongue grazed mine for the first time. He tasted of freshly picked strawberries and damson jam . . .

'It was just a kiss,' I said, dabbing at my suddenly damp forehead and exorcising the memory from my mind. 'No big deal.'

'You're still lying but what happened after?'

I sipped my drink and flipped my freshly washed hair over my shoulder.

'We came home, Joe helped my dad with setting up the party and I . . . worked.'

It was more or less the truth. When we finally broke apart, both of us shaking and panting, Joe pulled away without a word, walked around the car and got inside, until I found the strength to open the passenger side door. It took a minute. Neither of us said a word on the drive home and I couldn't remember what was playing on the stereo, a nineties station maybe? I could barely remember my own name. The Range Rover screeched into my parents' driveway, kicking gravel up the side of the garage, and before we'd even come to a complete stop, I let myself out and sprinted to the cottage, locked myself in the bathroom and spent the best part of an hour getting to know the new showerhead intimately. Which was sort of work, and I was certainly exhausted by the end of it.

'And that's that,' Sarah said, openly staring at Joe. 'You snogged once and now you're done.'

'Precisely,' I agreed. 'Scientific experiment complete. He is completely out of my system.'

It was such a useless lie. Before the kiss, Joe was under my skin, now he was in my bones. He ran through my veins, sweet and sharp at the same time, the kind of desire I'd only ever written about and never experienced myself. A dangerous downhill slide there was no coming back from. Joe didn't do relationships and I didn't do one night stands, so where did that leave me? Aside from locked in the bathroom for an hour with the showerhead, I wasn't sure.

'Is it weird that I couldn't find much about him online?' Sarah asked. 'What? Why are you looking at me like that?'

'Why were you looking for him online?' I replied.

'I wanted to check out the thighs so I wouldn't be overcome with lust when I saw them in real life,' she quipped. 'I'm serious, there's barely any personal information out there otherwise I'd have come armed with a full report.'

She was, as ever, a very good friend.

'Look, I know how much you love living in denial so I won't push,' she offered graciously. 'Happy to pretend nothing is going on until it all explodes in your face the way these things always do. Fun party, eh?'

'Nothing is going to explode in anyone's face,' I said, the fleeting memory passing through my mind of something pressed against my hip that definitely felt as though it was about to explode. 'And yes, it's a lovely party. Against all the odds. Can't believe no one's had a go on the bouncy castle yet though.'

She turned to look at the giant red inflatable pushed up against the hedge and raised her glass. 'The night is still young and I am still sober. Give me time.'

Along with the bouncy castle, Dad had hired a big-top-esque striped marquee, supposedly in case of rain that wasn't forecast but seemed to threaten in the dense, close heat. He'd also added some other circus-style flourishes to the back garden just to get the theme across. A giant stuffed lion that sat in an even bigger cage, a flying trapeze-style swing hanging from the oak tree in the middle of the garden and, to round things off, he'd rented an old fashioned test of strength, complete with wooden mallet and a bell that was yet to be rung. A few of his circuit-training friends tried it when they came in but almost all the men were steering clear. A quarter of the way into the twenty-first century and they were still too scared to have a go at a carnival game in case it made them look like a wuss.

The belle of the birthday ball was having the time of his life. After Mum had vetoed his clown outfit, Dad was now cruising around the party in a hastily put together ringmaster ensemble made up of black trousers, a white shirt, Mum's pink linen blazer speedily dyed cherry red, and a top hat William had hanging around the house for reasons best known to himself and his consenting husband.

'I'll say one thing about your dad,' Sarah said as he cracked a length of rope wrapped in black electrical tape masquerading as a whip at the head of international sales. 'He certainly commits to a theme.'

'Never knowingly failed to take things too far,' I replied, feeling oddly proud. 'I do wonder how he'll cope if he ever retires. He's never been very good at sitting still.'

'The bouncy castle kind of gives that away. Are you hungry?' She licked her lips as the scent of food floated across the lawn. The catering was the only thing that wasn't on theme, instead we had all Dad's favourite things, mini fish and chips and tiny toad in the hole from the local pub, prawn toasts and spare ribs by the Chinese takeaway down the street and enough sweets to give you diabetes just by looking at them. I shook my head, too on edge to think about eating. Things really were bad if I was off my food.

'I'm all right for now but please go and get something,' I told her. 'I'd rather not end the night holding your hair back over the toilet if it's all the same.'

'That's why I braided it,' she replied as she trotted off towards the big top. 'Meet you by the bouncy castle in ten!'

The warm afternoon had turned into a sweltering evening, the kind of English summer night when the air was so heavy you could feel it pressing down on you. A bead of sweat rolled down my spine underneath my beautiful black dress, finally making its debut. It had taken me a good half an hour to convince myself to wear it, trying the thing on and taking it off again three different times, getting as far as the front door in jeans and a T-shirt before finally forcing myself to put it back on, fasten the zip and walk out the cottage with my head held, well, not exactly high but I was doing OK.

'There she is, just the bestselling author we were looking for.'

At least until I turned to see my agent and my godfa-ther-turned-publisher stalking towards me.

'William,' I said, offering my cheek to my brother and then my godfather. 'Mal, you look very dapper.'

He removed his bowler hat and attempted to fan

himself but it was no use, there was no air to move. 'I'm sweating my tits off. If only I could go back in time and kill the bastard who decided men should wear suits, I'd be a much happier man.'

'Yes, that's definitely the first person we should take out when we come across that kind of technology,' I agreed. 'A nineteenth-century tailor.'

Neither of them so much as cracked a smile.

'Going to go out on a limb and say you didn't pop over for a lovely chat,' I guessed before tipping my champagne flute to my lips.

'Do you want to explain why Gregory Brent is telling everyone who will listen that his son is Este Cox?' Mal asked, straining to keep his voice quiet. Quiet was not his natural state.

'Not really,' I replied, looking past him. 'Where are your very patient wife and demonically possessed son?'

'Xavier is pitching a fit in the car because your little sister won't let him bring his iPad in with him, Rosa is trying to talk him down, and don't change the subject and I'd like an answer.'

Across the garden, Gregory was merrily holding court in another unmistakably ringmaster-inspired outfit. Not nearly as charming as my dad's but also not bleeding red dye onto the back of his neck.

'He shouldn't be saying anything to anyone,' I said, my mouth twisting into a frown. 'Charlotte will absolutely end him if she hears about this.'

'Silver linings,' William said brightly. 'It's not only Xavier who's off screentime, she took all our phones, put them in little sandwich bags and hid them somewhere. That girl isn't taking any chances.'

'Then that makes one bright spark out of the three of

you,' Mal said as I searched the crowd for our baby sister. I'd seen her earlier, flitting around in a gauzy transparent maxi dress with a silver bikini underneath, my Chanel bag slung across her body. Her hair was a dreamy lavender colour and full of glitter that trailed behind her like fairy dust. If only she wasn't going around the party demanding the guests turn out their pockets to make sure they hadn't snuck in any recording devices. Zadie Smith hadn't looked amused in the slightest and Kate Atkinson almost chopped her hands off. 'What were the two of you thinking mixing Joe Walsh up in all this?'

'It's not as though we planned it,' I replied, William shifting his weight and allegiance towards me when he realised he was also on the receiving end of this bollocking. 'Charlotte found the manuscript—'

'Which you should've given to me on Thursday.'

'And I didn't know what to do—'

'Besides tell the truth.'

'And Joe jumped in before I could say anything.'

'And I wasn't there,' William added quickly. 'I was having a slash, missed the whole thing, not responsible.'

'You're responsible for letting her go on with this pretence as long as she has.' Mal nabbed my drink from my hand and took a chug. 'Enough's enough. It's time to come forward, Soph.'

Charlotte came into view again, standing beside our mother and lecturing the crowd of assembled authors on some topic or another. The whole group looked impressed but no one more so than our mother.

'Not yet,' I said. 'There's no need to panic, Joe isn't going to tell anyone.'

'But Charlotte is,' William pointed out, getting a sharp

elbow in the ribs for his trouble as Mal finished off my drink.

'That's right, your brother tells me the young entre-preneur of the year is planning a TikTok reveal for us?' He glowered at me as though he hadn't thought things could get worse. 'Very thoughtful of her. The marketing team usually spends a fortune getting these things done.'

William reached into his pocket for his phone before remembering he had already been relieved of it, his hand coming up empty. 'True enough, she's got great numbers. It doesn't really matter where we announce, it's going to get picked up everywhere. Might be nice to keep it in the family.'

'I don't care if we do the reveal on social media or she goes door-to-bloody-door up and down the country, I want it done and I want us looped in so we don't look like idiots who aren't in control of our PR, and I want Joe Walsh out of the equation asap,' Mal barked. 'I don't like him anywhere near this. I *knew* I should've made you leave that bloody curry house.'

'Make me leave?' I choked out a gasp. 'I'm not a child, Mal, and seriously, what is your problem with Joe?'

He wound his neck in, leaving him with a not particu-larly flattering double chin. 'Aside from his father?'

'Aside from his father,' I confirmed.

'Well . . .' He waved a hand around as though he might pluck a better reason out of thin air. 'All right, it's mostly Gregory.'

'I've heard he's a bit of a slag if that helps?' William offered.

'Not really.' I gave Aunt Carole my best impression of a smile as she walked by dressed as an old fashioned fortune teller – or herself, I couldn't be sure. 'Do either of you know for certain that he's done anything unfair to anyone, I'm talking names, numbers, dates? Or is this standard office gossip?'

The pair of them pouted like toddlers caught with their hands in the biscuit tin. Whoever pushed the lie that women were the worst gossips had clearly never worked in the publishing industry. Or any other office. Or actually met a man.

'I know he went out for a drink with Zara from production and she texted him when she got home and he replied with a thumbs up,' Mal said. 'Then she suggested they go and see a film they'd talked about and he said no.'

'That's it?' I replied gobsmacked. 'That's all you've got?'

'Most of the stories I've heard were about New York,' William admitted, scratching his ear as he spoke. 'But my friend Saul is friends with an editor at MullinsParker in London and he knows Joe's deputy creative director and *he* says he's very cagey about his personal life.'

'Wouldn't you keep your personal life to yourself if your dad was Gregory Brent and five minutes after you moved to a new city, everyone you worked with had written you off as a wanker?' I asked, appalled with the pair of them. 'You're worse than kids. You don't know any more about him than I do so will you please both trust me to sort this out myself?'

'I'll trust you when I've got the sequel in my hands and a photo of your face on the dust jacket,' Mal said, the look on his face mirroring the storm clouds amassing above. 'Sort it out tonight.'

'Or?' I challenged.

'Or I'll sort it out for you tomorrow,' he said. 'Now

pretend we were talking about something else because that imbecile Anthony Khan is on his way over and he might be the only person in this entire industry I like less than Gregory Brent.'

'I'll remind you that imbecile Anthony Khan is my co-worker, thank you very much,' William said through gritted teeth. 'And since he represents some very big authors I'd appreciate it if you could pretend to be nice to him the same way the rest of us have to.'

'This fucking business,' Mal grunted into his empty glass. 'I need another drink.'

'William, there you are, I've been looking for you all night,' Anthony cried, hurling himself, chest first, at my brother as Mal slipped away. 'Hi, great to meet you, Anthony Khan. And you are?'

'Leaving,' I replied, moaning with exasperation when William caught my elbow in his hand. 'I mean, nice to meet you. I'm Sophie, William's sister.'

'Ahh, the lesser spotted Taylor sibling.' He spoke in a grating transatlantic accent that made me want to plug up my ears with a pair of the cocktail sausages that were piled up in one of Mum's giant John Lewis dishes. 'Great to finally meet you. I've heard all about you from William and CJ.'

'You're friends with CJ.' I wrinkled my nose and nodded. 'That makes sense.'

'Anthony was in the New York office for a few months,' William said while his fellow agent openly ogled my chest. 'Actually, didn't you pal around with Joe Walsh while you were over there?'

'Joseph? I certainly did,' he replied through a yawn he didn't bother to cover. Maybe the dress wasn't as revealing as I'd thought. 'We ran with the same ex-pat publishing crew. OK guy. Although I was relieved when he left for London, gave the rest of us a chance to have a go at the top tier totty. Haven't seen him in a while, is the old pussyhound here?'

Well, that wasn't a very endearing nickname.

'Nice to meet you, Anthony' I said with the fakest fake smile I had ever faked. 'William. You'll have to excuse me.'

Before I could go anywhere, I felt a hand on the back of my waist, and my shoulders snapped back straight as our group was joined by the old pussyhound himself.

'Anthony,' Joe said, an equally broad and equally fake smile spoiling his handsome face. 'How are you? I heard you'd moved back.'

'Good, busy, you know me, always making moves.' He gave a humiliating shimmy that I think we all regretted. 'I'm doing my civic duty by warning this young lady about you.'

'Yes,' I replied pleasantly. 'Anthony was just telling me how you're a total pussyhound who hogged all the top tier totty in New York.'

The four of us stood in an uncomfortable square, no one sure what to say next.

'I know!'

Anthony broke the impasse with a look of delight on his face. 'What happened to that editor girl you were so pally with over at Knoll? I haven't seen her in a dog's age. Was she American? Australian, maybe.'

'Canadian. She's fine.'

I'd only known Joe for a little more than forty-eight hours but I knew when someone was looking shifty. Perhaps I shouldn't have been quite so quick to leap to his defence with Mal and William.

'Heard all sorts about that one,' Anthony said, making a show of speaking out the corner of his mouth even though we could all hear him far too clearly. 'You did the right thing cutting your losses.'

'Anyway, what about those spare ribs?' William, always able to read a room, clapped his hands then rubbed his stomach. 'I'm ravenous, who wants to hit the buffet?'

'Bloody talented though,' Anthony went on, either ignoring or simply not caring about mine or Joe's discomfort. 'And I know you can't say it these days but, fit as.'

'But here you are, saying it anyway.' Joe turned his attention to me, lips pursed, jaw rigid. 'Sophie, do you have a minute?'

'Watch out, Willy,' Anthony gasped. 'He's cracking on to your sister, right in front of you. Before I even had a chance as well.'

'For fuck's sake, Anthony, give it a break,' William snapped. 'We both know you've only ever slept with one woman.'

'I told you that in confidence!' I heard him yell as Joe pulled me away, dodging one of Mum's newspaper colleagues dressed as the bearded lady.

'Khan is the worst,' Joe fumed as he strode away. 'No talent, no creativity, no business skills, the only reason he has a job is because his dad owns the agency.'

'Publishing nepo babies strike again.' I looked around at Dad's guests noting more than a few multi-generational groups. 'We're the worst.'

'We're nothing like him,' Joe countered.

'I know I'm not,' I replied. 'For starters no one has ever accused me of being a pussyhound.'

'You should try it some time, you might like it,' he tried to laugh but the joke fell flat and instead he rubbed the back of his ear with an anxious finger.

'Didn't you want something?' I asked, searching the crowd for a glimpse of Sarah. How long could it take to house a cone of mini fish and chips?

Digging one hand deep into the pocket of his charcoal grey trousers, Joe poked the toe of his shoe into the grass. 'Soph, I'm not going to pretend I haven't done my fair share of dating. More than my fair share probably, but I don't see why I should have to justify what happened in my past.'

'You shouldn't,' I agreed. 'You don't do relationships, you've been very clear about it. No one is judging you.'

'Are you sure about that?'

'I couldn't care less.' The words definitely came out more loudly than I would've liked. 'You can do whatever or whoever you want to. It's got nothing to do with me.'

Even though it was very difficult to turn on your heel and flounce away in a pair of slides, I did my best. The party was in full swing, dozens of guests were packed in the huge garden, laughing and talking under the string lights, Pimm's and champagne flowing freely. Mum was surrounded by a group of young writers as always, all of them trying to locate her good side and get on it, Dad was bouncing through the crowd, coiled whip on his hip, seamlessly introducing his pub friends to his publishing pals, William was still trapped in conversation with Anthony Khan, and Charlotte was still frisking latecomers like a very angry airport worker. Everyone, except for William, seemed to be having the time of their lives.

I took off down the garden and leaned against the back of the oak tree to watch the sun start its descent over the fields. The sky was beyond beautiful, shafts of light slicing through the gathering clouds, so clearly defined I felt I could almost reach out and touch them. The wheatfield that stretched out past the back of the cottage and out into the distance was brilliant in the fading sun, glowing and gold, uncut sheaths shimmering. Once, before Charlotte was born, while we were visiting, my grandfather took me and William out to pick the wheat and when I closed my eyes I could feel their feathery leaves and spiky heads against my palm, soft and sharp at the same time. When we got home, he showed us how to grind the seeds between two stones to make flour.

It was miraculous, the fact you could take one thing and turn it into something else entirely. It was the same with words. It never ceased to amaze me how many different books could be written by so many different people, all using the same words. And those words were available to anyone, everyone, all the time. One minute you could be writing an email or a text and the next, you're banging out a novel. Not to say writing a novel was easy but it was possible, there was nothing stopping anyone from giving it a shot as long as they had something to write on, an imagination and the time to do it. And from what I heard, time was usually the trickiest part. I was lucky, it was a gift CJ didn't even know he'd given me, unlike the edible underwear he left on my pillow on our last Valentine's Day together that went straight in the bin.

I felt something on my shoulder and saw a ladybird alighted there, settling for a moment before I lightly blew her on her way and she flew off towards the rose-bushes. Joe was wrong. I wasn't judging him. I didn't care about his past, not really. What I cared about was his future. I wanted him so badly, my body ached with it. I pressed my bare shoulders against the rough bark of the tree and told myself it was his hands. I let my own fingertips drift across my collarbone, wishing he was there in front of me, and tipped my head back for a kiss that wasn't coming. If this was my book, Eric would've appeared before a despondent Jenna, scooped her up off the ground and carried her away to relieve her frustration and smother her doubts with the unde-niable force of his love. But it wasn't my book, it was my life. And like he'd already told me, Joe was not Eric.

And I couldn't write his story for him.

CHAPTER TWENTY-TWO

'Have you seen Carole?'

Uncle Bryan pounced from behind the candy floss cart, wearing an upsettingly short pair of denim cut-offs.

'Sorry, no.' I scoured the crowd for Carole, more for my own benefit than his, but I couldn't spot her fortune-teller's silk turban anywhere. 'Maybe she's in the loo?'

'Looked in there,' he said with a sulky snort. 'Not like her to leave me alone at something like this. She knows I don't like . . .'

'People?' I suggested.

He looked so sad, I almost felt sorry for him. Then I remembered what a terrible person he was and got over it right away.

'You stay out here and I'll check the house,' I suggested, spotting Anthony Khan out the corner of my eye. To get through the evening with my sanity intact, I needed to be where he wasn't. 'If I find her, I'll send her down to you.'

'Tell her I've got the hand sanitiser!' he called after me. 'Don't let her touch anything!'

For one second, I considered licking my hands and wiping them all over his face but that didn't play well with my plan not to ruin Dad's party. I gave him a thumbs up, turned around and took myself off into the house.

I definitely deserved a prize.

A small crowd had collected around the downstairs loo and there was the usual, small party overspill in the kitchen but I couldn't see Carole anywhere. I tiptoed upstairs, drawn by the strange sound of voices coming from one of the bedrooms. One was Carole but she sounded distressed and she wasn't alone.

'Aunt Carole?' I called quietly so as not to scare her. 'Are you all right?'

No answer. I stopped outside her room and pressed my ear against the door.

'It's not that I'm not flattered but really, you don't know me. You don't know what you're doing.'

Unless I was very much mistaken, and I definitely wasn't, my aunt was in her bedroom, behind a closed door, with Joe.

'Yes. I do.' A strange quiver elongated the end of Carole's sentence. 'And I do know you, like you know me, inside and out.'

'I know you're Sophie's aunt,' Joe replied, the sound of panic in his voice. 'You were in the conservatory at lunchtime, weren't you? You're the one who asked if I was. . . oh Christ.'

'No more talk.'

Carole growled and I pulled back in horror at the

echo of creaking bedsprings. 'Your book has changed me, Joseph. When I started reading it, I expected nothing but mindless smut but I've never been so turned on in my life.'

I fought back a retch, very glad to have passed on the prawn toasts after all.

'Now my eyes have been opened. You can't expect me to let you slip through my fingers when we've been brought together by the forces of the universe.'

'It was not the universe, it was Hugh Taylor's birthday,' Joe said over the scuffling sound of small items of furniture being moved around the room. 'Please, you really don't understand the situation and you don't want to do this.'

'It's the only thing I want to do!'

A guttural and frankly terrifying groan carried through the heavy wooden door and, for a second, I considered calling the police. Joe was not safe and if I opened this door, I didn't know if I was physically or mentally strong enough to help him.

'I want you to make love to me the way Eric made love to Jenna on the rooftop, and at the lake, and in the woods, and—'

'Yes, I get the point,' Joe replied. 'But it's a hard pass from me.'

'The things you wrote,' Carole moaned. 'The things you could do to a woman like me . . .'

'I could do no things!' Joe asserted in response, footsteps still moving around the room. 'It's just a book. I'm very glad you enjoyed it but — no, don't take off your cardigan – but it doesn't mean anything.'

'Stop talking!' she shrieked. 'Take me, Joseph, take me now, and make me feel like a woman!'

'Fucking hell, I'm very sorry but would you mind putting your top back on?'

It was time to intervene.

'Aunt Carole?!' I bellowed, banging on the door. 'Are you in there?'

'Sophie?' Joe yelled. 'Help!'

Taking a deep breath and preparing for the worst, I pushed open the door. Joe was up against the wardrobe, Aunt Carole pinning him in place with two surprisingly muscular arms and the room in complete disarray. Someone had been working out. She was down to her matronly bra and pleated tartan midi-skirt, her face sweaty and red, and she was looking at Joe the same way I looked at a Greggs steak bake the morning after a heavy night which couldn't possibly be a good thing.

'Run along, Sophie,' she instructed without moving. 'Joseph and I are having a little chat.'

'Yes, that's absolutely what it looks like,' I replied, keeping my gaze firmly on her feet. 'If you're finished traumatising your favourite author, Uncle Bryan is looking for you.'

Taking advantage of the momentary distraction, Joe dipped out from between her arms and bolted past me onto the landing. Without him in sight, whatever had possessed her fell away and Carole staggered backwards and sat heavily on the bed.

'I don't know what happened.' She plucked her cardigan up from the floor and slung it around her shoulders, eyes still glazed over. 'It's that book, Sophie, it must be. The thing is wicked.'

'It has caused more than its share of problems,' I agreed, backing out the room. 'Anyway, I'd better be getting back to the party.'

'It would be much appreciated if you didn't mention this to your uncle,' she called after me. 'Or anyone else while we're at it.'

'Your secret is safe with me,' I promised, silently wondering who would believe me even if I did try to tell them.

'Then she asked me to help her get something down off the top of the wardrobe,' Joe said, looking pale and ghostly when I found him in the kitchen, washing his hands and splashing water on his face. 'The next thing I knew, she was bouncing across the bed and claiming we were twin flames with her hands on my—'

'Please don't finish that sentence,' I said, smiling politely at the other partygoers glancing our way with concern. 'You're safe now.'

He shuddered and pumped the handwash again.

'You've created a monster. What if there are other women out there, launching themselves at unsuspecting men?'

'The unsuspecting men should be so lucky.'

Turning off the tap, I passed him a hand towel. 'I'm sorry, that must've been really . . .' I paused and revisited the scene in my mind. 'Well, from my perspective it was mostly very funny. But I am sorry.'

'I'll never be clean again,' he muttered as he rubbed his hands violently with the towel. 'Is there any bleach around here?'

'No,' I said, 'but there's alcohol outside. Let's get you a drink.'

He followed obediently, completely silent as we passed through the party in search of booze. It was later than I'd realised and night was finally drawing in and the rain thankfully holding off. Dad's string lights glowed brighter by the second against a pinky-purple sky as darkness fell, and that soft, hazy, only by night feeling of possibility sparkled inside me as we poured ourselves large measures at the trestle table Mum had kept well stocked with booze.

'Thank you for the save,' Joe said, clutching his glass for emotional support without actually drinking. 'That was scarier than the time I got trapped in a lift with Courtney Love.'

'Don't mention it,' I replied. 'Please, I mean it, never mention it again. I'm just glad I made it before you did something you might regret.'

He stepped around me to block my view of the rest of the party, as though I could see anything but him in the first place. 'At the risk of sounding like a cliché, we need to talk.'

My head dipped low and my hair slipped over my shoulders to frame my face. 'About the book, I know.'

'Not about the book,' Joe said, one hand raising my chin so I could see the raw desire in his blue, blue eyes. 'We need to talk about you and that dress and whatever the fuck it is you did to me this afternoon because I haven't been able to think straight since.'

A wave of need rolled through me and my lips gently parted. I wasn't expecting it. I wasn't prepared.

'Joseph!' Gregory's voice cut through the night like a rusty bread knife, sawing away at my last nerve and shattering whatever fragile thing was between us. 'Get over here, I want you to meet my old pal!'

'Saved by the Brent,' I murmured, Joe's shoulders sagging at the sight of his dad, arm around the shoulders of a world famous and incredibly uncomfortable fantasy author.

'I'd better . . .' he said, letting his words trail off as he accepted defeat.

'You'd better,' I agreed even though I didn't want to let him go. 'He looks like he's had a few and the last thing we need is him pitching a *Butterflies/Coraline* crossover.'

With every step away from me, Joe's long, confident stride returned, the easy-going smile sliding into place for everyone to see. He only paused once, to glance back over his shoulder at me, his expression flickering for just a split-second.

'He doesn't do relationships,' I told myself unnecessarily and when I saw CJ approaching with a sickly-sweet grin on his face, added, 'And you don't get involved with wankers.'

'Who's a wanker?' he asked, sidling up beside me in his impossibly skinny black suit.

'You,' I replied with fluttering eyelashes. 'What do you want?'

He looked genuinely put out.

'What? A man can't say hello to his ex-girlfriend at her dad's birthday party?'

'Think about what you just said then answer your own question.'

I started to walk away but he placed a hand on my shoulder and my whole body shivered with revulsion. It felt wrong and painful, like stepping on a slug with one foot only to stand on a piece of Lego with the other. Looking up to the sky, I tried to remember the name of some ancient rain god and begged for divine intervention.

'You were missed this afternoon,' he said as I shrugged him off. 'I hope you weren't hiding away because of me.'

'Colin, please,' I begged. 'It's been a long day and I don't have the energy for your particular brand of bollocks right now.'

'CJ, please. And calm down, I only wanted to congratulate you on your book.'

'What book?' I stepped back, confused.

'*Butterflies*,' he replied, pushing his little wire-framed glasses up his nose. 'Walsh didn't write it, you did.'

All I had to do was deny it.

Or laugh in his face, roll my eyes or turn around and walk away. But there was something about the smug look on his face that stopped me from doing the sensible thing.

'What makes you say that?'

His mouth curved up into a wicked smile and I knew I'd given the game away.

'You forget how well I know you,' he replied, flipping a strand of hair off my shoulder, making me involuntarily gip. Did everyone feel this way about their exes? We'd been so intimate for so long but the thought of him touching me now made me want to run inside and take a shower with a bottle of bleach and a scouring pad.

'That book has got you written all over it, the references, the jokes, the lead character's obsession with Nutella. I only wish you'd been so forthcoming with your fantasies when we were together, maybe things would've worked out differently.'

'Happy to confirm they wouldn't,' I replied, pulling my hair away and very much wishing I had my cardigan with me. My cardigan, a used bin bag, a dead badger. Anything to cover up my bare skin.

'Sometimes we have to go through great heartbreak to unlock our art,' he mused, rubbing his designer stubble and looking up to the sky. 'I had to end things between us so we could both achieve greatness, I'm sure you understand that now.'

'I understand you wouldn't know humility if it kicked you up the arse and I understand my book has outsold yours by more than ten to one.'

'So you're keeping check on my sales.' He lowered his gaze, aiming for sultry but landing somewhere closer to extremely short-sighted, then took my hand in his. 'Sophie, I've been thinking. What if we were to give it another try?'

Just when I thought my day couldn't get any worse.

281

CHAPTER TWENTY-THREE

'Picture it,' CJ said with a purr. 'We could be a publishing power couple, the literary darling and his commercial superstar. A modern-day Henry Miller and Anaïs Nin, F Scott Fitzgerald and Zelda, Ted Hughes and Sylvia Plath.'

'And I'll be going the same way as Sylvia Plath if you don't stop talking immediately.' I stared at my ex-boyfriend. Who was this lunatic? 'You can't be serious.'

'Why not?' he reasoned. 'Things are different now.'

'How?'

'You're a bestselling author. Not just some little primary school teacher.'

Somehow he managed to misread the shock on my face for something altogether different and squeezed my hand with encouragement. It was a miracle he was still standing.

'You don't have to look like that, silly, it's not a trick,' he said happily. 'I'm prepared to give you a second chance.'

'You're prepared to give me a second chance.'

I had to repeat the words to make sure I was hearing him correctly. Of all the unpredictable things that had happened to me since leaving home on Thursday morning, this was, without a doubt, the most nightmarish. Not even Margaret Atwood could've come up with such a dystopic plot twist. I would volunteer for the Hunger Games before I got back together with CJ.

Disentangling my hand from his, I straightened his tie and patted him briskly on the shoulder.

'CJ, I don't know how to put this kindly but even if I received a solid gold telegram from a flying pig saying hell had frozen over and the only other two humans left alive were you and Boris Johnson, you would find me in the phone book under Mrs BoJo in less than two minutes flat.'

'I think, when people look back on the early twenty-first century—' he began but I was in no mood to hear the rest of it.

'You're a shitbag,' I said, filling my voice with conviction and forcing him to hear me. 'You're a user and an opportunist, you're beyond selfish, and I would never, ever even consider getting back together but I should thank you for inspiring me because if you had even an ounce of talent in the bedroom, I might never have put pen to paper.'

Of course, that was the only bit he really heard.

'As I recall, you weren't complaining at the time,' he said, nostrils flaring beneath his glasses.

'As I recall I wasn't providing much feedback at all,' I replied. 'I was usually too busy thinking about what we needed from the supermarket or wondering if I'd remembered to pay the gas bill. Thank god they invented rechargeable vibrators because I could not afford to keep giving Duracell half my salary. You know teachers are wildly underpaid.'

His beneficent expression twisted into something ugly and bitter and I felt myself tensing up. He never had been one to take rejection well. I thought back to all those torn-up letters I'd found on the living room floor until he finally found an agent who took pity on him.

'God, you're such a cliché,' he spat. 'That's how I knew you wrote the book, such lazy, predictable writing. It's not good, Sophie. I'm not surprised you wanted to keep your name off it. I'd be mortified if people thought that was the sum total of my talent.'

But his words rolled off me like lazy, predictable water off a duck's back.

'Of all the opinions I give a shit about, yours is at the very bottom of the list,' I said, pleasantly surprised by my own lack of reaction. 'I'll pass on the reconciliation but give me a shout when you've written your second book. If it's not shit and I've got time between counting all my money and writing the second and third books I already have contracted, I might blurb you.'

He scoffed, enraged. 'As if I'd want your endorsement. I've no interest in being a housewives' favourite.'

'At least then you'd be someone's favourite.'

'I'm going to tell everyone,' CJ cried, high on the bitter sting of a knockback. 'I'm going to tell your parents, I'm going to tell my debut author Facebook group—'

I looked away as he carried on with his rant, wondering how long I would have to endure his tantrum. It was strangely reminiscent of our sex life.

'—All those things people were saying earlier, to Joe,

they didn't mean it. Everyone was laughing at you behind your back. If your mother knew the truth, she'd never speak to you again.'

Out of the corner of my eye, I saw Joe excuse himself from his conversation and make a beeline over to us but CJ didn't notice, too busy conjuring up insults.

'You're not even a real writer,' he went on, tears in his eyes now. 'It's not even a real book, just a load of tropes and clichés strung together. You're not serious, you're not an artist like me. You don't even live in London!'

'Last time I checked that wasn't in a writer's job requirement,' Joe said, appearing by my side and making CJ jump out of his skin. 'Believe it or not, there are other places in the country.'

'When a man is tired of London, he is tired of life,' CJ sniped. 'To quote the genius wordsmith Oscar Wilde.'

'Been a minute since I was in a pub quiz but I'm pretty sure that was Samuel Johnson,' I replied. 'Not Oscar Wilde.'

'And to quote another genius wordsmith, Taylor Swift,' Joe added. 'Haters gonna hate.'

'As if you two know anything about literature.' CJ pulled out his phone to prove himself wrong. 'Here it is, when a man is . . . oh.'

'YOU!' Charlotte boomed, racing across the lawn when she saw my ex's Android and his crestfallen face. 'CJ, you chunt, give that to me.'

'What's a chunt?' Joe asked in a whisper.

'Use your imagination,' I replied in the same.

'You know it's no phones allowed.' She swiped it out of his hand and delivered a swift kick to the shins with her black and white Nikes. 'I can't believe you.'

'I assumed that didn't include family,' CJ said, blinking his cow eyes behind the magnifying lenses of his glasses but Charlotte the Gen Z genius was unmoved. 'It does but you're not family.'

She held the phone up to his face to unlock it then flounced off, scanning his photo album and howling with laughter as she skipped away.

'How is it possible your sister is as awful as you are,' he said viciously after she disappeared into the house to stash his phone with the rest of her bounty. 'It's beyond me how a woman like your mother managed to raise such a pair of—'

'If I were you, I'd be really careful how I finish that sentence,' Joe interrupted, stepping forward.

CJ sneered. 'Why, what are you going to do?'

'Say whatever it is you were going to say and find out.'

'Boys,' I cautioned, positioning myself between the posturing men.

CJ drew himself up to his full six feet of height and still came up short compared to Joe.

'I'm not afraid of you,' he said, even though both of his hands were visibly shaking. 'And she's not worth it, just so you know. Starfished her way through five years together and now she's begging me to take her back.'

'That's me,' I replied with a dramatic shrug at Joe. 'As you can see, I'm practically on my hands and knees over here.'

'Bitch.'

CJ whispered the word so quietly it almost escaped under the music and party chatter but I heard it and, if I heard it, Joe heard it too.

'Do you know where the nearest hospital is?' he asked.

'Yes?' CJ replied.

Joe clenched his huge hands into giant fists and rolled back his shoulders.

'Good.'

As a teacher, I believed violence was never the answer, unless it was between siblings in which case it was totally fine, but there was a dark little part of me that really wanted to see Joe knock CJ on his arse. There was an even bigger part of me that wanted to do it myself but my dress was new and the bodice tight and I wasn't sure how possible it would be to throw a proper punch without ripping it.

'Joe, leave the poor wretch alone,' William said, appearing just in time to join me for the standoff. 'Look at him, he's suffered plenty.'

'I don't know about that,' Joe replied, still staring daggers at CJ. 'He's an ignorant, overgrown toddler squeezed into a Topman suit and I've had enough of him.'

'How dare you!' CJ shrieked. 'This is Dries van Noten!'

It was a strange final straw but insulting a suit that was so tight we could all see the cut of his boxer shorts seemed to be the thing that finally pushed CJ too far. He launched himself at Joe but, before he could land a hit, William put out one arm to hold him back, and just a few half-hearted attempts at slaps in Joe's direction windmilled over my brother's shoulder before CJ gave up.

'Really?' Joe said, trying not to laugh. 'That's it?'

'I hate to interrupt CJ getting a pasting but your presence is needed.' Sarah hurried over with a worried look on her face. 'All of you,' she said before resting her eyes on CJ. 'Well, not you, obviously, you walking chocolate teapot.'

'Were we too mean to him?' I asked as we hurried away, following her across the garden. I shivered suddenly. The air had turned cooler and there was a sudden breeze.

'No,' William and Joe answered together.

'I don't even know what he said and I'm confident we're right,' William added. 'Please don't tell me or I might have to go back there and slap him myself.'

'You're going to be too busy breaking up another fight,' Sarah told him, pushing through the crowd that had gathered by the bouncy castle and leading us all through to the front.

CHAPTER TWENTY-FOUR

Right between the bouncy castle and the big top, and suspiciously close to the bar, my father and Joe's dad were bouncing around on their tiptoes, fists up in front of their faces and circling each other like they were starring in a senior citizen am-dram production of *Rocky*.

'What is going on?' I demanded, every guest at the party taking a single step back to leave me, Joe, William and Sarah alone up front. Behind our dads, I saw Genevieve Salinger and Nelson Allen looking on with very guilty expressions. So, the hot book deal news was out.

'Never mind,' I said as they both looked sheepishly away. 'How did this happen? Where's Mum? Where's Mal?'

'Your mum went to get the cake and the last time I saw Mal, he was holding a screaming child upside-down in the kitchen,' Sarah replied, as Gregory started hopping from side to side. 'I didn't know what else to do.'

'Saboteur!' Gregory yelled. 'You stole my author!'

'I did no such thing!' Dad yelled back. 'I'm a huge admirer of Gen's work. I made an offer for a book and it was accepted. Don't get your knickers in a twist.'

'Consider them well and truly knotted.' He swung at the air in front of him, completely missing my dad. 'This was your plan all along, drag me up here to the arse end of nowhere then humiliate me in front of my son and my peers.'

'No, Gregory, I did not plan my birthday party exclusively to put one over on you,' Dad replied archly as though it hadn't been in the back of his mind since the very first time he spoke to the *Llama Glama* author. 'It's just business, old friend. Isn't that what you said to me when you poached Nelson?'

Both authors choked on their drinks and backed slowly away from the bickering twosome as everyone else drew closer.

'You're a petty man,' Gregory said seething. 'I don't know how you can look at yourself in a mirror.'

'Very easily, thank you very much,' Dad replied. 'I assume you had to get special mirrors made to accommodate the size of your head.'

'Ignoramus!'

'Narcissist!'

'No, we're not doing this.' Joe jumped in between the two men as they started to scuffle, not so much boxing as exchanging awkward slaps and swipes, neither one wanting to commit to a full swing. 'Dad, it's Hugh's birthday. Apologise.'

'I'll do no such thing,' Gregory returned, the three of them all moving in unison, hands and arms flapping around in the most embarrassing display of violence this side of the 2022 Oscars. 'He stole my author!'

'You stole mine first!'

'Take your hands off me, son.' Gregory tore off his jacket and threw it to the ground. 'This has been a long time coming.'

'Might take him more seriously if he didn't have massive sweat stains under his pits,' Sarah whispered as she nibbled on a tiny sausage on a stick. 'I've got a tenner on your dad, Michael Cunningham is running a book.'

The low Motown soundtrack that had been playing quietly in the background all night suddenly became much louder as 'Eye of the Tiger' blared out over the speakers. Beside me, William quickly closed the Spotify app on his phone.

'What?' he said when I gave him a look. 'I already stopped one fight, I'm not the bloody UN.'

'And you think this one will be better?' I replied, looking at the two middle-aged men getting ready to duke it out.

'I think the other one would've been sad,' he answered. 'This should be a banger. They need to get it out their system.'

I crossed my arms over my chest and bit my lip. 'Trust me, that never works like you think it will.'

'Get your hands off Hugh!'

From out of nowhere, CJ hurled himself into the fray with a pitchy battle cry, charging directly at Joe's mid-section, head down, shoulders braced, and speared him right in the stomach. Joe barely flinched as CJ bounced off him, landing flat on his arse.

'What are you doing?' Joe said as our fathers continued to swipe at each other. 'I'm trying to stop them fighting, I'm not part of it.'

He held out a hand to help him up but CJ slapped it away.

'Oh look,' Sarah said as the second scuffle broke out. 'The men are menning.'

'The straight men,' William corrected. 'If you don't mind.'

'What was it you said before, you've had enough of me? I've had enough of you,' CJ declared. 'Twatting around like you're cock of the walk. Why are you lying for her? I hope it's not to get in her knickers because, trust me, it isn't worth it.'

'I've asked you to stop talking once, I won't ask again,' Joe replied with a growl.

But CJ didn't stop talking. His eyes sparkled with malice, thrilled to get a reaction.

'Don't be fooled by what's in the book,' he said. 'We were young when we first met so I'll be generous and put some of her poor performance down to inexperience but the fact of the matter is, some people are just shit in bed.'

'That's it.' Joe wheeled around, ready to fight. 'You tragic little weasel, I'm going to—'

'You're going to what?!' CJ yelped. 'You're going to what, Joseph Walsh, hit me? You can't, I'll have you fired!'

'He's right, Joe, you can't hit him,' I said, stepping forward. 'But I can.'

And I did.

Just once, landing my first ever punch square in the jaw. He reeled for a moment before careening backwards onto the bouncy castle, arms and legs flailing wildly.

'That's it, CJ!' Dad cheered. 'Someone had to be first on!'

'See, this is why women should be in charge of things,' Sarah said. 'Men mess around too much. We're efficient.'

'Oh my god, it hurts so much,' I gasped, shaking out my hand as the music ratcheted up another notch.

'Imagine how he feels.' Joe took my hand in his and kissed the throbbing knuckles in front of everyone. 'My knight in shining armour.'

'All right, everyone, it's time for cake!'

My mother's voice sang out across the scene as she and Charlotte emerged from the kitchen carrying her still very questionable cake, made no better for the massive number of candles she'd shoved in for effect.

'Joe, watch out!'

William's warning came a split second too late.

CJ launched off the bouncy castle and lunged at Joe, grabbing him around the waist and spinning him in a circle. With a look of perfect surprise on his face, Joe let go of my hand as CJ dragged him away, his arms still outstretched, and before he could attempt to recover his balance, he slammed into both my dad and his. Gregory went over next, stumbling into my mother and knocking the cake clean out of her arms as the two of them rolled to the floor. The cake flew through the air, landing right at my feet, somehow managing to look no less appetising than it had on the plate. At the same time, Joe and CJ continued to scuffle, rolling around in front of the bouncy castle, Joe holding a defensive position and CJ attempting to spike him with little jabs. It was like watching a cub trying to bash in a lion, almost adorable but also entirely pointless. There was a reason Simba waited a few years to take on Scar and we were seeing it play out in real time.

'Hugh! Gregory! Enough!' My mother's sharp voice brought both men to heel in an instant. 'I was gone for less than five minutes.'

Dad stooped, shamefaced, picked up the cake knife and held it out to my mother as the human tumbleweed of CJ and Joe spun towards them and Dad threw himself in front of his family.

'Watch it,' Dad yelled as Charlotte fished into her ill-gotten Chanel purse and pulled out her own non-contraband phone. 'I've got a knife!'

It wasn't a threat so much as a warning as the tangle of limbs swallowed him whole, the three of them hurtling back towards the bouncy castle, a blur of arms and legs thumping across the bright red floor. All four turrets jostled with joy as three adult male bodies and one ceremonial cake knife ricocheted around as one. We all held our collective breath as CJ stumbled and slipped like Bambi on his way to a funeral in his skin-tight suit. Dad scrabbled to gain purchase, long having lost hold of the knife and Joe, looking more confused than anything else, stayed exactly where he was, clinging to the last shred of dignity available to these men. As 'Eye of the Tiger' faded away, I heard the opening bars of 'Oops I Did It Again' emanating from the speakers and an ear-splitting squeal filled the air, drowning out even Britney, followed by a loud, insistent hissing.

'He's stabbed me!' CJ screamed at the top of his lungs. 'He's stabbed me! I'm dying!'

But it wasn't CJ who had been skewered, it was the bouncy castle. Joe rolled away from the human dogpile first, pulling my dad out next and leaving CJ to flounder as the castle wilted around him, deflating much faster than I would have expected.

'I'm sorry, Pandora,' Dad lamented as Joe helped him up to his feet, the bouncy castle deflating in the background. 'We're never going to get the deposit back.'

'At least you got to have a go.' She swooped down to pick up his top hat and placed it on his head with an affectionate pat. 'That's what matters.'

CJ crawled out from underneath the brightly coloured PVC, unstabbed and mostly unscathed. The only thing that seemed to have suffered was the seam up the back of his very tight trousers which had split in two, and much to my and Sarah's delight, he hadn't noticed yet. He stood up with indignation on his face, a torrent of abuse on the tip of his tongue and his arse on full display.

'You're pathetic! You're all pathetic!' he squeaked. 'Not you, Sir Ian, but him and her and him and you!'

'Moi?' Sarah coquettishly batted her eyelashes at CJ. 'I'll take that as a compliment.'

'Now, CJ, you need to calm down—' Dad started but he was already on a roll.

'I don't even know why I bothered coming,' he cut in with a grunt. 'A self-important, so-called critic, an editor who's so out of touch he wouldn't know a good idea if it slapped him in the face, a precocious brat who needs a good slap and William? Well, the less said about you the better.'

'My mere existence is offensive enough, I know,' my brother said with a quick incline of the head as my mother and father watched on in shock. 'But I really think it's time for you to shut up and piss off now, Colin.'

'Be quiet, I'm streaming,' hissed Charlotte under her breath as she held up her phone. 'This is gold.'

'Or what?' CJ challenged. 'You'll set your attack dog on me? Please, he's not going to do anything.' He looked over at Joe who bristled beside me, and above, the gathering storm clouds rumbled a warning. 'Couldn't even hit me, had to let a girl do it for him. Or were you simply returning the favour, Soph?'

'Colin, don't,' I said, keeping my voice cool even though I felt anything but. 'This isn't the time or place.' I started as I felt a single solitary raindrop fall on my bare arms.

He made a show of looking around, hands held out to either side as though what I'd said made no sense. 'Can't think of a better time or place. You've got so many fans assembled.'

'I know I might get the sack but please can I hit him?' Joe pleaded.

'No,' my dad replied.

'Yes,' answered his own father.

Strutting up and down in front of the crowd, grey underpants completely on show, CJ continued crowing. 'For the life of me, I can't work out why you're covering for her. You must be mad, even offering to put your name to a shit book that only appeals to little girls with no imagination and silly cows who lack the intelligence to understand and appreciate real writing.'

'Performance art at its finest!' boomed William. 'The cake's shot to shit but who fancies a Mini Milk?'

Half the guests raised their hands, people starting to shuffle away, glancing at the sky.

'Desperate wank fantasy with no more literary merit than a till receipt.' CJ however was still going. 'I could shit out something better. I could sneeze and come up with more impressive dialogue.'

'But you didn't, you one-hit-wonder-wanker,' Joe interjected. 'You wrote one very pretentious novel and you knew the right people so you got lucky. Every proposal you've sent in since has been rejected because not even someone as supportive as Hugh Taylor is prepared to put his name to them.'

'That's not true!'

'You write like an AI trying to impersonate Bret Easton Ellis only the AI would do a better job!' Joe shot back. 'Sophie writes rings around you.'

'Joe!' I exclaimed, pulling him back as more raindrops started to splash my face. 'Don't!'

'I'd rather publish one book and retire than have my name attached to something as vulgar and amateurish as *Butterflies*,' CJ wailed. 'Hugh, Pandora, I hope you're proud of what you've raised.'

'Sophie, before I beat him to death with the croquet mallet, what's he talking about?' Mum asked, tapping lightly on my arm.

'Nothing,' Joe answered for me. 'Don't listen to him.'

'Tell her,' CJ demanded. 'Or I will.'

Sarah squeezed my hand as William placed a protective hand on my shoulder and Joe gave me an almost imperceptible nod. Whatever happened next, at least I wouldn't be alone.

'Joe didn't write *Butterflies*,' I said, turning to face my family, their friends and Gregory Brent. 'I did.'

CJ said something, presumably even more hateful than before, but it was impossible to hear him over the crowd's collective gasp. Even Charlotte's arm fell back down by her side, livestream over.

'Sophie?' Mum said, blinking with disbelief.

'Este,' I corrected with a wan smile as a crack of thunder split the sky and the heavens opened. 'I'm Este Cox.'

It was a spectacular end to a spectacular party.

CHAPTER TWENTY-FIVE

For the first time, I could truly say William earned his commission. Right as the rain began hammering the party into submission, he stepped in, giving Sarah the nod and ordering us both to return to the cottage immediately. Mal reappeared at exactly the wrong moment, running down the garden with an umbrella, and the second he saw the looks on my parents' faces, I could tell he knew what he'd missed.

'I'll talk to them,' he promised as Sarah steered me in the right direction, barely able to see one foot in front of the other through the pouring rain.

'Thank you,' I said. Someone should and I didn't know where to start.

'Don't worry,' Mal replied. 'It's going to be fine.'

I only wished I had his confidence.

'Cup of tea?' Sarah suggested, pushing Joe's room divider out the way once we were safely inside, the noise of the party far away. 'Yep, this is clearly a tea situation.'

'It's also a my-parents-hate-me-and-I'm-going-to-lose-my-job situation,' I replied, tossing her a towel to dry her hair. 'Lots of milk, one sugar.'

I sank onto the sofa that Joe had folded neatly away. Considerate of him. Wet through and freezing cold, I stared straight ahead, my head full of helium but my body made of lead.

'Nixon?' I said, teeth chattering.

'Taylor,' she replied.

'I know you're going to say no and I know you're only trying to help,' I said with my best attempt at a reassuring smile. 'But I would really like to be on my own for a minute.'

'You look like you've been constipated for a week and you're trying to convince me you don't need a suppository.' She took a mug out of the cupboard and set it next to the kettle. 'You're a grown woman. If that's what you want, I'll leave you be. Unlike some people, I trust you.'

'You must be the only one,' I replied. 'No one out there would trust me as far as they could throw me.'

'I wasn't talking about anyone out there,' she said, dropping a teabag into the mug then coming back over to the sofa to press a kiss to the top of my head. 'I was talking about you learning to trust yourself. Your instincts were sharp enough to clock CJ, albeit two years too late, and you need to trust them now. This was always going to happen eventually, at least now you won't have to worry about when. It's time to bet on yourself.'

'Don't know if I like my odds but I haven't got a lot of choice, have I?'

'Nope.'

She fixed a fallen shoulder strap on my dress then pinged it gently. 'Get into some dry clothes before you catch your death. If it's all right with you, I might hang around outside for a minute, in case you change your mind and want some company to go with that cup of tea. Lights on or off?'

'Off please.'

Flipping the switch to leave me in gentle darkness, she let herself out, pulling the door halfway closed behind her.

So the news was out. The worst thing that could've happened, had happened. Although comparing the whole world knowing I was Este Cox with the idea of getting back together with CJ did sort of put it in perspective, and perspective was needed.

This wasn't the greatest tragedy ever to befall mankind. In the greater scheme of things, it wasn't even as bad as the fact they didn't sell Mini Eggs year-round or that Justin Timberlake was allowed to continue existing after Britney's book came out, but it still felt rough to me. Mum and Dad knew, Gregory Brent knew, along with everyone at the party and everyone who followed Charlotte on TikTok. The school would find out. And the most absurd part of it all? Even though my life had literally just been irrevocably changed, I wasn't sitting thinking about the damage to my teaching career, the reactions of my family or how much more pressure this put on me to deliver a brilliant sequel.

I was thinking about Joe.

'You're a disgrace,' I told myself as I kicked away my soaked slides, the wooden floorboards warm underfoot.

'I wouldn't go that far.'

His silhouette stood in the doorway, black against grey, as Joe leaned against the frame. Out the window, I saw an umbrella-carrying Sarah raise a hand in a farewell then walk away up the garden.

'You don't know what I was talking about,' I told him, one foot covering the other, my toes curling as he crossed the threshold, dripping wet.

He took off his shoes, leaving them by the door, white shirt clinging to his arms where the umbrella hadn't been enough to protect him, his grey trousers now almost black. He studied me for a long second with his damp hair falling in front of his eyes, little rivulets of rainwater creating a sacred circle around him.

Instead of joining me on the sofa, he walked across to the kitchenette counter and dug into the punnet of strawberries we'd bought at the fête. I grabbed one of the cushions from the other end of the sofa and held it tightly to my cold body.

'Want one?'

I shook my head and I watched him bite into his, filling the air with a fresh hit of sweetness.

'They're good,' he said, licking the juice from his lips. 'Nothing like English strawberries in the summer.'

'No,' I agreed weakly. 'Nothing like it.'

He reached for the fridge door.

'Don't,' I said and he paused.

'Don't what?'

'Don't put them in the fridge.'

I found my feet and forced myself across the room to take the punnet out of his hand, placing the strawberries on the kitchen counter. 'They taste better if you leave them out. They don't like the cold.'

'You learn something new every day.'

'Lots of people learned something new tonight,' I replied, prodding a plump, firm strawberry. 'What's the mood like out there?'

'The party mostly dried up, no pun intended, but no one was going to top what happened so probably good timing,' he admitted. 'Your mum and dad went inside with Mal before I could talk to them, William and his husband were returning phones and calling taxis, and CJ was crying hysterically on the shoulder of a very tolerant Michael Cunningham.'

'God, he's one of my favourite authors,' I whispered. 'He deserves better.'

'We'll send him a fruit basket,' Joe said. 'Or a stack of cash, whatever it takes.'

It was so quiet, all I could hear was the kettle clicking off and the heavy rise and fall of my own breath. If I'd run a marathon, I might understand why my body burned and my legs were weak but all I'd done was walk down a garden. I was exhausted but restless, the worst kind of tired.

'Your friend said you didn't want to talk.' Joe's blue eyes blazed like sapphires in the low light, the only colour I could see. 'Do you want me to leave?'

'No.'

It was the only thing I was sure about.

His hand reached across the short space between us and brushed my wet hair back behind my ear, and his fingers curled around the back of my neck for a brief moment before he pulled them away. I missed his touch immediately.

'I can't stand the thought of you sitting in here on your own, beating yourself up,' he said, his words tender. 'You've done nothing wrong.'

Flexing my bruised right hand, I frowned. 'Apart from when I punched my ex-boyfriend in the face?'

'You've done nothing wrong,' Joe said again, this time with a slight smile.

'Let's wait and see what Mum and Dad think before we commit to that.' I leaned back against the fridge, their disappointed faces right in front of my eyes. 'And my boss. And the parents whose children I teach. And the entire internet.'

'Because the internet is well known for their rational and even-handed response in all situations?' Joe pushed his own damp hair away from his face, newly defined waves curling around his ears.

'This isn't how I wanted everyone to find out,' I said with an exasperated groan. 'I was perfectly happy hiding.'

'Were you?' he asked. 'Perfectly happy?'

'I was happier than I am now,' I replied. 'It's like I've walked into one of those giant searchlights and everyone is staring at me.'

'It's not a searchlight.' He lowered his voice as his hand found its way back up to my face and neither of us pulled away this time. 'It's a spotlight. It's shining on you so the whole world can see things the way I do. Every facet of you is sparkling right now. You're so bright, you're blinding.'

My pulse quickened with the same heat and longing I saw reflected in his face. He was so close.

'If this is some kind of game, please tell me now,' I said weakly. 'I can't get involved with someone who's going to mess me about.'

'And I can't get involved with anyone full stop.'

His actions didn't match his words. He moved closer

still, until our foreheads touched and his palms rested on either side of my face, fingertips grazing my hair, my ears, my neck and both thumbs caressing my cheek-bones.

'Then what are you doing?' I whispered as one hand dropped down the back of my neck, his thumb trailing over my cheek and along my jaw until it found my mouth.

'I wish I knew.'

My lips parted as he tested the softness of the skin, lightly tracing the swell.

'The first time I saw you, at lunch with Mal,' he said, closing his eyes for a second to concentrate on the memory. 'Something about you connected to something in me in a way I can't explain. And I thought I could explain everything. Every time you moved, I panicked, sure you were going to leave before I got to speak to you. I told myself to stay where I was and let you go but I couldn't. You were like a test.'

'Did you pass?' I asked as his eyes fluttered open.

'The results aren't in yet.'

The pad of his thumb moved down my chin to my throat and paused at my collarbone. 'Then I came over and I know you felt it too. When you stood up to leave, your hair spilled over your shoulder. I literally couldn't breathe. The way the light hit, you were glowing. And you should've seen the look on your face when Mal told you to leave. I knew if you stayed, all bets were off. By the time we left the restaurant, I couldn't stand the thought of letting you out my sight.'

'Can't believe my singing didn't put you off,' I quipped softly. He grinned. No hesitation this time.

'There was nothing you could've done to put me off by then. There's nothing you could ever do. Even fighting with you is fun.'

My hands found the fridge behind me and cooled themselves against the metal finish, too afraid to touch him in case I couldn't let go.

'You're so passionate, you care so much. You're funny and smart, and you're ridiculously talented even if you aren't ready to believe it yourself. Anyone would be beyond lucky to stand beside you. Yes, I was trying to help when I said I was Este Cox but I was also being selfish. I was trying to keep myself in your life, same as when I brought your bag up here. Could've given it to my dad or taken it into work to Mal but it was an excuse. I needed to see you again.'

'Instalove is my least favourite trope,' I told him, hands shaking behind my back. 'You're not doing your-self any favours right now.'

'Then I'm not expressing myself very well and you don't understand how I feel,' he murmured, the soft rumpling of his shirt as loud as thunder in my ear. 'I wish it didn't have to be so complicated.'

'Why is it? You're the one who doesn't do relation-ships,' I reminded him and myself at the same time. If he didn't step away from me very soon, that wasn't going to matter much any more. 'I'm not a mind reader. If you want me to understand, you have to explain.'

He pulled away so I could see his face, flushed and full of need. 'You really want to know what I'm thinking right now?'

'I've got a vague idea,' I breathed. 'But clarification couldn't hurt.'

Joe stared back at me like this was another test,

searching me for something that might make him hesi-
tate but I knew all he would find there was my desire.
A desire I saw mirrored back at me in his blue eyes.

'I'm wondering how you like it,' he said, leaning in
to whisper directly into my ear. 'I'm wondering if you'll
pull me down on top of you or push me back and ride
me. I'm wondering what you taste like and how long I
can hold you at the edge before you come undone and
start to beg.' He moved around to the other ear and I
felt a shudder work its way down my body, rippling
along my spine and building to a crescendo between
my thighs. 'Will you say my name?' he asked. 'Or will
you scream? I want to know how far I can take you
before it's too much. I want to know if you will look
me in the eye when I finally let you come.'

The safe space between us disappeared and the hands
that had cradled my head so gently were on my hips,
his mouth hovering above the skin of my neck as he
breathed me in. Small whimpers escaped from my throat
even as I tried to contain them, my breath ragged and
uneven.

'If you don't like instalove, which tropes do you like?'
he asked, the rough promise of tomorrow's beard
scratching the tender flesh of my throat.

I placed my forearms on his chest, holding him at
bay and holding myself up, arms shaking, knees weak.
The sound of rain pounded against the roof of the cottage
and, as the anticipation grew, my resolve weakened
until there was nothing left at all.

'Only one bed has always been a favourite,' I replied,
casting my gaze across the room. My hands slid down
from his chest to his waist, thumbs hooking themselves
over his belt. 'Forced proximity, enemies to lovers.'

Slowly, so slowly, he began to unbutton his shirt, carefully manipulating each button, without taking his eyes off mine.

'Is this a good idea?' I said, my cardigan slipping off my shoulder all on its own.

'No,' he answered. 'It's a terrible idea. You're going to get hurt, I'm going to get hurt. You'll never speak to me again. It'll probably destroy my career.'

'Then we shouldn't,' I said as he pulled the fabric of his open shirt out of his waistband and casually discarded it on the floor. What little light there was cut shapes and shadows over his body, the indentation of his collarbone, the curve of his shoulder as it dipped into the swell of his bicep. 'I'll go back to the house, sleep on the floor or something.'

'That's a great idea,' Joe agreed, his words melting into me as he pressed his mouth against my neck, right where my blood pulsed under my skin, the taste of my heartbeat on his tongue.

'We're not animals,' I groaned, head rolling back when he slipped one black silk spaghetti strap off my shoulder, his kisses moving down my body and leaving a trail of sweet shivers in their wake. 'I can control myself.'

He ran his hand up my back and raked it through the hair at the nape of my neck, grasping a careful fistful and pulling gently until I moaned for more.

'Good girl.'

The words rumbled in his throat and I was done for. There was no need for even one bed, not when the wall was right behind me, the floor right beneath us. I tore at his belt, furious at the strip of supple leather for keeping him from me even half a second longer than necessary. The fastener, button and zip that held his trousers around his waist were an outrage, my fingers numb as they worked their way around each one. It was too hard to concentrate even on simple tasks with Joe's hands up in my hair, his mouth charting a course from one side of my collarbone to the other. Half of me wanted to let go and lose myself but the other half wanted to remember every exquisite sensation. I heard his trousers fall to the floor and pulled on the taut waistband of his underwear, slipping them down over his hips, his backside, his strong, thick thighs. He pushed me back against the wall in response, the skirt of my dress riding up and gathering between us as he found the slip of silky underwear between my legs, the last thing that separated us.

'This is the worst fucking idea you've ever had,' Joe growled into my ear as he worked his way along it, teasing and testing, one finger tracing a line right down the middle, gliding back and forth. 'We're going to regret this tomorrow.'

'Better make it something worth regretting then,' I said, forcing my eyes open and staring straight into his with as much defiance as I could muster. He held me still as his fingers slid inside me, watching the sharp intake of breath as it filled my body. Still I didn't look away, I watched him watch me, wonder on his face and a thick, hard erection throbbing impatiently against my thigh.

'Sophie, I—' he started but I shook my head.

'Don't.' I leaned into his body, the curve of his hand between my legs, my hips already moving to his rhythm. 'Don't say anything. Don't make promises you're not going to keep.'

'I can think of one I can keep.' The edges of his words

already frayed as my breath came faster. 'I said I'd make you come until you see stars.'

Finally, his lips found mine, his hot hungry mouth sweet with strawberries. But if he was hungry, I was ravenous. Two days of wanting, waiting, imagining this moment but it felt like a lifetime. I stood on my tiptoes to pull him as close as I possibly could and hooked one leg around his waist, riding the tide for as long as I could, even though I knew I would be overwhelmed and disappear beneath the waves without a trace. It was a mistake. I would regret it. But when he pushed inside me, filling me with sweet, sharp relief, I truly did not care.

CHAPTER TWENTY-SIX

It was dark when I reached across the bed for Joe, only to discover he'd been gone long enough for his warm side of the mattress to turn cold. There were no lights on in the bathroom, no sound coming from anywhere else in the living room, the curtain-less windows black. I rolled over, wrapping myself in a blanket as I left the comfort of the bed to search for him, relieved when it didn't take long.

'Storm's over. Clear night.'

He didn't turn around when I opened the back door, instead he stayed right where he was, sitting on the back step, staring out across the fields. I wasn't sure if it was very, very early or very, very late. The stars were still out, more here than I ever saw in Hertfordshire and the indigo blue sky bled into a deep, inky navy with the slightest orange tint to the line of the horizon. The promise of a new day on its way, whether we wanted it or not.

'Aren't you cold?' I asked, noting he was still naked. His body curled comfortably on the step, knees pulled up, arms wrapped around his shins. There was no self-consciousness or attempt to hide, he was entirely him.

'I'm fine,' he replied. 'Go back to bed.'

Carefully, I sat down beside him, keeping the blanket tucked around me.

'Can't sleep,' I said. It wasn't a lie. As soon as I realised he was gone, I was wide awake and, truthfully, I was surprised to find him so close by. The part of me that didn't trust either one of us was sure he'd have been long gone.

'Do you really hate the idea of love at first sight?' Joe asked, keeping his gaze steadily on the sky.

'It's not that I hate it but I personally don't believe in it,' I said. 'My favourite romances have always been the ones that seem vaguely possible. Love at first sight has never happened to me.'

He nodded thoughtfully.

'Did you love CJ?'

'I thought I did at the time. I'm not so sure now. It feels more like we were playing at it, pretending to be grown-ups. Even when things were good, it was never the kind of love you read about.'

'You mean the kind you write about,' Joe corrected sweetly before throwing out another question. 'Do you believe that exists? The all-consuming, overwhelming romance novel love?'

I paused before I answered, wanting to be sure I got it right. This wasn't the time for mixed messages. Or pretending.

'It has to,' I replied, choosing each word very carefully. 'Otherwise why would we all be chasing after it? Why have so many people dedicated their lives to trying to put inexplicable feelings into words? Love is the most incredible thing, it can happen to anyone, anywhere, at any time. You can't buy it, you can't force it, but almost everyone wants it and some people will do anything to get it. You could be walking down the street one day and pass a stranger, not knowing that six minutes, six days, six weeks, even sixty years from that second, you're going to be head over heels, hopelessly in love with them.'

We sat side by side, quiet and calm, and I tried to relax, pretending we weren't in the eye of the storm.

'What about you?' I asked. 'You've never been in love?'

The corners of his mouth turned up but it wasn't a happy expression, more a smile that existed in spite of itself.

'It would be fair to say I haven't had the best experiences with relationships.'

'That's not a no.'

'It's not a yes either,' he replied with the same wry expression. 'I always thought it was better to keep some distance in relationships, avoid commitment. I never took them very seriously. My parents were very good at showing me what *not* to do but figuring out the opposite has never been easy for me.'

'Is it ever?' I asked, studying him.

'I'm starting to think it could be.'

Only when I had him fully committed to memory, did I look away. Holding his hair back from his face, Joe took in a long, slow inhale then blew it all out at once.

'Have you ever heard of the Japanese phrase "Koi No Yokan"?' he asked.

I shook my head in response. 'What does it mean?'

He couldn't fight the smile that came with whatever it was that danced through his memory. 'I had a Japanese roommate at Harvard, Dai. He was, still is, the coolest person I know, but he would fall in love every other day. "Koi No Yokan" doesn't have a direct English translation but it more or less means the feeling you get when you meet someone and know that falling in love with them is inevitable. We mostly used it as a pick-up line.'

Even though I already knew the answer, I asked the question.

'Did it work?'

'Most dependable chat-up line I have ever used.'

'Can't believe I didn't give you a chance to use it on me,' I said, an uncomfortable non-laugh following my words. 'I should've held out for longer.'

Joe turned to look at me, squinting out from underneath his hair.

'It's difficult to use a line on someone when that's how you really feel.'

It was exactly what I wanted to hear. But he knew that, didn't he? Joe knew what everyone wanted to hear. Tall, handsome, clever, funny Joseph Walsh, with his instinctive chivalry, quick smile and impeccable manners. Charming parents, saving damsels in distress and swamped by women falling at his feet. There was no way of knowing which parts of him were genuine and which parts were finely honed tools crafted for a very specific job, just like his Japanese pick-up line.

He stretched his legs, flexing his feet, the muscles in his calves extending and contracting. 'I don't blame you if you don't trust me,' he said. 'I wouldn't.'

'Do you trust me?' I asked, deflecting his semi-question with one of my own.

'I don't know. I've never cared either way before,' he replied, frowning at his own answer. 'Trust is a difficult thing to identify in someone else when you know you can't be trusted yourself.'

He cocked his head to one side, lost in thought for a moment. It was an expression I was starting to recognise, his internal debate with himself. I waited patiently, in no rush, until his expression reset itself, eyebrows sliding back into place, forehead smooth, decision made.

'There are some things I need to sort out,' he said. 'I can't imagine you'll be shocked to hear I've occasionally acted on impulse and made a few mistakes in my time but I swear, you don't need to worry about anything.'

I pulled my blanket tightly to my body and looked back up at the sky. After all the rain, the air was clearer than it had been all weekend, a clean green scent cutting through the dense summer closeness. The storm had passed, we were starting fresh.

'There aren't any simple answers,' I said eventually, talking to myself as much as to Joe. 'All we can do is try to trust each other. No secrets.'

'Says Este Cox,' he responded with a sly grin.

'No secrets starting now,' I amended, placing one hand on the ground between us. 'How does that sound?'

His hand found mine and covered it.

'More than I deserve but exactly what I want.'

There was no hesitation this time, no waiting for permission. He brought his forehead to mine, nuzzling against me, and I let my blanket fall to the ground as he took me in his arms. The shock of his cool skin on my warm body struck like lightning, every inch of me awake and alive, inside and out. I explored his face with my fingertips, his lips, his eyelashes, the stubble that roughened his skin, then his strong, supple shoulders and the muscles in his back, his arms, his chest. A carnal sound ripped out of him when my hand moved down between his legs, melting me to my core before he laid me back on my blanket like a fallen hourglass, sands settling, time stopped.

It was the same but different. The first time, we'd been running a race, careening downhill and desperate to reach the finish line, unable to slow down even when we wanted to, but now the urgency, my need to answer all the questions he had asked, was tempered by the desire to savour every moment and commit it all to memory. The scent of his skin, which parts of me he reached for first, the way his lips parted when I took him in my hand, and the way I felt, knowing I had the exact same effect on him that he had on me. Bodies entwined, I arched into him, my heart beating faster and faster as the night wrapped us up in its last sigh and I surrendered, irrevocably lost, never to be found again.

When I finally opened my eyes and accepted Sunday was happening whether I liked it or not, Joe was already up, fully clothed and making tea. I laid in bed, watching him dunk two teabags and quietly swearing when he splashed boiling water on himself.

'You're dressed,' I said with disappointment.

'It is the way of my people,' he replied, dropping the teabags in the sink, splashing milk into both mugs and bringing them back to bed.

'But you said you'd never need clothes again.'

'And you said time is a construct, *The Muppets'*

Christmas Carol is the best Dickens adaptation of all time and Justin Timberlake should be tried in The Hague for what he did to Britney.'

He handed me a tea before taking a long drink of his own.

'When I'm relaxed, I tend to get a bit chatty,' I replied. 'But I stand by it all.'

'Good. Because you're right about all of it.'

One of us had pulled down the curtains that had divided the living space in the night and they lay in a pool of fabric beside the sofa. We hadn't slept much, or at least I hadn't. Every time Joe drifted off, I lay watching him, too overcome even to close my eyes. He slept on his front, arms under his pillow and his head to one side, the vivid red trails I'd scratched into his back burning in the darkness and I wished them into tattoos, marking him permanently the way I knew he had marked me. I didn't believe in love at first sight but, whatever this was, the way I felt when I looked at him now, hair messy, pillow creases still etched into his cheek, I believed in that.

'Not to spoil the mood but my dad is blowing up my phone,' Joe said, holding up his phone as evidence. 'I've got a feeling he isn't planning to stay for brunch.'

'He wants to leave?' I replied, putting two and two together and coming up with Joe going with him. 'Let him take the car. We can get the train back down together later.'

Later.

After.

I was going to have to talk to my family.

For one very long moment, I'd forgotten about everything that wasn't Joe Walsh.

'Or I could drive him to the train station and we could take the car,' Joe suggested. 'Either way, I was thinking. Maybe we should keep this between us for now.'

Another suggestion I didn't love.

'With everything that's going on.' He sat on the edge of the bed, cupping his steaming hot mug of tea. 'This is ours. I don't care what anyone else thinks and I don't want to share it.'

'Sounds to me like you don't want to be Mr Este Cox,' I joked but neither of us laughed. 'What happened to no secrets?'

'This is different, this is *our* secret,' Joe said. 'And it's just for now, just until everything gets figured out.'

Everything including but not limited to his commitment issues, my trust issues, our parents' feud and the true identity of Este Cox. I put down my mug and reached for the closest item of clothing I could find, Joe's white shirt from the night before.

'So we're basically Romeo and Juliet,' I commented as I slipped my arms through the sleeves. It felt even softer than it looked.

'Only I'm not sixteen, you're not thirteen and fingers crossed no one is getting poisoned or stabbed.'

'It's still early,' I replied, rolling up the too-long sleeves. 'Let's not rule out all the fun.'

With that crooked half-smile I already loved, Joe rose from the bed, put down his tea before taking mine. Bracing his hand against the wall, he leaned over to kiss me, deep and searching, and when we broke apart, I gasped, my hands cupping his face.

'You're staring at me,' he said, holding close, eye to eye.

'Because you're very pretty,' I replied. 'And I like you very much.'

'Stop it,' he instructed before kissing me again. 'You're giving me butterflies.'

He rolled me back onto the bed, his phone pinging quietly to itself as I worked on his belt. He tossed his T-shirt to the ground and I shrugged my way out of my borrowed button-down, laughing and happy and so close to calling it love, I could feel the words fighting their way out of my mouth until he kissed it closed. As long as the feelings were real, the words would keep. There was no rush, after all. We had all the time in the world.

CHAPTER TWENTY-SEVEN

There was so much yelling coming from the kitchen, it was a wonder anyone even noticed when we crept inside, Joe in front, me close behind but not quite touching. Mum was shouting at Gregory, Gregory was shouting at Dad and Dad was stoically brewing a pot of coffee while wearing a pointy cardboard hat that said 'Happy Birthday'. Charlotte sat with her back to the fuss, casually flipping through a limited edition version of the latest Victoria Aveyard in a pair of oversized men's paisley pyjamas, oblivious to the fuss.

At the same moment we came through the back door, William came in from the hallway, looking every bit as confused as I felt.

'It's simply abhorrent behaviour!' Gregory shouted, his very loud pink patterned shirt torn at the collar. 'How could you do it?'

'You're the one who was sneaking around in the middle of the night,' Dad replied. 'Texting unapproved counter offers to my authors.'

'My author!' Gregory's eyes bulged out of his head. 'Genevieve is my author!'

'Was your author,' Dad corrected. 'If you'd signed them to a decent deal in the first place, we wouldn't be having this conversation. Don't blame me for your lack of foresight and bad business.'

'You're a savage!' Gregory wailed, slamming his hand down on the kitchen counter and trying to hide his wince when he clearly hurt himself.

'Please lower your voice,' Mum moaned with one palm pressed to her forehead. 'We're all hungover, Gregory. Do we really need to do this right this very second?'

'Morning, Este!' Charlotte piped up from across the room. 'Sleep well?'

'Maybe we should come back later,' I suggested, Joe nodding beside me as his father continued ranting.

'What exactly is happening?' William asked, appearing out the blue to block our path before we could leave. 'Besides a re-enactment of *The Real Housewives of Salt Lake City* season four finale?'

Charlotte twisted around in her chair, resting her chin on the overstuffed cushion. 'Gregory tried to counter Dad's offer to Genevieve Salinger but they turned it down, and Dad has apparently had a message from Nelson Allen's agent, asking if he'd be open to pitching for *Nelson's* next book, taking him away from Herringbone and over to MullinsParker. They tried to fight again for a minute but it was all a bit sad so they stopped and started bitching at each other instead.'

'I always miss all the fun,' William sighed.

'Happy birthday me!' Dad picked up a small plastic noise maker and blew into it, the long strip of colour paper streaming out with a dull horn sound that couldn't quite manage to drown out the din of the room.

'Perhaps it's time the two of you made a move,' Mum said, glaring at Joe who stood up straight at the side of me. 'You don't want to get stuck in the Sunday afternoon traffic on the M1.'

But Gregory was still laser focused on my dad, who was busy spooning brown sugar into his new 'Birthday Boy' mug. 'I'm not going anywhere until he apologises and rescinds his offers to my authors.'

'Better set old Greggers a place for Christmas dinner because Dad's never going to go for that,' William said. 'You sticking around as well, Joe? If I put the extra leaf in the table, we'll have plenty of room.'

'We really should get going,' Joe replied, an embarrassed smile on his gorgeous face. 'Thank you so much for having us, Mrs Taylor.'

'Don't thank her!'

His dad was outraged, so upset that his entire head had turned the same colour as a plum. He looked to be seconds away from going full Violet Beauregarde in the middle of the kitchen. 'Don't thank any of them! They've already tried to drag you into their schemes, son, all this Este Cox bollocks? Can even one of you manage to tell the truth for one second?'

'I don't think Dad lied about anything—' William offered but Gregory cut him off before he could finish.

'Enough out of you!' he exclaimed. 'I want to know what's going on with little missus mouse over there, forcing you into saying you're Este Cox when she's the smut-peddler. I can tell when there's something rotten in the state of Denmark.'

'This isn't Denmark, it's Derbyshire,' Charlotte replied, kicking her legs back over the arm of the chair.

'And that brat—'

'Enough!'

Dad slammed his mug down so hard the handle snapped right off. 'Say whatever you like to me but you do not speak to my daughters that way—'

'Fine to talk to me like that though,' William said quietly with a thumbs up.

'—and I think you've overstayed your welcome. Time for the two of you to leave.'

'The two of you?' I repeated. 'What did Joe do?'

'Don't, it's OK,' Joe replied with a quick squeeze of my arm before turning to his father. 'Dad, go and get your bag, I'll meet you at the car in five minutes.'

'Five minutes longer than I want to spend in this shithole,' Gregory muttered, stomping down the hallway. 'Be outside in two or I'll leave without you.'

'Be right back,' Joe said to me, slipping out the back door.

'I'll help,' I offered but, before I could follow, my mum stepped in front of me and closed the door behind him. 'Or, I could stay here'

'Once our guests have gone, I think we need to have a conversation, don't you?' she said, her glasses slipping down her nose as she glared in my direction.

'What happened to CJ,' I asked brightly, closely examining my fingernails. 'Did he not stay over?'

'Last spotted mooching down the road to the pub in the rain with his arse hanging out,' William replied.

'Don't change the subject,' Mum said loudly, using her sternest, most chiding tone. 'The pair of you have got plenty of explaining to do yourselves before you start raising questions about other people.'

'Do you want to do it straight to camera?' Charlotte asked, peeping over the back of the chair again, phone in hand. 'Or are you feeling a notes app statement? It's a little retro but it could work if you let me draft it. You're not that great at spontaneous chat.'

'Thanks but I don't think I need your help writing anything,' I replied with narrowed eyes. 'Aren't you the one who said *Butterflies* was your favourite book of all time?'

'No,' she said, staring right back.

'Oh right, that was someone else,' I nodded. 'Never mind.'

The angry sound of Gregory's bag scraping against the walls and smashing into each and every step on his way downstairs filled the whole house.

'You better have the engine running, Joseph!' he bellowed. 'Get me out of this hellhole backwater ditch.'

'The average house price in Harford is seven hundred and fifty thousand pounds,' William said, stepping into the hall and holding the front door open for our guest. 'What drugs are you on and can I have some?'

Dad was still smiling a victor's smile but it was frozen in place, tight and uncomfortable, and he hadn't noticed the coffee trickling out from his cracked mug, spilling all over the kitchen counter. I grabbed a tea towel to mop it up, placing the broken mug carefully in the sink. I was picking up the handle to drop it in the bin when Joe passed by the window, heading down the side of the house.

He wasn't coming back inside.

With the sharp curve of ceramic still in my hand, I

raced through the kitchen and hall and out of the front door, where he was dumping his leather holdall into the boot.

Gregory marched over to join him, tossing his bag in the back beside his son's, toppling Walter the sad walrus squishmallow who had been in there ever since the fete.

'I left my number on the bedside table,' Joe said quietly. 'Call me later?'

My hand tightened around the mug handle, barely registering the sharp slice into my palm as I held myself back from him. But even without physical contact, the connection between us was as clear as day and on display for all to see.

'Get your son away from my daughter!' Dad shouted from the doorstep, storming across the gravel in his dressing gown, slippers and pointy birthday hat. 'Sophie, get back inside, I don't want you anywhere near him.'

'As if my son would go near your daughter.' Gregory howled with laughter and I squeezed the broken handle even tighter. 'Look at him, look at her. She should be so lucky.'

'In my defence, I'm not a morning person,' I said, trying to bite some colour into my lips. 'No one's a ten out of ten first thing.'

'All right, steady on,' William warned as annoyance flickered across Joe's face. 'Try to keep your weird little feud between the two of you and leave the kids out of it.'

Gregory gave a gleeful little giggle. 'It's one thing to think you can steal my authors but if that's the only bait you've got to try and trap my son, you'll have to do better.'

'Dad!' Joe exclaimed, one hand on the boot. 'Shut up and get in the car. Sophie, Hugh, I am *so* sorry.'

'He's going to feel very silly in a minute,' I whispered to William, waiting for Joe to tell his father just how wrong he was.

'Don't worry, darling, he wouldn't go near a girl like you on your best day,' Gregory declared with a condescending leer. 'Even if he weren't already spoken for.'

The boot of the car slammed shut to punctuate his sentence and Joe stared back at me, his face suddenly frozen.

'Dad, shut up and get in the car,' he ordered. 'Sophie, I'll speak to you later.'

'What do you mean, spoken for?' I asked, looking to his father for an answer.

'Ignore him,' Joe pleaded. 'He's talking shit.'

'Has he got a girlfriend?'

My voice sounded very far away but at least I managed to get the words out.

'He's got a wife.'

Gregory corrected my sentence in verbal red pen, bleeding every ounce of emphasis out of the word. 'Real stunner she is as well. Show them a photo, Joseph, the one on the beach in Hawaii. Canadian, isn't that right? She's an editor at—'

'At Knoll in New York,' I finished Gregory's sentence for him and, from the look on Joe's face, I knew I was right. 'I hear she's very talented.'

His dad squeezed his shoulders together as though talent was neither here nor there and I squeezed my hands to stop myself from crying. Behind me, I heard William suck the air in through his teeth.

'Soph, your hand.'

Tearing my eyes away from Joe's guilty expression, I held out both my hands, no idea what William was talking about. My right hand was slick with blood, bright red with a deep scarlet gash in the centre. The broken handle of Dad's mug slipped through my fingers and onto the floor, its sharp edge gleaming.

'I'll get a towel,' Dad said, immediately switching into parent mode.

Gregory retched into his hand and bolted for the passenger seat. 'I can't stand the sight of blood. Joseph, let's get going before I chuck.'

William wrapped a protective arm around my shoulder. 'We need to get you inside. You can't bleed out in the front garden, what will the neighbours say?'

But I didn't budge and neither did Joe.

'Are you married?' I asked him.

He looked away and I knew I had my answer. My brother, his father, the house, the car, everything and everyone else vanished, leaving only the two of us.

'You said no secrets.' I clenched my hands into fists, ignoring the rusty splatters on the gravel. 'You said I could trust you.'

'No. I didn't,' he replied sadly, finding his voice at last. 'I said I'd made mistakes and that I would fix them.'

'Forgetting you're married is quite a big mistake, pal.' William steered me away from the car and back towards the house. 'I think it's about time for you to fuck off now, Joseph, don't you?'

I put one foot in front of the other, moving so slowly, waiting for the sound of his voice calling my name, begging me to stop and let him explain everything.

Lindsey Kelk

Instead, I heard a car door slam shut and the growl of the Range Rover's engine, tyre tracks moving too quickly over gravel. And then, he was gone.

'Look at the state of you,' Mum muttered when we reappeared in the kitchen, irritated and anxious at the same time, a highly specific maternal mix. 'Get your hand under the tap so I can see how bad it is.'

'It's fine,' I replied, wrapping my hand in the wad of paper towel my dad was already holding out to me. 'It's not as bad as it looks.'

Joe was married. Joe was gone.

'What if you need stitches?' she carried on, still running the hot water. 'That'll be a nice end to the birthday weekend, twenty-four hours in A&E.'

'It's fine,' I said again, louder this time. Much louder. Slowly, she turned off the tap and started banging around in the cupboards, her irritation upgrading to agitation.

'A cup of tea then,' she suggested. 'We'll sit down and have a cup of tea and you can tell us what the bloody hell has been going on. Where the hell is my sodding lapsang?'

'Now might not be the best time,' William said, shooting Mum a meaningful look as Charlotte peered over the back of the chair again, uncertainty on her face. She knew she'd missed something but wasn't sure what.

Joe was married. Joe was gone.

'My daughter.'

We all turned to look at Dad, standing with his hands in the pockets of his dressing gown, shaking his head at me, and I held my breath, preparing for whatever came next.

328

'An international bestseller,' he said with a smile. 'Talk about happy birthday me.'

More confused and relieved than I had ever been in my life, I exhaled heavily and felt a fresh set of tears prickling at my eyes. Then, without another word, Mum walked out of the kitchen and the tears started to fall.

'Pandora?' Dad called.

She didn't reply and I heard her office door shut firmly and loudly. Pressing the paper towel against the cut on my hand, smarting at the sting.

'Would you drive me to the station?' I asked William.

He looked over at Dad for permission and grimaced.

'I'll drive you home,' he offered. 'Can't have you getting on the train in this state.'

'I'll go and get your stuff,' Charlotte said, shuffling out of the chair and leaving her book on the table. 'You probably shouldn't be using that manky hand.'

'You're just trying to get rid of me faster,' I said, leaning against my brother.

'And I get to go through your stuff again without you realising,' she replied as she let herself out the back door.

'Well, it's officially a birthday for the books,' Dad said with a sigh, sliding his hat over to a more rakish angle. 'Maybe you can use some of it in your next bestseller.'

'Maybe,' I said as he gave me a nod. 'I'm under contract, I've got to write about something.'

And I didn't know how I was ever going to write another love story ever again.

CHAPTER TWENTY-EIGHT

'Can we stop at a McDonald's?'

'No.'

'Can we stop at a Starbucks?'

'No.'

'What about a Marks & Spencer Simply Food?'

William's grip tightened on the steering wheel.

'No.'

Charlotte hurled herself across the backseat of his car, arms folded, face furious. 'What's the point in a road trip if we're not going to stop at the services and get treats?' she cried. 'If I don't get a frappuccino in the next half hour, I'm going to die.'

'I am prepared to test that theory,' William replied, smiling at the driver in the next car as he undertook our BMW then flashed a subtle wanker sign as soon as he was out of sight. 'We're not on a road trip, you little moose. If you don't be quiet, I'll leave you at the services and you can find your own way home from there.'

'That would be more fun than this,' she muttered

behind me. 'How come I had to sit in the back when she isn't talking anyway?'

'I'm talking,' I said as the screen of my phone lit up with the same number for the tenth time in a row.

'You've said three things in the last hour and none of them were particularly nice.'

'Sophie doesn't feel like being particularly nice.' William put his foot down, ignoring the engine's protests, and the time to our destination icon on his phone dropped by five whole minutes.

'She looks like she's having a nervy b.'

'I'm not having a nervy b,' I said as my phone screen went dark again.

Ten missed calls. Ten voicemails. Forty-three unread texts.

I closed my eyes and concentrated on breathing in and out. Joe was married. Joe was married. Joe was married. Nope, that wasn't helping.

'Still can't believe neither of you told me.'

Charlotte's right leg stuck through between mine and William's seats, just barely missing the gear stick with a black and white Nike, the same style as Gregory's, only Charlotte was eighteen and he was sixty-two. My poker face was terrible but she wouldn't even be able to hide her feelings about a game of snap. All of her emotions passed over her so clearly, it was like looking at a human mood ring.

'Leaving me out like usual,' she pouted.

'You're here now, aren't you?' William pointed out. 'We could've said no when you asked to come.'

I glanced in the rear-view mirror to see her contorted around her seatbelt.

'You don't give a toss about me,' she said. 'You don't need to lie, I know it.'

'That's not true, we give many tosses,' I replied, turning my phone over before it could come back to life. 'But we're both rubbish and, if I'm being completely honest, sometimes you make me feel old.'

'That's because you are old.'

William's eyes met mine and I silently begged him not to drive us off the road.

'Saying things like that don't help your case,' I cautioned her. 'I'm sorry we've made you feel that way. I definitely didn't mean to. William probably didn't.'

'On my eighteenth, he gave me fifty pounds and a card that said "In my day this was a lot of money, you ungrateful little monster",' she replied. 'And that was before I'd even had a chance to tell him this is my day and fifty pounds isn't a lot of money any more.'

Out of the corner of my eye, I watched a smile stretch across my brother's face.

'Insults are William's love language,' I explained. 'You'll get used to it.'

She ran her thumb over the tip of the fingernail of her forefinger, half her nails were covered by glittery almond-shaped press-ons while the others were short and bare, and her braided hair had faded down to a silvery-grey, a few little strands framing her pretty face.

'I can't believe you're Este Cox,' she said, gazing at me with a mixture of awe and disbelief. 'You wrote *Butterflies*.'

'I know,' I said. 'Sorry if that ruins it.'

'Why did you keep it a secret for so long?'

'Because.'

It was a complete sentence. There was something

about being in a car with only siblings that made it so much easier to regress to a teenage state.

'Because the *Guardian* called you the author of Britain's filthiest novel?' Charlotte guessed with a wrinkled nose, trying to remember. 'Or was that *The Times*?'

'It was *This Morning* and it's not even true, there's much filthier stuff out there.'

'Oh, much filthier,' she agreed readily. 'Have you read the one about the minotaurs that have to get milked? Or the *Shrek* reimagining where he's a CEO and—'

'I'm going to stop you right there,' I said as our brother began to turn as green as the swamp monster himself. 'Ogre smut is not my thing. And no, that's not why. I just didn't want to have to deal with it all.'

'All what?'

'Everyone's opinions,' I confessed. 'Mum and Dad, people at school. It's a lot.'

'You care too much about what other people think.' She yawned without covering her mouth and grabbed hold of her feet, performing a perfect happy baby pose on the backseat of a moving vehicle. 'Must be exhausting, seems like a waste of energy to me.'

'It must be amazing to be you,' William said, looking at her in the mirror. 'Promise me you'll never change.'

'Why would I?'

I looked over at William and he shrugged. Neither of us had an answer.

'If I'd written a book like *Butterflies*, I'd want everyone to know,' Charlotte announced. 'Imagine knowing there are millions of people out in the world, reading a story you wrote and it's making them happy. I don't understand how there's any more to it than that. Who cares what critics say, or pretentious twats like CJ? His book isn't inherently better than yours just because it's depressing. The whole thing where people shit on something because it's not what they're into is so messed up. When did we decide that was allowed?'

'Probably when Eve tried to get Adam to wear a different brand of fig leaf,' William said, swerving to miss an empty KFC bucket that made my empty stomach rumble.

'Well it's stupid. I love Mum and Dad but they don't know everything. Soph, Dad is in his *sixties*.' She hissed out the last word as though our father had been raised with dinosaurs. 'He's *so* old.'

'Sixty isn't old,' William clucked with dismay. 'George Clooney is in his sixties.'

Charlotte looked to me, blank-faced. 'Who's George Clooney?'

Before our brother could let out a wail of existential despair, she sat up and reached around the seat to grab my wrist, repeatedly whacking me in the side of the head with my own hand.

'Pack it in!' William yelled, locking in his arms at ten to two so the car didn't swerve when she didn't stop. 'Are you trying to get us killed?'

'I'm not going to stop until Sophie rejects the internalised misogyny that has been propped up by our patriarchal society and the expectations placed on her by our parents,' she shouted back, the strap of my Chanel handbag, which was currently hanging across her body, clanging against my seat. 'Why are you hitting yourself, Sophie? Sophie, why are you hitting yourself?'

'Because I've internalised misogyny and something about the patriarchy,' I squeaked as I wrestled my wrist free, rubbing it gingerly with my injured hand. 'You are so much stronger than you look.'

'I don't expect you to undo a lifetime of emotional self-harm overnight,' she said, flexing her miniature biceps. 'But you will need to figure it out before you do your first-ever author event at my bookshop.'

'Charlotte.' William met her eyes in the mirror. 'Leave it.'

But she wasn't about to give up that easily.

'As her agent, you should be behind this. Do you have any idea how many views my video from the party last night got?'

He sucked in his cheeks and I could see his commission senses starting to tingle. 'How many?'

'Last time I looked it was a hundred and thirty thousand.'

'Seriously?' He turned his head all the way to stare at her for a second before remembering we were doing eighty in the fast lane of the M1.

'Half of those might be watching it for the whole bouncy castle bit, but your confession has been stitched literally thousands of times.' She really went out of her way to hit every syllable of the word 'literally'. 'It's out now, everyone knows who you are. You're a superstar, Sophie, like it or not.'

'I'm an idiot,' I countered, checking my phone again as the endless grey of the motorway blurred by.

Fifty-two unread texts.

While the majority of them were from the same number that had been blowing up my phone for the last two hours, there were others from my friends, co-workers, the beleaguered head of PR at MullinsParker, and the woman who came round to steam my carpets once and ruined a rug but I didn't have the heart to tell her and paid anyway. Good news travelled fast. Salacious gossip moved like wildfire.

'Is she still talking about the book or is this about Joe?' she stage-whispered to our brother whose face took on a grim expression.

My phone lit up again, same number, one I refused to assign a name to, not even William's suggestion of 'Wanker the Weasel Do Not Answer'. I was so upset with myself for being so stupid and ignoring my instincts. It was a genius play when you thought about it, present yourself as an arsehole, surprise the woman by being a halfway decent human, then, once she's on the hook, briefly remind her you are in fact an arsehole so when the truth comes out and she finds out she was right in the first place, you're off scot-free, leaving her behind to wonder how she could ever have been such an idiot.

And by her, I meant me.

'Please answer it,' Charlotte begged as the phone kept ringing. 'Miscommunication is my least favourite trope. You're killing me with this.'

'It's not miscommunication, it's secret wife,' I reminded her. 'Which just replaced instalove as my personal least favourite.'

'Then let me talk to him,' she demanded. 'I'll end him in under a minute. Or I could post something? Set up a couple of finstas, ruin his life?'

'Imagine getting read filth by an eighteen-year-old.' William grunted behind the wheel as she opened an app on her phone I couldn't identify in the mirror. 'It would be easier to put your head in the oven.'

'No one is creating finstas or reading him to anything,'

I ordered. 'His name is not to be spoken ever again by anyone in the car and that includes on the internet.'

In the backseat, Charlotte grunted something under her breath and kept her finger pressed on the delete button.

'Secret wife in New York.' William blew out a long, surprised sigh. 'Not even stashed away in the attic.'

'Did you hear anything yet?' I asked, not really wanting to know.

His eyes flicked over to his phone, showing our route but nothing else. I knew he'd made some subtle enquiries before we set off for home, poking around some of the industry's more reliable gossips for details.

'Not yet,' he replied, gently smacking the heel of his hand against the leather-covered steering wheel. 'I just can't believe he's married. It's shocking. I am shocked. It's one thing to be a bit of a shagger but going out your way to get in someone's knickers when you're married?'

'Sociopath behaviour,' Charlotte, with her as-yet ungraded A level in psychology, agreed. 'Targeting someone like Soph as well. It's not as though she's going round hopping on a different dick every weekend, is it?'

William and I both turned around at the same time to stare at our little sister.

'What? We all know you're not a casual shagger. I don't think you were like, oh go on then, I'm DTF for the weekend then we'll never see each other again.'

'How do you know?' I asked, trying to remind myself she was in fact eighteen and not the little girl it felt like I'd just been playing Barbies with in the back garden. 'I might be out in London every weekend racking up my body count.'

She pulled a face and went back to her phone. 'Don't say things like body count, you can't pull it off.'

I turned back to face the windscreen and silently added it to all the other slang she had forbidden me to use.

'It is weird though,' William mused, gliding over into the next lane to get around a very old lady in a very large Land Rover. 'Why would he keep it a secret? He's been here for what, three, four months?'

'If I were a semi-reformed shagger, planning to put it about a bit until my wife left her entire life in a different country to be with me, I'd probably keep quiet about it,' Charlotte suggested from the backseat. Neither William nor I responded. It was as good a theory as any and I didn't care for it one bit.

'He did say he had some things to work out but he didn't clarify what those things were,' I said as my phone briefly went dark. Eleven missed calls. Eleven voicemails. Fifty-five messages. 'Was I supposed to ask if one of them was a wife?'

'I believe the correct etiquette is still for the married party to at least mention their status before putting their penis in the unmarried party,' William confirmed before moving back into the fast lane. 'The onus is definitely on Joe.'

'The onus might be on him but the joke's on me,' I moaned. 'I should've known better. This is why I'm better off single.'

In the back, Charlotte's expression shifted into something more thoughtful, a shadow I did not care for dulling the light in her eyes. 'Is that why you wrote Eric?' she asked. 'Because in real life all men are this terrible?'

An emphatic yes fought its way to the tip of my tongue, but I kept my lips pressed tightly together and shook my head instead. She was only eighteen, it wasn't fair, I wouldn't do it to her.

But William would.

'Yes,' he answered before I could sugarcoat a response. 'Straight men are human scum. And the shit-housery comes in all different shapes and sizes. They will go to any length to get what they want out of you and not a single one can be trusted, they are all, without exception . . . what was the word you used the other day? Chunts. They are all raging chunts, Charlotte Virginia Taylor.'

'No, they're not,' I said as forcefully as I could manage, twisting around to look right at her. 'Don't listen to your brother, this is his idea of being protective. I wrote Eric because I believed there had to be a man like that out there somewhere.'

She looked back at me with big eyes, traces of last night's glitter eyeshadow making them sparkle.

'Do you still believe it?'

I thought for a second.

'I want to,' I said, 'even though it isn't exactly an easy task at this precise minute.'

'Not all love stories are straightforward,' she replied with unearned wisdom as she leaned forward to pat me on the top of the head like a good dog. 'Maybe this is one of them.'

'Feels more like a thriller right now,' I muttered. 'I'm not sure this one has a happily ever after.'

'Maybe it's an epic. A grand tale for the ages where you find each other again in fifty years and realise he was your true love all along.'

'Fuck me, that's depressing.'

William's dry delivery managed to squeeze an unexpected laugh out of me and he grinned before his eyes moved up to the rear-view mirror. 'I can't remember the last time the three of us were on our own together. This is nice.'

'It'd be nicer if we stopped at McDonald's,' Charlotte grumbled. 'Sophie can pay. She's minted.'

Out the window, I saw a sign for the Watford Gap services and my stomach growled again.

'I could go for a six-piece of nuggets,' William admitted. 'And she's right, you are loaded.'

In the backseat, Charlotte let out an agonised gasp, suddenly pale and panicked.

'What is it? What's wrong?' I strained against my seatbelt to reach her, grabbing hold of her hand as William hit the hazard lights and swerved across two lanes of traffic to the hard shoulder.

'My Chanel bag,' she replied, clutching the leather and chain strap draped across her body. 'It's real, isn't it?'

Silently seething, William turned off the hazards and pulled back into traffic.

'Lottie, that bag is the least of my worries,' I told her, squeezing a tweaked muscle in my neck as I breathed out.

'Good because you're not having it back either way.'

'Just like William said,' I said, closing my eyes as he steered us along to the exit to the service station. 'Never change.'

CHAPTER TWENTY-NINE

It was almost nine o'clock when I heard the doorbell go.

'Who is it?' Charlotte asked, lying on her belly on my living room floor.

'I don't know, I'm not psychic.'

'You don't have a Ring camera?' she scoffed without looking away from the TV. 'Caveman.'

There was no need to tell her I did but I'd forgotten to charge it before I left to meet Malcolm on Thursday morning and next-door's cat had been having the time of its life, chasing foxes around all weekend long and draining the battery. She was sure to find that even more mortifying than the idea of my primitive, Ring-less existence.

She rolled over with a steely look on her pretty face.

'Do you want me to get it? In case it's him?'

'It's OK, I'll get it,' I said, closing my laptop and heaving myself off the sofa. Other than the chicken nuggets and spontaneous sibling road trip, one good thing had come out of today. I'd never felt so inspired to finish my sequel. As soon as the worst possible version of events happened in real life, it was very clear what I wanted to happen in the book.

'Bring him in and I'll defend you to the death,' she promised. 'I know how to hide a body, I've listened to "No Body, No Crime" so many times. Where's the nearest lake?'

'Actually very close,' I replied as I tiptoed along the hall to the front door trying not to give myself away to whoever was outside.

Four hours had passed since Joe had given up calling. Three since William set off back to Harford, leaving Charlotte with me supposedly for some unplanned sisterly bonding time but we all knew it was because they didn't want to leave me on my own, even if we wouldn't admit it, and because we wouldn't admit it, I couldn't say how much I appreciated it.

Frozen in front of the door, I shook myself down, cricking my neck from side to side like a boxer on his way into the ring. Joe could be right there, just a couple of feet in front of me, nothing but one relatively flimsy bit of wood between us. Would he bang on the door with the side of his fist if I didn't answer? Would he try, and probably succeed, to kick it down? He didn't strike me as a fall-on-the-floor-sobbing sort but I could imagine him standing in the doorway with fire in his eyes, demanding I hear him out. Yes, he was married to a really fit, super-talented Canadian editor from Knoll, but now he realised he'd never truly understood love until he met me. I would fight him at first, still burned by his lies, but he would sweep me off my feet and carry me upstairs, the bond between us too powerful to deny. Until he slipped on the loose bit of carpet at the top, fell backwards and we both broke our necks and died.

It would be all I deserved for even entertaining such a stupid theory.

'Time to switch to writing fantasy,' I mumbled, wiping both hands over my tired face.

When the doorbell rang again, I realised I wanted it to be him more than I didn't. I didn't know what I would say but that was OK, I just needed to know he was real, that I hadn't imagined the whole thing. When I unlocked the door and opened it slowly, I felt my heart drop when I saw who was standing there.

'Oh good, you are alive,' Mum said with an expectant look, waiting for me to move to the side and let her in. Out on the street, Dad waved from inside the car and I raised a slow hand to wave back.

'If you've come for Charlotte,' I started, leading Mum into the living room. 'Please take her because she's gone insane. Charlotte, where did you get a baseball bat?'

'Brought it with me. It was part of my Harley Quinn Halloween costume the other year,' she explained, standing in the middle of the room bouncing a baseball bat against her palm. 'What are you doing here?'

'I came to talk to your sister.'

If our mother was fazed by her youngest daughter wielding a weapon, she didn't show it. 'Why don't you go and wait in the car.'

'Because I'm staying here with Sophie like I told you on the phone.'

'If that's all right with Sophie, it's all right with me,' Mum replied, looking to me for my confirming nod. 'Go and tell your dad. He's got a bag of foul neon orange snacks in there and I'd rather he didn't consume the whole thing himself, birthday weekend or not.'

Charlotte didn't even stop to put on her shoes. So much for defending me to the death. I needed someone to protect me from my mother way more than I needed someone to protect me against Joe.

'Place looks nice,' Mum said as she settled down on the settee, testing the cushions with a splayed hand. 'Is this new?'

'New since you were last here.'

When was that? I couldn't remember. Neither she nor my father veered from the Harford to London route if they could help it these days. Mostly I went to them or we met in town and ever since I signed my book deal, my visits to them were less regular than usual. Still, I could count on one hand the number of times she'd been to my house.

'I'll put the kettle on,' I said, starting for the kitchen when she cleared her throat to speak.

'William called us on the drive back up and explained the entire situation.'

The tea would have to wait.

I scrunched my toes against my soft rug and leaned back against the rose-pink wall. I loved everything about my tiny house. After I'd moved out of mine and CJ's flat, I was determined to have everything exactly how I wanted it, from the decorating to the furnishings to the wattage of the bulbs in the light fixtures. It was strange to see Mum sitting on the sofa, sticking out like a sore thumb, when I slotted into place so cleanly at home. I made sense there but she didn't quite fit here, not quite comfortable.

'He didn't go into an awful lot of detail about your relationship with Joseph Walsh but the fact there was a relationship to gloss over at all is bad enough.'

The wall wasn't enough to support me any more. I lowered myself down until I reached the back of my midnight blue velvet reading chair and perched.

'I am pulling out all the stops to embarrass you this weekend, aren't I?' I said. 'Terrible timing, I'm sorry.'

'What are you talking about?' Mum replied, eyebrows almost meeting in the middle behind her glasses.

'Messing around with a married man, who just so happens to be Gregory Brent's son, secretly authoring a book you referred to as "predictable, badly written, misogynistic nonsense", lying about who wrote the book then causing a bit of a scene at the party?'

'If that's your idea of a bit of a scene, I'd hate to see what you consider a full-blown debacle.' She pulled on the silk scarf she had tied around her neck until both ends were exactly the same length. 'I'd also like to think you know it would take a lot more than that to embarrass me.'

'I saw Aunt Carole trying to seduce Joe in the spare bedroom when she thought he was Este Cox,' I blurted out and my mother blanched.

'Yes,' she muttered. 'That would do it.'

I slid over the edge of my chair and settled into its softness. I'd saved up for months to buy it, way before the book's success, my first grown-up, non-Ikea furniture purchase. Charlotte could have every Chanel handbag on the planet but I'd never part with this chair.

'None of what happened at the party was your fault,'

Mum went on. 'And I shouldn't have walked out of the kitchen this morning, but it wasn't because of anything you did. I had simply reached my limit with the entire fiasco.'

'Which brings us back to me messing around with a married man.'

'Which brings us back to me being horrifically hungover, your father acting like a complete fool, not to mention inviting way more people than he was meant to and ruining my favourite pink blazer, Gregory Brent merely existing and his monstrous son stringing my daughter along, when very clearly he is the one who should be strung up, preferably by a part of his anatomy he should never be allowed to use again.'

The fervour in her voice matched the fury in her eyes and my jaw dropped.

'You're not upset with me?' I asked, pulling a cushion out from behind me and hugging it close to my belly.

Both of her eyebrows eased up her forehead and she gave me The Look.

'Not about that, but I would like to understand why you felt it necessary to lie to us for so long.'

'Technically, I didn't lie, I just didn't tell you,' I corrected. 'Joe lied and maybe I backed him up but technically—'

The Look intensified by one degree and I shut my mouth immediately.

'Sophie, you wrote a book, you submitted it to Mal, you used William as your agent, and at no point in that process did you think it might be worth mentioning it to either of your parents? It's quite hard not to feel a bit hurt.'

'Can you really blame me?' I said when she stood

and crossed the room to my bookshelves where one single copy of *Butterflies* lay on its side, spine in, hiding on top of my most beloved paperbacks.

'Who else should I blame?' she asked, picking up the book and looking at it as though she was seeing it for the first time. 'William didn't tell you to keep it a secret, I very much doubt Malcolm did. As far as I can tell, it was your decision.'

Curling my legs up underneath me, I squeezed the cushion closer while she read the back cover copy, her finger following each line down, one at a time.

'When I first sent it in to Mal, I didn't want to say anything in case he said it was rubbish,' I began. 'I thought about telling you after MullinsParker acquired it, but it still felt too weird. And don't take this the wrong way but I didn't want the added pressure, people would've looked at it differently if they knew Este Cox was yours and Dad's daughter.'

'Because you're embarrassed by us.'

I couldn't believe what I was hearing.

'Charlotte's been very open about letting us know how out of touch we are,' she went on with a rueful smile. 'I'm very sorry that stopped you from sharing this with us.'

'I'm not embarrassed by you, you're embarrassed by me,' I said, sitting up. 'You hate romance novels, Dad has never, ever worked on one in his whole career. You know I've always wanted to write and it was really hard to know my parents were looking down on my book when I'd worked so hard on it and don't say you're not because you were very, very honest about your thoughts. At least until you thought Joe was the author.'

A rare blush coloured my mother's cheeks and she

returned to the sofa, still holding my book. 'I said some very unkind things about *Butterflies*. The fact my opinion changed had nothing to do with its supposed author and everything to do with my having read it.'

'Nothing to do with the author at all?' I prodded.

'Well.' She pursed her lips to temper her smile and ran her hand over the soft-touch cover. 'You can't deny you would be impressed too if you thought a straight man had written a woman-centric romance this good.'

It was the biggest compliment she had ever given me and it wasn't even direct.

'Your father hasn't published a romance novel because, to the best of my knowledge, a romance novel has never crossed his desk. I disregarded it because, and let me be brutally honest, I am a terrible literary snob.'

A laugh erupted out of me and I tried to capture it in my hand but Mum looked perfectly at peace with the fact.

'Very happy to admit it,' she said. 'Just because a bunch of old industry fogeys value my opinion doesn't mean it's the only valid one. And it's still only that, an opinion. It breaks my heart to think you didn't share this incredible achievement with me and your dad because I sit in my ivory castle handing out irrelevant pats on the head and he works on books by people who imagine themselves in the body of a llama.'

It was good to hear her say it and even better to see her holding my book without having to worry she was about to throw it into a bonfire, but the air between us wasn't quite cleared. A very loud imaginary voice told me to cut my losses while I was ahead but if I'd learned nothing else today it was that secrets festered and always came out to bite you in the arse in the end.

'The other night, when you were talking to Jericka and Aunt Carole in the kitchen,' I said. 'I was outside and I heard you saying how disappointed you were that I'd gone into teaching rather than publishing.'

'Oh, Sophie, no.'

Mum's face fell, the hard-earned smile I'd already saved to my memory box vanishing in an instant. She was up on her feet and beside me on my chair before I'd even had time to blink away the tears that threatened as soon as I spoke.

'You must think I'm an absolute monster,' she said, combing her fingers through my hair, something she hadn't done since I was a child. 'That's not what I meant at all. I'm not disappointed because you're a teacher but I have worried about you making that choice, only because I suspected that your heart lay elsewhere. Sometimes things come out wrong after a long day, especially when talking to your Aunt Carole. Obviously if I'd known you were listening—'

'It's all right,' I told her, even though it wasn't. 'You get used it. Middle child stuff.'

'But you're not my middle child,' Mum corrected. 'You're my eldest daughter. William got away with blue murder by being the first and Charlotte has been spoiled to death, and we're all suffering for it now. But you had the weight of the world on you from the very beginning. Trying to live up to everybody's expectations, suffering all the lessons we learned with William, trying to win your big brother's approval, and just when you started to come into your own, along comes your little sister. But you always handled everything with such grace.'

'Except for when I punched CJ in the face,' I suggested.

349

'I missed that so we'll pretend it didn't happen,' she replied. 'Although I did hear from your father that it was a decent swing. Good follow-through, were his precise words, I think.'

Squeezed onto the chair next to me, she placed my book on top of my cushion and smoothed one hand over the cover.

'I should've had more confidence that you would find your way to it in your own time,' she said, pulling my head down onto her shoulder. 'You have excelled in everything you've ever done and I am so proud of you. So is your dad and your brother and so is your new little shadow.'

She nodded out the window to where Dad and Charlotte were still digging into a giant bag of Doritos and singing along to something on the stereo.

'Not quite managing to excel in my love life,' I said when she went back to the sofa and started rummaging around in her handbag. 'I can't believe I was so stupid.'

'I can,' she replied without looking up. 'Sorry, that came out wrong. Do you know your father proposed to me the same day we met?'

'Yes but that was a million years ago,' I said. 'You've been together forever.'

'We have now but we hadn't then.' She pulled a Sharpie out of her bag and came back to the chair. 'We were fools for each other from the very first day we met. Sometimes it happens that quickly and you don't get to control it,' Mum said, tapping the cover of my book. 'I'd have thought you knew that.'

'Dad wasn't married though,' I reminded her. 'And spoiler alert for book two, neither is Eric.'

'He wasn't married but your father wasn't entirely single either. Scandalous, I know, but here we all are today, no regrets. The course of true love never did run smooth.'

'Yes but also, *one must not live one's life through men but must be complete of oneself as a woman of substance*,' I quoted wisely.

'Very good, I like that,' Mum said, impressed. 'Austen or Brontë?'

'Fielding,' I replied. '*Bridget Jones's Diary*.'

There was no restraining her grin this time.

'That expensive education was worth every penny,' she commented with a loving nudge. 'And regardless as to how you feel right now, there is no shame in falling fast and falling hard. Joseph is very charming and if I didn't know what I know now, I would've readily believed he felt the same way you evidently feel about him.'

'Plus he's really fit,' I sighed, giving the tall, dark haired illustration of Eric on my cover the filthiest look I could muster.

'It does help sell the package. More intelligent women than you or I have been taken in by a pretty face and a pair of strong arms. And a very nice back-side. And—'

'All right, you've made the point. Hot, charming, not my fault.'

'Even if it feels like it is.'

She took my hand, turned it over and placed the Sharpie in my bandaged palm.

'What's this?' I asked as she pulled off the lid. 'I've got the message, you don't need to write a warning on the back of my hands, I'm not going to call him.'

'No, you're going to sign my book.' She opened *Butterflies* to the title page and drew a thick black line through the name 'Este Cox'. 'After that, I'm going to get your dad and your sister and we're going to order a pizza and you're going to tell us the whole story, starting from when you very first had the idea to where we are now and you're not going to leave out a single word. Deal?'

'We both know I will do anything for pizza.'

I scrawled my signature under the crossed-out name and stared at the page.

'What's wrong?' Mum asked. 'Please tell me you didn't spell my name wrong.'

'This is the first book I've signed,' I said, slightly stunned.

'The very first signed first edition of *Butterflies*,' she said with the greatest reverence. 'If you add the date, this should see me and your dad through our retirement. And for the record, I never said you shouldn't call him. There could be more to the story than you know.'

'He's going on the DNF pile,' I told her, shaking all thoughts of Joe Walsh out of my head. 'I can live without his unnecessary exposition. He isn't a morally grey hero, he's an arse.'

She pulled me into a hug and, over her shoulder, I saw my phone light up on the arm of the chair. Same number, calling again. But this time when the screen faded back to black and my heart sank, there was a little lifeboat there to catch it before it hit rock bottom, and I smiled against the tears that fell anyway.

'That cut needs some antiseptic, I think it's deeper than it looks.' She broke the hug and took my injured hand in hers, softening her grasp when she saw my tears. 'But it'll heal,' she promised, wiping them away one at a time. 'Given time.'

'I know,' I said, blinking my eyes dry. 'And I've got all the time in the world.'

CHAPTER THIRTY

Three months later . . .

'Are you ready?' Charlotte asked, slipping into the stock-room and securely closing the door behind her.

'No,' I replied. 'I want to cancel the whole thing.'

'I'd kill you and do the event wearing your skin like a Snuggie.'

'You're truly terrifying, you know that, don't you?' I told her, a chocolate Hobnob frozen halfway to my mouth as she folded herself into a deep and elegant bow.

'It's a full house, we've sold every copy of *Butterflies*.'

My mouth dried out and I traded my Hobnob for a swig of Diet Coke.

'Oh good. Exactly what I'd hoped for.'

She poked through an open box of chocolates on the table and helped herself to a nut truffle. 'William set up a screen outside for the overspill and anyone who misses the livestream can watch the replay. For a fee.'

'You're going to be a billionaire,' I told her with a

mixture of admiration and genuine fear. 'Please spare me when they put you in charge of the entire universe.'

World domination looked good on my little sister. Her emerald green jumpsuit made her newly platinum hair shine and if I ever found the confidence to wear bright red lipstick out in public rather than in the comfort of my own home, I hoped it would look as good on me as it did Charlotte. In the three months since Charlotte's Bookshop opened, she'd already established herself not only as a destination store, hosting events with every kind of author, but as an authority on the industry, appearing all over international media and even deigning to do a radio interview after Mum explained it was very much the same as a live podcast for older people. In their own way, I was sure *Woman's Hour* took it as a compliment.

She pulled out the card from the enormous bunch of flowers on the table and scanned the short but sweet message. *Congrats on your first event. Don't fuck it up xxx.*

'These from Mal?' she guessed.

'How did you guess?' I confirmed. His assistant subscribed to the bigger is better school of thought when it came to gifts and the oversized spray of roses, hydrangeas and blue delphiniums filled the space literally and figuratively, knocking us all out with its overpowering scent. 'He said he would try to come but it depends on the trains.'

Charlotte snorted out a pretty laugh. 'If he's relying on trains, we should expect him by Christmas. I'd say I'll save him a seat but seats are for paying customers.'

I glanced out the tiny window up at the frozen November sky, not even the slightest amount of light to let in now. No matter that it happened every year, the dark winter nights always came as a surprise. On the drive over, William said it was an evolutionary thing, we forgot how painful winter was, so we didn't throw ourselves off the edge of a cliff when the nights started drawing in, but then Mum reminded him that was childbirth and started talking about her episiotomy and he shut up soon enough.

'Knock-knock,' said a voice as the door opened again, allowing the excited chatter from the bookshop to crackle into the stockroom. I gulped down my Diet Coke and wiped damp palms on my jeans.

'Thank god you're here.'

I jumped to my feet, immediately tripped over Mal's floral arrangement and fell face first into Sarah's chest, smushing my shakily applied make-up against her freezing cold coat.

'Your fans are rabid,' she replied, visibly quaking. 'I didn't think I was going to get through alive. Some of them even knew my name?'

'We should look into doing a collab,' Charlotte said, snapping her fingers. 'Buy a copy of *Butterflies*, get a free cookie at your coffee shop.'

'You scare me,' Sarah said to my sister who, as ever, took it as a compliment. 'It's not sane out there, Taylor. I hope you're ready or they're going to devour you whole.'

'I should've said yes to *I'm a Celebrity*,' I whispered, Hobnobs churning in my stomach.

'You hold out for *Dancing with the Stars* or you don't do anything,' Charlotte corrected. She picked up her phone and scowled

'Is there a problem?'

'Uninvited guest,' she replied, hammering away at the screen. 'Not an issue. I'll be back to get you in two minutes.'

The door slammed shut, closing out worryingly raised voices, and Sarah sat down beside me, digging into the open box of chocolates. 'You'd better get changed if you're starting soon,' she said as she unwrapped a strawberry cream. 'Show me what you're wearing.'

'This is what I'm wearing?' I pulled at the sleeve of my new striped cashmere sweater to demonstrate. 'You don't like it?'

'It's jeans and a jumper,' she said, completely unimpressed. 'I thought you'd be wearing something a bit more, you know . . .'

She waved her hands around, Sparkle Motion-style.

'Brand new jeans and a brand new jumper,' I amended. 'And the jumper is cashmere. I won't even tell you how much it cost.'

'No, please do,' she insisted. 'I had to spend two hundred pounds on new school uniforms for the boys last week because they decided to tag team on a growth spurt and have already grown out of everything I bought them in September but, do enlighten me, Este Cox, how much *was* your cashmere jumper?'

'It was a bargain,' I muttered, wrapping a strand of my carefully curled hair around my finger. 'Also remember to send me their Christmas holiday dates so I can book the Disneyland Paris tickets. And the Eurostar. And the hotel.'

Smoothing the empty chocolate wrapper into a flat sheet before folding it into a neat little package, Sarah nodded. 'Will do.'

The three months since Dad's birthday might've passed quickly but that didn't mean they'd been uneventful. Charlotte's accidental TikTok reveal went viral and it didn't take long for the internet detectives to find me, but it wasn't as awful as I'd expected. Getting a new phone number was annoying and having to set up all new private social media accounts was an inconvenience but so far the only people who had turned up at my house were some very sweet Brazilian bookstagrammers who pushed dozens of gifts through my letterbox, and the only reason they had to do that was because I wasn't home to let them in. I would've been powerless against them if I'd been home; I'd seen the videos they posted, they were so incredibly cute.

Staying away from the Goodreads reviews had been good practice for avoiding all the posts and articles that came out after the reveal. Sarah occasionally took screenshots and sent me the more absurd rumours. We were both thrilled to find out I was having an affair with Austin Butler after casting him in the movie adaptation, especially since I wasn't and we hadn't. There was only one thing that really pissed me off and we all should've expected it: the 'Saucy Author's Ex Tells All' interview that ran in one of the tabloids with CJ's best attempt at a heartbroken face splashed right across the page. Only there was very little to tell and ninety-five percent of the feature was concerned with how annoyed he was not to have been featured in the acknowledgements, something I could relate to.

'My main goal was comfort,' I said, picking a bit of imaginary lint from my shoulder. 'I'm here, ready to be trotted out like a prize cow. I didn't think gilding the lily was necessary.'

'Only if you consider yourself a lily in the first place,' Sarah clucked. 'And I wouldn't say *prize* cow.'

With one eye on the door, expecting Charlotte to burst through any minute, I took another chug of Diet Coke. 'I do feel more like a regular dairy heifer. All I've done for the last three months is churn out pages.'

'Better to be churning out pages than trying to decide who gets to play Mary in the Nativity,' she said. 'Remember last year?'

'It's not easy to forget a seven-year-old performing a dirty protest on the school stage because they were asked to play a shepherd,' I replied, pushing the chocolates away. 'But it is still weird to think I won't be going back to school any time soon.'

Sacrificing my job was the one thing I'd been absolutely right about. I'd talked to my head teacher, Mrs Hedges, on the phone after the party but she didn't seem to comprehend what I was saying. It was only after some of the less understanding parents saw CJ's newspaper interview I was summoned into school during the summer holidays, something that felt wrong whether you were a teacher or a student. We had a very awkward conversation, followed by lots of crying on my part and annoyed grunting on hers, and agreed the best course of action would be for me to resign.

'Still can't believe they managed to replace me in less than a day,' I said with a distinct edge of grumble to my tone as Sarah pulled a theatrically sad face.

'I bet they'd have you back in a heartbeat.'

'No,' I assured her, remembering Mrs Hedges deeply unimpressed face when she held up a copy of my book. 'They wouldn't.'

'Better not fuck this up then,' she said brightly, patting

the card from Mal that shared the same sentiment as the door opened.

'One-minute warning,' Charlotte bellowed over the racket outside. She beckoned Sarah, cocking her head out the door. 'I saved a seat for you, but you'd better go and claim it before someone starts a riot.'

'Please, I'm a single mum of two boys,' she replied with a scoff. 'They haven't a chance in hell.'

'I thought seats were for paying customers only?' I said as Sarah stuffed a handful of sweets into her pocket.

'She gives me free croissants,' Charlotte replied, one finger delicately pressing the earpiece of the headset she'd acquired since she was last in here. 'Put more lipstick on and get ready. Sixty seconds to *An Evening with Este Cox.*'

With a double thumbs up, Sarah followed my sister out the door and they left me alone. The first time I'd been by myself in here since my very first visit, sitting in the chair behind the desk I'd avoided like the plague with Joe on his knees in front of me. It already felt like something I'd read in a book. It couldn't possibly have happened in real life.

I hadn't heard from him since that Sunday. I deleted all his voicemails and texts without reading them, reminding myself over and over I'd known him less than three days and the whole thing was meaningless. But weeks later, I was still half hoping to see him every time the doorbell rang, my heart still in my throat whenever flowers arrived, just in case they were from him.

They never were.

Mal never mentioned him. My books had been passed on to a super-talented new creative director who I loved and had no interest in shagging whatsoever and the only time Dad had spoken Gregory's name in my presence was when he called with the good news that not only had he signed Nelson Allen, but Nelson and Genevieve Salinger were also collaborating on a project together, having hit it off during his birthday party. Funny how things turned out.

'Soph.' Charlotte stuck her head around the door one more time as I gave the desk a longing look. 'We're ready to start when you are.'

'Ready as I'll ever be.'

I stood up and brushed out my hair with my hands. Should I have worn it up? Should I be wearing something more glamorous? Would I regret necking that Diet Coke before my first-ever public appearance? Possibly, probably and almost definitely.

'You've got a Taser for any trouble-causers, right?' I asked, only half joking, and she threw up her fists and put on her most threatening face.

'Don't need a Taser when you've got Take 'Em Out Taylor,' she said, raising her fists in front of her face. 'Anyone even looks at you the wrong way and they'll be eating their Christmas dinner through a straw. My dad was a boxer in his youth, you know.'

'I have heard that,' I replied, kissing my little sister on the top of the head as we walked out into the shop, arm in arm, and the screaming began.

'Yes, the lady with the amazing pink headband.'

I pointed towards the far side of the bookshop and a young woman with an impressive amount of gorgeous curly red hair stood up, holding out her hand for Charlotte's roving mic.

'Hi, I love the book and I read that there's going to be a film. Do you get any say in casting and can Sebastian Stan play Eric?'

The room erupted in conflicting roars of agreement and dissent and I sat back in my comfy armchair, almost unable to believe all these people had such passionate opinions about a book I'd written in bed after CJ fell asleep, trying not to type too loud because the sound of clacking keys 'gave him nightmares'.

'I haven't talked to anyone,' I replied, speaking up before a fight broke out. 'Honestly, I have no idea, I haven't even seen a script yet, but I'll definitely let the people in charge know all your suggestions.'

So far, the event had been a huge success, my most pinch-me moment yet. I'd wasted so much time worrying about the people who would look down on me for writing *Butterflies*, I hadn't given myself a chance to think about the people who would celebrate it. And they so desperately wanted to celebrate it. We started with a reading then Charlotte asked me some annoyingly intelligent and insightful questions, Mum, Dad, William and Mal all lined up along the side of the shop, beaming with pride. I could've done without the dreaded un-invited guest, CJ, gurning at me from the doorway but the family had decided it was easier to let him in than risk a scene outside. Personally, I'd have voted for a scene. Preferably one where I got to punch him again.

'Any more questions?' I asked, already wiggling my fingers to prepare for what my sibling assured me was going to be a mammoth signing session. I would have happily sat there all night long chatting with them about everything from which Taylor Swift album was Jenna's favourite to my most-watched *Real Housewives* franchise, but it was getting late and there were so many people crammed into the bookshop, I couldn't even see the faces in the back three rows. If we didn't start the signing soon, we'd all be here until midnight which probably wouldn't go down very well with the people who needed to catch a bus home.

'Why do you think romance novels are so popular right now?' asked a voice in the middle of the room, a girl in a sparkly lavender T-shirt dress with arms full of friendship bracelets. Everyone's arms were full of friendship bracelets, including my own, and I planned to treasure each one forever.

'I'm sure there are a million reasons,' I replied, having practised the answer to this one plenty of times over the last few weeks after Mal forced me into media training, something I was grateful for now. 'For me personally, I love romance because it gives me hope. When I was very unhappy and lonely—' a brief pause to glare at my ex in the background '—these were the books that kept me going. Not that I want my life to be as dramatic as Jenna's but writing her story helped me convince myself I would find someone too. Someone better. Someone who really saw and appreciated me for who I am. That's why I think modern romance novels are so brilliant, they celebrate women exactly as they are.'

'We've got time for one more,' Charlotte announced as a dozen more arms shot up. One reached much higher than the others, a large hand coming out of the cuff of a white shirt. 'Right there, in the back?'

'Thank you, appreciate it.'

I heard the voice and every muscle in my body tensed. The entire crowd turned in their seats to see who was speaking but I already knew. I'd know that voice anywhere. Slowly, Joe rose to his feet at the very back of the room and accepted a microphone from my traitorous baby sister.

'First, I wanted to say thank you for *Butterflies*. It's an amazing book and I know I speak for everyone here when I say we cannot wait for the sequel.'

He paused to allow for the cheering and stomping, not even flinching at the death stare coming from the stage.

'And since you've written my favourite romance novel of all time, I was hoping I could get your advice on a romantic predicament.'

'I'm the last person who should be giving out advice on love,' I replied, the back of my neck prickling with sweat. Definitely should've worn my hair up. 'Trust me, I make terrible decisions when it comes to my own love life.'

'I told you she wanted to get back together,' I heard CJ stage-whisper to a disgruntled-looking man in an 'I'm a Swiftie Dad' T-shirt at the side of him. 'She's probably going to make some big romantic gesture right now. Try to look surprised if she proposes.'

Joe's hair was slightly longer, his skin a little paler, but he still filled out his beautiful white shirt like it had been tailored to his body. Maybe it had, I wouldn't know. I didn't know anything about him.

'I'd still like your opinion,' he said. 'We've all made bad decisions.'

'Not as bad as mine,' I insisted, wishing he would disappear. 'Take this summer for example, I thought I'd met someone amazing.'

The crowd let out a chorus of oohs.

'Don't get too excited. It turned out he was married. Can you even believe it?'

The oohs turned to boos with record speed.

'What's she talking about?' CJ asked too loudly.

'Not you,' Sarah replied wearily from the front row. 'Never you.'

'He sounds like a complete arsehole.' Joe shook his head with feigned shock. 'Unless he had a good reason not to tell you.'

'What reason could possibly be good enough?' I replied. 'How could anyone justify lying to someone, cheating on their wife and then disappearing completely?'

'He didn't disappear completely, did he?' he said. 'He called you about a hundred times and left millions of messages, but you didn't answer any of them. He thought that meant you didn't want to speak to him.'

'He was right,' I agreed as he left his seat and began edging down the row. 'I didn't and I don't.'

'He'll never forgive himself.' He kept going until he reached the aisle in the middle of the shop, his dark hair shining under the halogen lights. 'And he doesn't expect you to forgive him either but he does need to explain.'

'No, he doesn't, he needs to piss off.'

The happy mood of the bookshop had turned into something electric. Phones were out, everyone was whispering, heads were on a swivel. The only people who looked unhappy to be there were me, my parents, CJ and Mal, who was clearly beginning to regret bothering with the train.

'I didn't want to speak to him then,' I said, determined to keep my composure. He would not see how much he'd hurt me. He would not know about all the nights I'd cried myself to sleep. 'And I don't want to speak to him now.'

Anyone who hadn't worked out what was going on, suddenly figured it out and Joe had to duck to dodge a barrage of flying friendship bracelets and assorted projectiles. He pressed a hand to his face when a random copy of *Butterflies* struck him on the face.

'OK, ow,' he said, looking for the culprit. It could have been anyone. I wished it had been me.

'A thrown book is a sold book,' Charlotte yelled. 'Do not trash my shop. All angry mob participants will be asked to wait outside where you'll be able to kick him after the signing.'

'I'm sorry, I can't do this,' I said, moving to stand. 'Charlotte, can we skip to the next bit?'

'Sophie, I miss you,' Joe shouted over the din. 'I think about you constantly, all day, all night. I hate myself, *hate myself*, for what happened.'

'What exactly did happen?' Sarah asked, turning all the way around in her seat to follow him up to the front, the rest of the audience following suit. 'Soph might not want an explanation, but I'd like to hear it.'

'None of it was planned. Every word I said to you that night was true.'

Joe was in front of the crowd now, his words only for me. I sank back into my seat and he set his microphone down on the floor. He was so close, I could see the dark circles under his eyes, the bloodshot streaks of red, the determined set of his jaw. But he wasn't nearly as determined as I was.

'Except for the no secrets part.'

'Except for that,' he replied softly. 'If I'd had one more day to fix things, I would've told you everything.'

'Cool story,' Sarah sniffed. 'Soph, say the word and we'll tear him limb from limb.'

I shot her a thankful look but couldn't afford to risk a smile. My face was fixed, angry and hurt, and I knew even the slightest emotional variation would see me in floods of tears.

'My best friend Caitlin and I got married last year,' Joe said, moving very slightly closer as I moved very slightly further away. 'So she could keep her job in New York.'

'Marriage of convenience plot twist,' mumbled a woman in the front row, the girl beside her nodding with wide eyes.

'She forgot to renew her work permit and it expired. I have dual citizenship through my mum and I was trying to be helpful.'

'You really do have a terrible track record with that.' I dug my fingernails into my palms before relaxing my hands suddenly. The scar on my right hand had taken forever to heal; hands that spent all day flying across a keyboard did not recover quickly. 'And to think I called you inconsistent.'

'You'll be thrilled to know I've taken a vow never to try to help anyone ever again,' Joe said, the slightest hint of a smile on his face that fluttered and died when I didn't respond. 'I married my friend for a visa, that's the short version. The longer one is, I did it because I'm selfish. She was my best friend in the world, maybe my only real friend in New York, and I didn't want her to leave, and I honestly thought I would never get married. I'd always said I wouldn't, not after growing up with my parents. No one knew except our closest friends and family. As you know, I made the mistake of telling my dad but, obviously, he didn't understand.'

'Predictable,' my dad muttered somewhere across the room. 'Classic Gregory.'

'It worked out great for a while,' Joe went on, the rest of the room so quiet, you could've heard a Post-It drop. 'Then my mum got ill and I needed to move home which messed everything up. We had to fill in all these extra forms, do more interviews, get letters from my mum's doctors to prove why I was coming back to the UK and Caitlin wasn't. It was a whole new mess. We made a pact to keep things clean; no social media and no serious relationships with other people. To make sure we didn't get rumbled, no one else could know.'

He reached one hand out towards me but I jerked backwards. I couldn't bear it.

'But things were serious with you from the first moment we met,' he whispered. 'From the first moment I saw you.'

'And your mum is OK?' I asked.

'Mum is OK,' he confirmed, the room sighing with relief.

'If you weren't really married-married, why didn't you just tell me?' I could feel my resolve weakening when he raked his hair away from his face, close enough for me to smell his clean, warm scent, and feelings I'd fought off for what felt like forever came flooding back, consuming me too easily. 'If you'd explained it like this, I would've understood.'

'Would you?' There was a genuine and reasonable question in his voice. 'Oh, hello woman I just met and have completely fallen for, this is incredible and everything but, heads-up, I'm married and I can't get a divorce for at least another six months and, until then, we'll have to keep our relationship a secret, cool? Cool.'

'You didn't give me a chance,' I said.

'Because you didn't trust me to begin with,' he pointed out. 'And I wanted to trust you but if things went badly, and they always go badly for me, that put Caitlin at risk. If I didn't tell you and you found out, you'd never trust me again. It was a Catch 22.'

'Overrated book,' I heard Mum comment followed by Dad gasping in horror.

It stung because it was true. We'd made it very clear we didn't trust each other. Only I thought we'd agreed to try.

'After that night, I knew things had changed. All I needed was one day to go home, call Caitlin and explain before I could even attempt to explain everything to you. She's been my best friend for years. I couldn't break our agreement.' Joe took a deep breath and held it in his chest. 'Even if I had fallen in love.'

He must've known the crowd's intake of breath would suck every atom of oxygen out of the air. It left me light-headed, reeling against my chair.

'If this is all true and you got only married to help your friend, how come you're telling me now?' I asked, recovering myself and catching sight of Sarah's warning glare melting into begrudging acceptance behind him.

'Because when I talked to Caitlin yesterday, she could see this was killing me,' he answered. 'She's decided to move back to Toronto. The whole thing was a terrible idea and I never should've suggested it in the first place but I really was—'

'—only trying to help, I know.'

'You still should've trusted her in the first place,' called out a boy with furiously red hair and an even more furious expression.

369

'He's right,' agreed the girl in the pink headband. 'Eric would never do something like this.'

'That's because I'm not Eric.' Joe's eyes were still on me, fixed and focused. 'I'm real and real people make mistakes, they apologise then try to earn forgiveness.'

My front teeth dug into my bottom lip to hold all my words in until I was absolutely certain about what I wanted to say. Joe had no such intention of holding back.

'I did not see you coming, not ever,' he said, shaking with determination. 'I made myself stay away because I was so sure you were better off without me but, even when I managed to keep my distance from you, I couldn't let go of this.' He held up his copy of *Butterflies*, so well-read, the writing on the spine was completely illegible. 'Every time I was lonely, I read your book. Every time I missed you, I read your book. Every time I woke up in the night and couldn't understand why you weren't beside me like you were in my dreams, I read your book. I know every word off by heart, because they're your words. They're sacred.'

'That's quite good,' Pink Headband Girl whispered to Red Haired Boy. 'He's been practising that.'

'Are you still streaming this?' I heard Sarah ask my sister.

'No,' she replied, somewhat unhappily. 'I turned it off right before that idiot confessed to visa fraud. No one likes a prison romance.'

'Sophie, these have been the worst three months of my life,' Joe declared, grabbing hold of my hands and falling to his knees in front of me, stoking a fire in the pit of my belly my body immediately tried to put out with tears. 'Please, I'm begging—'

Whatever he said next was drowned out by the roar of the crowd, almost everyone in attendance screaming so loudly, I had to cover my ears with my hands.

'I'm not proposing, I'm begging!' he said loudly, only slightly panicked. 'This is the begging position, both knees, not one. I love you and I want you to give me a second chance but I know you're not insane.'

A mix of sighs of relief and murmurs of disappointment filled the room and I had to wonder for a moment whether or not he was right about my mental state. I could hear other voices but far as I could tell, we were the only two people in the room. The only two people in the world.

'Sophie Taylor, you are my favourite author and my favourite person. Whatever it takes, I will do anything to earn your trust. Complete honesty. You're going to know more about me than you do yourself. You can have the password to my phone, I'll show you my browser history, anything you want.'

'I don't know what to say,' I whispered as the real world crept back in and I felt all two hundred pairs of eyes on the two of us. 'Except I really don't want to see your browser history.'

'That's better than no,' Joe replied with a crooked smile. 'Can I take you out for dinner after your signing and we'll go from there?'

'Sorry, Joe,' Sarah said. 'She's got plans and I paid for a babysitter. There's no way she's weaselling out on me.'

'Wouldn't dream of stepping on your toes, Sarah,' he said, holding up one hand but keeping his gaze on me. 'Tomorrow?'

'She's got an event in Paris,' called William. 'The day

after that, she's in Amsterdam and the day after that, Berlin.'

'The day after that?' Joe asked. 'How about I sit outside your house until you've got five minutes spare?'

'It's supposed to get very cold after tonight,' Dad commented behind us. 'I hope he's got a proper coat with him.'

We faced each other, me still clutching my microphone with his hands wrapped around mine, and I flashed back to the first day. Hot and sweaty in that karaoke room, singing and laughing before everything got so complicated.

'This is all up to you,' he promised as I turned off my microphone and placed it on the floor. It protested quietly, a soft whistle tone sounding under his words. 'Tell me to go and I'll go. Ask me to stay and I'll stay. Tell me you're not sure and I'll wait until you are. You make the rules.'

Joe Walsh was everything I said I didn't want.

He was frustrating and impulsive and he couldn't help but complicate everything he touched, even when he was trying to help. Especially when he was trying to help. He was arrogant, overly charming and altogether too sure of himself, even this grand romantic gesture was testament to all of that. But he was also kind and good-hearted. He listened to me when I talked and he saw me in a way I couldn't see myself. He could be raw and vulnerable, and much braver than me. He was real. And if I wanted him, he was mine.

'Stay,' I said eventually, falling forward onto my knees, my arms looping around his neck like they belonged there. There was no other choice. 'I want you to stay. But if it goes badly, you'll have to answer to Sarah and Charlotte.'

'Then I'd better behave because they would never find my body,' he said, holding me tightly, as though he might never let me go. I pulled back, just far enough to find his lips, smiling at the fluttering feeling in my chest. It floated down to my belly and exploded inside me right as his mouth met mine.

Butterflies.

'There were other things I wanted to say but not in present company,' he murmured against my lips as the crowd went wild. 'They aren't suitable for the under-eighteens.'

'Please,' I replied as I lost my hands in his gorgeous hair. 'There's nothing you could say that could shock a single person in this room. They're romance readers, they've heard it all.'

'I still don't think your family want to hear what I'm planning to do with you the moment I get you alone.' His teeth grazed the soft skin of my ear and my body flushed from head to toe. 'Remind me to make sure Charlotte turns off that livestream. We've got unfinished business in that stockroom and I would prefer not to broadcast it across the world.'

'How is it possible that I missed you this much?' I asked, incredulous as the crowd began to ebb and flow around us, my sister joyously declaring the event over and shuffling everyone into a signing queue.

'You tell me,' Joe replied, his eyes full of love. 'You're the romance writer.'

I had no idea what I was doing, no clue if we'd find our way to a happily ever after. This was the beginning of a new chapter, a fresh page that hadn't been written yet. Maybe we'd find ourselves living in a castle in a faraway land or end up fighting dragons for the rest of our lives. There was no way to skip to the end, no guarantees, no easy promises.

But when he kissed me again, I knew enough to kiss him back with my whole heart.

Whatever came next, I knew our love story was far from over.

ACKNOWLEDGEMENTS

As ever, I remain completely gobsmacked that I'm still allowed to do this as a job and that is in no small part due to my amazing agent, Rowan Lawton. Thank you, Rowan, and all at TSA, especially Eleanor Lawlor who always gets it.

Books really are the biggest team effort and even though my name is on the front, this one wouldn't be in your hands right now without the incredible hard work of everyone at HarperCollins who makes the magic happen. Lynne Drew, is it weird that this is basically my longest relationship outside of family and a handful of friends? What's that? I just made it weird? Excellent.

Olivia Robertshaw, Vicky Joss, Philippa Cotton, thank you for your work on the front lines of this bad boy, and of course, thank you to Maddy Marshall and the world's greatest train sleeper, Felicity Denham for everything ever. Thank you to Ellie Game and Ana Hard for the cover of dreams, and thank you to everyone else at HarperCollins – I MASSIVELY appreciate you. I will inevitably miss off a thousand people who deserve individual appreciation but whether you're in sales, marketing, publicity, production, legal, art, audio, design, customer service, logistics or anywhere else in the entire company, please believe me, your contribution to this process does not go unnoticed.

Thank you to all my friends and family who (mostly) help keep me in one piece, especially Jeff, Bobby, Kevin and Guns, who have all pulled at the very least a double shift this last year. No thanks to the cats who only want me to lie on the sofa and double no thanks to the lady who takes terrible care of Chester, but shoutout to the good people of the WWE, all ASMRtists and Ms Taylor Swift for giving me something to think about that isn't words. Are you still reading? Yes, this is a test. Comment on my last IG post with a strawberry emoji or I won't believe you. And massive thanks to all the screwballs comedies that inspired this book, especially *Theodora Goes Wild* and *It Happened One Night* but also anything with Cary Grant or Barbara Stanwyck, because, swoon.

Special authorly thanks to Elena Armas, Victoria Aveyard, Andi Bartz, Julia Bartz, Poorna Bell, Holly Bourne, Daisy Buchanan, Anna Carey, Andie Christopher, Sophie Cousens, Juno Dawson, Lizzy Dent, Jane Fallon, Becca Freeman, Mike Gayle, Kirsty Greenwood, Rachel Hawkins, Jenny Hollander, Milly Johnson, Emily Henry, Lauren Ho, Christina Lauren, Lia Louis, Sarra Manning, Mhairi McFarlane, Justin Meyers, Beth O'Leary, Adele Parks, Chip Pons, Alex Potter, Laura Stevens, Paige Toon, Lucy Vine and probably another million amazing people for existing and doing what you do.

And to everyone in Book World, this one really is for you. Whether you're an author, a reader, a reviewer, or all three, I'm so happy to share this sandbox with you. For what felt like a very long time, the romcom playground was a pretty lonely place and it's been beyond thrilling to watch the romance world grow.